SIM

JC

30 MAY 2017

D0514066

FLE
GRT
LOG
SAH
SUM
SUS 8/22

WITHDRAWN

Books should be returned or renewed by the last date above. Renew by phone **03000 41 31 31** or online *www.kent.gov.uk/libs*

Libraries Registration & Archives

CUSTOMER
SERVICE
EXCELLENCE

CSE

Kent
County
Council
kent.gov.uk

C334083770

Praise for Jane Lark

'Jane Lark has an incredible talent to draw the reader in from the first page onwards'

Cosmochicklitan Book Reviews

'Any description that I give you would not only spoil the story but could not give this book a tenth of the justice that it deserves. Wonderful!'

Candy Coated Book Blog

'This book held me captive after the first 2 pages. If I could crawl inside and live in there with the characters I would'

A Reading Nurse Blogspot

'The book swings from truly swoon-worthy, tense and heart wrenching, highly erotic and everything else in between'

BestChickLit.com

'I love Ms. Lark's style—beautifully descriptive, emotional and can I say, just plain delicious reading? This is the kind of mixer upper I've been looking for in romance lately'

Devastating Reads BlogSpot

Just for the Rush

JANE LARK

A division of HarperCollins*Publishers*
www.harpercollins.co.uk

Harper*Impulse* an imprint of
HarperCollins*Publishers*
1 London Bridge Street
London SE1 9GF

www.harpercollins.co.uk

A Paperback Original 2017

First published in Great Britain in ebook format by Harper*Impulse* 2017

Copyright © Jane Lark 2017

Jane Lark asserts the moral right to
be identified as the author of this work

A catalogue record for this book
is available from the British Library

ISBN: 9780008139889

This novel is entirely a work of fiction.
The names, characters and incidents portrayed in it are
the work of the author's imagination. Any resemblance to
actual persons, living or dead, events or localities is
entirely coincidental.

Typeset in Minion by Palimpsest Book Production Ltd, Falkirk, Stirlingshire

Printed and bound in Great Britain

All rights reserved. No part of this publication may be
reproduced, stored in a retrieval system, or transmitted,
in any form or by any means, electronic, mechanical,
photocopying, recording or otherwise, without the prior
permission of the publishers.

Author Note

Before you begin reading let me say a quick thank you to Suzanne Clarke my editor who has helped me pin Jack down a little. He is a very challenging man but as always I like to stretch the boundaries of perspectives with my characters and so you are about to go on another Jane Lark journey of emotions. Enjoy!

Ivy

November

'Are you ready yet?' Rick called from downstairs.

'I'm just doing my makeup. I'll be down in a minute.'

I stared at myself in the bathroom mirror. Into my eyes. Trying to look inside myself. Why did I feel so miserable? It was my birthday. A birthday celebration should penetrate through the darkness and dispel at least some of the shadows.

I lifted the mascara brush and swept it up along my eyelashes.

When I finished with the mascara I put the brush back in the bottle and the bottle in my makeup bag, then took out the mauve lipgloss that matched my hair.

My hand shook as I opened my mouth to apply it.

The wobbliness in my stomach expressed itself with a desire to be sick. I didn't want to do this. I wasn't in the mood for a quiet, romantic dinner with Rick. It wasn't the way I wanted to spend my birthday. I'd rather be in a club with Milly and some of my other girlfriends. I'd rather spend the night sharing large cocktails with a dozen straws, jumping up and down and dancing badly because I could barely stand up.

But Rick would be upset if I told him I didn't want to spend my birthday with him.

I shoved the lipgloss into my makeup bag, then zipped it up and looked at myself in the mirror. My hands ran over the creases of my black dress, trying to straighten the clinging material. I pulled the hem down to the top of my knees. It would ride up again when I walked. But so what? I'd have my coat on and we'd spend the evening sitting down at a table.

I breathed out, steeling myself for this. It really wasn't a good thing that I had to force myself into going out with my boyfriend, but I was just down. I'd been down and trapped in this darkness for months, though.

'Ready.' As I walked downstairs, he smiled at me in the way that said *you look gorgeous*.

My lips lifted in a quick, answering smile.

'You look good,' were the words he said aloud.

'Thanks.'

He had his coat on already, a bomber jacket. He was so broad and muscular that the fitted styles rarely fitted him.

'Hey, cheer up it's your birthday.'

I looked down so I could slip my feet into my sparkly gold stiletto heels. His hand ran over my hair then settled on my shoulder for a moment.

I glanced up and smiled at him. The thing about Rick was that he was so nice I could never say anything bad to him. I couldn't tell him no, or shout at him, or argue with him. But inside I was screaming. His kindness was confining. I was trapped. How foolish was that? Other women would think their fairytale had come to life with a guy like Rick. It was selfish and mean to not be happy. I should be happy.

I wasn't.

I was in a prison with glass walls – and comfy slippers, and soaps to watch on the TV and cardigans to snuggle up in.

'What is so bad about that?' My mum would say on the rare occasions I dared to complain.

Nothing. Nothing was wrong. So why did it feel like this life was strangling me.

'Come on, then.' He held my parka coat up for me to put my arms into the sleeves. He was such a gentleman. Other women would scratch my eyes out to get at Rick if they knew about this offer of a perfect masculine package that I was not appreciating as I should. He picked up the keys, then turned and opened the door.

'Where are we going?' Please God tell me we were not walking around to the local Chinese that we went to at least once a month, at least let it be somewhere different.

'You'll find out.'

Oh, whoopee! A surprise! How fucking radical!

I was such a mean bitch to him at times in my head, even though I would never say the words aloud. He was too nice to be sworn at.

A black cab waited outside our two-storey flat in a terrace in a London suburb.

Rick walked ahead and opened the door of the taxi. 'Here.' He held the door as I got in, then sat next to me and pulled the door closed.

Sometimes the glass walls on my prison closed in and became solid.

'Did they tell you the address I gave when they took the booking?' he asked the driver.

'Yep.'

'Great, thanks.'

I looked out at the houses illuminated by the streetlights. The year was heading towards mid-winter. Christmas. Time was going so fast. I held my clutch bag with both hands because I didn't feel like holding Rick's hand. We'd had loads of settling-down conversations this year, and the number of them had been building since September. 'Do you want kids?' 'What would you prefer first, a boy or a girl?' 'Where would you get married if you had a choice of anywhere?' 'Do you see us always living in London?'

Maybe that was the problem – I didn't see me and Rick *always* doing anything. I could never imagine the future. I only thought about now. And since I'd been depressed, I couldn't even imagine being happy again. So why would I care about five years from now?

Rick had ignored my lack of enthusiasm every time I'd shrugged off his questions, with comments like, 'I never thought about it.' 'I'm not sure if I want kids.' 'I'm too young to think about that.' 'We're fine as we are, aren't we?' 'Isn't living here, okay?'

The cab driver put the left-hand indicator on. There was no street to turn into. 'Oh.'

'Yeah,' Rick answered.

The cab turned into the car park of the boutique hotel that was just up the street from us. The taxi had been a decoy; we could have walked. But at least it was something different. We hadn't been here before and I'd heard good things about the restaurant.

The cab stopped and Rick got out without paying, so I suppose he'd already covered it.

When we walked up to the door leading to the reception, his arm lifted and hung around my shoulders. My heart thumped. I was so miserable I felt uncomfortable when he touched me. But possibly because I felt guilty about being such a bitch to him in my head.

Sex was the worst. Sex had become endurance, and that was cruel. Because he played rugby, so he had a good body; it shouldn't be awful to do it with him. But it was.

I kept telling myself it was the depression, and he was really understanding, as ever. He didn't push me if I said I wasn't in the mood, and he kept telling me I'd get better. I'd kept telling myself that the depression would go away too. But I didn't feel like it would.

The hotel had a fun vibe; the walls were decorated with dark glass and deep-purple colours, and there were gilt accessories everywhere.

He smiled at the receptionist as we walked past, then pointed at a door as his arm slid off my shoulders. 'Go on.'

I pushed the door, but it didn't open easily. I had to push both of the double doors to get either one to open. Then the music kicked in, Katy Perry's 'Birthday'. The room was dark but at the far end disco lights were flashing, green, mauve, pink and blue.

'Surprise!' The room full of people yelled at me.

I turned to look at Rick. He grinned at me. 'You said you wanted to do something different.'

'Yes.' I could hardly breathe. I hadn't imagined this. See. He was soooo nice. Sooo thoughtful. How could I not love him any more? Or had I never loved him and only just started realising it? Maybe I'd grasped at all his niceness because he'd loved me, and how could I have turned my back on that?

'Ivy, darling.'

'Mum.'

'He is a clever boy, isn't he? You didn't have a clue, did you, when you spoke to me this morning?'

I shook my head as Mum hugged me.

Then Dad hugged me. 'Happy Birthday, darling.'

'Hello, dear.' Rick had even managed to get my frail Nan here. I hugged her too.

'Ah! You look gorgeous!' My best friend, Milly, squealed, before wrapping her arms around me. 'I've been bursting to let this slip for weeks. Steve has been threatening to stitch my lips up.'

The stream of my family and Rick's family and our friends, who wanted to wish me well, kept coming and they all thought Rick was amazing for doing this for me. I hadn't even taken my coat off yet.

'Let me take your coat.' Rick was still near me. I turned and then his hands were holding my coat on my shoulders so I could take my arms out. Soooo nice.

'Good job, mate.' Steve slapped Rick's shoulder. Steve, Milly's partner, was Rick's best friend. It made for perfect couples' nights out – or in, my inner voice snapped sarcastically. I was such a bitch in my head.

'Come and dance.' Milly grabbed my hand.

'I'll get you a drink! A G&T?' Rick shouted after me.

I nodded.

I should be happy. I still felt sick and miserable. I was glad I could dance, though. Glad I was dancing and not sitting at a table facing Rick on my own, and I was going to get drunk.

Maybe Rick was right. Maybe this would pass. Maybe if I hung on, tomorrow I'd wake up and be madly in love with him and happy again.

But I couldn't remember when I'd been truly happy. Had I ever been properly happy?

Not for years.

I danced a lot and Rick kept handing me glasses of gin and tonic.

I drowned myself in the music and gin, to the point that I didn't care that the hem of my dress had ridden up to the top of my thighs and was way too short and probably showing off the lacy tops of my holdup stockings.

When the DJ started playing slow songs Rick came over. I'd kicked my heels off in the centre of the circle of friends I'd been dancing with. I put them back on as Rick held my arm, steadying me.

'Are you having a good night?' he whispered into my ear.

'Yes, thank you.'

'You're welcome.'

Suddenly the music stopped playing and the lights went on. I blinked.

Rick descended on to one knee.

No! No!

'Ivy, you know how much I love you, and I have loved you for a long time.'

Shit! Shit! Why was he doing this now? Why here, in front of everyone? Oh, my God. Rick!

'So, I thought it was time...' His hand went down and dug

6

into the pocket of his black trousers. '…to…' he glanced up and gave me a grin as he was still struggling with his pocket. But then his hand came up and between his finger and thumb a solitaire diamond caught the electric light and sparkled.

Oh, my God.

'…ask you to marry me. Will you marry me, Ivy?'

My mouth opened, but I didn't say a word. My throat was dry. Shit. Shit! Why had he done this? 'I…' I couldn't say yes. I couldn't. 'I'm sorry.' I swallowed, steeling myself to say the word. 'No. I can't.' Oh, my God.

I turned away from him, shaking all over. My mum and dad stared at me. His parents stared at me. Nan stared at me. Milly stared at me. Everyone was staring at me.

Shit.

I walked across the empty dance floor. The entire room was silent.

He knew I didn't want to commit yet. Why had he done it? What did he think, that because everyone was here I'd be forced to agree?

Images of his slippers, pyjamas and cardigans spun around in my head.

I wasn't ready to settle down into a quiet domesticated life. I wasn't a dog to be sat with and stroked on the sofa every night. I wanted to live life, to see and do things I hadn't done yet; to be allowed to go crazy when I wanted to.

I wanted to do lots of things. New things. Wild things.

I didn't want to be sitting at home forced to look after the kids he wanted me to breed.

I hid in a cubicle in the toilet still trembling.

The door into the toilets opened. 'Ivy.'

Milly.

The door into the toilets slammed shut behind her. 'Are you okay?'

'No.' I opened the cubicle door. 'Will you get my coat for me?

I need to get out of here. I can't stay with Rick. I can't go home with him.' My eyes filled with tears that ran on to my cheeks, probably smearing the mascara I'd so carefully applied before I came out. I wiped the tears away.

'It's okay. Wait here?'

Shit. Steve was his friend. If I went home with them, this was going to be so awkward. But I couldn't go home with Rick.

Chapter 1

Today, December 24th

The phone rang out its sixth ring. It was annoying me. Jack hadn't come into work yet so the phone in his office wasn't going to be answered. The answer machine would kick in on the next ring, like it had done four times in the last ten minutes. But whoever was calling hadn't left a message and I was guessing it was the same person.

Oh bugger. I snatched up my phone and keyed in the number to pick up the call. Jack didn't like his calls answered unless he'd transferred the calls to someone. But whoever it was wasn't going to stop ringing and I wasn't in the mood to listen to it. 'J's Advertising.' I glanced at the clock; it was after twelve. Jack was really late. 'Good afternoon. This is Ivy. How may I help you?'

'It's Sharon. Where is he?'

Shit. What did I say? I had no idea how my boss would like me to respond to the wife he was divorcing, and I had no idea where he was anyway. That was probably why he hadn't transferred his phone to anyone. 'Hello, Sharon. I'm sorry, he's not in the office.'

'Well, where is he, then? I want him to do something for me.'

I opened up his e-calendar to take a peek, although I didn't plan on telling her. It said 'private appointment'. 'I'm sorry, I don't know. I'm afraid he hasn't let anyone know.'

'Well, tell him to call me when he does come in.' The call was cut off, with no goodbye, and no thank you.

'Who was it?' Emma, Jack's business partner, called over.

I turned and smiled at her. 'Sharon.'

'Oh.'

A couple of glances passed around the office.

Rumour had it that Sharon had caught him cheating. But that was Jack; he flirted constantly with clients, it was part of his winning sales approach. But Sharon had been as bad – and the two of them put together—

The door into the office opened. 'Morning, all you lovely happy people!'

Talk of the devil.

'Nice to see you all smiling at me, but not surprising, seeing as you're about to get a few days off. I suppose you're going to the pub after work.'

'Aren't you, then?' Mark asked him.

'No, I need to work on the Mack's account, seeing as you are all finishing early.' Jack said it with a smile. 'But you can knock off at two, and have several on me, so you can get thoroughly drunk.' He stopped at the desk near the door, pulled out his wallet, and selected two fifty-pound notes, which he let flutter down on to the table. 'That should do for a few rounds.'

He shot a smile around the room, gave us a nod, then walked on.

He was a good boss in many ways. Fun-loving and a little crazy, even if he had tendency to be a control freak. He liked laughter and noise. He said laughter and noise had energy, and energy was inspiring, and as we were an advertising agency we needed to be inspired.

He was the thing that inspired me. He had magnetism. It was in his smile and his enthusiasm. He pulled me along like the Pied

Piper of advertising and his levels of positivity gave me more energy.

'The Mack's account isn't urgent! They don't need the idea until mid-January! You can come for a drink!' Emma called over as he walked into his office.

He turned and gripped the doorframe, leaning back out. 'Thanks, but no thanks, Em. I'll pass this year anyway.'

'Jack Rendell passing on a drink…' I said in a low voice.

He heard and looked at me. 'Jack Rendell working late, now that is nothing different.'

'No, that is true.' I smiled at him. He had nice eyes; they were a very pale blue.

'Good morning, Ivy.' His gaze skimmed over my hair and my face, then settled on my eyes.

'Good afternoon, Jack. You've missed an hour or two.'

He glanced up at the clock, then shrugged. 'Yes.'

He was being weird today. He wasn't himself. He was missing his usual exuberance.

'Sharon called you. She asked me tell you to call her when you came in. She said there was something she wants you to do.'

'Well, she can get lost and find another fool to do her chores, and if she calls again you can tell her I said that.'

I didn't know how to answer. But he didn't expect me to. He turned and went into his office, a glass walled box to one side of the room, then took off his coat.

When he hung it up on the coat rack in there the movement pulled his jumper up a little and his shirt out of his waistband, revealing a line of pale flesh. He was always well dressed, in designer clothes, mostly. Today he was wearing skinny-cut black trousers and a black pinstripe shirt beneath a burgundy jumper. The jumper was tight and I'd guess the shirt beneath it was fitted. From side on, his stomach was like a board. He was slender and muscular. He must spend hours in a gym at his house – or somewhere.

11

His hands slipped into his pockets and he walked over to the window, looking out at the view the office had of London. After a moment he turned around and caught me watching. He smiled. I smiled back and when he sat down I picked up my phone.

'Jack,' was all he said when he answered.

'You don't seriously expect me to get in the middle of your messy separation do you? Because I'm not up for that.'

He laughed. 'Not if you can't take a dozen rounds with Sharon; she fights hard and she has a cracking left jab.' He sighed out a breath. 'Okay, if she calls again put her through.'

'Okay, but she was calling your phone.'

'Then why did you answer?'

'Because she kept ringing and it was annoying.'

'Well, expect lots of 'annoying' in the next few months, Ivy, because she's not letting our ship sink easily.' He put the phone down.

Ten minutes later his phone rang, the tone announcing it was a call from outside. I looked over and watched him. He waited until it went to the answer machine, then lifted the phone off the hook. Two minutes later I heard his personal mobile ring; he didn't answer that either. Then he got up and stuck his head out of the office. 'Hey, Em. Are you up for changing our number?'

I laughed.

He came over to my desk. 'My life is not funny, Ivy.'

'I know, sorry.'

'It's ok. I was only joking. Do you want a coffee? Does anyone else want a coffee? If someone heads out to Nero's you can line your stomachs before you go out and get pissed up on me at two o'clock!'

'I'll get you a coffee.' I stood up.

His lips lifted only at one side. 'I offered one to you.' He was flirting, but he flirted with everyone.

'I'll get it. You pay.'

He smiled fully. His mobile rang. 'Oh, sod it. We'll both go

12

fetch the coffee. Listen up, guys! The boss is doing the coffee run! This has to be remembered!'

A few people laughed. We all knew he'd remind us that he'd gone out to do a Nero's run for at least a year.

His phone stopped ringing.

My office phone started ringing with an outside-line tone.

'Don't you dare answer that,' Jack said.

'And what if it is a client and not Sharon.'

'It's Christmas Eve. If it's a client they'll call again in the New Year. Come on, let's go get coffee. Make a list of what people want.'

I picked up a post-it note and went around everyone. There were ten of us. It wasn't a huge team.

Jack had picked up his coat and was putting it back on. His mobile rang again. He knocked it on to silent and left it vibrating on his desk as he walked out of his office, hands in pockets. 'Come along, then.'

I stuck the order on the sleeve of his duffle coat before I turned and grabbed my parka off the back of my chair. I pulled it on as we walked out of the office.

He tilted an eyebrow at me while we waited in the hall for the lift, and recited the list of coffee orders. 'Are they taking the piss, seriously, gingerbread lattes with cream and iced mochas. I mean who wants anything iced in the middle of winter?'

I made a face at him. 'You offered.'

'Yes, I did. Mug that I am.'

The lift doors opened. 'You're not a mug. You're a nice boss.'

'Nice… That's shit praise. It's sour when you know there are words like 'great' and 'awesome' that have not been used.'

'You're in a bad mood today, aren't you?' I folded my arms over my chest and watched the light behind the numbers as the lift went down through the floors.

'Is it any wonder, with Sharon on my back?'

I glanced at him as the lift doors opened again. 'Yeah, but you did bring that on yourself.'

13

His lips quirked sideward, sharply. It wasn't a flirtatious expression; it was a challenge. I'd annoyed him. His eyebrow lifted on one side once more too and his pale eyes looked their objection through his dark lashes. The expression said, *what?* Then asked, *why?*

A pull of attraction caught in my stomach. Jack was too good-looking and his flirtatious nature had always made my stomach somersault. I laughed, but it sounded awkward. The hit I got was not just an appreciation of his looks; it was sexual. My body was saying it would love to have sex with him. It had been a secret desire of mine for years. But it was one of those things that I thought about but would never do. It wasn't going to happen because he was my boss.

He looked away and held an arm out, telling me to walk ahead through the revolving door. I had a feeling, even though I had my parka on, that his gaze dropped to my arse. He was such a player.

But that side of him had always been exciting. I liked him looking at me, like I looked at him. I smiled to myself, my hands slipping into my coat pockets to keep them warm. It felt like a compliment to be admired by a man like Jack.

On the far side of the spinning doors, the volume of London, on the last day before Christmas, roared into life. The traffic was bumper to bumper, and there were people everywhere, with hands full of shopping bags.

Jack came out of the spinning doors behind me.

I sighed out a breath as he walked next to me.

'So what are people saying about the mess I made of my marriage? Did Sharon tell you what she'd like to do with my private parts? I've heard several versions. That was probably the chore she had in mind. She probably wanted me to pick up some nutcrackers on the way home.'

I looked at him. It wasn't surprising Sharon wanted to do him harm. If he fancied me, I doubted he felt guilty. I used to feel

14

guilty when I was with Rick, when my stomach flipped at the sight of Jack, like I was being disloyal to Rick. But Jack was one of those men you'd have to be blind not to have some feeling for, and he played up to it.

'Is Sharon still at your place?' I asked as we wove a path through the Christmas shoppers. There were thousands of people walking up and down the street, but it was the heart of Knightsbridge. They were here for Harrods; to see Santa and the windows and look at the Christmas lights as well as shop.

'Yes. I moved out.'

I couldn't play judge over their separation; I'd instigated my breakup too, and I'd moved out too. I'd rammed a stiletto heel right through Rick's heart in front of an audience. Santa was going to be slipping a lump of coal into my stocking tonight. I was not on anyone's nice list.

But I wasn't sorry. Santa could leave me on his bad-girl list. I'd rather be on it than miserable still. It had been amazing how my depression had lifted since I'd left. But there was guilt. I'd hurt Rick, and that was the one thing that was preventing me from being wholly happy now.

'Here.' Jack pushed the door of Nero's open and let me go in first. We were welcomed in with the sound of Wham, singing out 'Last Christmas'…

The place wasn't too busy. Most people were buying Christmas Eve bargains, not wasting time in a coffee shop.

I joined the queue. Jack stood behind me. I looked back to see his face, 'So go on, then, what's the truth with you and Sharon?'

'It's none of your business.'

'Harsh.' It wasn't all that harsh; he'd said it with a smile.

'I don't fancy talking about it. I save those conversations for my lawyer.'

'Are you trying to get your place back?'

'No. She can have it.'

Jack had many edges. As well as always bursting with enthusiasm.

15

There was the risk addict and the control freak. The big picture that others glimpsed seemed ten miles wide when Jack described it. He was a true entrepreneur; an ideas man and a money-maker. Emma always said if you gave him a pound, tomorrow it would be ten thousand. Everything with him worked fast, his brain dodged all over the place and he loved long shots – loved anything that made his heart beat. You could see the light in his eyes get sharper when he had an idea or was after something. The harder a client was to convince the more Jack wanted the contract and the more he pushed us to win it. He worked stupid hours fighting to win new work. But that was why he was so great to work for, his energy was infectious and he was passionate about what he did.

The only thing that freaked me out sometimes was the intensity that came with the passion. He sucked us all in and had us screaming for more, no matter how heavy the workload was, but then he would suddenly stop and lean back and look at all the work, and my heart would be going like crazy because I wanted what I'd done to be what he was looking for.

'She's not getting a share of the agency, though.'

I'd never considered that his breakup might affect us. 'Shit, I'd never thought—'

'Of course she was going to be after it. Why would she not try to get her claws into the treasure trove of J's Advertising?'

'Sorry.'

He laughed sharply. 'No. I'm sorry, I shouldn't have said that. I shouldn't be telling you. Don't worry, your job's safe. And I'll shut up. You didn't ask me to rant at you and I said I wasn't going to talk about it.'

'It's okay, I understand.'

'No, I doubt you do.'

He probably didn't know Rick and I had split. Jack didn't sit around and talk much; he was always too busy.

I looked forward again and moved along with the queue, my hands slipping into the pockets of my parka once more.

16

Jack's hands suddenly gripped either side of my waist and he shook me a little, sending my tummy into a backflip. 'Hey. Sorry again. That was mean. I heard you split from Rick. But if you're thinking it's the same thing – it's not.'

No probably not. I hadn't cheated.

'So, who got the house in your split?'

I looked back again and laughed, but it was a shallow sound. 'Him.'

'Where are you living, then?'

'In a tiny flat; an attic room. I like it. Rick is in the place we used to rent together still. I think he's hoping I'll go back.'

'There see, very different. Sharon wouldn't want me back.'

'And you…?'

'Want her back? Are you kidding me, that money-grabbing, self-centred bitch. I'm celebrating being rid of her.' His pitch didn't say celebration, it was bitter – and maybe a little twisted.

'Can I help you?' The barista called along the counter, picking up the orders along the queue.

'Hi, Susie.' Jack smiled at her. 'Here you go; there's the list.'

The barista smiled at him. 'Be with you in a minute, Jack.'

'You're on first-name terms with the Nero's staff,' I whispered as she turned away.

He smiled at me. 'Why, aren't you?'

My smile quirked. 'Do you flirt with her?'

'I talk to her. What's wrong with that?' His hands slid into the pockets of his coat, as if he was the most innocent guy in the world. He was so on Santa's naughty list too.

But what was wrong with it? Flirting. Nothing. Flirting was fun and I hadn't been able to do it for years because I'd tied myself down to Rick. 'Nothing… But… I give up with you.'

'That's the sort of thing my mum would say, and I didn't even know you'd started with me, Ivy.'

We moved three people along. 'It's no wonder Sharon is pissed off with you.'

His eyes widened, the pale blue challenging me as his lips formed a firm line, like he was going to blow off into a storm of rude words. His Adam's apple shifted as he swallowed them, then he said, 'What do you guys think?'

Awkwardness wrapped me up with a nice bow. But he should know what everyone thought. 'That you cheated.'

'That I cheated,' he said it in a disparaging way and his eyebrows lifted, saying, *are you kidding me*.

I'd guess he hadn't cheated.

'Well, if that is what you all want to believe...'

'Sharon told Emma.'

'That was good of her, and good of Em to repeat it.'

Shit, I was digging a deeper hole. 'You didn't cheat?' I took a step out of it.

'Oh, no, she's absolutely right. I cheated. *Loads*.' He'd leaned forward when he said the last word, and it shivered down my spine. Being up close to Jack was more than a metaphoric slap around the face, it was like I'd eaten a mouthful of the hottest curry; he made me sweat, as my temperature soared.

I turned away and faced the counter as we reached the till. He'd given the list to Susie and so I started reeling off the drinks we had on order. He pulled out his wallet. I stepped out of his way so he could hold his card over the machine.

'Sorry, that was declined. Do you want to try putting your card in the reader?'

He slotted it in, then typed in his PIN.

'Sorry, it's still declined.'

'Oh, fuck,' he said under his breath. 'Try this one. It ought to work. It's just mine.' He put another card in. The payment went through.

We moved out the way to wait for our coffees as the Christmas music aptly changed to The Pogues, 'Fairytale of New York'.

'Has she cleaned out your account?'

'She cleaned out our joint account a month ago. Fortunately

18

I didn't have much money in there. Now she's maxed out the credit card. I only left her access to one. She was meant to use it wisely. So if she hasn't bought her Christmas dinner already she's going to be hungry. That is probably what she was calling about. I had the limit lowered and didn't tell her. It's a full-on war I'm in, Ivy.'

'Sorry.'

'Again, not your fault, just me moaning.'

I hadn't heard Jack moan until today. He was always upbeat. Where had he been this morning? To see his lawyer? He'd been managing his split with Sharon since the summer, but he hadn't been like this before. 'Well, I am sorry. I don't like seeing you down.'

His smile tilted, then his hand gripped the back of my neck and his fingers squeezed. 'Thanks, and, for what it's worth, I think Rick is an idiot.'

He didn't know how Rick and I had split then. 'You know I dumped him?'

'So Em said. What I meant was, Rick is just an idiot.'

I laughed. I didn't know what to say to that. His long fingers slipped away from my neck, but I could still feel them there.

As we waited watching Susie make all ten drinks and load them into a box, the music changed to 'Happy Xmas (War is over)'.

'If I hear one more Christmas song…' Jack whispered under his breath.

I laughed. But I knew what he meant. I was not in the spirit of the season this year. Rick hadn't only taken custody of the house; he'd got custody of my parents and my friends. Everyone was on the side of team-Rick. But he was so nice, any woman would be stupid to say no to him, and so everyone had seen the complete and utter bitch in me.

I probably was the stupid one.

I glanced sideways at Jack. He was about four inches taller than me and I was five-eight, so he was tall. I caught his gaze as it shone through his dark eyelashes. 'For what it's worth,' I whispered, 'I think Sharon is a bitch.'

A bark of laughter left his throat.

'Here you go!' Our box of coffees was handed over, I moved to pick it up, but he leaned over and took it before I could. Really he could have done this on his own. Except maybe he needed someone to hold the doors. I pushed it open for him as we walked out.

The street was so crowded with shoppers it was like playing dodgems. I opened the disabled access door into the office block so he didn't have to navigate the rotating doors with the box.

'Back to the madhouse,' he said as we stepped into the lift.

I looked at my watch. 'There's only an hour left before two...'

'I can't see much work being done, but maybe this coffee will charge you all up, so we can get all the account work wrapped up—'

'Before Christmas.'

It was like he cringed at the word Christmas, as his face screwed up and one shoulder sort of ducked. But after that weird reaction, once his face had straightened up, he said in a flat voice, 'Yeah.'

'Weirdo...' I said as the lift doors opened and I stepped out.

I got the office door and held it open.

'Heartbreaker...' he said when he walked past me into the office.

He was such a flirt, but so fit that even though I knew he flirted with absolutely everyone, it still had an effect. It was that pitch in his voice, the look in his blue eyes, and the quirk to his mouth, as much as any of the things he said – oh and how hot his body looked.

'Coffee!' he yelled as he set the box down on the desk, then he pulled a cup out. 'Vanilla latte.' He held it out to me.

'Thank you.'

'You're welcome.'

My fingers touched his when I took it and my tummy did a backflip, excited by a sexual jolt of attraction.

He turned away and looked into the box again, then pulled

out his triple-shot espresso. He drank his coffee like the drug it was, taking shots to charge up his exuberant personality. He walked back into his office and shut the door.

I shouted out the types of coffee and people came over to collect them as I watched him take off his coat. He hung it up on the rack in there, then went over to his desk, picked up his mobile phone and made a call. He walked around as he talked, making large hand gestures. Then his hand gripped in his hair and he looked up, as if he was seeking Divine intervention.

It didn't look as though he'd received it. He looked like he shouted something into the phone before ending the call. Then he put his mobile on his desk as if it had burned his hand and stood staring at it for a moment. His hands slid into his pockets. A look of exasperation played across his face.

When he sat down at his desk, he picked up his office phone. The phone two desks behind me rang. Tina answered. 'Hi, Jack.'

'Your lawyer… Okay, on to it.'

As I walked over to leave the empty box by the recycle bin, about three minutes later, I heard Tina say, 'He's on the line. I'll put him through.'

I felt sorry for Jack. He'd worked hard to build up the business. But then he had cheated.

I sat down to finish off the project I was working on. I wanted to get it completed before Christmas. I wasn't allowed near the big accounts, but I'd recently been given one of the smaller ones to manage as a trial. I was trying really hard to come up with a new concept that would blow their minds.

If I was going to make my mark on advertising, this was my moment to start.

After about half an hour I sat back in my chair and sighed. The right idea wasn't coming. I'd listed, in a mind map, all the things the client wanted, the demographics we knew about their market, the things that were unique about their products, looking for an angle, a hook, a catch… But I couldn't spot one.

My stupid brain was absorbed with Christmas, and Rick.

He was going to my parents with his parents. The plans hadn't changed since my birthday – I'd just been dropped from them. 'Ivy, I think it's best you stay away from home this year, Rick is very upset.' Those were Mum's precise words. Everyone loved Rick and so now everyone hated me. The only person who was sort of with me still, was Milly. But she couldn't openly be on Team Ivy because Rick was Steve's best friend – the two of them had paired us up at school. They could not have been more wrong.

Then why had I stayed with Rick for six years? *Six years!*

Because I'd been lazy. It had just been easy. I'd liked him. I still did. He was nice – why wouldn't I like him? I even loved him, in a quiet way. But he'd never made my heart pound or my tummy backflip. I didn't want to settle for 'like', or 'comfortable', or 'kind'. I wanted a passionate love. I regretted hurting Rick by letting him think everything was okay. But I didn't regret leaving. I'd wasted six years of both our lives staying in that relationship when I'd known it was wrong.

When the clock hit two, everyone started packing up. Emma knocked on Jack's office door. When she opened it, she asked, 'Are you sure you don't want to come for a drink?'

I didn't hear what he said, but it was obviously a reiteration of no.

'Have a good Christmas,' Emma concluded.

She stopped at my desk then. I hadn't stopped working; I wasn't in the mood for a rowdy pub on Christmas Eve. 'Are you not coming either, Ivy?'

'No, I don't feel like it.' Emma knew all my troubles, she was my direct manager, and she'd been good about everything – she'd given me time off to look for somewhere to live after my life had crash-landed, and the place I'd found had actually been one she'd spotted advertised on Gumtree.

'You're sure?'

'Yes.' It wasn't only the crowds, I wouldn't be able to stand the

Christmas music; Christmas was not happening for me this year and I didn't need reminders of what I was missing out on. It was depressing and I was trying to leave my depression behind.

'I don't like leaving you here.'

'I'm alright, honest.'

'Why don't you go home?'

Because there was no one and nothing to go home for. 'No. I want to finish up what I'm doing on this account. I'll use the creativity room while it's quiet and try and generate some ideas before I pack up.' I looked back at my computer and clicked on print, then stood up.

'Well, if you want to come down to the pub later, text me, to check we haven't moved on somewhere, and if you need me over the Christmas break you can call.'

'That's really kind, but I'll be okay. Have a good time.'

'Take care.'

When she went over to get her coat, I collected the printout of the mind map I'd done and then walked to the door with everyone. They were smiling and laughing, and they talked excitedly. Christmas had an atmosphere that was different to any other holiday; everyone was *jollier* – using the Christmas word. But there were the gifts, decorations and feasting to look forward to. I wasn't doing any of those things this year. I was going to sit alone in my room and dine on baked beans on toast. I wasn't very good at cooking for one. Rick had been the homemaker, not me.

A couple of the guys air-kissed me at the door and I hugged Tina and Mary, and wished them all a good time, and a Happy New Year, because this was it until the 2nd of January; we were finishing up for the whole period between Christmas and New Year.

So as of… Now. When the door shut. I was on my own.

I walked into the creativity room. It was four walls of blue-sky posters that you could write on and then wipe clean. 'To encourage blue-sky thinking,' that was Jack. Emma was the organiser, planner and manager out of the two of them and Jack was the off-the-wall ideas and sales man. He did most of the client work; Emma managed the office and the accounts. The things Jack would find boring.

'Right. Forget them, forget what time of year it is, I am going to do this. Come on, brain, give me some inspiration.'

I wrote up all the key things I'd thought of so far, then I used the computer in the room to Google relevant images and printed them off and stuck them up against all the facts and inspirations. As the images began to build, I started to think I was getting somewhere, that any moment the idea was going to come, but then suddenly the door opened.

'What are you doing in here?'

I jumped. 'Oh, God, you scared me.'

Jack stepped into the room. 'Ivy, why aren't you at the pub? I was just about to put the alarm on and lock up when I saw the light on in here. I nearly locked you in for the holidays.'

'I didn't want to go to the pub either. I've been working on an idea for the Berkeley account.'

'I can see that.' He glanced up at the wall. 'But it's Christmas; they aren't going to do anything with it until the New Year and anyway I'm going now so you're going to have to leave too.'

I picked up all the stuff I'd been working on, but left everything I'd put up on the walls. He stepped back and let me walk out. Then he knocked off the light, shut the door behind us and followed me.

I went over to my desk. The light was out in his office and his coat was in a heap on the desk next to mine.

'I shut your computer down. I thought you'd gone and been sloppy and left everything out.'

I poked my tongue out at him as he dropped into the chair before the desk next to mine. One ankle lifted to settle on his opposite knee as he sprawled back in the chair, watching me.

I put everything down on my desk and then opened the drawer in the pedestal.

His skinny black trousers hugged the muscular definition in his legs as he leaned back in that cool, nonchalant pose.

He picked up a pen that had been lying on the desk tapped one end of it, twisted it over with his fingers and then tapped the other end, and kept on turning it and tapping it in an absent-minded way as I shoved all my work into the drawer.

'So what are you doing for the holidays?'

'Nothing.' I locked my drawer, then looked at him.

'Me neither. Have you got anyone to go and visit, or anyone coming to you?'

'No. I'm all alone.' I gave him an awkward smile as I straightened up, ready to go. He didn't make a move to get up.

'Me too.'

His blue eyes looked at me and his fingers stopped turning the pen, then lifted to brush his black hair off his brow. There was that tug and my tummy did a dozen backflips like it had taken on a tumbling act.

'You know, Ivy, we needn't spend the holiday alone.'

Shit. What was coming?

'We could spend it together, if you want?'

'If I want...'

'I'm going away. I've got a cottage in the Lake District. It's my haven. It's entirely isolated. You could come, if you want?'

'If I want?' I repeated. Where was this going?

His eyebrows lifted. 'Ivy, come on, you get it. You could spend Christmas here alone. Or we could go away together and spend Christmas having naughty sex and leave the world to get on with their happy families' celebration.'

I should feel insulted, I should feel shocked. What I felt was nothing like that – I felt – tempted...

He stood up. 'You fancy me. We've had chemistry going on since you started here. Admit it.' He was standing close to me, arms at his sides, looking at me like he wanted to reach out and touch. I wanted to reach out and grab, I always had.

25

'Give into it,' he said, as though it was the most normal thing for him to come on to me and ask me to go away with him.

'Oh. You're so tempting,' I said sarcastically and turned my back on him, deliberately, to cross the room and fetch my coat. My heartbeat raced manically. God, my body would love to do that. Sex! Naughty sex! The wicked side of me, the girl on Santa's bad list, wanted to ask *how naughty?* But I didn't really need to ask; I'd seen the glint in his eyes that had implied very naughty. But he was my boss.

'I can be more tempting.' I heard him getting closer as he followed me to the coat racks.

His voice ran fingers across my innards like they were guitar strings.

After I'd taken my coat off the hook I turned and faced him. A part of me was terrified and it yelled, *don't be more tempting!* While the wicked me, the bitch that had refused to marry Rick because he was boring, wanted to leap at Jack's offer.

I smiled.

One eyebrow and one side of his lips lifted. 'You are tempted. I knew you fancied me.'

'I didn't know you fancied me that much.' I slipped my arms into the sleeves of my parka. It would be entirely reckless of me to say yes.

His hands lifted, saying, *look at you.* 'Seriously, Ivy, you must know what you look like, who wouldn't?'

'That isn't a compliment that'll win me over.'

'I'm saying you're gorgeous.' He stepped closer and then his hands gripped the edges of my coat. 'And there is one thing I've always known about you, you were too good for Rick. That guy was never right for you.'

My tummy did pirouettes. 'I am tempted.' My answer was a broken, dry-mouthed whisper. He'd had me at 'Rick was never right for you'.

He glanced up at the ceiling, his head tilting back. 'Yes. Come on temptation.' His gaze dropped back to me. 'Actually, why don't we scrap naughty sex and go for all-out nasty sex, a whole week of it.'

'And what happens when we get back?' I could hear the words in Rick's voice. *Don't be crazy, Ivy, he's your boss.* I'd spent too many years listening to Rick's cautions.

'Nothing happens. We act like normal.' He looked around. 'I don't see anyone here; who's to know we went away together?' Then he looked back at me. 'It'll be our secret.'

'But you're my boss—'

'I'm not going to sack you if you have sex with me.'

'Or you have sex with me. This is your suggestion.' I'd only ever done it with Rick. Was that desperately sad? It felt sad, and I was one hundred per cent sure that doing it with Jack would be incomparable to doing it with Rick. My bad girl wanted to know what it would feel like.

His eyes glinted. He still had a hold on my coat. The expensive aftershave he wore filled the air around us.

I breathed in and ended up breathing in his out-breath, he was so close.

'As far as I remember, sex takes two people. If we have sex we agree no one's to blame, no one's leading the other one. We're doing it for a bit of fun because we have nothing better to do and we'll come back feeling much better than if we'd sat at home pissed off with everyone else enjoying themselves.'

Naughty. Nasty. Sex. My heart thudded, adding a bass beat to the moment, and my tummy was wobbly like a jelly shot. This was what I'd turned Rick down for – to feel a rush like this – this pounding and excitement in my blood. 'Yes okay. Alright.' The words left my lips without any bidding from my brain.

'You're sure?' He sounded surprised.

But I *was* up for this. This was what I'd thrown my life up in the air to feel. This feeling was the thing I'd craved. Excitement.

He let go of me. I'd expected him to kiss me. But then it wasn't romance he was offering.

27

'I promise you, you won't regret it.'

'You…' A nervous laugh escaped my throat. 'You're so full of yourself.'

His hands suddenly pressed either side of my head, his long fingers sliding into my hair. Then he did kiss me. It was hard and dominating. Nothing like the soft, gentle way that Rick kissed.

Oh, no, she's absolutely right. I cheated. Loads.

I hadn't ever admitted it, not even to myself in my head, but I'd wanted him to kiss me since I'd started here two years ago even though I'd been with Rick. Maybe I'd even have loved it if, at the end of my interview, he'd have pinned me up against a wall, kissed me, and whispered into my mouth, 'You got the job.' But there had been Rick at home and I wouldn't have cheated. I'd never have let it happen before.

I cheated. Loads… Jack would have, and the whole idea of that made my tummy backflip when it should be turning in disgust. Maybe I'd dumped Rick not so much because he was too nice, but because I was too bad. Maybe all my family and friends were right to be on Team Rick.

When Jack's lips lifted off mine, I rose on to my toes and captured his bottom lip with a nip. I was up for this. I wanted to be the sort of person who played. I wanted to try it. There was a rush inside me, inspired by the risk of who he was, and what he was – even though he denied it, if this went wrong, he employed me. But Jack would not even think of stuff like that, he thrived on risk. I wanted to think like him. I was up for a seven-night stand of naughty, nasty, sex.

He smiled then let go of my hand. 'There's one thing we need to make a deal on before we go,' he said as he turned and walked back to pick up his coat, before looking at me again. 'Let's not mention the C word, I'm really not up for that this year.'

He meant Christmas. I laughed. 'Deal. Me neither. We'll make every day a normal day. '

He grinned as he slipped on his coat.

I should feel scared. All I felt was excited. This rush was amazing.

He held my hand, which wasn't intimate because he'd put his suede gloves on, and then he led me out of the office, setting the alarm with his free hand before closing the door.

When we were in the lift, his free hand gripped the back of my neck and he kissed me again. The heat in my blood whizzed up to the four-chilli symbol temperature, as his tongue touched the seam of my lips. I opened my mouth. What was the point of playing shy when we'd agreed on sex already?

The way he kissed was purposeful, adamant and domineering. I pushed my tongue into his mouth. I was not going to let him be the boss of me in this.

When the doors opened he pulled away.

'There is one thing I want to make a deal on before we go,' I said. 'You're not my boss now, from this moment, until the 2nd of January. I'm giving you notice and you can re-employ me then.'

'Deal,' he breathed.

This was crazy.

'Where do you live? I'll drive you back, then I'll pick you up at six-thirty and we'll go up north tonight, okay?'

'Yeah, okay.'

Jack

Six months before – in June

I shut the door to my office. This weekend was going to be different. Not the same old clubs and same people. I was journeying into the past.

'Good luck with the reunion, Jack.'

'Thanks, Em, enjoy your weekend.'

Em and I had shared a house through the last two years of university and now we shared a business. We were polar opposites but the two of us together were the perfect blend for success. I was the insanity and ideas and she was the voice of reason and a planning genius.

Ivy, one of the women who worked for us, was leaning on my personal assistant's desk as I walked towards the door, telling Tina something, and her bottom was prominently aimed in my direction. She was wearing her chequered trousers; the ones that exaggerated her curves and made my groin heavy with longing.

'Bye, Jack.' Tina lifted a hand in parting.

Ivy straightened and turned around. She had the most amazing eyes. They were a lavender colour, purple-grey, and she dyed her hair a quirky pale mauve to match them. It made the colour of her eyes a dozen times deeper.

My diaphragm shoved all the air out of my lungs every time I looked at Ivy and those eyes. She was tall and slender but she had curves in all the places a woman should and a face that looked like something an artist would paint. Plus she had the purest ivory-white skin. Who kept their skin white these days? None of the girls I knew, but Ivy shied away from the sun and fake tan and kept her skin pure.

I'd have put her in front of the camera in one of our adverts but I had a feeling if I did that I'd never see her again; some modelling agency would pick her up and steal her away. And the thought of not having Ivy around to look at, and get my kicks over in the day, was gut wrenching.

But my kicks were all safe and innocent – she was with someone – and she was not the sort of girl to go anywhere near me when I had a wife. Plus Em would kill me if I tried it. And anyway I wouldn't; Ivy was a nice girl. Too nice to treat like a throw-away.

'Have a good weekend, Jack.' She smiled at me.

I smiled too. 'See you on Monday – have a good one.'

Nice, and someone else's or not, though, every time she looked at me her eyes told me she fancied me too.

When I rode the lift downstairs I stared at myself in the mirror, looking into my eyes. I didn't like who I saw in the mirror any more. I was getting bored of me. This school reunion had made me do a lot of reflecting on the boy I'd been and the man I'd become.

I changed into my leathers in the toilets on the basement floor, then lifted my hand to the security guy when I walked out.

This used to be the part of the week I looked forward to most. Friday night. Spending the money I'd earned, showing it off to win girls.

I preferred being at work now.

I shoved my clothes and the shoes I'd taken off into the pannier on my motorbike. Then I straddled the machine, revved the engine and gloried in the roar and vibration between my legs. I rode it

31

out of the car park with a good feeling about going to do something different this weekend.

It was a warm night. The sky was pure blue. I dodged through the traffic, weaving in and out, avoiding the queues, unless I saw a police car and then I waited and queued with the rest, my feet on the floor as the engine rumbled between my thighs.

I loved the bike. I loved the anonymity of being behind a helmet and the freedom of speed. But it was getting out of the city on it that was the best. Then I could speed, especially in the middle of the night when hardly anyone else was around.

Riding the bike absorbed my thoughts and my mind needed to be absorbed in something else when I was heading home to my wife. Tonight I hoped Sharon would be out.

I used the word 'wife' loosely. My marriage wasn't really a marriage; it was more like regular sex for the investment of half my income, the cost of a penthouse and every other thing Sharon wanted.

When the lift opened on to the top floor I owned, I sighed as I walked over to put the key in the lock. I hated coming home. I came home because this was where I lived, but the place didn't feel like a home.

I turned the key and opened the door. 'Sharon!' I called out her name because I never knew what I was walking into and I wanted to give her the chance to stop if necessary.

I unzipped my leather suit and left my helmet on a chest by the door.

There was nothing wrong with the apartment. The place was amazing. It would be perfect if it didn't house Sharon.

A part of me sulked all the time over the fact that Sharon had ruined this place for me.

I'd got myself tangled up in something stupid with her; every room in this place was tainted by it and I didn't know how to untangle myself from the mess I'd made.

The place was a massive open space with three walls of glass.

32

There was a Jacuzzi in the bathroom and a pool on the roof outside that had a view across London through another glass wall when you swam. I'd thought the place was 'us', me and Sharon, when I'd bought it. A wild place for a wild couple, who loved to live without limits. We had orgies up here and took drugs that made the skyline and the world distorted. We lived life to the extreme – on top of the world. Riding the world like the world was a motorbike, to be raced and dodged through the stationary and slow traffic.

I still loved the place, despite it not being homely. But I didn't love Sharon any more. I probably never had and I didn't like the way we lived any more. I think I'd just been in lust with Sharon in the beginning and excited by the way she lived – so fast and far on the outside of normal.

The life I led with Sharon ran parallel to everything else. It had felt like unleashing the true me in the beginning. The rebellious, fast-living, independent, unboundaried me. But if this was the real me, why didn't I like it, or myself, any more?

Maybe I'd always known this wasn't right for me because I'd never told my friends about it, not from school, not from my climbing club, uni, work or anywhere.

'In here!' Sharon shouted from the bedroom. I hoped this wasn't going to be another gift. She knew my interest was waning and so she'd started trying everything she could to keep me in the game with her.

I didn't want to play.

Ever since I'd had the invite to go back to my old school I'd been evaluating my life and nothing fitted. I'd been ambitious as a kid and Em and I had the business, and I had my investment properties and ten times more than I could have expected to achieve at my age – except that it all tasted sour because I'd never been ambitious for this empty fucking marriage. This was not how I'd seen myself. This was not where I wanted to be five years from now.

33

Sharon was on her own in the bedroom, in her underwear – just old-fashioned suspenders and stockings. Maybe she hoped I'd be motivated to react to her nudity before I left. I wasn't. I started stripping off my leather suit. After I'd released my arms, it hung from my waist

'What time are you going out?' she asked.

'As soon as I'm showered and ready.' I removed my boots and took the leather suit off my legs. Then straightened and stripped off my t-shirt.

'Is it okay if I ask some people over?'

By 'some people' she meant her friends – I used that term loosely too – and a mix of strangers, who'd take cocaine that I'd pay for and drink booze that I'd pay for. Then they'd come in here, into my bedroom and have sex on my bed, a twisting puzzle of tangled bodies. Or maybe not in here, maybe in the Jacuzzi or in the living room, or in the pool… 'Do what you want.'

I left my clothes in a pile on the floor for the cleaner to pick up, then went to have a shower.

I washed my hair and let the water teem over my head, tipping up my face, then I sighed. I spat out the water that had run into my mouth and turned to face the wall. Fuck. The thought of tangled bodies and long legs wrapping around me and the tongues and mouths that would be all over me, if I stayed here, did still turn me on. With one hand flat on the cold marble slab lining the back wall, and the water running over my head and down my back, I took my dick in my hand.

The images in my mind had made me hard.

I gripped it with anger, because I really didn't want to be like this. Then I shut my eyes and let thoughts of sex wash over me with the water.

Sharon would be willing to murder me if she knew I'd rather wank than have sex with her. She thought I was going to pick someone up at the reunion party. I had no intention of doing that. The girls I'd been at school with were not like Sharon.

34

But maybe that was why I'd been so absorbed by Sharon when this had started.

I groaned when the orgasm rattled through my bones. My head fell forward and I took another breath.

That would keep me going without sex until I got back.

I washed off the marble in front of me, then washed the soap off my body and turned off the shower.

When I looked at the guy in the mirror to shave, I still didn't like him.

I walked back into the bedroom with a towel hanging low on my hips and droplets of water still on my skin. Sharon looked up at me from where she sat before a mirror painting on her lipgloss. She'd put a robe on. She turned around on the stool. 'We could mess around before you go, if you come over here.'

'No thanks. It's a long drive. I'm going to be late already.'

I found a shirt and trousers out of the wardrobe and got dressed. She watched me, but she didn't say anything else.

I picked out a dark-blue, thin tie just to break up the white of my shirt, but I left the tie loose, the top button of my shirt undone so the collar was open. Then I rolled up my sleeves. It was too hot to put a jacket on.

Tonight we were meeting for a drink in the hotel, then tomorrow the school were holding a formal dinner. I'd packed this morning when Sharon was asleep, so at least I didn't have to do that with her watching me, like I was a panther she was trying to work out how to trap.

Two nights away. Two nights to look at my life and think about where I wanted it to be in another five years. I needed to work out what my end game was.

I turned and looked at Sharon. She uncrossed her legs, with her back arched, so her breasts looked good. She never said, *don't you fancy me any more?* But the words were in her eyes all the time lately.

Yes, I did fancy her still. I'd have to be blind not to; she had

35

an amazing body. I could still get hard for her and enjoy every minute of sex with her. But emotionally – she did nothing for me.

I walked over and gripped the back of her neck, pressed my lips on hers for an instant, then wiped the gloss off my lips with the back of my hand. 'See you on Sunday. Have a good time.'

Her eyes, which some people called green, but were really hazel, stared at me. Ivy's lavender eyes came to mind. She was the only woman I'd ever seen with really distinctive eyes. I'd never seen anyone else with lavender-grey eyes.

'You have a good time too. Don't shag anyone I wouldn't.'

I gave her a crooked smile. 'That leaves the field open, then. You'd shag everyone.' She liked girls as well as guys. That had been one of the novel things about her, when I'd first met her – that she loved bringing other women to bed with us and she loved watching me fuck them as much as messing around with them herself.

She gave me a half-hearted laugh. 'Bye.'

'Bye.' I walked out and grabbed my leather jacket off the hook by the door. Then picked up the keys to the Jag. I was going on an adventure. Stepping into the unknown. I probably felt as excited as most young guys felt when they were invited to join an orgy.

I was bored of orgies. They were full of self-centred, greedy people.

I was looking forward to going back to the simplicity of the life I'd led as a youth – with a heart-wrenching need. I wanted to be who I'd been then – the boy I used to look at in a mirror and like; the one who had dreams in his eyes. The person I'd been before I'd made my first million and had to fight off the parasites.

As I drove down there, I wondered what people would say if they knew how I lived. Some of the others had become involved with drugs too. I'd heard that. When you had money to waste and youth on your side it was too tempting. But some of them… most of them… would probably turn their backs on me if they knew

36

everything about me – like my parents had. And my parents knew hardly anything.

Nostalgia hit me in the stomach with a punch when I drove into the small town where I'd gone to school. It was old-world. Dickensian. I'd spent years of my life here. This school had formed who I was; it had made me a stronger person and given me the confidence to believe in myself – and my belief had made me a millionaire by the age of twenty-two.

Loads of people here had money. It wouldn't be exceptional turning up here as a rich man. But I would be one of the few who'd made it himself. Most people had trust funds; money given to them on a plate by mummy and daddy. Not that I hadn't had that too; my parents' initial investment had started me off, but I'd paid them back and I was still rolling in it. Advertising and my brain full of the weird and wonderful were my pots of gold. I had a skill for concepts and big corporations loved it, and I'd invested my profits in property.

I parked up around the back of the hotel, took a breath, then steeled myself to walk in there.

The guy at the reception desk signed me in, gave me my room key, said they'd take up my luggage, and then pointed me in the direction of the bar where everyone was meeting.

There were probably a hundred people in there; there would be three hundred plus tomorrow. I recognised a few faces.

'Jack!'

Edward. He'd shouted from about ten feet away. He lifted a hand.

'You made it,' he said, when I got over to him. 'It's great to see you. I was looking out for you.' He held my arm for an instant, pulling me into the group of people he'd been talking to. We'd been best friends at school – we'd kept in contact. He worked for a bank and sometimes I went over to Canary Wharf and met him for a drink after work. 'This is Helen, my fiancée…'

'Hi. Nice to meet you, Helen. Edward's talked about you, and nothing else, every time we've met for the last year.'

The conversation they'd been involved in cracked up again. My hands slid into my trouser pockets as I stood there and listened.

I'd known you could bring partners; I'd never considered bringing Sharon. She'd have embarrassed me. She'd have tried to get into all the guys' trousers and if she knew it made me uncomfortable she'd have been trying ten times harder. And if she'd succeeded with anyone, I'd have died if she'd expected me to share my bed with people I knew from school.

That was the thought that had made me start reflecting harder. If my life was not something I'd share with friends because my wife was embarrassing and the way I lived so bad it had to be a secret – what was I doing living like that?

Edward had never met Sharon. I'd been married for nearly three years.

When we were younger, maybe he'd have whacked me on the back in applause if I'd told him I was in an open relationship, which meant shagging anyone you wanted in any mix of people, anywhere and anytime. But we were meant to be grown up now; it was a very different thing to say it now.

It was weird. I lived a weird life.

I turned to the bar. I needed a drink to hold so I didn't feel like a prick. The guy serving lifted an eyebrow at me to ask what I wanted. He was probably pissed off with the posh twits that must haunt this hotel all the time – people with more money than sense. 'Champagne. A bottle. A good one.' But you had to play the part if you had money. He showed me a list of the bottles they had. I picked one.

When he opened it, he gave me a taste. I nodded that it was okay, then he poured me a glass. 'Put the bottle back in the chiller and keep it for me.'

'Sure.'

When I turned back to the room I noticed someone I recognised in a way that was more than mental.

Victoria.

I knew her smell and her taste.

We'd dated for a year while we'd been at the school, but she'd left before year thirteen. She'd gone home one summer and I'd never heard from her again. I'd texted her a few times, but then I'd given up chasing her. I'd had enough girls chasing me. I didn't have to chase them.

Her head turned and her gaze stretched across the room, catching a hold of mine, as though she'd felt me looking. She was still really pretty. Blonde and slim. I smiled. I'd have gone over to talk to her but she looked away, her expression saying, *shit, not him.* She didn't want me over there, then.

I turned to the group Edward and Helen were among. The crowd around them were the guys he and I had hung out with at school. I didn't listen to what they said, I thought of Victoria. Of the nights when we'd snuck out of our dorms in the dark and found quiet spots down by the river – of how it felt to slide my hand up under the long skirts the girls had had to wear. Of how soft her thighs had felt and how I'd discovered heaven between them.

Victoria had been my first. This was a true walk down memory lane.

But shit, if she knew how I lived my married life I'd bet her nose would screw up in disgust. She wouldn't be into this me. I'd bet Victoria was a 'normal' person.

When the evening wound up I walked upstairs to my room alone. A little drunk but not high on anything. I stripped off, then lay on the bed staring at the ceiling.

I needed drugs or sex to sleep. I had neither thing to bring my constant adrenaline rush down.

I got up and opened the window on to the street. The shop windows were still lit up across the road. It was past midnight

39

but the sky seemed light. It wasn't much past the longest day and to me this was the best part of the year. I liked being up in Cumbria when it was like this, maybe I would go up next weekend. Maybe getting away from London and the people and the life there would put my head straight again.

Sharon hated the place I'd bought in the Lake District. It wasn't her scene. There was no one else to have sex with when we went up there. It was quiet, peaceful and idyllic. To me it was better than the best trip I'd ever had on drugs, and it went on forever when you were up there. Nature was addictive. Life was addictive when I was there.

I dropped back on the bed and stared up at the ceiling, which was grey because the night was so bright.

Things churned around in my mind. The work I had to organise for clients next week. What Sharon would be up to in our bed back at the apartment. What I had got up to in that bed all week, and in the Jacuzzi, and the pool.

I took a breath, longing for some weed to smoke at least, so my mind could come down from its height of activity enough to sleep.

I couldn't sleep. I never could. I'd been a raving insomniac for years.

Victoria came into my mind and I wondered how different things would have been if I'd stayed with her. But that was stupid, because I hadn't loved her, just liked her a lot, so we'd have split at some point between then and now, either in year thirteen or when we'd gone on to university.

I slept for about an hour, maybe, I think, or maybe I'd lain there thinking all night, wishing I'd done what Sharon had thought I'd done and found an old school friend to fuck. One of the girls would have been up for it. I'd seen a few of them who'd used to sleep with me in year thirteen, looking.

There was something about a woman's eyes that gave the game

away when they were up for it. Sharon had taught me that. She was good at spotting the people in bars who were cool for a night of naughty sex. She said it was because their pupils flared. The easier measure was who stared back at you when you stared at them.

After breakfast everyone walked down towards the school. I walked beside Edward and his fiancée. None of the guys I'd kept in contact with had asked me why I hadn't brought my wife. Every one of them who had a partner had brought them. I suppose they were used to me not taking her whenever I saw them. I guess they all thought I was just a bad husband. I think that was what everyone outside of the bubble I lived in with Sharon believed.

What would happen if the bubble burst?

The shit would fly.

My hands were in the pockets of my trousers, pinning my suit jacket open as I walked. I had skinny-cut trousers on and a pale-blue shirt. My suit was a dark blue. We were probably meant to wear black, everyone else was in black, but I'd always liked to be different.

I mentally heard one of the masters shout at me, '*take your hands out of your pockets Mr Rendell!*' as we walked through the doors of the Harry Potter-ish school.

It was an amazing place. The building made you respect it. It had always gripped at my soul but today it seemed to look inside me and prod my conscience. It didn't like what it saw either. It didn't approve of what I'd become. It was ashamed of me.

We listened to speeches from the school heads about the achievements of our year's alumni group and the achievements of the school since we'd left, as we sat in rows like we had as kids – only this time on chairs not the floor or a bench.

My theory was we'd been brought back because we were of average child-bearing age and they hoped we'd send our kids here.

Kids. That was one mistake I'd not made with Sharon and I had a very firm condom rule in our sex games. A child wouldn't

41

want the sentence of a life with me as their parent, or Sharon acting as mother.

After the speeches, we were given time to wander about the ancient halls and rooms, re-familiarising ourselves with the place. It was weird. I could see myself at desks, talking to people in halls, kissing Victoria and some of the other girls after Victoria had left, up against the walls.

Victoria had been three rows in front of me in the hall, but if she'd sensed me behind her, she hadn't looked back.

As I wandered around the halls alone, wondering how my pathway from here had ended up where it had, I saw her walk out of a room with a friend. When she saw me, she walked back in.

I carried on, walking past the room she was in, as she clearly didn't want to speak to me. I ended up outside on the lawn on my own, walking about the rugby pitch, wishing for a joint again. I hadn't ever smoked cigarettes. I only smoked when the tobacco contained something with more punch.

Hands in pockets, I walked along the recently re-marked white lines, viewing me then and me now in my mind's eye. I suppose the two of us were not that different. I'd been a self-obsessed shit then too, only then I'd valued it as self-belief. But it had helped me create a successful business. It was not to be knocked too heavily.

It was that cocky attitude that had made me tell everyone else they were wrong about Sharon when I'd met her. My parents and Em had warned me I was taking a wrong path. I'd told them to fuck off out of my personal business. But it was the wrongness and forbidden nature of the life I led that had made me get involved in it. It held a sense of risk and that made my blood pump with adrenaline. And, of course, anything that had pissed my parents off, and got my adrenalin raging, I'd been into it when I was younger. My self-focused attitude had made me rebellious and I wouldn't have let my parents set boundaries around me when I'd just made a million. In my eyes, then, I'd been a genius and they'd been beneath me.

I'd been a big-headed dick, and now—

'Jack.' I turned around to see Victoria walking towards me, in a pair of pale-pink stiletto heels that were sinking into the grass of the pitch. She had a light flowery summer dress on, one that covered her breasts entirely and fell down to her knees. One that showed the outline of her body as the sunlight shone through the cotton and made me want to guess what everything looked like beneath.

I was more used to women who wore tops that shoved their breasts up in your face, or showed you the first curved edge in a dress secured by tape. While their skirts were so high you had no leg left to imagine, and if they opened their legs, which they frequently did deliberately, you had nothing at all left to imagine.

Imagination was nice and Victoria's simplicity and prim dress had me hornier than any of the half-naked women Sharon liked us to play with.

I was glad Victoria had come looking for me. Maybe she'd been waiting for a moment to speak quietly. Just the two of us. Maybe I would do what Sharon expected me to do tonight and share a bed with Victoria, for old times' sake.

'Hi,' I said, as she came closer. 'I got the vibe you didn't want to talk to me, otherwise I'd have come over and said, hello, last night. How are you? Is life treating you alright?'

She gave me a faint smile and looked me in the eyes. *The look* wasn't there. Her pupils didn't flare. She just looked awkward. It didn't look like she even fancied me.

I had another sleepless night to look forward to… My internal voice, which never fucking shut up, laughed.

'Hi,' she answered. 'I do want to speak to you, but I've been building up courage.' She swallowed as if she had a dry throat.

I held her arm and turned her away from the school towards

43

the edge of the narrow river where there was a path her heels wouldn't sink into. She didn't try to shake my hand off.

Was she thinking about the times we'd lain out here and used the grass as a bed? I remembered. I could remember every element of what it had felt like because she'd been my first.

I let go of her when we reached the river path, but we kept walking, following the path further away from the school. My hands slipped back into my pockets. I looked ahead, not at her.

'You're married,' she said. 'I heard Edward tell one of the others when she was asking about you.'

A sound of amusement slipped out of the back of my throat. So Edward had been guarding me from propositions. He definitely would not agree with mine and Sharon's open way of life. 'Yes, I'm married. What about you?'

'But you didn't bring her.'

'No, this type of do isn't her thing. She's high-maintenance.' It was the only way I could describe Sharon to people. She was, though – I had to invest eighty per cent of my mind and money on her to keep her happy, or to make sure she was not up to something that would make me unhappy. It had got to the point that I only really took part in the orgies because the argument if I didn't take part took too much energy, Sharon never backed down.

I'd rather be with someone quiet like Victoria. It would be like going away to Cumbria. The solitude and solidity of having sex with one woman was currently the best fantasy I had. 'And you? You didn't answer. Are you married, settled down, single… What?'

'Married.' She looked at me with the smile I remembered from our school days and lifted her left hand to show me the ring. On top of it was a beautiful white-gold engagement ring too, with a sapphire and a diamond entwined.

'Is he here?'

'No. I have a daughter…' Her breath caught for a second, but then she carried on. 'She's at home with him.'

44

'Are you happy?'

She smiled. 'Yes. Very.'

It was weird, because if I took Sharon out of the equation, the two women who'd counted in my life were the complete opposite of me. The sensible part of me was drawn to level-headed women like Victoria and Em. The wild me…

Here was Victoria settled into a quiet life with a husband and a kid, in her below-the-knee length print dress that covered all of her breasts, and I'd bet she only went out to a restaurant for special occasions because her world was all wrapped up at home. It was nice. I was glad for her.

Then there was Em, with her accountant's brain, and her black-and-white way of looking at life. She had everything in our business and her personal life sewn up tight; she never let anything slip. I liked to be all over every project at work, but I didn't need to be, with Em, because she was always there before me. But even she did not know how I lived my life with Sharon, and I saw Em every day. What did that tell me?

Sharon loved trying to rock that relationship; she hated me being close to Em. She even sent girls into work to try and get Em riled up with me, so that Em and me would fall out. My wild side laughed it off, and in the early days I'd indulged with one or two of the really pretty ones, because my attitude then had been 'why not?'.

Now it was – *why?*

'Are you happy?'

I should have known I'd get the same question back.

'Yes.' No. The white lie was easier.

'There's something I need to tell you, Jack. It's the only reason I really came here. But I was a coward last night. Can we sit down and talk?'

'Sure, shall we sit here and watch the river.' The grass was dry. We'd sat down out here on the grass a thousand times before.

She let her handbag fall off her shoulder and dropped it on

the ground, then swept her skirt beneath her and sat. I hoped the pale cloth wouldn't be stained by the grass.

I slipped my jacket off, but I couldn't offer it to her – it was too expensive to sit on. I folded it and dropped it on the ground, then sat down beside her with my legs bent up and my arms resting on my knees.

She twisted sideways, her legs bending so she could face me. One of her hands settled on the grass to balance her.

I smiled at her. 'What do you have to say? That you're really sorry you ran out on me at school. Don't worry, I received the message, even though it was silent I got used to you not being here. And you were allowed to make choices that didn't include me.'

'It wasn't a choice.' She looked down, her gaze falling as if she found it hard to look at me. She hadn't used to find it hard when we were at school. Her free hand picked a daisy out of the grass and then she spun it between her fingers, looking past me at the river. The sound of the water played on the air around us.

She was still being cowardly because whatever she'd come out here to say to me wasn't erupting from her lips. 'Did something happen, then?' Maybe she'd left school to avoid me? Perhaps she was holding some blame against me because life hadn't gone in the direction she'd wanted and she'd pinned it all down to not staying at school? But she'd just said she was happy. And I hadn't done anything bad to her.

She took a breath and looked at me again, as if she'd spent the last couple of minutes trying to slot words into place. 'My daughter is really beautiful. She's made my life what it is. I love her – like you cannot imagine. She says funny things all the time and every new thing she does and learns… It's beautiful… I have a picture on my phone.' The daisy fell from her fingers and she turned to her bag.

That was nice for her, but I didn't want to look at her photo.

When she found her phone she tapped in the code to unlock it and I saw her hand shake as she brought up her pictures. Then she held it out to me. 'She's seven years old, Jack.'

I looked at the image of a little girl, not really looking.

'She's yours,' Victoria said.

The words hit me. Shit. 'What?' She'd punched me in the stomach and followed it with a slap around the face. 'What?' I rocked back, as though she'd really hit me.

'I fell pregnant when we were here.'

'We used a condom every time.'

'Most times – not every time, when we were just messing around, and they aren't one hundred per cent safe. You managed to get me pregnant, anyway. I did not sleep with anyone else, if that's what you're thinking.'

I looked back at the phone and took it from her. My free hand shook. Like hers had done. My fingers brushed back my hair.

No. This was insane.

The words, 'you're fucking with me', spun around though my head in a sharp growl. But why would she?

The girl had black hair like mine and blue eyes like mine, and her face shape was mine. I stared at it. 'Why are you telling me now? If she's seven, why tell me now?' I was looking at a picture of a child that was meant to be mine.

'Because you should know. You should have known then, but my parents are old-fashioned, they didn't want anyone told. I pretended it wasn't happening, because I didn't know what to do. They found out about Daisy when I had her a month early on the floor in my room. Mum found us there and they rushed us both to hospital. I was lucky I didn't kill Daisy.

'Afterwards Mum and Dad told everyone the child was a maid's and they were going to adopt her and look after her. It took three years for me to stand up to them and tell them I was going to let people know Daisy was mine.'

'I don't know what to say.' I stared at the image on her phone.

47

My child. I had a child. Those words kept spinning through my brain. 'What do I say?'

'I met David after that, and he's a great dad. He didn't want me to tell you. That's why he isn't here. But when I got the letter from the school, it was like it was telling me I had to come here and let you know. You should know her, and she should know you.'

I stared at the picture. My daughter. I'd never choose to have a child. Never. My life was too fucked up. But I had a child. I'd had a child for all the years I'd been acting like a selfish bastard with Sharon. This little human being was made up of part of me. 'You should have told me.' I was a father. Me.

'I should have. I know. I'm sorry. But at the point I felt capable of speaking to you about it, she was already four and I didn't know how to begin.'

When she'd been five I'd married Sharon. Would I have made the same decision to lead a hedonistic life if I'd known about this child? Shit. I'd come here feeling introspective and nostalgic—questioning my life. This spun everything on its head. It was like someone had put my life in a box, picked it up and shaken it.

A child. I looked at Victoria, a frown probably making a line down the middle of my forehead. 'Am I allowed to see her, then?'

'Yes. David's agreed.'

'I doubt I need David's agreement.'

'Don't be like that, please. If we're doing this, if you want to see her and get to know her, then you have to do it sensitively. She's a child. It will be a massive thing for her. You'll need to take it slowly.'

'This is a massive thing for me. I just discovered I have a seven-year-old daughter.' When I'm not fit to be a father.

'You'll have to see her in my company, at least to begin with. I can't let her visit someone who's a stranger. You'd scare her.'

Scare her, my own child. But I had a legal right to her. I looked back at the picture. 'Does she know about me?'

'Yes, since she was four I've shown her your pictures from school, and said you're her daddy.'

I looked at Victoria again. 'So I'm not a complete stranger to her, but she is to me.' I shut my eyes as a wave of pain washed through my soul. 'You should've answered my messages that summer and told me. I would have helped you.'

'Jack you liked me but you didn't love me. You'd have felt guilty and made choices that changed your life, we'd have been stuck—'

'It changed your life. If the two of us made her, shouldn't the two of us have had equal impact? I would have loved her. I'm capable of love...'

Did I even know that? God, I hadn't experienced it. I loved my parents and they were probably the only people, and look at what I'd done to them; we'd only spoken on birthdays and at Christmas since I'd been with Sharon.

I stared at the picture. My child. The emotion in me was like flowing ripples on a pond racing outward after someone had dropped a stone in the middle. Her eyes were so like mine. There was no point in denying it. I'd made a child. Me. God! I wasn't going to mess her up. I had to do this. I had to be that man. As Victoria had said, there was no choice. I would love this child. I would shift heaven and earth. I would turn my fucking life around to be good enough for her. I had flesh and blood in this world.

How different would my life have been if Victoria had told me she was pregnant when I'd been seventeen?

There was no knowing.

Jealousy threw another fist into my stomach and clasped around my throat. I was jealous of Victoria, of her normal life, of her happiness – of the fact she'd brought up my daughter and seen her start to walk and learn to talk. 'Tell me about her.'

I asked her everything. When did Daisy ride her first bike? What was the first word she'd said? What did she like to do? Was she a fast runner, like I'd been? Did she swim? Was she reading? I spent an hour talking to Victoria about Daisy, with her picture held in my hand, as odd emotions twisted over in my stomach.

The school clock rang out the hour.

It brought back a hundred memories of being in school here. I had a daughter who went to school somewhere… I was going to start asking questions about where she lived and what school Daisy went to but Victoria gripped my arm. 'We'd better go back. I want to get ready for the ball this evening.'

'Okay.' I stood up, suddenly numb. This level of shock was like being hit by a car that had then reversed and run over me; it wasn't just my feet that had been taken out from underneath me. 'When can I see her?'

She smiled. 'Talk to her on the phone first, Jack.'

I didn't want to wait, I wanted to follow Victoria home. I didn't want to stay for the ball. Patience had never been a skill I possessed.

She held my wrist. 'I'll see you at the ball tonight and we can swap numbers and organise something in the next couple of weeks.'

Weeks. Uh-uh. No. I wanted a deadline. Days. But I bit my tongue and nodded.

I didn't ring Sharon when I got back to my room, I rang Mum. 'Hi, it's Jack.'

'Hello dear. This is unusual. How are you?' She never asked how Sharon was; they ignored her existence, sweeping the embarrassment I'd made of my life under one of their nice ornamental carpets.

'I'm feeling a bit weird.' I was sitting on the edge of the bed with my elbows on my knees and my forehead balanced on my free hand. 'I'm at my old school. There's a reunion thing.'

'That's nice.' Her voice made it sound as though she was surprised I'd bothered to go. But I'd earned, and created, every ill opinion they had of me. Rebellious, self-centred bastard that I'd been. I think money was bad for you when you were a kid. It had made me take everything, including them, for granted.

But right now, Mum was the only person I wanted to talk to.

'Mum, one of the girls told me I got her pregnant when she was sixteen. She had a baby when she was seventeen. A girl. A daughter. The child's nearly eight now, and she's mine. I have a daughter I've never seen, and you're a grandma.'

The connection went silent. I didn't know what I expected her to say, but despite the fact I'd hardly spoken to her in three years, Mum was the only person I'd had an immediate urge to tell because I was looking for reassurance – *come on*.

'Well…'

The single word ran through my nerves. Was *well* good or bad? Mum's perfectly rounded upper-class accent made it hard to tell what emotion was in her voice sometimes.

'That is a shock.'

I was still not sure of her tone.

'How do you feel?'

'Numb. Weird, like I said.' But beneath those, 'excited too.' I had a reason to turn my life around now the box of my life had been shaken. If I opened it up all the pieces inside would look different. I had a reason to pick the pieces up and put them back in a different order. I sighed down the phone. 'Like I can change.' I needed to tell Sharon and set down some ultimatums. 'I wish I could turn back time and start over. I want to know her.'

Mum breathed in deeply. It sounded shaky. 'It's wonderful, Jack, and it will be lovely if you have a relationship with her. Children need loving parents who are involved in their lives.'

I choked back a laugh. I'd spent my life in boarding school while she and Dad had travelled on business; they hadn't been all that involved. I didn't say anything. She hadn't been thinking of herself; her pitch was challenging me.

'Children need consistency. I know you hated us leaving you in school but it was better for you than being on the move every other month. But what you must remember with this girl, if she's yours, is that children are not toys. You have a tendency to lose

51

patience with things, Jack, you always have. If you step into this child's life you cannot walk out a few months later when you're bored.'

'Mum, I have a business I've been running for years. I've been climbing since I was a teenager. I don't get bored of everything.' But she was right, I did get bored of a lot of stuff. I was bored of my life. But I would not become bored of my child. Daisy. She would be a constant. Like Em. Like the business. Like my male friends. I had constants. 'I know, Mum.'

'Then I'm glad for you. I'd like to meet her.'

'She looks like me; I've seen her picture.'

The sound of another deep breath slipped through my mobile phone. 'I hope this turns into a good thing for you.'

'This is a good thing. I know it.' Hope… No. There was no hope about it.

'Thank you for calling me, Jack. I'm glad you did.'

I took a breath, words wanted to come out of me which were not natural to me. 'I'm glad I did too. I'm sorry I don't call you enough. I love you.'

'I love you too.' That emotion was in her voice – loud and clear. She ended the call.

I couldn't remember the last time I'd said those words to her. Years ago.

Maybe this was already starting to heal over the errors I'd made. A granddaughter could build a bridge to reach my parents. Maybe even Dad would forgive me for messing up.

When I stripped off and showered, my mind span through what I would need to do to become a man who'd make a good father. I'd never have planned this, but it had happened and I didn't want irregular phone calls and hour-long visits, watched over by Victoria. I wanted to change my life. I wanted to be a dad. I needed to get a DNA test done and then I'd get my lawyer on to it, to get proper rights. I wanted part-custody, agreed by a judge – and if I was going to get that, then I needed to clean up my life.

I didn't even drink at the ball, I watched Victoria as she talked to people and danced with friends. Now I'd had time to digest the news, I was angry with her. She should have told me. I'd made a mess of my life. I could have stopped myself doing it if I'd known there was a reason to live life differently. Suddenly everything wrong with my life was her fault, which was bollocks, but I was looking for someone to blame because it was easier to blame someone other than myself.

We swapped numbers at the end of the night, having hardly spoken to each other, so I bet people thought something weird was going on, but she hadn't told anyone, so I didn't. Then I said goodbye to the other people I'd caught up with and afterwards I made the decision to drive home.

What was the point in staying here? I hadn't drunk and I wouldn't sleep.

While I drove back, my mind ran through what I'd need to do to turn myself around – grow up. I had to become someone who wouldn't make me feel guilty. Someone I'd be happy for my daughter to know. Someone who could invite a child over for the weekend. Someone I could stand to look at in a mirror

I called John, my lawyer, as I drove, even though it was two-thirty a.m., and left a message on his work phone. 'Hi, John, I've got a new job for you. Please keep this quiet. I discovered I have a child. Call me on Monday and I'll give you the mother's details, then you can contact her and ask her to get a lawyer. I want a DNA test done and I want to apply for access rights. I want to be able to have the child stay with me.'

I was going to be the person who could have my daughter stay over. I'd needed a new ambition for the next five years of my life. I had it. *Become a decent man who could be a father.*

When I got home it was four a.m. I lifted a hand, acknowledging the security guard as I drove into the basement car park. He nodded at me with a smile. He'd know who was in my apartment, he saw everyone who went in and out, and at what time they went in and when they came out, because there was a camera in the lift.

He'd probably seen a lot of parts of Sharon and me in that lift too, and parts of the people we brought back. God, if Victoria wanted to stop me seeing my daughter she'd have a ton of evidence against it.

But I hadn't known I'd had a reason to be respectable.

It was a pathetic excuse. I got out, locked the car up with the button and walked towards the lift, carrying my bag. I'd left my suits hanging in the car.

As I rode the lift up to the top floor I thought about the security guy watching me when I'd let Sharon suck me off in here, or fucked her, or fucked one of the girls we'd brought in. I bet he thought I was an arrogant prick. He'd probably watched it like a porn show and laughed at me.

I hadn't cared before.

When the doors opened I walked into our private hall and unlocked the door. The place was quiet.

I didn't shout. I had no doubt there would be people in here. I ran upstairs first and checked the spare rooms on the mezzanine level. There were no people in there. Thank God. This would be easier than I'd thought. I checked the bathroom and looked outside, no one.

I went into our room last, my heart pumping hard.

They were sleeping.

There was a guy I didn't know on the bed, tangled up in the sheets with Sharon, and one of her girlfriends was cuddled into his back. She must have gone out with Sharon. Another girl, who I didn't know, was sleeping next to Sharon. My guess would be they'd pulled a couple in a club and promised them the night of their lives. It was the promise Sharon always made. She'd used the line on me when we'd met.

I stood there looking at them for a minute. If Sharon was awake, her hand would be lifting out to me, begging me to join whatever tangled cobweb of sex they were in. I was her handsome, rich plaything. I don't think she loved me any more than I loved her. I'd been kidding myself in the beginning and she'd been having fun. But this was the end. It was time to call stop. I couldn't bring a child into a life like this.

I kicked the sole of the guy's foot. 'Get up.'

He groaned. He was going to feel like shit. They'd probably snorted cocaine and Sharon loved picking out people who didn't normally do that sort of thing.

I kicked him again. 'Get up.'

He rolled over, on to Sharon. 'Where the—what the fuck?'

The women woke too.

'Get up and get out. This is my place. I don't want you in it.'

He sat up, looking back at Sharon. He was a bulky, muscular guy. If he wanted to fight me he'd probably win. 'I thought you said your boyfriend was cool with this…'

'He's my husband—'

'And he is cool with it, very cool,' Sharon's friend Karen, who had fairly regular sex with us, answered.

'Not any more. Get out. All of you. I pay the bills here, I own the sheets you're fucking on, and I am not cool with it. So, fuck off.' I grabbed the top sheet and pulled at it, revealing some of their tangled-up naked bodies.

The guy got up. 'Alright, mate, no need to go fucking mental.' He walked past me and picked a pair of jeans up off the floor. Then looked back as he put them on. 'Come on, Pen.'

'You too, Karen. Get out.' I glared at her.

She got up, all long skinny limbs. She was into heroin, not just cocaine. She had needle marks all over the inner sides of her arms.

My conscience kicked; her relationship with Sharon and I was probably a part of her addiction. I don't think I'd ever looked at her when I was sober and clean before. I saw a different person.

55

She smiled at me, came over and touched my crotch. I gripped her wrist and took her hand away. 'Just get out.' She smiled as if she believed we'd call her in an hour and ask her back.

Never again. I'd received my wake-up shout and Daisy was my get-out-of-jail-free card.

When they walked out, clothes thrown on or hanging in their hands, I went into the hall and watched until they walked out the main door. It clicked shut behind them.

For the first time I thought about what all the hangers-on in my life might have done with the freedom of my apartment while I'd been out of my head. But I didn't have much to steal. Sharon and I didn't spend money on trinkets, we spent it on sex and drugs – and clothes – but Sharon did have some jewellery. We'd probably had stuff stolen and not even known.

I went back into the bedroom and looked at her. She was leaning up on her elbows in the bed. 'What's brought you back in a bad mood?'

I stared at her. I didn't know what to say to this.

'Come and get into bed. You'll feel better.'

'No.' Oh, just say it. 'I have a kid with one of the girls I was at school with. I found out today.'

She sat up and the sheet slithered to her lap, revealing her body to the waist. 'What?'

'My daughter is seven years old. I got a girl pregnant and she didn't tell me.'

'Oh, my God. That was a riot, then.' It was said in a dismissive, sarcastic tone.

'I need to change my life. I want my daughter in it, and this is not the sort of life a child can see. We're not having any more parties and no more cocaine.'

Her face screwed up, as though she was annoyed and she thought I'd gone crazy.

'I mean it.'

She slid across the bed and got up, then grabbed a dressing

gown off the floor, walked past me and went into the bathroom. 'Don't be pathetic.'

'I've had enough of living like this. I don't want to do it any more. I'm not this man.'

'You've never complained before.'

'No. But I'm complaining now. We need to settle down. I want to be normal. I want to be able to invite my daughter here. I want to stand up in front of her and not feel dirty.'

She made a face at me, then squatted down over the toilet and weed, with the door open. 'How do you know she'll even want to see you? How can you know you'll even like her?'

'I like her already.' Victoria was in my mind and through Victoria I could imagine our child. She'd be sweet, polite. If I'd had a child with Sharon, it would be a spoilt brat. 'I called John. I'm getting a DNA test done and then he'll start working on legal rights and I'm going to set up a trust fund for her.'

'You haven't even met the kid—'

'I don't need to meet her. She's mine and I have seven years of her life to make up. So, Sharon, you need to change or we're over.'

'What?' She shouted as she wiped herself. 'What have you taken?'

'Nothing.' For the first time in a long time.

Only Sharon would have this sort of conversation with me while she was using the toilet. She had no decency. But even that had turned me on in the past.

'Then where's this sudden burst of anger come from?' She walked past me, her dressing gown hanging open. Then she climbed on the bed. 'Come to bed, Jack. You'll get bored of the kid and forget about this and think differently in a few days. Come on. I'll make you forget your bad mood.'

'No thanks. Me and my bad mood are happy together. I like it. You can go back to sleep.'

I walked out and went into the living room, then sat on the floor with my back up against the sofa and my knees bent up, and watched the sun rise over London through the glass.

Sharon wouldn't change and she wouldn't go, and I didn't want to be with her. If I was going to change my life, I had to be the one who left.

At seven I went back into the bedroom and started packing. She was out cold in the bed. I packed my clothes into five suitcases. She didn't wake. My clothes were all I wanted – everything else I'd leave for her and buy new.

I took the cases down to the car, then went back up to tell her I was leaving her.

I shook her shoulder. Her eyes opened. 'I've decided. You won't change. But I'm changing. So I'm going. I'm leaving you. Don't bother calling – and find a lawyer. I want a divorce.'

I took a room at the Hilton, left my car and my things there, then caught a tube back and got my motorbike out of the underground car park and rode that over to the Hilton too. Then I started looking on the Internet for somewhere new to live and rang Em.

'Hi. Sorry to interrupt your Sunday, but I wanted to warn you, I won't be in tomorrow. Can you run the meeting and tell everyone I'm off because Sharon and I have split? I'm going to get somewhere else to live. I want to do some viewings and then I'll be back in.'

'You split up?'

'Yes, and do not say I told you so, or thank God, or anything. We split up because I discovered I have a daughter, a seven-year-old daughter.'

'Oh my God. You—'

'Say nothing.'

'Saying nothing. I'll see you on Tuesday, with any luck. I hope it goes okay. If you need me, call.'

'Cheers, Em.'

I sat on the sofa in the hotel room and scrolled down through the pages of apartments. I'd done it. I was making a new start.

At one o'clock I called Victoria. 'Hi, it's Jack.'

'I know, your number's in my phone.'

'Can I speak to her? Daisy. Have you said anything?'

'We're eating, Jack.'

'Shall I call back, then?'

'No. I'll call you later.'

'Do.'

'I said I would, Jack.'

It was two hours later when she called. I grabbed my phone. 'Hi.'

'Hi.'

My heart pounded like the bass rhythm from a speaker in a club. 'Is she there? Is she with you?'

'Yes.' Victoria sounded nervous. 'Daisy, do you want to speak to him still? His name is Jack, remember.'

Victoria's voice had become more distant at the end of the sentence, as if she held the phone out, then I heard some short, sharp breaths. She was there. 'Hi. Daisy?'

'Hello.'

Tears clouded my vision. 'Hello. It's nice to talk to you.' What did I say?

'Mummy said she met you at the party she went to.'

'Yes, she did. I've only just discovered you, Daisy. I'd like to come and see you sometime.' Sometime soon.

She took a breath. 'Mummy said your eyes are like mine.'

'Yes.'

'I want to go and play again.' The sound dropped away.

'Sorry, she has about as much patience as you did.'

It felt like something had been ripped away from me. 'When can I see her?'

'Jack, don't start pressuring me. It's not only Daisy who needs to get used to this, it's my husband too, and I'm not risking my marriage for you. Take it easy.'

'You can't dangle her in front of me and then say no.'

'I'm not doing that. Please don't start being awkward.'

'Wanting to see my daughter is not being awkward.' I was tired and desperate and falling to pieces. 'But I will play it how you want to play it.'

John would fight my case. In the meantime I needed to do everything right, and if I was lucky, maybe by Christmas, I would have a daughter to spend that day with. That would be something. That was a goal worth aiming for.

Chapter 2

Today, December 24th

When I got out of Jack's car, he said, 'I'll see you later.'

I looked back at him. He was leaning on the passenger seat, while his other hand still gripped the steering wheel. 'Yeah, see you later.'

He smiled as I shut the door.

Shit. I must be mad. This was a stupid thing to do. When he drove off, I lifted a hand and stood there like an idiot, waving at him. A big guy was walking down the street. He looked at me. I turned to climb the steps up to the front door then glanced over my shoulder to take one final look at Jack's car as it turned the corner. The stranger caught my eye, smiled at me like he was laughing at me, then pulled his beanie hat lower and carried on walking.

I keyed in the code to get into the house and up to my flat, my heart playing out a manic dance rhythm. I was excited and terrified all at once.

I'd never done anything crazy before.

My hands shook as I packed, while the adrenaline dripped out of my blood, the excitement draining out and leaving the nervousness behind. I didn't put a lot in my case. I didn't need clothes for staying in bed for a week—having naughty, nasty, sex.

The words gave me shivers. I heard them in Jack's voice and I felt them in naughty places.

The buzzer on the intercom sounded.

I answered, 'Hi.'

'Are you ready?'

I looked back at the case on my bed. I'd shove some heels in and my black dress, then… 'Yes.'

'Do you want me to come up and carry your case?'

'Oo, you're such a gentleman when you're not talking about sex. No. I'll manage. I'll meet you outside.' My heart bounced against my ribcage, partly excitedly and partly terrified. The adrenaline was kicking back in now I'd heard his voice.

This was so random. When I'd woken up this morning I'd imagined spending a week in my pyjamas, streaming constant films so I could avoid all the C-word specials, with Ben and Jerry's on tap.

'*You're being stupid,*' Rick's voice said in my head, with a sharp note of warning.

I squeezed my favourite high-heeled shoes into the backpack I had my makeup and toiletries in, grabbed my dress out of the wardrobe and lay it on top of my clothes in the case, then closed the lid. There. Ready. I was done. I was going. Doing this.

I smiled as I left my room and let the door slam shut behind me. But then I turned around and pushed it to check it had shut. In the way Rick would have done. It had shut.

I smiled again as I walked downstairs. I hadn't left Rick to spend the rest of my life in an attic flat for one. And I didn't want to begin breeding cats to fight the loneliness. I'd turned the opportunity of life with Rick down because I wanted to do different things. Exciting things. To live in the moment. To feel my heart race. I wanted to be one of the fast-living, uncaring, naughty people – like Jack.

When I opened the downstairs front door, Jack was leaning with his bum against his F-Type Coupe, his keys in his hand.

He was wearing the same black trousers and shoes, but he'd swapped his duffle coat for a waist-length leather jacket.

He shifted into movement when he saw me and came over to take the case out of my hand, with one of those tummy-flipping smiles.

'I was half-expecting a text calling it all off.'

'Why?'

'I thought you might go cold on the idea.'

'No. Still hot.' I followed him down the steps.

He pressed the button on the key fob and the lights on the car flashed as the locks released, then he loaded my case into the boot, came around and opened the door for me.

'Are you this much of a gentleman in bed?'

'You'll have to wait and see. But probably not. I wouldn't get your hopes up. Nasty and a gentlemen… Nah.' The sound at the end of the sentence implied… *not a good fit.*

My heart raced through the steps of *River Dance. How naughty and ungentlemanly/nasty would he be in bed?* The idea blew shivers through me.

The seat in his Jag felt like it hugged me. 'I can't believe we're doing this. You do realise it's nuts,' I said as he dropped into the driver's seat. 'I have no idea how I'm going to work for you after this.'

'With good memories,' he said, as he started the engine.

I pressed my head back into the leather. Yes. With memories. That was a good currency; I was only going to trade in making amazing memories from now on – memories that made me go, *wow did I do that?* Memories that made my heart pound years later. Even if I ended up lonely, with loads of cats, I'd have memories.

Memories of Rick slipped through my head. But they weren't anything to look back on in ten years' time. They were like watching YouTube clips of cute kittens. There had been 'ah' moments. But never 'wow, what was that?' moments.

Biffy Clyro played out from the speakers in the car, 'Animal Style'. Jack turned the music down a little.

'I feel like I'm back at school, playing truant,' I said when he pulled away.

He glanced over and smiled.

'How long will it take to get there?'

'It depends on the traffic: about four hours-ish, maybe five.'

He drove into the high street. 'I have to keep my eyes open, as I'm driving, but feel free to shut yours if you want to avoid the C lights.'

I smiled, but it was twisted. He didn't see my expression; he was watching the road. 'You really are bitter. Is this offer of yours more to do with Sharon than me?'

'Why? Would that make you ask me to turn around and drop you back home?'

My heart danced another Irish jig. 'No. I'm not here for a relationship, am I? January 2nd, this is over. And you didn't offer me anything but sex, so why should I care if you're trying to shut Sharon out. This isn't anything to do with feelings. So whatever the reason, I don't care.'

'Who is bitter?'

'You. I split with Rick because when he asked me to marry him I couldn't imagine spending my life with him. And before you ask why, he's dull. I'm not bitter; I'm just seeking some excitement.'

He glanced at me, with an eyebrow-lift. 'So your motive for fucking my brains out is to get the boring Rick out of your head. You're right, I don't mind if you make me your Rick-eraser. This isn't about feelings. So that makes us even.'

A laugh came out awkwardly, then I turned the conversation off me. 'Do you take women up to this place a lot?'

He glanced over again. 'What, because I'm such a cheat?'

'Jack, you flirt all the time. And you didn't deny you've had affairs. And we aren't blind at work, we see them flouncing into the office, and then you disappear—'

64

'Flouncing into the office…' He chuckled.

'Have you ever done it with Emma?' They were close, they'd been together for about six years. They'd become friends at uni and then built the business up from the ground together.

He looked at me with a twisted expression. 'No. She's my best friend, and she'd be really annoyed with me if she knew I was stealing you away for a dirty, extended weekend. I can hear her voice. *Jack, you idiot, what do you think you're doing? Ivy is one of our best people.'*

'Am I one of your best people?'

'Doesn't Em tell you that? She tells me it. She's been warning me off you ever since you started.'

A surprised laugh was pulled from my throat. 'Since I started…'

'She's seen me watching you.'

'You watch me?' I smiled, because I'd guessed he glanced at me at work, and it felt good to hear him admit it.

'You watch me too.'

'I do no—' Him knowing that didn't feel so nice.

'Don't you dare lie.' He glanced over. 'I'm not blind.'

I poked my tongue out at him as the traffic slowed and he stopped. His hand came over and squeezed my knee, then let go and returned to the gear stick.

'But I've only seen you looking, because I watch you. The best view is when you wear those black-and-white chequered trousers and lean on to someone's desk to talk. Your bum looks amazing in those. But then your bum looks pretty amazing in anything. I told you, people who look like you should not be with people like Rick. I cannot imagine, for one minute, that he knew how to deal with you.'

'Deal with me…' I discarded the comment, because it made a tremor run up my spine. I couldn't imagine how Jack was going to, *deal with me*. 'You're such a player. I bet you watch Susie in Nero's, and every other woman's bum.'

'No. Only the bottoms of the girls I really like. You're one of them.'

A blush caught alight and flared into a hot flame under my skin.

'See, Em doesn't know what I know, that you fancy me too. I wouldn't have made my suggestion to you tonight if I hadn't known that.'

'How could you know that?'

'How could I *know*… ah, that's nice, you admit it.'

I pulled a face at him as he stopped at a red light behind a scarlet double-decker bus.

We were driving along the Embankment, past Battersea, out of London. The dark, flowing water of the Thames was visible beside us, in places, reflecting the lights of the city.

His hand reached out again and his long fingers ran up my thigh, over my worn, faded, skinny jeans. 'I've known it from the moment we interviewed you. Your eyes looked at mine through the whole thing. You barely looked at Em, like you just couldn't take your eyes off me. You always look at me like that when I'm in a room. I like it.'

He made it sound cringe-worthy. 'Have you fancied me since you interviewed me?'

'You fancied me, remember. That's a pretty good aphrodisiac to a man.'

'And here was I thinking this invitation was a spur-of-the-moment thing, to get over a bad day.'

'It is that. But also a good excuse to fulfil a few fantasies. Since you walked into the room for your interview, with those ridiculously long legs, I've been imagining some fun things.'

'You're far too sure of yourself, Jack.'

'And you are far too unsure. I know you had no expectation this would happen.'

We'd flirted at work for years, but this wasn't flirting, it was honesty. 'If you fancied me, why didn't you make a move earlier?'

'I told you, Em's been warning me off. Plus you had Rick on the scene, and I never got the vibe that you'd be up for cheating.'

'No, I wouldn't have done anything when I was with Rick, or you were with Sharon.'

'Well then, perfect timing. A whole holiday of naughty to get over our sexual buzz, which has been crackling around the office for two years.'

'And then what?'

'Don't be a woman, Ivy. Be a predator. 'After' doesn't matter. Don't think about it. 'Now' matters. Thinking about after is what makes life dull. You said you didn't want dull.'

Thinking of 'after' is what makes people sensible. The retort Rick would have given raced through my head. But I wasn't Rick. Think of now, I chanted in my head. That was what I'd wanted to do. That was why I was here.

Jack turned the music up as he navigated through the traffic in the city. There were thousands of people making their way out of London tonight, going home to family.

He glanced over at me. 'What do you normally do this time of year?'

'Go home to my parents, or Rick's parents, it was an alternate-year thing.'

'The parents fought over you two, then?'

'No, what I mean is, alternate years his parents came to mine, or my parents went to his. They're good friends.'

He glanced over again and laughed. 'Oh shit. Now I get why you're alone.'

'I'm disowned.' I laughed, in a weird way. I'd been trying to laugh it off, but it hadn't been working. It hurt. 'I was told to stay away. Mum's embarrassed by me. She hasn't worked out how to be in the middle of all the mess I made and she didn't feel like she could cancel the dinner invitation. So Rick and his parents are with my parents and I'm here.'

'And his parents?'

'Think I'll come around. They say what Rick says; it's just jitters.'

'Is it jitters?'

I looked at him, watching him drive. He was more of a silhouette in the dark as the streetlights and shop windows flashed past. 'No, it's not jitters. I like him, he is a really nice man, but I don't love him. Or maybe it is love, but in the way I'd love a friend. I can't build a life on that. I'd hate him in the end.'

'Well, I know how that feels.'

'What do you normally do?'

'Me?' He glanced over. It made me realise how rarely Jack spoke about himself. 'One thing I never did was see my parents. They'd have considered it hell if I brought Sharon over for lunch. Sometimes we took Sharon's parents out to a restaurant if they came to London, but not every year. Sharon preferred to party Christmas Eve and paid more weight to that than what we did Christmas Day. Christmas and Boxing Day were about recovering.' He breathed in, like he thought of something else he would say, but he didn't say it.

'Do you realise you said that word three times, then?'

'Oh fuck, I did, didn't I? Alright, from now on, if either of us says it, the other gets to think of a forfeit.'

I smiled at that, imagining all sorts of forfeits I'd choose for him, while my tummy quivered, wondering what he'd pick for me. 'I might start using the word to make you give me forfeits.'

He laughed. 'Then I'd change the rules. I seriously hate that word now. I hate the whole notion of it and everything it stands for.'

'Ooo, got it. Bitter… much…'

He glanced over at me and laughed, shaking his head.

'When did you meet Sharon?'

'The year we started the business up, oddly enough, although now I realise not oddly at all. I met her the night we won our first big contract. Em always had Sharon down as a money-grabbing bitch.'

'If Emma didn't like Sharon, why did you go ahead and marry her?'

'Em is my friend, not my minder. I listen to what she says in business, I don't listen to her when she is commenting on my private life, and that's exactly why you're in this car, Ivy.'

Point noted. I grinned at him. 'But—'

'No buts, leave it. I don't want to talk about Sharon, not tonight anyway. I've had my fill of her today.'

'Sorry.'

'You don't need to apologise, just avoid the subject.'

'We seem to be setting a lot of rules that are narrowing down our conversation, so I'm just going to shut up. Do you have any quieter music on your phone?'

'Take a look. You can manage the music.' He reached into his inside pocket and pulled out his phone. It had been playing the music via Bluetooth. I opened up his music and scanned through the albums as he drove out of London. I chose Ed Sheeran's album *Multiply*, then shut my eyes, listening to the songs as we hit the motorway. The car was warm with the air-con up high and the seat was comfortable.

When I woke up Jack had *Maroon 5* playing, and his hand tapped on the steering wheel as he sang along to 'Sugar'.

I stretched my arms up. I'd dreamt he'd been watching me through the whole of the Monday meeting and then before he closed the meeting he'd walked up, taken my hand and pulled me out of there and we'd run away.

It was sort of real; I was in a car with him.

I looked through the windscreen into the middle of nowhere. We were on a virtually deserted motorway.

'What time is it?'

'Hey, sleepy-head.' He glanced over and smiled then looked at the clock in the dashboard that I could have looked at. 'It's eleven-ten. I was just going to stop, stretch my legs and get a coffee.'

'I need a pee.'

'That too. These are the last services before the Lake District.'

'How far away are we from your cottage?'

'About an hour, maybe a little less.'

I yawned, even though I'd slept for hours. I hadn't slept well for days. I'd been too messed up over everything going on with Rick.

The services sign was up ahead, and then the white bar signs counted down to the turning. Jack flipped the indicator on and turned on to the slip road.

There were only about a dozen cars parked in there. I guess most people were not in a motorway services at nearly midnight on… I didn't say the word, not even to myself, he was right, we should treat this like a normal day.

After he parked up, he looked at me. 'Pull the hood of your parka up, then you won't have to look at any of that festive shit. I'm wrapping my scarf around my head.'

I laughed.

'We're going in, doing what we need to do, then we'll grab a coffee from Burger King. They're right by the door and they'll be quick, and we can drink it out here.'

'Don't you want a longer break from the car?'

'No. I'd rather not put up with that fucking merry music playing.'

He pulled a beanie hat out of his pocket, slid it on and pulled it down to his eyebrows. Then he reached over the back, through the gap between the seats, and grabbed a scarf, folded it double and wrapped it around his neck, then pulled one half through the other. Finally, he settled both his beanie and his scarf so they covered his ears and nearly covered his eyes. 'I'm ready.'

I flicked my hood up. 'Come on, then.' I opened the door when he did.

It was cold outside. I'd swear it was colder than London had been. I shoved my hands into my pockets as I shivered, walking towards the services. He caught up with me and his arm came around my shoulders. It felt nice.

We walked up to the door like that, with me leaning against him.

As soon as we walked in, though, we realised his plan wasn't going to work, there was a metal grill barring access to Burger King – they'd already closed up and gone home.

Wizzard's, 'I Wish It Could Be Christmas Every Day', played out.

'Shit,' he said under his breath.

'I fancy a change of seat for a bit, anyway, a hard chair in the café will wake me up.'

'Alright, I'll brave the good cheer for you. But I need the toilet first.'

'So do I. I'll meet you in the café.'

'Okay.'

We parted ways.

When I came out he was standing at the entrance to the café, with his hands in the pockets of his jacket, looking stupid with his hat pulled down and his scarf pulled up, but of course his striking blue eyes against his dark lashes and brows, and the bone structure of his cheeks were still visible. I'd bet, even half covered up like that, the women in here thought he was the best-looking man who'd been through here for days. The women in the café were watching him.

'You owe me big time for making me stand here listening to this merry fucking music.'

The merry music, was now 'Last Christmas' by Wham.

'Can we get something to eat? I'm starving.'

'Sure, go on then. I'd be mean to make you wait another hour.'

I picked up a tuna-melt for the server to heat up. 'Are you having something?'

He took a look at what was left in the chiller and chose a pasta salad. Then he shouted over to the girls who were waiting on our order. 'I'll have a cappuccino but with three shots, and a skinny, vanilla latte…' He glanced at me with an eyebrow lift to check that's what I wanted. I nodded.

71

When he got to the till he took out his wallet. While he looked out his card, he said, 'Can you put that sign down for a minute please. I don't want to see it. Not everyone is happy about that shit.'

The girl made an odd face, then knocked it over. I guess the customer was always right.

He held his card over the machine so it paid on the contactless connection.

'We'll bring the tuna-melt over, Ha—'

'Don't you dare say it.'

'Who are you? Scrooge.'

Jack threw the woman a glare.

She flipped up her sign.

I laughed and grasped his arm, pulling him away before he decided to make it a full-on argument.

He picked up a plastic fork to eat the pasta with, and napkins and sugar. I'd never seen him take sugar before, but then he didn't usually drink cappuccino either.

I took a sip from my latte, watching him as he opened his salad and took a forkful. I liked his hands. He was right, I had watched him a lot at work, but it wasn't just his face I watched, and his hands were fascinating. I think he actually had his fingernails manicured; they were always perfectly shaped, with no cuticle. He had hands he could model with, his fingers were long and slender, and yet they looked as masculine as the rest of him.

I glanced up. 'Can I have one of the serviettes?'

He smiled at me, 'Sure, knock yourself out.'

I took one then leant down to get my handbag; I'd put it by my feet. I couldn't find a pen, but I had a black eyeliner. I took the lid off and then I wrote on the white serviette.

When I finished, I slid it across the table. 'Just to make things official.'

Dear Jack
I'm giving you my notice. I don't want to work for you any
more. As of right now, you are not my boss. You're my lover.
                                                    Yours sincerely
                                                    Ivy Cooper

He looked up and laughed. Then he folded the serviette and slipped it into his inside pocket. 'I'm keeping that as evidence that you said yes to me. I might even have it framed and put up in my office.'

'Don't you dare.'

He gave me a grin as the woman brought my tuna-melt over.

Chapter 3

We'd come off the motorway about thirty minutes ago, and since then the roads had been gradually getting narrower and darker. The place looked like Middle Earth, the little of it I could see in the headlights.

I'd never been this far north before. I hadn't known what to expect, but it hadn't been gnarly woods, broad glass-like lakes and tall hills hemming us in on every side as Jack drove through twisty, narrow roads. It really was like something out of the *Hobbit* or *Lord of the Rings*, even the little whitewashed cottages were like hobbit houses. 'This place is cool, Jack.'

'It's more than picture postcard, isn't it? It's knock-you-off-your-feet stuff. Sometimes I just stand around here awed by nature. But you haven't even seen it in the daylight.'

'Have you brought anyone else up here?'

'I brought Sharon here. But she hated it. I'm hoping you don't.' He glanced at me, then flicked the indicator on.

'Are we here?'

'We are.' He turned off on to a track that ran across a field. 'This is the driveway to the cottage and the house that's next to it.'

I didn't think I'd dislike it – it looked like I'd love it. 'I can't believe how out in the sticks it is.'

'I told you, it's my haven. This is where I escape to.' He smiled, but he wasn't looking at me.

Then I saw it. The moon had been hidden by clouds most of the way since I'd woken up, but now the clouds parted and I could see a two-storey whitewashed cottage glowing in the moonlight, nestled in a valley, in a meadow amidst the hills. It had a slate roof that glistened when the moonlight caught it. I saw the bigger house behind it, but the cottage was perfect. 'That's really awesome.' Literally, the awe he'd talked about hit me.

'Isn't it? At least because Sharon hates it I know she won't be going after this as part of the divorce settlement.'

I looked at him. 'I love it.' My words came out breathless as he pulled up in front of an old- fashioned-looking porch with a wooden carved frame and lamps on either side of it.

Someone had left a light on inside.

He got out of the car and stretched. I got out too.

He looked different; his shoulders had relaxed. He looked as if he'd dumped the weight of work and his problems from London in the car. He looked over at me, waiting for me to come around the car. 'Thanks for saying yes and coming up here. I think I'd have hated being here on my own this time.'

He sorted through his keys and then held them out to me with one separated. 'Open up. I'll get our stuff.'

'Thanks.' My heart went bump, bump, bump in my chest. While my stomach was no longer doing backflips, something warm and elemental was stirring within it instead. In this cottage was a bed, and I had come up here to get in that bed with him.

I unlocked the door as waves of surreal washed over me.

Was I really doing this? Who was this Ivy? *The bad girl who'd turned Rick down.*

'There should be wine and food in the fridge!'

'How come?' I shouted back as the door opened.

'There's a woman who comes in and looks after the place. I had her stock it up ready for me!'

The door opened straight into the living room, there was no hall, and on the far side there was a staircase, and to one side a fireplace with a log-burner full of wood, waiting to be lit. But in the corner beside it there was a very bare fir tree. I dropped my handbag into a chair.

When he came in behind me, I turned. 'You forgot to tell whoever bought the food you aren't doing Christmas.'

His smile twisted with a bitter look, but then he leaned forward. 'That's a blindfold.'

A forfeit. I smacked his arm and laughed with a nervous sound, because the way he'd said it, and what he'd said, made my tummy do even weirder stuff. It was like a coil twisted down through it.

'You check out the fridge. I'll put the cases upstairs.'

He had my rucksack on his shoulder, my case in one hand and his in the other.

I didn't ask which room he'd be putting my case in.

'There'll be some champagne in there. Get that out, for a start, and anything else you fancy.' I watched him walk upstairs, my gaze hovering on his bum. He'd said he liked watching mine, but his was nice too.

I turned to the kitchen. Ravenous, suddenly, but probably not for food. My heart pumped so hard. I couldn't wait to find out what sex with him was going to be like, but I was terrified of making myself look stupid.

I sighed when I opened the fridge. Rick would be playing charades with our parents about now. Go him! He could keep 'nice'.

There was caviar, paté, smoked-salmon mousse, prawns, salad stuff and chicken, along with a dozen varieties of local cheese. Jack knew how to eat well. The problem was, I didn't.

My phone buzzed in the other room.

I pulled out the champagne and looked in the cupboards for glasses. I found wine glasses. They'd do. I took out two and held them with the stems between my fingers, then picked up the champagne and went back into the living room.

Jack was just coming downstairs.

I held the champagne up.

He came over and took it from my hand. 'Take your coat off.' He'd taken his leather jacket off.

I put the glasses down on the table, which stood in the far corner of the room, then slipped off my coat. There were coat-hooks behind the door and I hung it up there. But the room was really cold without a coat. I rubbed my arms.

He'd undone the foil on the champagne and had the cork ready to pop. His thumbs gently pressed it up. Bang; it went off and made me jolt as it flew up and hit the ceiling while a mist of champagne evaporated out of the bottle, but there was no spray. I guess he'd learned how not to waste any over the years.

He picked up a glass and filled it, then filled the second glass before putting the bottle on the table. He handed me a glass. 'To a holiday of naughty sex.' He tapped the rim of his glass against mine, just as a clock somewhere in the house chimed midnight.

'I feel like Cinderella. Shall I peek out and check the Jag didn't turn into a pumpkin. Something must be suddenly going to change or disappear.'

He shook his head. 'I wish a week of sex could change stuff. But no. This isn't going to change anything, Ivy, except it'll either mean we look at each other more in the office, or we look less. More if we have hot memories we are continually thinking about. Less if we manage to burn out the flame of lust entirely.'

'Have you done this before?'

'Brought people up here? As I said, no. Had sex with people to kill my desire for them? Yes. It works. But some infatuations take a little longer to burn out.'

'So, is that why you invited me, because you want to stop getting hot when you look at my bum in the office.'

He grinned rather than smiled. It was a more relaxed expression. This place changed him. He drank a large gulp of champagne, then set his glass down. 'It's cold in here. I'll get the fire going.'

He knelt down at the hearth and picked up a pack of matches. The log-burner was set up, ready to be lit – all he had to do was light a match and when he held it to the paper on the fire, the paper burst into flames. He shut the door on the burner. The fire raged into life as it sucked oxygen through the grate.

He knelt back on his heels, watching the fire.

'Why is that here?' When he looked at me to see what I meant, I glanced at the naked fir tree.

'I may have forgotten to tell the housekeeper that Christmas wasn't happening.'

'You said the word. Now I get a forfeit.' I drank some of my champagne, pretending to think, but I already knew. 'When you've finished with my blindfold, I'm going to use it to tie you up.'

'I might say the word more if you're going to come up with that kind of forfeit.'

'Then I'd change the rules.'

'You can't change the rules, it's my game.'

'But you're not the boss any more, Jack. You're just my lover.'

He stood up suddenly and came towards me. 'Do you know how sexy that sounds?' His hand came about the back of my head. 'Feel.' His other hand gripped mine and pressed it against the front of his trousers.

'Shit. I'm in for some fun.'

'You are.' His lips came down on mine and I spilt champagne on the stone-flagged floor as his tongue pushed into my mouth. Forget jelly, my stomach was lighter than that; it was soft snow melting into slush. A sexual tingle teased between my legs, while heat raced across my skin, four chilli symbols of heat. I'd felt nothing like that when Rick kissed me. Had I never really fancied him?

Jack broke away. 'I think you spilt your drink down my jumper.'

'Sorry.'

'No need to be. It was my fault.'

'I feel guilty about Rick—'

'You're not pulling out now we're up here?' He looked at me, his body stiffening.

'I wasn't saying that. I meant I feel guilty for staying with him so long. You're right. I've fancied you since I started. I don't think I ever fancied Rick. I should have let him move on years ago. Oh, I forgot. I got a text.' I finished off the champagne, put the glass down and went over to my bag. I pulled out some tissue to wipe up the spilled champagne, but took my mobile out too.

'Rick: Hey, I miss you. You should be here. If you change your mind over Christmas I can drive up and get you. I still love you, Ivy.'

Daggers pierced through my chest, a hundred of them... All dipped in guilt.

'What is it?'

I touched my thumb against the screen to unlock my phone, then went into Rick's messages and held the phone out to show Jack.

He took it from my hand. 'He wants you back,' he said after he read the first one, but then he started scrolling through them. 'Oh shit. Are you sure he hasn't got some sort of problem?'

'I think his problem is just me. I walked out on him.'

'There are hundreds of these things.'

'I know. I stopped replying a fortnight ago. He still sends them. They generally start about ten and then, as the night goes on, they get more and more desperate. I think he's drinking a lot.'

Jack looked up from the phone, at me. 'You must feel like shit.'

I closed my lips and nodded. Stupid tears welled up. He pulled me into a hug. Crazily that did stuff to my innards too, just in a different way than the kiss.

'It's alright to feel shit when you're breaking up. No matter what side of it you're on. And you're not obligated to have sex with me just because you came up here.'

I pulled away. 'But I want to have sex with you.' I sounded petulant.

He laughed as he dropped my phone into an armchair, then his fingers braced the back of my neck and he kissed me.

My arms reached around his neck, one hand still gripping the tissue I'd got out to wipe up the spilt champagne.

He was taller than me, but in my heeled boots, not all that much. We felt like a perfect fit physically—but otherwise, I only knew him professionally, getting personal and touching and exposing myself was scary. But that was why this felt so tummy-churning.

He broke the kiss. 'If you had a skirt on I'd lift your legs up right now and do what I've been wanting to do to you for two years.'

'What's that?'

'Have sex with you on my desk.'

'Your desk isn't here.'

'No, but the table would do.'

He let me go and I squatted down to wipe the champagne off the floor. He turned to the fire, opened the burner door and poked it with a metal poker to make sure the wood caught properly, then shut the door again. 'I thought we could get the cushions off the sofa and the chairs and put them out on the floor.'

'Okay.'

My phone buzzed again. Jack picked it up and then read out the text. 'Ivy. Please. I want to spend, the C word, with you.'

I looked at him. 'See, it's like the first text is a nice tester to see if I'll reply and now I don't, then he dives into being more and more pressing. But even when I was replying they used to end up desperate when I wasn't saying what he wanted.'

'You have two options. I call him and tell him to get lost – you're here with me. Or we switch your phone off. I'm not listening to him texting and you shouldn't be reading them.'

'Just switch it off.' It was nice to have someone else know about them. I hadn't been able to talk to anyone because everyone was on Rick's side.

'Done.' His thumbnail flicked the little switch, then he threw my phone back down on the chair.

'Thank you.'

I went into the kitchen to throw away the soiled tissue. When I came back in Jack had spread out the sofa and chair cushions in front of the fire, and he was stripping off his burgundy jumper. His body was so firm and his black pinstripe shirt was fitted to every lean contour.

I loved watching his body. In the summer, when he just wore a shirt and trousers at work, when we were doing something in the blue-sky room, and he reached up, stretching, or bent down and twisted, my brain had me working on how his body might look beneath his clothes. His stomach was so flat and hard, and his pecs were not pronounced, but they had definition. Like his arms. He didn't have massive biceps, but they were marked, slim, sculpted shapes. He was a man someone would love to sculpt in bronze.

He threw his jumper on to the now-bare sofa. 'Are you going to come and get cosy with me? Do you want some music on?'

'Yes, and yes.' I threw him a smile.

He pulled his phone out of his back pocket and toed off his shoes, while I bent and unzipped my boots then pulled them off. I left them near the door, but I was cold, so I didn't take my hoodie off.

I sat down on the cushions, upright, facing the fire, with my knees bent up and my arms hugging my legs.

He'd put his phone in a docking system and the music played out through speakers, Maroon 5, 'Maps'. He went into the kitchen and came back in a couple of minutes with a bowl of nuts and a bowl of olives, then he handed me my refilled glass and finally sat down near me, leaning back against the sofa, holding his glass. His knees were bent up too but slightly parted.

'Oh fuck it…' he said it out of nowhere, for no apparent reason, and then he drained his glass, set it down on the hearth in front of the wood-burner, and moved the bowl of olives there too, and the nuts. Then he lay down, with his knees bent upward and one hand behind his head.

He looked up at me as the next song came on. 'Animals', it was the V album. It was what he'd been listening to in the car when I woke up.

His eyes shut. Then he started singing.

'You know your phone is full of breakup music, don't you?'

His eyes opened but he still sang the next line, smiling at me. He had a good voice. I hadn't heard him sing before, but his voice blended with the song and made it better—

'So what, I bet you have a freezer full of cartons of Ben & Jerry's.'

'You got me.'

He shut his eyes again, and sang – the song was really laddish. 'Did you love Sharon?'

'That is a banned subject.' He hadn't opened his eyes.

I sipped some of my champagne then twisted sideways so I faced him. 'I know, but answer the question please? I'd like to know, seeing as we're planning on having sex.'

He stopped singing and his eyes opened. 'Yes, I sort of did.'

'When did you stop loving her?'

'I probably never did, properly, but I didn't start realising that until about a year ago.'

'How did you decide what you felt wasn't true any more?'

He stared at me, one hand still behind his head. 'We weren't like you and Rick, we lived fast and we played hard. We weren't in each other's pockets the whole time. And, believe me, it's been pretty easy to cut her off. She's proved herself to be an absolute bitch. But anyway, I really don't want to talk about that. What about you and Rick?'

'I do still love him like a friend. But there's no desperation. I want to feel desperate when I love someone.'

His gaze held mine, the pupils at the heart of his eyes wide in the electric light.

I drank the last of my champagne.

'Do you want more?'

'No it'll give me a headache. I wouldn't mind a lager, though, if we're going to stay up.'

'I don't drink lager. Ale? Do you want a bottle of ale?'

'Yeah, okay.'

He got up and went into the kitchen. Then came back with two open bottles. He flipped the light switch off when he came past it.

The only light in the room then came from the flames in the burner. He handed me a bottle, then tapped the neck of my bottle with the base of his. 'Happy morning. Technically we're not staying up late, we're up early.'

He put his bottle down on the hearth beside his empty glass, then turned his back on me and walked around behind the sofa.

He opened the cupboard under the stairs and reached into it to get something off a high shelf, something that he'd obviously had hidden away so his cleaner wouldn't find it. He pulled out a tin. 'Do you smoke cannabis?'

'Shit, I didn't know you did that.'

'Do you smoke it?'

I breathed out, my heart dancing to the beat of his music. 'No.' Not even when I was at school. Rick and I had got together a month before my sixteenth birthday; I'd never had an adolescent stage when I'd tested out life.

'Do you want to try it?'

'I don't know. What does it do to you?'

'You sound like you're fourteen. It relaxes you. It's a downer.'

'A downer?'

'I'm not so good at relaxing; my head races with too much stuff—'

'You drink too much coffee.'

'I know, that's an upper, it keeps me punched up and thinking fast at work, but I keep cannabis up here so when I get away from the city I can chill out.'

'You don't smoke it in London.'

'Not so much now.'

'Is it addictive?'

'Do you want me to look up FRANK on my phone? There's a whole website there that'll tell you the risks and what it does. Or are you going to call the police…' He dropped down on the cushions next to me again and settled his back against the sofa. 'They wouldn't do anything, you know, there's hardly any here. I'm not a dealer, only a casual smoker.'

He opened the tin, then glanced up at me and smiled. His look took the piss, calling me naive.

I sipped from the bottle of ale and watched him pull out a long, white bit of paper. He lay it on the lid, then put what I thought was tobacco in that. I'd never been a smoker at all, so I knew nothing. Then he lifted out a bag of greener-looking stuff and sprinkled that along the tobacco.

He glanced up. 'I haven't put too much in, so you can see if you like the feeling first. But I wouldn't put too much in anyway – you only want enough to relax and feel good.' He looked back at what he was doing and rolled the paper up into a tube about the tobacco with his dexterous long fingers and thumbs.

I drank my ale while I watched him.

He licked the edge of the paper, then grinned at me as he rolled the joint so it sealed.

The last thing he did was tear a little bit of card off the packet he'd taken the paper from, then he rolled that up and slotted it into the end of the joint.

He looked up and grinned at me again as he lifted it to his lips and then, sucking on the other end, he held a lighter flame to it. It flared as it lit. He took it out of his mouth and blew out the flame, so the end glowed and nothing more.

'You don't smoke,' I said really stupidly.

'No.' He sucked on the joint again, breathing it in deep, and held the smoke in his mouth for a while, then blew the smoke out upward.

'But you smoke that.'

'I don't smoke it all that much now.' After he'd inhaled from it three times, he held the end he'd put to his lips out to me. 'Do you want some?'

'You can still get cancer from that if it has tobacco in it.' God, that was such a Rick thing to say.

'Yeah, but one isn't going to give you cancer, and you can get cancer whatever. Do you want it?' He lifted it up in my direction, his arm out, like now is your moment, take it or leave it.

My heart knocked against my ribs. It was telling me to choose – not to do it – or do it. Heat and adrenaline pulsed in my blood, a rush of life, a rush of feeling. I wanted to feel like this. I wanted to take risks. 'Yes.' I reached out, took it and put it to my lips, then drew in a breath and choked.

He laughed. 'I take it you've never smoked.'

I shook my head, still coughing.

When I stopped coughing, I took a mouthful of ale and swallowed it, my throat had literally burned.

'Just put it to your lips, breath in a little, let the smoke fill your mouth, then blow it out for now. You won't get the hit so hard, but it won't make you cough.'

I did that; it still felt a weird thing to do.

I blew the smoke out upward. Then I took a swig of ale, and then tried again, this time I breathed in slowly. It didn't make me cough. I handed the thing back to him.

He was smiling at me, like he thought I was funny.

I poked my tongue out at him. 'How did you get so successful?' I knew he worked hard, but where had it started.

'I'm a natural entrepreneur, Ivy. I have ideas, I put them out there, and I work my arse off to make them a success. And my brain buzzes with stuff. That's why I need things like this to bring me down.' He lifted the joint. 'That's why Em and I work so well together – she has all the qualities I don't. She's calm, cool and organised.'

He inhaled from the joint.

'You two are good together.'

'I know.' He breathed out smoke. 'She knows it too.' He laughed.

'I like you,' I said to him as he held out the joint to me.

His smile quirked as I took the joint from his fingers.

'I mean, I haven't just always fancied you. I've always liked you.'

'Thank you. I've always liked you too. That's why I employ you.'

'You don't employ me any more, I gave you my notice.'

He laughed as I breathed in some of the smoke. I felt different already, woozy, like being drunk but sober. Weird.

'Oh yeah, right, I'm your lover now.' His eyes looked at me in a different way when he said it.

I wondered what the cannabis was doing to him.

After my third turn smoking his joint I handed it back. I could feel it in my blood. The music seemed to play louder and I could pick out the sounds within it more: the beat, the lyrics, all seemed – separated out.

He watched me as he inhaled, then said, as he let the smoke slide out of his mouth, 'How do you feel?'

'Different.'

He handed me the joint again. I breathed the smoke in and held it in my lungs for a minute, like he was doing. Then breathed it out.

Shit, it hit my bloodstream hard and my head spun. It *was* like being drunk, except when you were drunk you had no control. I still felt in control.

I handed the joint back to him. It was making me feel sick.

'You okay?'

'Yeah.' I nodded. The room spun.

He took two more puffs, then leant and opened the burner and threw the rest of it into the fire.

I drank the last of my ale.

He drank his, set his bottle down on the hearth, then took my empty bottle and put that down too.

'Take your top off, Ivy.'

I still had my hoodie on. I slipped it off as he got up, and I toppled on to my back, with my hoodie stuck on my arms.

I laughed as I stripped it off.

He'd gone into the kitchen.

When he came back. I threw my hoodie on to the empty sofa.

He had a tea towel in his hand.

'Blindfold, remember.' He waved it at me. His forfeit. Then I remembered my choice. After he'd done whatever, I was going to tie him up with it.

His legs straddled mine when he dropped on to the cushions and he lay the tea-towel over my chest and folded it over several times on a diagonal until it was a band. 'Lift your head.' He set it over my eyes, wrapped it around and tied it behind my head. It was tight. I couldn't see.

My heartbeat was a sound joining in with the music; I could feel its rhythm in my chest. It reverberated through my body. Then there was a rush of adrenaline, but the rush came in an odd way, it was as if someone had pressed slow motion.

I wanted him.

I wanted to do things with him.

I wanted him to do things to me.

'Ivy. Ivy. Ivy.' His words danced on the air as he began unbuttoning the blouse I'd worn into work this morning – I was never going to be able to wear it to work again.

His fingers brushed against my skin – he wasn't hurrying, he was doing it slowly and I could sense him watching what he did and looking at the skin he revealed. It made my pulse race, and my body hotter, and both sensations were amplified by the cannabis.

'Oh, my fuck… You have abs.' His fingers slid another button

87

loose and then began tracing lines on my belly. 'I always knew you were fit – I mean fit as in the amazing-looking sense of the word. But you are beautiful.'

His fingertips skimmed over the hollows on my stomach. Following the lines with reverence.

Rick had never made me feel appreciated physically like this.

'I'm lucky, it's in my genes.'

'Natural… But you must exercise. What do you do?'

'Yoga.'

'Phew, I might find out where you do yoga and come along.'

'I do Bikram yoga – it's in a heated room.'

'I can imagine doing yoga in a room with you would be pretty hot.'

I poked my tongue out at him as he released the last couple of buttons, then his hands swept my blouse back, so it hung at my sides. The next thing he did was undo the front hook opening my bra, he brushed the cups off my breasts and the air caught my skin.

The heat from the fire was warm on my legs, but with him kneeling over me I didn't feel it on my breasts. My breasts were cold.

His fingers touched, cupping the sides of my breasts gently. My brain was completely focused on what he was doing. I could feel and hear everything clearer: the tingle in my skin, his touch, his breath on me, the abrasion of his trousers against my jeans, and the feeling between my legs was a desperate need. I wanted him to take my jeans off and just do something to give me some sexual relief.

'Jack…' I said, when he hadn't spoken.

But then I felt him lean down and the next thing I felt was his warm mouth cover my nipple. He sucked it gently at first, then suddenly so hard it made me cry out. 'Ow.'

He laughed – it rippled over my breast. Then he turned his attention to the other breast. 'These are very pretty.'

'Just pretty?'

The cannabis was stealing my inhibitions. I didn't care what he thought of what I said, or did. I wanted an orgasm. I wanted my boss, the beautiful Jack Rendell, to give me an orgasm. Only he wasn't my boss any more. He was my lover.

It was getting more like being drunk, except drunken sex was crap. When you were drunk you were numb and senseless. This… I felt everything.

'Okay then, gorgeous.'

He sucked my other breast while he played with the first one.

I couldn't see anything but blackness, and so I could do nothing but enjoy – and touch.

My hands lifted up and gripped in his hair. He had slightly wavy hair, about an inch and half long. I'd always liked watching how it moved when he moved. When he leaned on someone's desk, talking, it fell forward and when he was in his office, he combed his fingers into it, lifting his elbows out to the side, when he was thinking. I liked touching it too.

My hips lifted, pressing up against him.

'I'm not going fast, Ivy,' he said it over my breast, 'so don't push. We're going slow and relaxed. That is what I need and that is what we're doing.'

'Yes, lover.'

He laughed against my breast, one palm settling over my abs.

'Anyway, I'm not pushing, I'm just enjoying it.'

'Okay, you can do that.'

'Carry on, then.'

I think I preferred having the blindfold. Being blindfolded meant I could hide and pretend this wasn't me.

He kissed a path along the hollow between my abs, then ran his tongue along it as he came back up. Then he kissed me, his tongue delving into my mouth. My fingers clung in his silky, wavy hair as his tongue danced around mine in an appreciative, assured way, making the place between my legs tingle with want even more.

I wanted Jack. I'd always wanted Jack. I'd thought this year I would have nothing to look forward to in the holidays, and now I had this.

I wanted my jeans off. I wanted his trousers off. I wanted to feel his naked skin. I'd never had desperate sex with Rick. I wanted desperate I-need-to-get-my-hands-on-you sex. But that wasn't what Jack wanted.

He kept kissing me, slowly, while his fingertips slid all the way down my middle. He did really like my abs, he kept touching the run from my neck to the top of my jeans, sliding his hand up and down, but this time he undid the button when he hit my jeans.

My mouth filled with saliva, but he didn't go farther, he pulled away. The heat from the fire reached the skin on my stomach.

'Where are you going?'

'You'll find out, and don't you dare peek.'

There was a noise in the kitchen, like he was getting something out of a cupboard, and then the sound of a fridge or freezer door. Something was poured into a container with a clattering sound. 'Ice?'

'Maybe!' He shouted from the kitchen. Then he was back in the room.

The cushions by my hips dented as he knelt, straddling me again.

'Ah.' It was cold. He trailed a single piece of ice around one nipple, then he sucked my nipple, making it warm again and trailed the ice around the other. My cannabis-confused brain was totally absorbed by every intense sensation as the music played like it danced around us.

He picked out another piece of ice and trailed it down my middle, the tip of his tongue following. When the ice reached where he'd undone the button of my jeans, he left it there – and slid down the zip.

My hips lifted, urging him to do more, and the piece of ice slid off sideways, I presume on to the cushion. 'Green-lace pants to match your bra. There's a naughty side under your clothes, Ivy. Or did you change your underwear when you were getting ready.'

'No, this is what I wear and you can think about that when you look at my bum in the office'

He laughed. 'Are you trying to make sure I never work out my lust for you?'

'Maybe.'

'We'll see. I'm going to try. I'm going to work hard to satisfy us both so well we'll be too exhausted to ever want sex with each other again.'

'So we'll look at each other and think, that was too knackering?'

'Maybe not that, but you'll look at me and feel exhausted by the memory.'

'I feel exhausted now, just waiting for you to take my jeans off.'

Another note of humour escaped his throat. 'My pace.'

I poked my tongue out. He swooped down and bit it. 'Ah.'

He didn't touch me then as he lifted away, not for ages. But he was moving.

'What are you doing?'

'Taking my shirt off.'

'Ooo let me see, I want—'

'No. But you can touch.' He gripped one of my hands and pressed my palm against his abs, he had really clearly defined abs, much tighter than mine, and I'd been right, there was no layer of fat beneath his skin. My other hand found his body too and ran over the contours. He was all velvety skin and firm muscle beneath, and his pecs were shallow and not hairy; he just had a few hairs dusted around his nipples, but nowhere else.

I slid my hands down across his skin, over his abdomen. There was a little hair in a line leading into his trousers. My fingers found his belt buckle.

'Uh-uh, my pace.' He pulled my hands away.

The room was warm now and I could hear the fire crackling. He slid my jeans off my hips but didn't take them off, only slid

91

them to my upper thighs. Desire ran up the back of my throat—a deep urge to grab him. There were new sensations everywhere in my body, not just the places he touched.

A piece of ice ran around the edge of my pants. 'Ivy Cooper, are you wearing a thong?'

'Jack Rendell, I am, but I wish you'd hurry up and get it off, and get all your clothes off too.'

A deep laugh rang around me. I felt it on my skin as the cannabis continued easing into my body.

'My pace.'

'Fuck your pace.'

'Fuck it or not, still my pace.'

He kissed my pelvic bone over the top of the lace, playing with the ice, running it over my abs. Then, suddenly, he gripped my hips and flipped me over to lie on my stomach. 'Ah!' A squeal came out of my mouth, as my heartrate leapt.

A cold ice cube settled between the top of my bottom cheeks and was left there to begin to melt as his tongue played along the line of my thong and his fingers pulled my jeans down so they cupped my bottom.

He was such a tease.

'I'm hard as hell, Ivy.'

'I didn't know hell was hard, but I guess you've been there.'

'Ha. Ha.'

He breathed in, a sound that said all his senses were appreciating me. 'I'm undoing my jeans.'

Oh wow. No. 'What are you going to do?' I shivered, as he stripped my blouse off my arms and threw it somewhere, then took off my bra. I was half-nervous now the moment was nearly here. But the nerves made the rush kick back in, the adrenaline pulsed inside me, full of anticipation; whatever Jack did to me, it was going to be good. It was going to make me feel good.

'I'm going to do all the things I dream of doing when I look at your bum. Every time you bend over a desk, you are going to think of me doing this.' He came down over me, his hands either side of my shoulders and then he settled between the cheeks of my bottom, his firm, velvety warm skin a contrast to the ice, then he rocked against me, his cold belt buckle pressing into my buttock. He hadn't taken his trousers down, just opened them and pushed them down a little. The material brushed against my skin as he rocked against me, sliding up between my bottom cheeks, where my thong was buried.

Sounds left his throat, pleasant sounds, satisfied sounds.

My face was pressed into a cushion and my fingers clasped the edge of it, my toes gripping on the cold stone flags, while the soles of my feet burned from the heat of the fire.

This was crazy. This was Jack.

'I could come like this, but I'm not going to.'

'I could come with you just doing that, if you'd actually touch me.'

'Wait. Patience—'

'I am waiting. Your pace, I know.'

He pulled away and smacked my bottom. It wasn't even a gentle smack – it was really hard. 'If you aren't going to do as I say, Ivy.'

He smacked me again. 'Ow.'

'Is that as loud as you can shout?'

'Ah. You're vicious!' He kept smacking.

'Doesn't it turn you on?'

'No. It hurts!'

'It turns me on.' He smacked me again.

'You prick. Ow!'

He laughed.

'Ow!'

When I expected the next smack, though it wasn't that, but about three cold lumps of ice were pressed on to my bottom.

'Ow,' I said it for a different reason.

He laughed again. 'Does it feel better?'

'A little.'

He did the same to my other bum cheek – smacked it about a dozen times, the bastard, then put ice on it. Then he kissed both my bottom cheeks and slid my thong down below them.

I was so wet for him, even though he'd hurt me when he'd smacked me.

'Oh, Jack.' He slid himself into the slot between the gap of my thong as it gripped beneath my bottom, and my flesh, so that he slid through the moisture between my legs. The weight of his hips came down on to me, pressing down like he was actually having sex with me, but he wasn't penetrating me at all, just taking his own pleasure and making a game of it, a delicious game.

If I had not split up with Rick I'd have been at home playing charades, or Scrabble, or something.

My breathing followed the pace of his strokes and my fingers curled about the cushion again, clutching tight as I tried not to cry out. Even Jack doing this was mesmerising.

He stopped then and yanked my jeans down more, then moved out of the way and pulled them off my feet.

'Thank God,' I whispered.

He laughed. Then he pulled off the stay-up stockings I'd left on when I'd put on my jeans after work. I felt the whisper of the light materiel touch my calves as he threw them away.

I could hear him moving but I couldn't—

'I'm taking off my trousers, Ivy. Stripping them down my legs, along with my boxers.'

He was saying it to make me anticipate what was coming next. I was anticipating, and my insides were anticipating.

He stripped my thong off last, leaving us naked.

'Open your legs a little.'

I did. I was still lying on my tummy, in the darkness behind the blindfold.

I thought he was going to come into me, but instead his fingers gripped my bottom cheeks and pulled them apart, and then his tongue touched me.

94

'Oh.'

He lifted my hips with the pressure of his fingers. I bent my knees up and tilted up in his face in answer.

He laughed, and then, finally, his fingers slipped into me. 'Ooo,' it was a sound of gratitude, of longing for more. I desperately wanted more. My heart pounded out a rhythm that played through my veins, as he used his tongue and fingers, still teasing me, toying with me. I pushed back against the invasion of his long fingers when he tried to make them shallow. He let me play along with him, not avoiding my attempts to join in, but using them to increase the anticipation – sometimes allowing it, sometimes avoiding it.

I rocked back against him as his tongue skimmed over me.

I was so horny and yet I was nowhere near coming, and I felt like that was how he wanted it.

With Rick I'd had to make myself come before he started if I wanted to get anything out of sex… This was so different.

'Oh God.' Those were his words, and he said them right before he slipped into me, his full length.

It was the most heavenly thing I'd ever felt. I lifted up on to all-fours, kneeling before him on the cushions, still blindfolded, as he gripped my hips and pulled me against him when he pushed in, then he withdrew and pushed me away at the same time, creating a slow, intoxicating rhythm.

I was panting as he filled me up – every time he filled me up – and sweating in the heat from the fire, and the heat of his adoration.

An ice cube touched the top of the cleft between my buttocks, and he held it there with one hand, letting it melt as he kept moving, and I kept moving. The water trickled down over where we joined, cold and different, and then it dripped from the front. His cushions were going to be a mess.

I didn't care. Let him care.

I pushed back against him.

Once the ice had melted he gripped my thighs, and then his rhythm was no longer slow and gentle it was fast and hard and desperate as he pounded into me with firm, hard strokes. Rick had never once, in all the years we'd been together, set my heart pumping like this. My breaths were shallow. I couldn't breathe. I couldn't waste any thoughts on breathing.

'Oh, Jack.'

Feelings, sensations danced around in my nerves. It was as if I hovered a step away from an orgasm. Just one step more, just one…

'Oh.' It spun out into my blood, a raging storm of sensation whizzing through my nerves with the extra intensity from the cannabis. It washed through me on a flood, then swelled and ebbed like waves rolling in then pulling out as he carried on shoving into me.

I hadn't ever known an orgasm like this – it was different to when I played with myself when I'd been messing around with Rick; that's what my old sex life felt like now – only messing around. This… This was a universe away from what Rick and I had done.

Then suddenly Jack stopped and leant over me. 'You're on the pill, aren't you? I didn't check.'

'Yes, Jack, I'm on the pill. Don't stop.'

He laughed and then he was moving again, more determinedly, desperately, as his fingers slipped forward and gripped my waist. 'I love your figure. You're so beautiful.'

I came again because he'd said that as he pushed into me. I was swept away with the sensations. They made tears fill my eyes – in the darkness behind the blindfold.

'Oh.' It was a breath of sound on my lips.

His hand slipped to grip my thighs again, and then he breathed out on a low growl, pushed in hard three times and spilled himself into me. His fingers clawed into my thighs, pressing into them as he ground himself against me in a circular motion.

Then, finally, he slipped out of me with a sigh of relief.

I tumbled on to my back and tried to take the blindfold off, but it was too tight.

'Here. Sit up.'

I did.

What felt like the back of his fingers brushed over my breast before he undid the tea towel. It took him a while to get the knot undone, but when it slid away I saw the beautiful chest I'd touched before.

I touched it again as he pulled back. He was still kneeling, with his buttocks settled back on his heels, so I had a full frontal of Jack naked.

He was beautiful.

His head lowered and he kissed me hard on the lips, then turned away and snatched up the metal tin with his cannabis in it. He sat on the cushions facing the fire and began making another joint.

This was the craziest day of my life.

I sat forward and clasped my knees in the same position I'd been sitting in before the sex had begun.

We were still naked.

He lit the joint and took a drag, then held it out to me. 'Here. I'll go get the duvet. You must be cold.'

I took a drag as he stood up, looking like a piece of moving artwork from the Tate Gallery. He went upstairs. I didn't take another drag, the first one had made my head spin.

It had been a really long day.

When he came back down, he carried a duvet and pillows too. I suppose he planned to sleep down here.

'It'll be warmer down here, there's no central heating. I never had it put in. I felt like it would spoil the rustic style of the place, and the range cooker in the kitchen keeps the place lukewarm.'

I nodded, feeling weird now.

He tossed the pillows down and dropped the duvet, then held

his hand out for the joint. I gave it to him, then lay down, pulling a pillow beneath my head and yanking the duvet across, so it covered me. The linen smelled fresh, with a hint of lavender.

With a hand under my head on the pillow, I watched him. He dropped to his knees, then sat back on his haunches, smoking. 'Do you want some more?' He lifted the end of the joint out towards me.

'No. It makes me dizzy.'

He smiled. 'More for me, then.'

I lay there, watching him. It all felt odd now it was over. Awkward. Like there was no need for me to be here, like I shouldn't be here. But I was still hot and sticky between my legs and my blood hummed from the sex. I was glad I'd come here.

He opened the wood-burner and threw the last of the joint into the fire, then put another couple of logs on and shut the door. Then he lifted the duvet and joined me underneath it.

'Come here.' He lifted an arm, I settled against his chest. I felt better there, calmer.

His fingers stroked through my hair as I drifted into sleep. His breathing didn't sound like he was falling asleep.

Chapter 4

The weight of Ivy's head rested on my chest. I opened my eyes. It was daylight and it was probably late morning. It had taken me ages to get to sleep; I'd been too wound up, and the second joint had only ended up making me think more not less.

Anyway, now I was awake I wasn't going to be able to get to sleep again. I'd always suffered with insomnia, but since everything had kicked off, I found sleeping even harder.

I looked up at the ceiling, absorbing the sound of Ivy breathing and the feel of her hair stirring on my chest.

Ivy was special, I'd always known that – different. When I'd interviewed her years ago, I'd spent the whole time looking at her eyes as she'd stared at me, trying to work out if they were really blue, because –who had lavender eyes? Elizabeth Taylor was the only other woman I'd heard of with eyes like Ivy's.

I liked looking at her smile too. It was why I'd gone to the coffee shop with her, because I'd needed a few doses of her smile… and then she'd still been at work, and the need in me had roared. I hadn't been with anyone in weeks and I'd always wanted her, and I'd been lonely and in a miserable mood and it had been too tempting. But Em was going to kill me – if she found out.

I sighed and, my chest lifting, woke Ivy. Her palm pressed down on to my stomach and she turned to look at me.

Her dark eyelashes seemed to make the lavender an even deeper colour, and she looked pretty, even with her hair messed up and her eyes cloudy with sleep.

'What time is it?'

'I don't know. I haven't looked. I was trying not to wake you.'

She blushed as her breast stroked over my chest when she moved. My dick came to life. But I didn't want another round right now. There was something I wanted to do, even if it did annoy Victoria.

I untangled my legs from Ivy's. 'I need the toilet.'

The room was cold. The fire must have burned out hours ago.

I glanced over at the naked fir tree as I threw the duvet back. It wasn't naked any more. One of Ivy's stockings hung from it. It slid off and fell among the ashes around the hearth.

'Perfect timing,' she whispered. 'That's Santa's judgement.'

I looked back at her and smiled weakly as the humour caught in my chest – it was mixed with an odd sense of pain. Everything around me was reminding me of what I didn't have. I hated it. I was pissed off again today, even though I'd run away.

'Happy—' Ivy began.

'Don't say it.' I covered her mouth.

She laughed beneath my hand. But I wasn't joking.

She bit my hand gently, so I had to lift it off her mouth, then said, 'I need the loo too.'

'You go first, then, but hurry.'

She got out from the beneath the duvet, all beautiful long, pale, slender limbs, and ran towards the stairs.

I followed her up there and waited outside the bathroom for her to finish, then I pointed to my bedroom door. 'Your case is in my room, if you want to cover up a bit. After I've been to the loo, I'll go down and cook breakfast, so feel free to have a shower if you want one.'

She nodded.

I went into the bathroom, stood over the toilet and peed. I smelled of Ivy. She had a nice smell.

I washed my hands and washed her scent off me. I'd shower after we'd eaten.

I walked into the bedroom. Ivy was sorting out something to wear, pulling clothes out of her case. I went over to mine and found a pair of my trunk-style boxers to put on. 'Are you going to shower?'

'Yeah.'

'I'll see you downstairs, then.'

It was weird having her here this morning. When I'd asked her up here, it had been a knee-jerk reaction. I hadn't thought beyond what I wanted to do last night – and now I'd have her hanging around all week.

My heart pumped in a quick rhythm as I went back downstairs. The bathroom door shut upstairs. I walked over and grabbed my mobile from the stereo's docking point. Turmoil rioted and gripped at my gut as I looked at the phone. I wanted to call. Just a quick call.

I slid up Victoria's number, then touched the call icon.

It rang five times, I was going to hang up, but—'Jack?'

'Hi, can I speak to her?' I was breathless, and my heart was jumping in my chest as if it was raving. My first Christmas with a daughter. I'd wanted her here.

Victoria sighed, as though it was an inconvenience. 'Yes, okay. Hang on.'

I breathed deeply as shivers trembled through my muscles. I still wasn't used to this.

'Hi!' Her breathing was hard, as though she had the phone too close to her mouth.

'Happy Christmas, honey!'

'Hey! What are you doing? We had an agreement no 'C' word! Your forfeit—'

Oh my God. Ivy was meant to be in the fucking shower. I

turned around sharply, lifting a finger to my lips. She was halfway down the stairs, clutching some of her clothes against her chest.

'Who are you—' she began.

Fuck it. I tapped the loudspeaker icon. 'Hello, Daddy!' The words rang out from my phone. I loved the word 'daddy', it kicked me in the chest every time.

Ivy's jaw dropped. I looked away from her and carried on talking to Daisy.

'What are you doing, sweetheart?'

'Playing with my new Barbie. Thank you for my Polly Pocket.'

'You're welcome. Did Santa bring you a whole pile of presents?'

'Yes. I woke up at six and I opened them all.'

'Awesome, honey.'

'Mum said I have to go.'

'Okay, I'll see you soon. We'll go skating or something?'

'I like it when we go ice skating.'

'I know. Have a good time.'

'Thank you, Daddy!' The phone went dead. I wished she'd handed me back to Victoria; I'd not been allowed any time with Daisy on my own yet. I wanted some time alone with her, I wanted to be a proper dad, but unless Victoria gave me some space… I was using my solicitor to fight for my rights, but Victoria wasn't budging on the pace of things. I wanted to see Daisy alone. I'd wanted to bring her up here for Christmas and be the two of us for a couple of days, but Victoria had denied it. She'd had Daisy for seven years of Christmases. I'd just wanted one. The eighth was meant to have been mine.

Emotions skidded around in my chest.

'I thought you were playing me already.' Ivy was still standing on the stairs. 'I didn't know you and Sharon had a daughter.'

I didn't answer but walked into the kitchen to start breakfast.

Ivy followed me in there.

I picked the stuff out of the fridge to make omelettes. Ivy's hands slid around my waist and gripped over my middle.

102

She ought to know that Daisy wasn't Sharon's. 'Sharon and I don't have a daughter.'

'Then whose—'

'Daisy's the daughter of my first girlfriend. We had a high-school reunion in the summer. I came out of it with Daisy.'

'What?' She let me go and stepped back.

I turned around and watched her. 'Yes. My first girlfriend had our child in her bedroom when she was seventeen, and the family never told a soul, including me. She had Daisy in the summer and never went back to school; they kept her a secret. I think they were ashamed. The first I knew about Daisy was six months ago. She's eight now.'

I turned away, opened the cupboard to get a bowl, then started breaking eggs into it. 'That was the end for Sharon and I. She wasn't into me playing daddy and definitely wasn't up for calming down and playing mummy, or for Daisy to have any access to my money. You should see Daisy, though.' I glanced back over my shoulder. 'She looks like me. She's the best thing I've created.'

'That's saying something…' Ivy was referring to adverts and the business. Those things were not the same, but I guess if you didn't have kids you didn't get that feeling of – did I really create this little person? I wouldn't have got it a year ago.

'I was hoping to bring Daisy up here for…' My lips twisted. 'I got the tree organised for her to decorate. But her mother wouldn't let her come. I'm fighting Victoria in the courts for a share of custody.'

'Wow.' The word was a breath of sound behind me.

I turned around. 'Has that spooked you?'

'Everyone at work thinks you and Sharon split because you played her so much.'

'I know. You said yesterday.'

'I'm sorry.'

'What have you got to be sorry for?'

'I don't know.' She laughed then.

103

'Are you going to get in the shower?'

'There was no towel.'

'They're in the cupboard at the top of the stairs.'

She stepped towards me and hugged me again suddenly, her arms slipping back around my middle, as if she was offering me comfort. She was a sweet girl. But she'd given me far more comfort last night.

When I made no move to hug her back she let go and hurried off to shower.

I broke all the eggs into the bowl, then turned a ring on on the hob. Good idea, or bad idea, Ivy was up here with me, and I guess I ought to make the most of her company – and if my lust burned out, or if she was annoying – then I could drive her back to London, drop her off and come back up on my own.

'Where are we going?' Ivy challenged as I led her out of the house. I'd put another blindfold on her. I'd wrapped my scarf around her eyes. She'd probably looked out the windows anyway, so this wasn't going to be all that much of surprise, but I longed for her to feel the awe that I felt up here. Sharon had never got it and if Ivy didn't, then her company was going to be immediately irritating. I led her around the cottage, pulling her by the hand, and then around the corner of the barn.

I loved this place. It was my favourite place in the world and I'd been to Switzerland, Dubai, Paris, Cairo, Monaco, Rome, South Africa, New York, the Grand Canyon, but none of those places gave me the rush of wow I felt when I was here. This place hugged me and yet, at the same time, it punched me in the gut with its magnificence.

'I'm going to step in a puddle and fall over or something, Jack.'

She had her stiletto-heeled boots on and it was a little frosty. 'It's not far, just a few more steps, then you can see.'

Once I thought I'd led her to the point where she'd get the best view. I undid the scarf. 'Oh my God, that's beautiful!'

104

Right answer. I watched her. Her eyes darted around the view, looking at the hills, which were almost mountains, with their snowy caps, and the fir-tree woods that covered their skirts, and then her eyes settled on what I called the 'big house'. But it wasn't all that big – it was five bedrooms. But it was a traditional house for the National Park, with a central porch and sash windows at either side and three large sash windows along the top floor, then little dormer windows in what used to be the servants' rooms in the attic.

'Do you want to look inside?' The fields around the house would have been sheep-grazing land in times gone by. I'd thought about getting some sheep, but I hadn't gone for it yet.

'Why?' She looked back at me. 'Do you own the house too?'

'Yeah, but I rent it out to holiday-makers when I'm not up here. The place is too big for me; I'd rattle around in it, so I stay in the cottage.'

'You're nuts.' She looked back at the house and walked over.

I followed, my scarf swinging in one hand as I took the key out of my pocket.

Ivy stomped her feet on the stone step, knocking the dirt off her boots, then gripped her hands around her middle to fight off the cold as I unlocked the door. When I looked over my shoulder at her, she smiled. She'd put a little makeup on, but not much, her lips were a pale pink and her eye shadow a pale gold.

I pushed the door inward and encouraged her to walk ahead. The place was cold and her boots echoed on the bare wooden floorboards, which had probably had two centuries of wax rubbed into them.

Her gaze spun around the hallway, following the wooden staircase as it rose up and turned a corner, then carried on. 'I love this place,' she said it to the room not me. Then she turned to a door. 'Can I look?'

'Sure. Go ahead.' It was fun watching her. I bet I'd looked like her when I'd first seen this place.

105

'Oh…' The sound of appreciation echoed into the hall when she discovered the parlour. I'd filled the place with lots of antique furniture, although the sofas were modern but with a style that fitted in with the place. There was a dark oak dresser on the other side of the room, a writing desk, and the pictures were antiques. She turned around and smiled at me, then walked past me and crossed the hall to open the door to the dining room.

'Did you decorate it yourself?'

'I didn't do the work, but the ideas are mine.'

'I like your ideas. Can I look upstairs?'

'Yes, but look at the kitchen first.' I held her hand and pulled her along the narrow part of the hall, beside the stairs. The door at the back opened on to the kitchen – it still had a black, iron range, with a hook for the kettle and a bread oven in the wall.

'This is like being on the set of a historical drama. I love it.' She turned and stared at me. 'I'd never have thought you'd be into something like this.'

'Then it proves you didn't really know me.'

'I think I worked that out. You have an eight-year-old girl.'

My smile faded and a sharp pain dug into my ribs. I was still hurting over the fact that I couldn't see Daisy. My first… C… with a child to play Santa with and I couldn't see her. It wasn't fair. I'd missed years with Daisy. It was cruel.

It was Daisy I'd wanted to show around.

'Can I go upstairs?'

'Yeah, you go explore…'

She walked out and headed upstairs. I heard her heels on the wooden treads as I looked out of the kitchen window at the view. The views from this place did things to me, eased my soul. But there were better views upstairs. I followed Ivy.

I found her in the room that had the best view. She was leaning on the windowsill, looking out.

'So what's your verdict?'

She turned around, her eyes full of wonder. 'This place is amazing. But why don't you stay in it?'

'Because if I lived in it, I think I'd spoil it.'

She didn't answer, just looked at me like she still thought I was mad. Maybe it was a bit crazy.

'Do you want to go and explore the great outdoors? I thought we'd go out for a drive around. If that's alright?'

'That's okay.' Her arms had folded over her chest, her hands gripping the sides of her jumper.

'Come on, then.'

Sharon would've pouted if I'd suggested driving around to her. Sharon would have considered it boring. Ivy didn't. But she wasn't smiling either and she looked a bit uncertain, with her arms over her chest – or nervous, maybe.

She had the same pale skinny jeans on as yesterday, but today she was wearing a loose, mauve jumper, and it looked like the wool had silver woven through it because it sparkled when it caught the sun. It suited her hair, though, and it suited her figure, having something loose on top and her slender legs wrapped up in a second skin of faded denim.

But Ivy had the figure of a model as well as the face – anything she wore would look good.

She shivered as she walked out on to the landing. Maybe she was clutching herself because she was cold? Her arms fell and she gripped the bannister before she started walking down.

I felt like Gollum out of *The Lord of the Rings* when I locked the place up – my precious. There was a huge weight of pride in my chest.

Sharon had agreed with Ivy on one thing. She'd always said it was stupid letting other people stay here when I thought it was so precious I wouldn't use it. But it would be a crime for it not to be lived in and enjoyed. I just wasn't the person for it.

I pressed the button to open the car, following Ivy over there.

'I prefer to be on the bike than in my car. But it's not the time of year for the bike.' I slid into the driver's seat and threw the scarf I was still carrying into the back.

'Your bike…' she said, settling into the passenger seat.

'Motorbike. I have two in the barn here. I have one in London too. I prefer riding a bike, but I want to take you up over the hill passes and it's too icy.' We'd have some fun in the car, though. The roads would be quiet.

I didn't speed when we were in the single-track narrow lanes – that would have been stupid, but once we were on the wider roads, which I knew like the back of my hand, I started playing rally driver. I revved up between bends, then dropped down through the gears, before racing up through the gears again.

'Jack!' Ivy squealed when I let the back of the car slip out around a corner. But then she laughed.

I glanced over at her. She wasn't scared, or maybe she was scared, but whether she was scared or not she was enjoying it – her eyes were bright with excitement. I pulled on to a straight and put my foot down. I loved speed – or rather I loved the risk of speed – doing something all out that other people were too scared to do.

Ivy's fingers gripped the edges of the passenger seat and she pressed herself back into it as we neared a bend. I dropped through the gears as I slowed down fast. It was completely the wrong way to drive on a cold, icy day, but I knew the roads that were salted. I wasn't taking foolish risks, I was taking controlled risks.

She laughed when we came out the other side of the bend just fine.

I took her to Ennerdale Water first. It was my favourite lake – it wasn't commercialised and the quietest I'd found. From where I parked you couldn't see the lake and I deliberately hadn't driven past any on the way out here.

Ivy looked at me.

Sharon would've said, 'why have you dragged me out into the middle of nowhere?' But Ivy seemed to get this place. Her head

108

had been spinning around looking at every view, even though I'd been distracting her with dangerous driving.

Ivy's eyes held expectation, she knew, without knowing, that I'd brought her out here to appreciate something.

'Come on.'

It was like my church; there was a sense of reverence hanging over me when I got out of the car and walked around to Ivy's side, to open the door for her.

After I pressed the switch to lock the car, I gripped Ivy's hand, which was clothed in a stripy glove. She had entirely the wrong footwear on for this, but girls liked their heels, especially when they were trying to impress, and I hadn't told her what this place was like. She'd dressed for a week away with me in London.

Her parka coat hung open, revealing her mauve glittery jumper, and her equally sparkly nature, to the world.

I drew her along the grass path towards the lake, without saying anything. Then as though I'd created the hills and the lake, when she got her first view I held her hand and stood beside her, silent, so she could experience the awesomeness of the place.

It spoke – or it did me anyway. It whispered serenity and beauty, and the complexity of the world and it reminded me to keep my feet on the ground. Not that I needed the feet on the ground reminder much any more, Sharon and Victoria had achieved that this year, dropping me back on my arse with a bump.

'Wow,' Ivy said.

'You can walk right around it. It's one of my favourite places up here. I like to run around it, but on the far side it's more of a scramble – the path becomes a steep pile of slate shingle.' I glanced at her feet, then back up at her lavender eyes. They were an awesome view too and her jumper accentuated the colour – she was clever at picking clothes that did that. 'You'll never do it in those boots. We can walk as far as the shore if you want, though?'

She nodded, but she gripped my hand hard as her heels sunk into the turf pathway. We were probably lucky it was frosty, otherwise it would've been even harder for her. 'Did you bring any flat shoes, your Converse or something?'

She shook her head.

'Looks like we might hit the sales tomorrow, then.'

When we reached the shore, I picked up a stone and skimmed it. It bounced along the surface of the water.

'How do you do that?'

'Like this…' I showed Ivy the technique of finding the right-shaped stone, bracing it in your forefinger, then using that to power a spin as you threw.

She had a go, but she failed. I stood behind her and held her hand, my arm braced against hers. The stone bounced twice, she bent down and picked up another, her bottom rubbing against my groin in a way that made me recall every beautiful detail of last night. My lust hadn't died.

I turned away and found a couple of stones to skim.

'Have you got any brothers or sisters, Jack?'

I threw a stone and counted as it bounced on top of the lake fifteen times. 'No. I'm the single point of failure in my family.'

Her stone plopped into the water and sank. 'You're hardly a failure.'

'Talk to my parents; they will tell you different. Have you got brothers or sisters?'

'No. I always wanted a sister. I think if I had a sister now, I might not feel so isolated—'

'I thought we were having fun.'

'I don't mean right now. I mean over the thing with Rick. I think a sister, or a brother, might have been on my side—'

'Or just another person to be against you.'

'Maybe.' Another of her stones plopped into the water.

I looked at her. I hadn't heard her on the phone this morning. 'Did you call them today – your parents?'

'No. I thought it best to leave it. There were two dozen texts on my phone from Rick this morning. It sounded like he was really upset. If they know he's doing that, if he was drunk and crying… I don't think Mum would want to hear from me. It would make things more awkward for her while he was staying there.'

'She's your mum…'

'I know, but she's still angry with me and embarrassed and… They thought Rick and I were a sure thing for grandkids and his parents are their friends, and well… Whatever. It's over, and I don't regret ending it, and I'm not going back and she needs time to get used to that fact.' Her head tipped sideways as something sparked through her thoughts, and the question appeared in her eyes. 'You said you left Sharon and this morning you said you split up because she didn't want anything to do with Daisy. Was that why you left?'

I didn't usually discuss my personal business with anyone, even Em, not all the detail. But out here in the middle of nowhere, knowing it was a special day, and she was so lonely she'd come up here to spend it with me, who she didn't even really know… I felt guilty… I felt like I should let her in a bit. 'I ended it because Sharon isn't the mother type. I told her to clean up her act, but within hours I realised it was pointless asking her to do that, she never would, and I didn't love her. I wanted to change my life anyway. Daisy just gave me a good excuse.'

She gave me a judging look.

'Sharon married me for money, Ivy. Don't feel sorry for her. I bought the most expensive champagne from the bar and then there was Sharon beside me, hands all over me… She basically moved in with me that night. I should've known. But Sharon has a way…' Disgust, guilt, embarrassment twisted inside me. I'd been as bad as her. I hated myself when I looked back. I didn't go on. Ivy wouldn't understand the life I'd led with Sharon. 'She leached off me. She's never worked.'

'Sharon is pretty.' Ivy punctuated.

Yes she was, in a model way, just like Ivy, but not like Ivy.

Sharon's hard, grasping edge showed in her features, like Ivy's gentleness showed in hers. 'Yes, she is pretty, and selfish, and pushy, and opinionated, and—'

'I get that from her phone calls. But you said you thought you loved her in the beginning?'

My hands slipped into the pockets of my leather jacket and we started walking along beside the water as it lapped at the pebbles. Ivy's hand gripped my arm as she struggled in her heels.

'Sharon liked to party. And you know me, so do I.' I glanced at Ivy. Fuck it, it was better she knew who she'd had sex with. 'Sharon led me by the dick, as Em puts it. Only Em doesn't know one-hundredth of it. I like things that make my heart beat. I like the rush of surprise and excitement. I like doing different things, risky things. Sharon got that. She's like that too, in different ways to me, but the same in some ways. I was addicted to all her little tricks. I'm not going to tell you some of them because they'd blow the mind of a nice girl like you. I don't want to shock you. But I will tell you, the girls who flounced into the office, they were prostitutes… I didn't have affairs, they were presents from Sharon. Yes, I played around, but everything we did was mutual and agreed.'

Ivy's mouth opened and her eyes framed by dark, now mascara-coated, eyelashes, widened.

Sharon would've had fake lashes on.

'You've slept with prostitutes, and then you did it with me last night with no condom…' The accusation was high in her voice.

I was surprised she'd let me. But I was clean. That had been the first time I'd ever done it without a condom and I was one-hundred-per cent certain she was clean, otherwise I'd have used a condom. She was a nice girl.

I turned away and picked up a stone to throw. 'I'm clean. I know. You're absolutely safe. And I didn't do it with every prostitute she sent. She only sent them when I wasn't paying her enough attention – or money. Mostly I turned them around and sent them away, but there were a couple who were too pretty to pass on. But I used condoms.'

'*I used condoms…*' It was said in an insulting, cutting tone that mimicked the arrogance that might have been in my voice— 'You're disgusting.' Ivy turned around and began walking off the shingle-covered shore. But if she was aiming for an impressive stomping-away exit she didn't achieve it in her heels.

Disgusting… Yeah. I felt it. I wasn't arrogant about it on the inside. I knew how my story of sin sounded. But for years Sharon's little tricks had kept me charged up with adrenaline and suitably tamed – and my bank account open. I'd given her everything she wanted. She'd never really cared what I wanted.

This was what I wanted. This place. Speed for my dose of adrenaline. Climbing. Lake-swimming. I didn't need orgies and prostitutes, and sex games.

Yes, I still wanted sex, and I'd been sleeping with girls I hooked up with in clubs. I couldn't switch my sex drive off. But it had been normal sex with normal women. And single women. Not the conveyor belt of orgies with innocent strangers Sharon had had me on.

'Hey.' I caught up with Ivy and my arms surrounded her, then I lifted her off her feet.

'Ah.' She thumped my shoulder as she squealed, to make me put her down. 'You should have told me before last night.'

'What? Like I can't drink, I'm an alcoholic… but, I can't have sex, I've done it with prostitutes. They were high-end; I didn't take them off the streets. They were paid a fortune. It wasn't dirty like you're thinking. God, most of the stuff Sharon had us getting up to was a lot worse than that…'

'How does that make it better?'

'It's all in the past. It ended when Sharon and I ended. Give me credit for being honest. You're the only person, other than Sharon, who knows that, and I'm not proud of it, but those years happened. I told her, I wasn't getting involved in that shit any longer. I needed a home Daisy can visit. I grew up. Sharon will never grow up. So there's no more marriage, and that was a relief for me. I'd gone to that reunion wanting it to be over anyway. I hadn't taken Sharon with me because she'd have embarrassed me. She'd have probably tried to get my best friend and his wife back to our room and expected me to fuck them…' I received a punch on my arm for trying to shock Ivy. 'To Sharon that's fun.' I leant nearer Ivy, because her bad judgement was starting to piss me off. 'Risky… Exciting… It made her blood rush through her veins…'

'You're twisted.'

'I *was* twisted.' I straightened up. 'I'm straightened out now and out of rehab.'

She poked her tongue out at me, then had another go at storming off towards the car. It didn't work. Her heels sunk in the grass and slowed her down.

'Sharon's found a replacement for me already. Some guy in banking. She went over to the bars the guys drink in at Canary Wharf and probably waited for someone to buy the best champagne.'

'Is that meant to make me feel sympathetic? It doesn't. You give me the shivers.'

'But good shivers or bad shivers?' I knew what girls could be like – if they liked naughty stuff. Sharon had used to get turned on by me even telling her about sleeping with other girls. She'd have loved tales of Ivy—

'Bad shivers!'

I popped the lock as Ivy neared the car.

Her hand rested on the roof and she started trying to wipe the mud off one heel with the other.

I opened the boot and found the penknife I had stashed in my emergency kit.

I squatted down in front of her to scrape the mud off her stiletto heels with the back of the penknife.

Afterwards she climbed in the car while I walked back down to the lake. To wash the knife off and take a breather.

When I came back to the car and got in, I told her, 'I'm going to take you somewhere else you'll want to see.'

I heard the air sweep into Ivy's lungs on a wave of awe when she saw the pass up ahead. 'Wow.'

'Hardknott. It's an ancient track-way through the hills. There's a ruined Roman fort up there. There's also no other way through the Lake District at this point, so the only way is up.'

And it was up, straight up – although the road snaked its way up there, you'd never get up it if you drove straight. I revved the engine to spook her and drove. There were no other cars in sight behind us and I could see for miles in the rear-view mirror. I'd bet there were no cars on the other side, either. People generally didn't come here in winter, it wasn't salted, but the day wasn't that cold, and the sun had been bright all day. I was gambling on the ice having melted up there.

Ivy gripped her seat again as I kept roaring the engine when I could. Like the car was struggling to get us up the gradient. It wasn't.

'Oh my God, you're mad.'

I smiled, but I didn't look at her. We hadn't talked much since my declaration at the lake. But I was glad I'd been honest. It felt good to have someone else know what a depraved shithead I'd lowered myself to be – at my worst. But the worst was behind me.

'I feel like the car is going to fall off.' Her fingers gripped the leather even tighter.

I laughed at that. The road wasn't vertical, but it was the steepest road in England.

'You ought to know, I'm scared of heights, Jack.'

'You're on the ground.'

'Yeah, but I feel like I'm hanging off the edge of the world. Oh my God! Jack!'

We were nearly at the top. I revved the engine harder, more genuinely to get us there.

'Oh.' She turned and glanced across her shoulder looking back as we reached the brow of the pass and went over. 'This place is amazing. I didn't even know England had anywhere that looked like this.'

'It's hardly a secret. It's packed with tourists fighting to get up here in August. There's a whole snake of cars on this road.'

She looked at me, her eyes bright. 'That would spoil it.'

'I know. I don't come up to the house in August ever, and if I come up in any of the summer months, I tend to stay on my own land.'

'Your land…'

'I own ten acres around the farmhouse.'

'I didn't realise you had land with it.'

'It's worthless, really. It's protected up here, everything is, so you can't build. It's so it stays picture-postcard. A little part of England caught in a time warp. But I bought the place because it was like that. I don't want to build. I'm even considering getting sheep.'

'Ha. Ha.'

'I'm not kidding. I'm seriously thinking about buying a small flock of sheep to keep the grass down.'

'I don't see you as a shepherd. Get a ride-on lawnmower.'

I looked at her and gave her a listen-to-me look. 'I'm serious.'

'Well, I will look forward to watching you looking after your sheep, because that will be funny.'

I doubted she'd get to see it, but— 'I won't be the one looking after them. I'll pay someone who knows what they're doing. I'm not an idiot.'

I pulled the car over and parked up.

'I'm not sure about that, Jack. You slept with prostitutes.'

'I didn't sleep with them, they didn't spend the night. I had sex with three prostitutes, and all of them over a year ago. Does it make you feel better knowing the detail?'

'No.'

'Whatever, Ivy.' I opened the door. 'I'm going to go up and look out from the ruins. Come if you want.'

116

It looked like I was going to spend tomorrow driving her back to London.

Whatever.

I walked on up to the old fort. Most of the stone in the walls had been robbed away, or fallen down, so it stood at varying heights, marking out a world that had been here a thousand years ago. It had been like a small village up here, with rows of dwellings and military buildings within the perimeter walls. I climbed up on to one of the walls and just stood there, looking at the view. It was an awesome view. You could see for miles up here – all the way out to the sea, and it was so quiet today; there was no one else here and no cars crawling up either side of the pass. I'd never been here when it was like this.

I breathed in the clean, fresh, cold air. It made me feel better. No, I didn't need sex or cocaine for my rush of adrenaline any more. I used this place, and if I couldn't get up here... because I was too busy, or someone was in the house, then I took my motorbike out of the garage in London and rode out of the city late at night.

But I guess it was foolish of me to think Ivy would understand. She was sweet and sensible, and level-headed. Why would she understand me?

'Sorry.'

I turned around. She was there.

I jumped down off the wall. 'What have you got to be sorry for? That you slept with a prick who's had sex with prostitutes?'

'I'm sorry I was so angry. If what you said is true, that it was over a year ago, it doesn't affect me. I shouldn't be kicking up about it.'

Damn right you shouldn't. 'What I said was true. So where does that leave us? Do you want me to take you back to London tonight?'

Her eyes looked into my eyes, like she was measuring me up, probably judging the depth of any lies I'd told. I'd told quite a

117

few in my life, but none to her in the last twenty-four hours. 'No. I want to stay here.'

'With me…'

'With you.'

I took a breath. Maybe this wasn't the moment, but it was a one-off opportunity. 'Do you want to have sex up here?'

'Are you kidding?'

'No.' I lifted an eyebrow at her. 'There's no one around, and there's never normally no one around; it'll feel like having sex on top of the world. I bet hardly anyone has done it up here. It'll be a better invisible badge than the mile-high club.'

'Where?'

'On one of the walls.'

'You're mad.'

'I was disgusting half an hour ago.'

'You're disgusting and mad.'

I wrapped an arm about her waist and pulled her closer, then whispered in her ear. 'And horny as hell after last night.'

She reeled back, pulling away. 'I'm not sitting on one of those walls, it'll cut me.'

I smiled at her. She was sweet, I didn't want her pretty little bottom to be sore either, and nor did I want anyone to catch us up here with her jeans stripped off. Which meant. 'Lean your hands on the wall and I'll show you.'

She stood there, staring at me for a minute; I'd lay a bet on the fact her heart was racing. I had a feeling Ivy liked things that scared her and made her heart pound as much as I did. Maybe that was why she'd let me off for sleeping with prostitutes. I didn't think it would have turned her on, but I did think that the risk involved in having sex with me turned her on. She was a little scared of having sex with me.

She turned around and stood in front of me. 'The view is amazing isn't it?'

'Yes.' I slipped my arms around her middle and just held her

118

for a moment, but I didn't want to be too slow in case someone else came up here. I undid the button on her jeans.

Her hand covered mine before I got the zip down, as if she was going to stop me, but instead her hand moved along with mine.

I freed my hand from hers and tugged her open jeans down to her upper thighs.

'Oh.' The sound from her throat was a mix of shock and excitement. She liked risk. I knew it. Her blood would be rushing right now.

My thumbs pressed against her naked bottom cheeks, under the first curve, pushing them up as I looked down, checking out the colour. Today her thong was dark purple.

If she knew how sexy she was she wouldn't be here with me, she'd be somewhere else making a fortune out of it, but not on her back. Ivy was not like that – not like Sharon.

'Rest your hands on the wall,' I said as I slid her thong down to her thighs too.

'What if someone comes?'

'You can see down the hill.' I undid my belt.

'But what if someone comes up the other side?'

I freed my button. 'We'll hear the car doors shutting if anyone is coming up here.' I slid down my zip – *and this isn't going to take long.*

I gripped her hip. Her pale bottom cheeks were cold already. 'Lean over more.'

'Jack…' My name was said with a plea that was half terror – *I don't think we should be doing this*, and half – *please get on and do it.*

I angled everything and pushed into her.

The air was cold, but she was warm inside, really hot. I withdrew and pushed back in, my fingers gripping at the point where her long legs joined her hips. My middle finger could feel her pulse racing. I watched myself withdrawing into the cold, steaming from

119

the heat of her, then slid back in to get another dose of her warmth. Her body embraced me, giving me far more comfort than the hug she'd given me this morning.

But we weren't up here for a slow ride. 'Look out at the world, Ivy, look at it. Now you and I are the king and queen of it.'

She was looking, and I knew she was feeling the awe of sexual bliss and nature's magic combined. I bet she really did feel like a queen. I felt like a king.

I powered into her, over and over, my belt buckle banging against her leg as my hips hit her backside. She couldn't move, her jeans and her thong had her tied up. It made this sexier, and her sweet little sounds misted in the air each time I pushed in, with a note that was like she couldn't help herself from making noise.

My fingers gripped her harder as her scent lifted on the cold air. I pulled her back against me and shoved myself in. Her bottom was beautiful, so pretty.

When she came her body was like a furnace of molten gold, and it pulled at me to come too, drowning me in fluid as her scent became the headiest perfume, infusing the air all around us.

I fell, toppling off the world, absorbed in the flood that washed around my limbs, sweeping in like a wave crashing against cliffs. This was why I'd played along with Sharon's games, because there was a rush that only came from sex.

I let go of Ivy, slid out of her, with a sigh, then pulled my jeans up.

She pulled up her thong and then her jeans as I did up my fly.

She'd be sticky for the rest of the day, walking around marked by me, and I'd smell of her for the rest of the day. I liked that idea.

She glanced at the entrance to the ruined fort as she did up her button.

'If anyone had come up here, Ivy, I would have stopped.'

She looked at me, her eyes saying contradictory things. 'You said we'd have nasty sex; I do feel dirty. Sharing you with prostitutes doesn't feel nice.'

You still did it with me! 'Oh fucking hell. Let it go or say you want to go back to London and we'll drive down there now. I'll post your stuff via Parcel Force when they're open again. I was honest with you because you aren't some random girl, I just… Oh I don't know. It doesn't matter. If you don't want to be up here with me, I'll drive you back. I guess I broke our contract. There was probably a clause I missed in the small print on it that said tell me if you've had sex with prostitutes before I let you fuck me.'

I reached into my pocket and pulled out the napkin she'd written on. 'Here, in fact, take your contract back. The only thing we agreed on was that we'd come up here and have sex. Agreement fulfilled. Coming out here and looking at all of this, that wasn't in the deal. We had an agreement for a moment in time, Ivy, past and future didn't come into it, they shouldn't matter – this was about now.'

She didn't take the napkin.

'Was that you doing a sales pitch on me? Remember I know how easily you influence people. I know you know what to say and how to control clients.'

The napkin scrunched up in my hand. Generally, in her presence, the sales man in me was switched on all the time. I was surprised she even knew I had another side. I'd thought Sharon was the only person who knew about the pissed-off and heartless me. But I knew what Ivy meant, and she was right. I could flip into selling mode in a second and I had probably pushed the point to make her cave in.

'Maybe. But we're here because we like each other. Can't we just ignore everything else and get on with liking each other? Please? You can't even imagine how much I regret meeting Sharon. I hated who I was. But that isn't me now, and – I don't know what to say. If it's a deal-breaker for you, I guess it is. I don't want to spend a week up here arguing with you. I can call Sharon or Victoria if I want to argue.'

'Victoria…'

'Daisy's mum.'

I walked over to Ivy, still gripping her screwed-up statement saying she was going to be my lover in my hand as I looked into her eyes. 'If you stay, then don't mention any of the stuff I told you again. No sales pitch. Just because I don't want to think about the past up here. Look at the place…' I threw a glance at the view. 'It's too beautiful to waste time arguing about things I can't change.' When I said beautiful, though, I wasn't looking at the view from the hill. I was looking at Ivy.

She looked from the distance to me. Her eyes said her brain was weighing up whether I deserved a second chance. But she had just let me fuck her again. 'Okay. I won't mention it any more.'

I slid the napkin into my pocket.

From this moment on… You're my lover.

'Come on.' I held her hand. She still had her stripy gloves on. We'd had sex with her leaning on the wall, with her bum exposed to nature, and her silly stripy gloves on.

I laughed.

'What?'

'Nothing. There's other places I want to show you today, but the next place is going to be busy by the time we get there. I'm sure there will be loads of people out walking off their lunch.

Chapter 5

Ambleside was a small town on the edge of one of the lakes and I walked around it gripping Jack's arm, my woollen gloves sliding on the leather. Nothing was open but he was right, it was busier. We had to keep stepping off the narrow pavement to walk past other people.

It was a pretty place. We walked along past a tiny picturesque house, which was built over the top of a stream. He said that's what he'd wanted to show me. We leaned on the wall watching the river flowing underneath the house for a while, looking for fish in the clear water, and then walked past a giant water wheel.

Further along he took me down a path leading away from the high street. There was a sign pointing like an arrow, saying 'waterfall'. It took about half an hour to walk up the path to it, and all the time you could hear the water as the pathway wove across the clear stream, through a wood.

'Nice place?' he asked when we stood just below the head of the roaring waterfall – watching it.

'Yes.'

He was standing behind me. His arms wrapped around me. I leaned back against him and rested my head on his shoulder.

It felt good, despite what I knew about him, and despite the fact that he'd slipped into control-freak mode today. A part of me liked the alpha-male masculinity of his control-freak side. The other side wanted to slap him when he got arrogant and began ordering me around. Captain Control; that was what people called him when he was like that at work. But the way he'd ordered me last night and at the fort, and what he'd asked me to do – that was sexy.

He had his beanie hat on and his scarf wrapped right up around his neck. It was getting colder, especially in the shade of the trees.

We got back in the car after we'd seen the waterfall and he drove for about half an hour, but he drove sensibly because it was on a busy main road. I watched the scenery all the time, looking through the passenger window. Everything was beautiful around us. The road dropped down and followed the edge of a glass-like lake that reflected back all the hills around it. There were so many places you could just stop and walk, and so many places you wanted to capture in a photograph.

When he turned off the road I saw a brown sign saying 'Castlerigg Stone Circle.'

'This place should be quiet by now, I hope. It isn't ever all that busy, but sunset is one of the best times to see it. I like it most in winter, when the sky is a metallic grey and a little threatening; it adds to the mystery of the place.'

'What mystery?'

'You'll see.'

He was being Mr Cryptic today, as well as Captain Control. I'd never known Jack be cryptic or spellbound like this. He was like a child showing off his favourite toys – only it wasn't toys, it was places.

'Shut your eyes,' he said, once we'd walked through a wooden gate on to a pathway into a field. I did, but my heels sank into the turf. His suede gloves covered my eyes, like he didn't trust me to keep my eyes shut, and his strong body moved behind me, the leather of his jacket making creaking sounds.

'Walk forward slowly.'

124

It was awkward because my heels were sinking and we were walking up a slope, so it was slow progress, but he kept his hands over my eyes. I was getting used to him keeping me in the dark. But I didn't mind it. Not when I thought of last night. But then there'd been the sex on the top of the world with my eyes open looking out for miles, feeling like I owned the world – as if I *had been* the queen of it. My heart did a little skip behind my ribs, then it thumped in a steady beat. It was waiting for Jack to throw something new at me. Sex on the wing of an aeroplane!

I laughed aloud.

He didn't comment.

But then… *Prostitutes…* The memory swept through me on a chilly breeze.

I wasn't over the news, but I was trying really hard not think about it. It was in the past. He was right. It just made me feel weird to know I'd gone with a guy who did that sort of stuff. But he'd said he wasn't carrying any nasty diseases, so it shouldn't matter, I suppose…

'Okay, here's a good view.'

His hands slipped away and my heart burst into a full-on thud like the bass beat that had pulsed through his speakers in the car. I opened my eyes. 'Oh…' I didn't know what to say. 'Wow.'

The air was colder as I breathed in, but it tasted really clean up here. 'My God. That's the most beautiful thing I've ever seen.'

'I've thought about suggesting this place for adverts, but I can't bring myself to do it, it would feel disloyal, like I was breaking some unspoken code. It would ruin it if loads of people started coming up here.'

I looked at him. 'You're more complex than I thought.'

He smiled.

I turned around, looking at the ring of stones. Then walked towards them. 'How old is this?'

'Stone Age.'

It wasn't the stones that were beautiful, though, it was their setting. The stones themselves were no higher than an average person, or below that, but they'd been brought up here, to a place, to a particular hill, which seemed as if you were balanced in the clouds with God, speaking with the other hills around you. Perhaps ancient man thought these hills were gods and they'd come up here to try and speak with them.

I looked at Jack. 'What was this place used for?'

'Look at the panel. It gives you all the information. Last time I read it, it said for trading—'

'I can't imagine anyone just coming up here to buy or sell a pot.'

He laughed at me. Probably because I had a dopey look of awe on my face.

But I *was* awed by this place, like everything around here. I hadn't been abroad, my parents had never travelled and Rick and I had never had the money to go anywhere. This place had nothing to be compared to for me, except itself and as itself. It was the most perfect part of the world I'd ever seen.

I looked at Jack. I was still in awe of what had happened last night, too, but then I hadn't travelled around guys either, not like he'd journeyed around women. I suppose nothing had been special for him last night.

I looked back at the view. I was also still shocked to know he had an eight-year-old daughter. But the thing that knocked my feet out from under me most was the relationship he'd had with Sharon – *prostitutes as presents* – I was never going to be able to look Sharon in the eyes if I saw her again.

Oh, but I was trying hard to do what he'd asked and not think of that; I just wasn't winning.

They had been in the office. Emma couldn't have known.

I walked into the centre of the ring of stones and stood there for a moment looking at the view, then I opened out my arms and spun around. The place had a magnetic pull. I was trying to live in the moment, but I didn't ever want to forget this. This was a perfect memory to be filed away and kept forever.

I slipped my hands around Jack's middle, over his stomach. 'Hey...' He was washing up. By hand. He didn't have a dishwasher here. My fingers reached to his belt buckle and undid it.

'What are you doing?'

'Acquiring this for when you've finished in here.' I started pulling his belt out of his dark jeans.

'Why?'

'You used the forfeit you won from me yesterday. I haven't used mine.'

He glanced over his shoulder at me, smiling, as his belt slipped free from his jeans. 'I'll finish this up right away.'

He'd cooked for us. He hadn't let me do a thing. He'd cooked prawns and stir-fried vegetables. I was impressed. He was a better cook than me. But then he was better at everything than me.

I wrapped the belt around my hand and went into the living room. There was no TV; he had nothing to do in the cottage, not even a bookshelf. All he had was the tin of cannabis in the cupboard and the music player. It was playing the Arctic Monkeys, 'AM', and the cannabis, his other entertainment, was left open on the side as we'd had a joint with our after-dinner coffee. 'What do you do when you come up here alone?'

'Relax. Think. I'm busy in the day and generally I just sit and think in the evening!' He shouted from the kitchen

'You're so weird, I don't get you...' I bent and pulled a cushion off the sofa, then threw it on the floor as he'd done last night.

'I think you get me more than most women I've known,' he said when he came into the room.

I turned around. I didn't know what to say. We'd agreed to forget the past, and I didn't want to consider what other women thought about him. Or think about how many of them there'd been. 'Turn out the light, then sit down in that chair.'

He smiled.

I forced my mind to focus on now, and fun, as the cannabis played in my bloodstream. And maybe a little revenge. We'd had sex twice and both times he'd controlled it – and after his confession I didn't feel so great about it. This was my turn.

I was going to mess with his freaky need for domination.

I smiled to myself and scattered more cushions on the floor as he watched from the chair with a smile twisting his lips. The sort of smile he gave me at work if we were flirting – before he disappeared into his office.

The wood-burner threw out heat behind me, but I wanted the room hot like it was when I did yoga, hot enough to make Jack sweat, so I opened the wood-burner door and threw a couple of logs into the flames.

When the room was ready I turned around and looked at him, my hands on my hips.

His fingers gripped the chair's arms and his lips parted in a wider smile, saying, *what do you want to do with me?*

Everything, Jack.

If I was a nice, decent girl, I should be back in London by now. I should have grabbed his offer to get out of here. Jack was depraved when it came to sex. But the truth was, knowing he was so bad made my heart race harder, being here was like living the best dare. I'd bungee-jumped into bad-girl status. But I'd needed this to get over Rick. This feeling – the way my heart had thumped with adrenaline all day, because I never knew what to expect – this had been what I'd missed out on with Rick.

I was going to enjoy this.

I unwrapped the belt from my hand, put it down on the sofa, then stripped off my jumper and top and threw them on to an empty chair, so I stood in front of him in my purple bra and jeans.

He breathed out. 'You look good, Ivy'

'Give me your hands.'

He held his hands out. 'But think about it. Don't you want me to take my top off first, babe?'

'Oh.' I made a face at him. Trust Jack to be clever. Like I'd said, he was better at everything. 'Take your top off, and don't call me babe, in that patronising tone.'

He gave me one of his twisted smiles, his eyes dancing with life and humour as he stripped his sweater and his t-shirt off. The flickering orange light from the wood-burner played over him.

His body was incredible. His stomach was stupidly firm. I imagined you could hit him with an iron bar and he wouldn't flinch, and I could see every muscle moving beneath his skin when he moved, even tiny ones you wouldn't be able to see on most men. His skin creased at his side when he threw his sweater and t-shirt on to the sofa, with mine.

The sight of him danced through my nerves, a line of Irish dancers drumming out their steps, and the muscle around my womb clenched tight because it had the instinct to make babies with him. My body knew what was coming and every sensation was amplified by the cannabis.

'Hands!' My order was sharp because I felt so weird inside.

He held them out. I wrapped his belt around his wrists in a figure of eight a few times, then I pulled the end through the buckle and yanked it tight.

'What now, Ivy?'

'Wait and see.'

My guess was that me getting naked first would be the thing that would torture him and turn him on most. I smiled and unbuttoned my jeans, then slowly slid the zip down.

'Phew.' He laughed after he'd said it.

I'd played stripper for Rick a couple of times, but this wasn't the same, probably because Jack was a ten-out-of-ten man with a depraved, extreme alpha-male sexuality. I was playing with fire stripping for Jack, teasing a tiger.

I put my thumbs into the waistband of my jeans, then slid my jeans down over my hips, just my jeans. 'Arabella' started playing on the stereo. What a song to strip to.

I stripped my jeans and socks off my feet. That wasn't all that sexy.

He'd probably watched a hundred women strip. *Don't think of the past. It's you stripping for him now.* But the past was still intimidating. 'Arabella' played on. I rolled my hips, dancing to the music in my thong and bra, in the heat that the fire threw out into the room.

He leaned forward and rested his elbows on his knees to get closer, his tied-up hands lifting to brush over the crotch of my thong. 'No touching! My pace!'

He laughed at that and tumbled back into the chair.

I turned around, turning my back to him, and carried on rolling my hips as I played with the edge of my thong over my bottom.

'You're being mean. I want to touch.'

I undid my bra strap then slid off my bra. He huffed out a sigh. He couldn't see anything more as my back was turned to him. For ages I just kept teasing him, swaying my hips, dancing, then I squatted back, gripped the arms of the chair and wound my hips across his lap, not touching him and twerked a couple of times.

He didn't even try to touch me.

It was the sexiest thing I'd ever done and if he'd touched me he'd have known I was turned on too.

I stood up and turned around. The heat in his eyes said it all, and the beat of the music throbbed through me. The dark small room here, out in the middle of nowhere, away from anything I was in real life, gave me the confidence and freedom to be wicked too. I could be anyone I wanted here. Make up a new me.

The cannabis in my blood urged me on.

I played with my breasts, squeezing them and rolling my nipples between my fingers. I could see from his face he was painfully hungry for sex, plus there was an obvious sign in his jeans.

I slipped my hand into my thong and touched myself there as I swayed to the music, still gripping one breast too. He was only watching my thong now. I put my other hand down there and ran one hand over the top of the silky fabric while the other played beneath. He sighed with a low growl. His face moody.

I turned around and played with the material that ran between the cheeks of my bottom, then leaned forward and touched myself from behind.

'Come closer and let me touch with my mouth…' It was a plea, not an order.

I did, but only because that was what I wanted too. I was as turned on as he was.

His tongue danced around where my fingers played, but I couldn't really let myself go when I was standing – without something to lean on. My legs were getting weak.

'Shit…' I breathed as I un-seductively stripped off my thong and then I turned around and climbed on to the chair, with one foot either side of his thighs as he leaned back, so I could stand over him, straddling his legs in the chair.

I hissed out a breath when his tongue slid over me, then I touched myself again.

His hands came up and touched my bottom. He couldn't grip me, but he did slide a finger into me while his tongue played around and I caressed my sensitive spot with little circles.

I came in minutes.

He wiped his chin on his arm as I collapsed on to his lap with a sigh.

This was Christmas Day. I'd never imagined I'd spend a Christmas day like this. Rick, his parents, my parents and my nan would be full of Christmas lunch, lounging in their chairs watching specials on TV and I was here…

I undid his button and his fly and freed Jack from his jeans and his designer-fitting boxers that hugged his hips and bottom in luxurious cotton, then dropped down to kneel on a cushion on the floor, and I played with my tongue and my hand and mouth, while his tied hands rested on my head and his hips pressed up in the rhythm of sex, enjoying my games.

'If you carry on, I'm going to come.' The music speakers played out 'One for the Road'. I didn't stop. I wanted to be in control and make him come. I liked having control over him; it had become a to-and-fro game, and now I was winning.

He swore when he came. 'You fucking bitch.' But it wasn't said aggressively. It was said because he'd hit bliss and he hadn't wanted to go there yet. Joyous control. His salty fluid filled my mouth when his hips jerked up. I swallowed it away, then rose up and kissed him with the taste in my mouth. 'Bitch.' He breathed over my lips when I pulled away.

'Get up!' I ordered.

He stood up, his erection bouncing, slightly falling forward because he'd come.

'Strip your jeans off.'

He caught his thumbs in the front of them and slid them down, then used his feet to work them off the rest of the way, along with his socks. It was very deftly done and I watched every inch of his beautiful body moving. 'Now take off your boxers.' They were still at his hips, below his erection and his balls. He slid them down his dark hair-covered thighs and then off his feet.

I stepped back a couple of paces. 'Lie on the cushions, on your tummy.'

I was going to have some real fun now.

He reached his hands above his head as he lay down.

I was faced with the beautiful arch, from his broad shoulders into his narrow waist and hips, and I could see the intricate patterns of muscle beneath his skin. Who knew how he managed to tone them all? His pert bottom begged me to repay some of his sadistic games from last night. I knelt down and smacked him with a hard, quick slap to leave an after-sting.

'Ow!'

I laughed. But it felt like it wasn't hard enough. I did it again.

'Ivy! If you're trying to get me hard again, not the way…'

I laughed in a way that mocked him. 'Doesn't it turn you on, Jack?'

I didn't wait for the answer. I stood up, then ran upstairs, remembering my leather belt in my case. I ran back down with it, naked and uncaring, because with Jack I felt like I didn't need to care. He didn't care what he did.

'What are you doing?'

'Getting some pay-back,' I answered as I straddled his thighs, then I whipped his arse with the end of the belt.

'Ow! Fuck! I didn't use anything!'

'You're stronger than me – this makes it fair.'

'Ow! I won't be able to sit down tomorrow!'

'Shut up.'

'Ow!'

I laughed as I carried on, but I wasn't hitting him that hard, only enough so he would feel the same pain I had last night. 'Aren't you turned on yet, Jack?'

'No.' He breathed out, getting my point. 'But are you? Is it turning you on, Ivy?'

Okay, so he'd made his point too because yes it was… A lot.

I didn't stop or answer. He knew the answer. The sound of the leather cracking hit my senses through the cannabis. It marked his skin with red welts and made his body jolt under my legs. He could probably feel the moisture from me on his leg.

After I threw the leather belt aside, I kissed and licked every sore, red mark and I was horny as hell by the time I asked him to turn over.

So was he.

His eyes tagged me, the pupils really wide, and his erection was a stiff straight-upward column that begged for more attention. I shuffled upward, straddling his hips and his hands came down from above his head and held his erection, aiming it at me with hope.

I laughed, then rose up, to give him what he wanted. I positioned myself, watching his face as he watched where we'd join.

When I let his tip slip in, his hands slid out of the way and then I pushed all the way down, impaling myself as his arms lifted above his head.

The control was still all mine; he couldn't control anything with his hands tied.

I lifted and rocked, rose up and slid down, playing the role of a seductive stripper. I didn't have to be shy, reserved Ivy with him, the person who Rick had placed in a glassed-walled prison of average life. I was free. I could do what I wanted. Find out who I was without Rick.

But somehow I couldn't see myself as the sex goddess Jack was making me. I wouldn't be into the things he'd done with Sharon. If he wanted to sleep with other people and me, I'd run. But I was glad I had this moment to live a little of his life. I'd experienced the extreme end of heart-pounding sex – or at least the extreme as far as I was willing to go. I'd look back on this Christmas my whole life and treasure that I'd dared to do something so crazy – even if I only did it once.

I lifted up and dropped down on to him as his hips pressed up and he pushed into me. Even with his hands above his head, his body was so muscular he could move and participate easily, undulating underneath me to the rhythm I'd set.

His eyes were closed and his lips set in a firm line, as though he was biting the inside of his lip trying not to come. His whole body glistened orange with a thin sheen of sweat in the heat and the light from the fire.

I moved down, sheathing him and broke apart. The orgasm flooded me with the strength of a tsunami sweeping through my body, obliterating everything else. I collapsed, falling on to his chest.

'Oh, fuck. Ivy.' His arms came down and rested on my shoulders, capturing me in the bonds I'd tied around his wrists, and his body kept undulating, thrusting up into me, as he moved his feet so his heels could press down on the floor tiles to give him more purchase, and more strength. 'Fireside' played out from the stereo, in a manic rush of sound, confusing my cannabis-distorted brain. There was nothing seductive in what Jack did, there had never been in anything he'd done since we'd been up here, it was just hard, naughty, and sometimes desperate sex, the sort of sex I'd imagined to turn myself on when I was with Rick.

When I recovered from my orgasm I joined Jack in the hurried battle for pleasure, my hands on the cushions either side of his head, as his arms rested on my shoulders, and our gazes clung to each other, just looking, absorbing. I thought about nothing but the feel of our bodies punching together at our hips, my thighs gripping his, my breasts catching on his chest – and all the sensations inside me.

I came again, and he followed; a deep, primal sound erupting from low in his throat.

Chapter 6

'Ow.' A hand slapped my naked bottom. It wasn't the nicest alarm.

'Come on, wake up, beautiful. We have shopping to do. I want to get into town before it's too busy.'

'Shopping?'

'Yes, I want to get you some things. If you're staying the rest of the week, then those high-heeled fancy boots you brought for walking around London won't do.'

I looked at the clock. It was nine a.m. and he was dressed and his hair was wet as though he'd had a shower. He smelled nice.

I rolled over on the bed. We'd come up to his bedroom and had sex again last night, with me lying on my tummy and him lying over me. I'd fallen asleep afterwards without moving.

'I'll make some French toast while you shower, if you like?'

'Thank you. I like.' I slid off the bed. He watched while I found some clothes out from my case.

It was funny, because this was the second day, after the second night, and yet I felt just as I had yesterday – really awkward now it was daylight. The sex-goddess role I was playing with him was fine when I could hide in the darkness and the low light of the fire. But in daylight I had to face that woman and look her in the eyes. Who was she?

She wasn't me.

When I walked into the bathroom, I heard his footsteps on the stairs.

An hour later Jack and I stood outside a sports shop in Keswick, watching a guy open up. He looked at us queuing on our own like we were weirdos who should have something better to do. It wasn't a large shop and they didn't seem to be going too much for the whole Boxing Day-sale thing.

Jack immediately started walking around the shop pulling things off racks and handing them to me. 'Try these too.' He gave me another pair of leggings that looked like jogging pants. I already had an arm full of things to try on: bottoms, tops and coats.

He turned back and looked at me. 'Go on, then, try them on.'

'You're not my boss, Jack. Stop ordering me.' But I turned away to find the changing rooms anyway.

'Whatever. Remember you're going to need enough until the thirty-first and you'll want something to wear every day. You'll be getting dirty—'

I looked back. 'Why, what are we going to do?'

'Wait and see.'

I went into the cubicle. None of it was sexy. It was all like jogging stuff. If he wanted me to go running with him, I wasn't very fast.

I made the shop guy get a couple of alternatives and then picked four pairs of leggings and a couple of warm tops and a lightweight coat that was meant to be really warm even though it was thin. I didn't show Jack any of my choices on. I didn't like giving Captain Control the chance to tell me exactly what to wear, which was why two of the leggings I chose were ones the shop guy had given me.

Jack didn't challenge my choices, though. When I came out of the changing room he threw a woolly hat at me and a pair of leather gloves. 'You'll need those, and shoes.' He looked at the shop guy. 'Something she can climb in... What size are you, Ivy?'

'Seven.'

The guy immediately disappeared through a door, into a store-room as Jack took the clothes I'd picked from me and carried them over to the till. He left them piled on the counter as the guy came back with three different boxes. Jack watched as the shoes were revealed. He selected a really light, thin pair of trainers for me to try on.

I didn't argue, only looked at him and said, 'Captain Control' before I tried them on. His expression twisted with a look that questioned my comment.

When I said they were comfortable, he said we'd have them. The store guy had got over his reticence about his only Boxing Day shoppers as soon as he'd realised how much money Jack was willing to spend.

Jack chose some walking boots for me too.

'Climb in?' I whispered while we stood by the till and he found out his card.

He looked sideways at me and gave me the sort of twisted smile he'd have given me the day we'd begun all this, when we'd been queuing for coffee in Nero's. Then he said, 'Captain Control?' with a lift of his eyebrows and a pitch that made the words a question.

'Captain Control is you in a bossy mood, when you think no one else at work can get the project right, 'cause Jack's way is perfect.'

He made a face and shrugged the comment off. 'One more place to go to.'

We walked out of the store loaded down with bags.

The one more place turned out to be a motorbike shop that sold leathers, helmets and boots. He bought me a helmet and he checked it fitted securely. I chose it, though. It was white and mauve, with silver trims so it would catch the light well. He picked out a leather outfit that fitted like a second skin; but was black with purple and white markings, so my colours. There was nothing sexy about it, yet my heart went pump, pump, pump... wondering what he wanted me to do now.

138

When we were back in the car, with all our purchases stored safe in the boot, I said to him, 'Where are we going?' It was past twelve o'clock. 'I'm hungry.'

'I'm taking you to one of my favourite villages. We can get something to eat there.'

'Where?'

'Grasmere. *I wandered lonely as a cloud that floats on high o'er vales and hills—*'

'Uh?'

He glanced over at me as he changed gears and flicked the indicator on. 'It's Wordsworth: *When all at once I saw a crowd, a host of golden daffodils, beside the lake, beneath the trees…* and so on and so on.' He looked over and laughed. 'He wrote that poem up here.'

'I never knew you were intellectual.'

'I went to private school; you can't avoid that stuff there.'

'I didn't know you went to a private school.'

'Boarding school, but let's not turn the conversation to that.' He drove into another old-fashioned-looking village with grey-stone buildings, white-washed cottages and picture-postcard streets.

When he'd parked up I opened the door.

He grabbed the back of my coat before I could get out. 'Wait a minute. Stay in the car.'

He got out and walked around to get something out of the boot, then he came around my side with the walking boots he'd bought me in his hand. 'You'll need these.'

I looked down at his shoes to make a point. His shoes were not walking boots.

He laughed. 'Mine are in the back.'

I unzipped my heeled boots and took them off, then sat side-ways in the front of the car and pulled the walking boots on and laced them up. When I stood up, I saw him lift a foot down from the boot; he'd been leaning on it to do his boots up. He shut the boot down.

'Where are we going?'

'To get something to eat and then to see another of the most special places in the world.'

We walked into the village, which had a charm all of its own including the tiniest shop I'd ever seen where they made an old gingerbread recipe. But the shop was shut so I couldn't try any.

We stopped in a pub for lunch and ate steak-and-ale pies before walking out of the village and through a gate into a field.

I gripped his arm as I looked up a steep hill. 'Where are we going?'

'*Up yonder hill and down dale.*'

'Stop talking in riddles. What are we doing?'

He freed his arm from my grip and, instead, wrapped it around my shoulders. 'We're walking up this hill because at the top of it there's a really beautiful tarn: a lake, to ignorant people.' His fingers squeezed my shoulder, then let go. 'It's called Alcock Tarn. You're going to love it.'

His leather-gloved hand gripped my woollen, stripy glove and pulled me on.

He was right. I loved it. Oh my God, I loved it. It was so peaceful, an idyll. Right on top of the hill, like a secret paradise.

'I've swum in it,' Jack said, letting go of my hand and walking forward. He took his gloves off. 'In the summer this year, I came up here at daybreak.'

He leant down and touched the water, sending out ripples. 'Ah, shit that's cold.' He looked back at me. 'It was fucking cold then too.'

I laughed when he stood up. We were making so many memories to keep a hold of up here. My lips parted in a wider smile.

'Do you want to swim now?' He rushed at me and picked me up.

'Ahhh. No!'

He moved as if he'd throw me in, and he was so toned he controlled it until the last minute, making me really think he would. But he didn't let go; instead he set my feet down on the edge of the grass. I turned and faced him. His eyes seemed darker. That look did weird things in my tummy, it was like a penny rolling around in a spiral dropping down inside me – and my internal muscles clasped at it.

His head bent down, then his lips were on mine. I wrapped my arms around his neck and kissed him back. It was the first time, except for the moment we'd made our agreement, that we'd kissed without any expectation of more.

I was still breathless from the kiss when we walked back down the hill. I was glad I'd come here with him. I didn't regret it. I wouldn't ever.

Jack picked up my plate. 'Today you're going to discover why I bought you all those clothes.'

'I'll wash up. You keep doing everything.'

'Because I don't care for other people's cooking, and you'd damage your nails washing up.' He threw the tea towel that was on his shoulder at me. 'You can dry up.'

I watched him walk back into the kitchen, then stood up and followed. It didn't feel as awkward today. Last night we'd had sex in the shower before dinner, then eaten dinner and played a game of truth or dare, with sexual consequences.

The truth questions included him asking me how many people at work called him Captain Control? I told him everyone, when he took a project over.

'Tell me what we're doing?'

'We're doing what I spend most of my time here doing.'

'What?'

He looked over his shoulder at me. 'Climbing.'

'You said climbing yesterday, but climbing what?' I picked up a plate and started drying it.

'Rocks.' He lifted an eyebrow at me. 'Cliffs.'

I wanted to punch that clever eyebrow. 'I'm scared of heights.'

'Perfect chance to get over that, then.'

'You can't just get over it.'

'You can if you want to.' He wasn't looking at me any more – he was focusing on washing up. I couldn't imagine him being scared of anything and if he was scared I think he would do what he was telling me: face up to it and ignore it.

I wasn't like him.

He glanced back at me. 'Look if you want to watch me and stare at the rock, that's what you do. But I want to get some climbing time in up here. So sorry if it'll be boring, but if it is, then it'll be your fault for not taking part.'

I'd gained a new insight into his relationship with Sharon from things he'd said in our truth-or-dare game. They were both self-centred. I bet they hadn't done much together – except have sex. But actually, even that they'd done apart too. They'd probably gone off and done their own thing all the time. Rick and me had been the opposite. He'd wanted us to do everything together: I'd endured hours on the edge of a rugby pitch in the freezing cold, watching.

I sighed. I didn't have much choice about going today, though, unless I sat in here and listened to music, or aimlessly wandered around the field outside. It wouldn't harm to go with him and watch him.

I wiped up the frying pan as he washed up the last of the stuff.

He leaned back against the Belfast sink, watching me as I finished drying up. 'Okay?'

I looked at him as I put the last of the cutlery in the drawer. 'Yeah.'

'Well, let's go get into our gear. You're going to need the leggings and a top that I bought you yesterday, and that coat. You need stuff that's easy to move in.'

I hadn't agreed to climb, though.

We got dressed together in his room and he pulled on a pair of legging-style bottoms too, and a thermal top like the one he'd bought me, and a black jacket to cover it. 'You'll need your bike helmet too.' He threw it at me. I didn't ask why. I'd given up trying to keep up with the pace he lived his life.

All kitted out and ready to go, with my new gloves on, and my woollen hat in my pocket, I stood outside waiting as he opened the barn that had been converted into a garage.

There were two bikes in there beside a four-by-four: an off-road bike with big wheels and a basic frame, and a Ducati, which was gleamingly clean, like his Jag had been in London.

He walked over to the off-road bike and glanced at me. 'Put your helmet on.'

I put it on as he put his on, and I did it up how he'd showed me in the shop yesterday, checking it was tight. He straddled the bike. 'Come on.' He beckoned me to get on the back, behind him.

My heart played out an Arctic Monkeys' loud, aggressive rhythm as I climbed on, straddling the bike behind him. He started the engine. I'd never ridden pillion and this bike wasn't even designed for it.

He tapped my thigh and pointed at the footrests. I looked down and put my feet on them as I gripped his waist.

'Hold on tighter!' he shouted. He was sitting as far forward as he could.

I wrapped my arms right around his waist and held him, pressing my head to his shoulder. When he drove out of the barn the door automatically closed behind us.

I held on tight as he drove on to the track leading back to the main road, my heart pumping hard with adrenaline. His body was rigid. His core was made of iron.

He turned off the track and on to the grass before we got to the road. The bike bounced across the uneven meadow. I pressed closer to him, hanging on, but he wasn't going too fast. Probably because I was behind him and slowing him down.

At the edge of the field he turned the bike sideways and slid it

143

down a muddy hill. I squealed. He ignored my outburst, carrying on along a narrow mud track.

It looked like he rode the bike along here a lot; there were tyre marks everywhere.

It only took a few more minutes to get to where he was headed – a cliff face about twenty meters high at its highest, and about five meters at its lowest.

He stopped the bike and pulled off his helmet. 'You can let go of me and get off.'

I leant away from his back and let go, but my hand touched his side to steady myself as I climbed off. My hands and legs were shaking, and my heart raced so badly I struggled to catch my breath.

He slipped his helmet off. 'So, first off, I'll show you how to do it.'

He threw his helmet at me. He was lucky I caught it, but he wasn't even watching; he unzipped his coat and tossed that on top of his helmet. I balanced the helmet on his bike and hung his coat over the handlebars, then took off my helmet as he walked towards the highest part of the cliff.

When I looked around he was about three meters up the cliff, with no fucking rope on. But it was like he balanced on the air; I couldn't see him putting any weight into his feet or his hands. When he gripped the edge of a rock and pulled himself up it looked as if he gripped the rock with his fingertips, all his weight and his balance was in the core of his body.

He looked for another handhold, gripped, then moved his foot up higher. It looked effortless. He was Spiderman. He was about six meters off the ground now.

I swallowed against the dryness in my mouth. Willing him not to fall.

He didn't even look nervous. He was just doing it, like he did everything – full-on and full-force.

He was insane.

He carried on climbing, looking from one side to the other for holds. At the top there was a ledge that jutted out, which he'd have to lean outward to climb over. I couldn't see how he'd do it. A tight knot of anxiety caught in my throat. But he knew what he was doing. He climbed around it, moving sideways to reach an easier point and then found a solid handgrip and lifted his leg up.

God. I wanted to pass out just looking at him as he hauled himself up on to the top of the cliff. I breathed in properly for the first time in about ten minutes.

He waved at me.

'You're crazy!'

He smiled, then turned away and disappeared out of sight.

A few moments later a rope came over the cliff, unravelling and tumbling down to the bottom, about four meters away from where I'd last seen him. The end of it hit the ground. A couple of minutes later, another rope came over the cliff at the lowest part.

I saw him then, standing at the top and wrapping the first rope he'd thrown down around his waist, then he abseiled down, walking down the rock as his hands controlled the slip of the rope around his body. It wasn't safe. He wasn't properly attached to the rope he was using.

'If you want to climb, this is the bit you can climb.' He pointed at the lowest part of the cliff. 'See, it's not so scary.'

'Is this on your land?'

'Yes, that's why I have all the ropes set up. This was the deal-clincher when I saw this place.'

'I didn't know you climbed.'

'I've climbed since I was a kid. I have friends I climb with. We go all over. But I still love messing around here.'

'Where do you climb in London?'

'There's a climbing club, with mocked-up walls. I climb there to keep my toning up.'

When he was climbing I'd had a pretty good view of that toning. His clothing was skin-tight, his thighs strong and his bum firm, and his torso and arms were, as I'd thought before – like something you'd cast in bronze.

'While you're deciding if you're going to be a chicken or not, I'm going to time myself on this face.' He looked at his watch, pressed a button, then turned away and ran to the edge of the cliff.

This time he did wrap a rope around him, and pulled it so it was taut, but he didn't keep it taut as he climbed. He wasn't safe. He climbed anyway, reaching for footholds and handholds in a hurry, swinging on his fingertips at one point. Jack was crazy, but despite being terrified he'd fall, I was impressed by his Spiderman impression. He was clever.

I didn't want to be Spiderwoman, though. I found a rock to sit down on and turned on my phone. Oh shit, there were about thirty messages from Rick, and two missed calls from him late last night, and ten missed calls from Mum. Awesome. I turned it off again. I'd have gone into games but if I left my phone on I'd hear the messages and the calls coming in. I didn't want to answer. I wanted to hide away from it all for a little longer.

'Ivy, come on. You've got to give it a go, at least.'

I looked up at Jack. He grabbed my hand that held the phone and pulled me up, then took the phone away and dropped it on to the ground, on the mud. 'For me, Ivy. Think about how you'll feel when you conquer that rock.'

'I thought we were living in the now, and right now I'm standing at the bottom of it. I can't think about conquering it, that's not now.' The whole idea turned my tummy over. The thought was beyond heart-pounding; it was petrifying.

He pulled on my hand.

'Jack.' A cold sweat made my hands damp as I looked from the rock to him.

His eyes said, *please try it for me.* 'There has to be a first time

146

for everything. A moment of discovery. You can't know what it's like until you try it, and if you conquer it and conquer your fear – think of the rush – the adrenaline pulse you'll get from that.'

He was a full-on adrenaline junky. I'd only been dabbling, dipping my toes in at the edges. 'That's what you'd feel. I feel terrified.' This was where he and I were very different.

'But you need the fear the first time to make it exciting – if you didn't know it was hard and risky, what would be the fun in having achieved it?'

I shut my eyes.

'I'll give you a harness. I'll put it on for you. You'll be safe.'

I didn't answer and kept my eyes closed, shutting out his persuasion.

He let go of me, and I sat back down and opened my eyes.

He sat down next to me and his hand settled on my thigh and tapped it.

I shook my head. 'I'm not you.'

'No. You're you: beautiful and determined, full of fire and passion. You liked the night you had me all trussed up didn't you?'

I looked at him. 'Yes… But so what?'

'Because you liked getting control over me. Well, imagine being in control of that cliff?' That annoying eyebrow of his tilted.

I made a face at him, but I was imagining it. 'You're sales-pitching me. Stop it.'

He laughed. 'Works, though, doesn't it? You can see yourself, can't you, climbing over the top and thinking, shit did I do that? Me. Who used to be scared of heights.'

The face I'd made distorted further. 'You're so fucking clever.'

He laughed and stood up. 'It's up to you, Ivy. Feel that rush of success, or keep watching.'

I really wanted to hit him. How could he make me want to do something I was terrified of?

I looked at it, the cliff. Then looked at him.

'Okay.' I stood up.

I couldn't believe I was going to do it. But it wasn't a rush of anticipation and excitement in my blood – it was pure panic.

'Hang on, I'll get the harness.' He scaled the five-meter climb he wanted me to do in about three minutes, with no rope. Then he threw down two more ropes and abseiled back down, holding a small helmet and something else in one hand.

My heart thudded out its rhythm in my ears.

'Here.' He handed me the helmet to put on first, then squatted down. 'Step into this.' It was a set of straps that together made up a seat-like harness. Then he attached the rope to that with a metal clip.

'Okay, you're ready.' He picked up the other rope, which turned out to be the other end of the rope he'd strapped me to. 'Watch.' He stepped up to the cliff face and cupped his fingers on a tiny narrow ledge. 'This is the sort of thing you're looking for; just something you can grip or get the tip of your toes onto. Keep your body light. Don't put too much weight through your grip… and you can't fall because I have you on the rope, alright? So you don't need to worry.'

He had no concept of what being scared of heights meant. It was irrational. It wasn't about whether you could fall or not – it was just fear.

'Go on then, Ivy.'

I started climbing. It was easy starting. I wasn't up high when I started and the first couple of handholds were easy to find.

When I lifted my right foot for the second time, he gripped the sole of the thin trainer I had on and moved my foot to a ledge. 'That's it.'

My heart played out the rhythm of the Arctic Monkeys' 'Crawling Back to You'. I was getting too used to his break-up music. I started singing the song in my head and found a few more holds and climbed up a little higher, focusing on the song.

But then I couldn't find anywhere to put my foot. My fingers clung while my toes blindly felt for a hold and there was nothing,

I couldn't look down because I was too high… I lost the music in my head and it became a massive blur of panic. My lungs were solid. Petrified. I had no breath. I couldn't move. I just clung. 'Jack!' My voice was shaky with desperation. 'I can't do it! Jack!'

'You can. Just take a couple of breaths, concentrate and you can control the fear. There's a foothold about ten inches away from where your foot is. Lift your leg and it's a little to the right.'

'No. I can't do it, Jack. I want to come down.'

'Coming down is harder than going up.'

'Please? I can't do it.'

'Wait a minute. I'll tie the rope around a tree.'

The next thing I knew he was there. His hand gripped my foot and moved it to the hold he'd meant, then, when I lifted my other foot he moved that too. 'The rope is going to go slack, Ivy, but if you fell you won't hit the ground. Just be careful you don't bash yourself on the rock. Don't put your hands out, just curl up.'

'That makes me feel better. Not.'

He laughed as he climbed up beside me. 'Just remember, I'm not wearing a rope, so don't fucking fall.'

Why had he had to say that? 'Thanks for adding to the pressure.'

But talking to him and having him close made me feel better; he was talking deliberately, taking my mind off the panic.

'Lift your weight on to your right foot and go for this handhold up here.' His fingers were gripping it, but he let go when I did what he said. He was balanced easily on two points, up to his Spiderman tricks.

'Your other hand can go there. Then you can move your left foot.'

He talked me all the way to the top. When I reached it, relief flooded me as I clutched the grass and pulled myself over the top of the cliff on to the turf. I rolled to my back, shutting my eyes, breathing hard as pure adrenaline, and no more fear, pulsed through my blood. I was shaking. 'Thank you, God.' I breathed into the air as 'Crawling Back to You' played in my head again. Only this time the memory of the rhythm and the words to the song were joined by the image of me whipping Jack's arse with my leather belt.

'Did you enjoy it? Would you do it again?'

My heart thumped against my ribs as if it wanted to get out of my chest, and it didn't feel cool. 'No.' I wasn't like him. If he'd scared the crap out of himself like that he'd be buzzing from it now.

He laughed, then he held out a hand to take mine.

He pulled me up. 'But you mastered it. You're now the master of that little bit of rock. You won. You got the control over your fear and the stone.'

'You don't need to sales-pitch me after the event.'

'I do if I want you to do it again.' He looked over the edge.

I tried it, but it made the world spin. It wasn't ever going to happen again. *But it had happened once.* The memory was mad. I'd done it – and his sales pitch was working. I did feel proud of myself.

He pressed a quick kiss on my lips. 'You know if you'd really wanted to come down, you could have just let go of the rock, you'd have just hung on the rope. I had you. I'd have just lowered you down.'

I hit his arm. 'You bastard!'

'You conquered it, though, you'll be thanking me later.'

'I was terrified. And what if you'd fallen?' Oh shit, I heard Rick's voice again. He would be yelling at Jack if he was here; he'd never condone a guy climbing with no ropes. He'd call it irresponsible, and most of the time Jack came up here and climbed alone.

He did a few more climbs, while I sat on the rock shaking with cold in the aftermath of the adrenaline. Then we went back to the cottage and I cooked lunch – cheese on toast – because I didn't know what to do with any of the fancy food he had in his fridge. After we'd eaten lunch Jack told me to put

150

my motorbike leathers back on then threw my helmet at me again.

'Where to now?'

'Just out for a ride.'

He drove the off-road bike and we went out on to the road, to a forest of fir trees that covered one side of a giant hill where he turned on to a mud track.

The ride became a fast-paced mud-spraying scramble through the forest, going up and down the steep tracks, with the bike sliding on the soft ground, while the echo of the engine's sound buzzed back from the trees.

This made my heart pound excitedly. It was dangerous, but fun.

Chapter 7

'Jack, can we sleep in the big house tonight? It's my last night and I want to wake up to the view of the hill.'

I glanced over my shoulder at Ivy as I threw the keys down on the side. I'd taken her out for dinner, because it was our last night. I'd decided to go back on New Year's Eve. I was hoping Victoria was going to let me see Daisy on New Year's Day and I wanted to call around to see her and just… I don't know, cement the deal. But she'd agreed to it in one of the numerous texts that had been passing between us since Christmas. She'd said I could have Daisy on my own for two hours. So I needed to work out what to do with a child for two hours, when most places were shut.

I leaned back against the kitchen worktop and folded my arms over my chest.

Ivy gave me one of her sweetest, brightest smiles, saying, '*please?*' with her lavender eyes.

I never slept in the big house now. But Ivy got this place; it had been good having her here. Fun. Cool. She'd been good company. The only downside was she'd hated the climbing, but the rest of it, she'd loved everything about it.

'Maybe,' I answered. 'We'll see.' The bed would be made over there, it would be cold, though, the fires wouldn't be lit. But coldness just gave sex another edge.

Maybe…

I turned and took my jacket off then threw it over the back of a chair. 'Do you want wine or anything?'

'Just ale.'

I laughed to myself. That was generally all she drank; she hadn't liked the champagne. She was such a cheap girl compared to Sharon. I turned to the fridge and took out two bottles.

I held one out to her. 'Do you fancy a game of gin rummy?'

'What is gin rummy?' She took the ale bottle from my hand.

'Didn't you play it as a kid?' I turned to a drawer and found a pack of cards, then held up a hand, encouraging her to head into the living room. 'You get seven cards to start with, then the top one is turned over on the pack so you can see it, and you have to pick up a card and throw one away every time it's your turn. You can pick up cards I throw away instead of the one from the pack, too. Then with the cards you hold in your hand you have to make runs of three or more cards, so like two, three and four of hearts, or jack, queen and king of spades. Aces can be either high or low.

'You can collect a set of three or four cards the same number too. So, for instance, you could gather three or four sevens. When you have any set of three cards you can choose to lay it down, or you can wait until you can lay all seven cards down, but the winner is the one who puts all their cards down as sets first.'

'Okay. I think.'

'But my extra rule is, every time one of us lays a jack or an ace down on the table in a set, or as a throw-away, the other person has to take an article of clothing off.'

'So, let me guess, you're collecting jacks and aces.'

'Or just hoping to pick them up so I can throw them away…' I laughed internally and turned to pick up my jacket. I took it into the other room and hung it up, then pulled a low table over between the chairs we'd used the last couple of nights. Although last night we'd been in only one chair, having sex.

When we played, I watched as she picked up the game, focusing on the cards in her hand. She let me see them twice when she leant too far forward to pick up a card, her mind on the desperate need to fight my attack. I'd laid one ace as a throwaway, and she gave me a stocking, peeling it off, but she picked the ace up off the throw-away pile and then put it straight back down again. I gave her a sock. Not so sexy.

She had a black dress on, which had a neckline that was off both shoulders and a narrow silver chain with a snake pendant hung about her neck. It swayed forward every time she picked up a card.

She looked a little like she did at work tonight. She had the look of concentration I saw on her face when she was typing something on her computer, with a line between her brows. I couldn't see her eyes, she was looking at her cards, but they never really showed lavender in the firelight anyway.

I picked up the fourth jack and smiled. I didn't lay my four jacks. I was enjoying watching her just as she was, fully clothed. Another round went past, and I didn't lay them.

She bit her lip when she picked up a card and then slotted it in between what I knew was the five and seven of hearts, so I guessed it was the six.

'You have to put a card down.'

She glanced up, flashing me a sharp *shut up* look. She was deciding which of the two possible sets she had to go for. She had the king and queen of clubs and she wasn't going to get the jack. I had it. But she might get the ace.

She'd never win, then, if she laid—

She put down the five, six and seven of hearts. I wanted to laugh, but it depended on what card she threw away.

The two of spades.

She couldn't win now. I had the jack she needed to get a set of four.

I could keep playing with her... But... Why not do it? Why not go over to the house? Just this once.

154

I didn't even bother picking up a card. I threw down the four jacks and lifted my eyebrows. 'Strip.'

'I'm only wearing five things.'

'All the more fun for me, then. That only leaves your thong or your bra – your choice which.' She huffed at me, then stripped off another stay-up stocking, lifting her dress up to the top of her thighs to tease me with the view.

My dick was very nicely teased, thank you.

Then she slipped off the cardigan she'd put over her dress to keep her warm – item two. Then came the only thing she could take off next, except her thong – her dress – item three.

She stood up, gripped the figure-hugging viscose and elastane fabric at her thighs and pulled it up. It peeled off her. It was, I'd guess, a cheap dress, but it did a lot for her figure anyway. She'd look good in anything, though; there was nothing imperfect about Ivy. Pale, glorious skin caught the firelight as she threw her dress on to the sofa. Then she reached behind her to free her bra.

I stood up and turned away, to get my leather jacket off the hook. 'We're going for it. Come on, then.' I turned and threw my leather jacket at her. 'Put that on. I'll get the key for the house.'

I slipped my walking boots on because they were by the door, but I left them unlaced, and with the keys in hand, I turned and scooped Ivy up into my arms. She was barefoot and naked bar my jacket and her thong.

I juggled her with the use of one knee, as she shivered in my arms while I locked the cottage up. Then I carried her over to the house. It was a cold night, our breaths misted in the air all around us. The grass in the field around the cottage was already turning white with frost.

After I'd unlocked the house and carried her over the threshold, I let her feet fall to the floor. She was shivering like crazy and the noise of her teeth chattering filled the large hall.

'Run upstairs and jump into bed. I'll get some stuff to get the fire going up there; there'll be wood up there, I think.'

When I went upstairs, I knew which room she'd be in; the back one that looked at the hill and the wood, it faced the daybreak too and sometimes you could see deer up on the slopes. Sometimes there were deer right outside the house, grazing, at dusk.

She was in the bed, with the duvet tucked under her chin; her mauve hair a sharp contrast on the white-linen pillowcase.

I squatted down and shoved the paper I'd found into the open grate, then stacked on some kindling wood I'd picked up from the log store out back, before putting a couple of the dry logs on top. They'd been in the room; I had an efficient property manager. I lit the paper and the flame burned up bright and strong.

When I straightened up, I stripped off my jumper, then undid a few of the buttons on the navy, paisley-print shirt I'd worn out, then stripped that off over my head too. She was watching. Her eyes peeking over the top of the duvet.

Moonlight poured through the window. It cast a white rectangle across the bed, over her.

I released my belt, thinking of her beating me with hers a few nights ago and smiling. Then I began unbuttoning my fly. She watched my fingers.

I hadn't got all that dressed up, just worn black trousers and a shirt. But we'd only gone to a local gastro pub – nowhere like the London places that wouldn't have let me in looking like this. Maybe one day I'd take her to a decent place in London.

I slipped my remaining sock off, then stripped off my trousers and boxers.

'Come on, get in.' She flipped the duvet back and slid across the bed to make room for me, it wasn't the master bedroom – it was a normal-sized, narrow double bed.

The white rectangle of light captured her beautiful body. I took a mental picture for my memory. 'Let's get rid of this.' I climbed on to the bed and pushed the covers back further as I gripped either side of her thong.

'Hurry up, lie down. It's cold.'

Not until her thong was off.

Her legs lifted, slipping her feet free. I tossed the thing away. Who knew where? I didn't care.

Ever since we'd come here, I'd been having sex with Ivy as if she was one of the random women Sharon and I used to play with – or a prostitute. She'd hate it if I told her that. But Ivy had played along and acted like that – dancing for me, stripping for me, letting me smack her and whipping me. Tonight I just wanted clean, honest sex with her, soul-touching sex. That was the sort of girl Ivy really was. The cold room, clean linen sheets and the moonlight, were enough stimulation. We hadn't even smoked any dope tonight.

She lifted up her knees, parting her legs so I could come between them, and her hands came up to my shoulders as her eyes looked into mine.

The girl was amazing. I pushed into her. No foreplay. No games. No sexy tricks.

She pulled the duvet over us, while I worked inside her, pressing in, and up, moving slowly.

I think I felt it more than I'd done when I'd smoked a joint before we'd done it. She was so warm on the inside, and soft and smooth, and I could feel the muscle in her tummy tightening as she worked in counter moves to push up against me when I pushed into her.

It was a slow, sensual dance for ages. It was the first time I'd had sex in the missionary position for I don't know how long, and with the clean sheets releasing a vanilla and lavender smell around us and the fresh wood crackling in the fire, and Ivy's soft pale-skinned body beneath me – it was the best sex I'd had in months, maybe years. This was the sort of sex I'd been dreaming of when I'd become tired of the way I'd lived with Sharon.

Ivy came first, and that felt amazing, because her internal muscle sucked at me, massaging me as I pushed in, trying to tempt me into spilling into her. Not interested. Not yet.

I smiled and knelt up. The duvet slid down my back so the cold air touched our skin, but I don't think either of us cared any more. I held her hips and thrust into her until she came again, then I leaned over once more and made her come in the missionary position another time, because to me that had just become the best position ever, and her coming was a beautiful thing.

I came too, with a sigh of ecstasy. Then I rolled off her, collapsing back on to the sheet. It was cold where she hadn't been lying.

She pulled the duvet up again and curled into me, her fingers resting on my stomach, and her head on my chest. I was exhausted, but in a really pleasant way, really relaxed. I fell asleep.

Something tickled my chin. I opened my eyes to find Ivy looking down at me. Her hand was braced on my chest.

'What?'

'Nothing. You just look really handsome when you're asleep. It's the first time I've woken up before you since we came here. I haven't seen you asleep before.'

'What's the time, then?'

'I don't know. We didn't bring anything over with the time on it, but by the level of the sun, I'd take a guess at nine o'clock.'

I sat up and Ivy slid off me, tumbling on to her back. 'We need to get up.' I stretched. I felt refreshed.

The fire had died down and gone out at some point in the night and the room was freezing.

I looked at Ivy. 'I'll turn the bath on for you. You can have a soak in the roll top. You can look out over the fields even when you're sitting in it, and I'll go over and get something for breakfast. Do you fancy anything particular?'

'Just toast and marmalade.'

I smiled at her. I'd got used to that amazing look she had with her hair messed up, and her eyes sleepy, and I loved the little smile playing with her lips.

'Toast and marmalade… Okay.'

When I took her toast up to her, she was lying in the bath, her head back on the rim and her arms stretched along the edges as she absorbed the view amidst the steaming water.

She didn't want to leave. I knew she didn't. But this place was an escape, it wasn't for everyday life, and real life called. I needed to get back to see Daisy and in two days' time we'd have to be at work acting as though this had never happened.

'Toast and marmalade.'

She took the plate from my hand and sat upright, making the water swirl around her, so her breasts swayed too.

I stripped off, then climbed into the other end of the bath. She gave me a funny little smile. The water was nice and warm. I stretched my legs out around the outside of hers and lay my head back on the rim, then shut my eyes. I hadn't stayed in the house for a long time. I'd stopped staying in it when Sharon had begun refusing to come up here with me.

Ivy sloshed water at me.

I opened my eyes.

I felt as if I'd been asleep again and Ivy had finished her toast. The empty plate was on a chair beside the bath. I must have fallen asleep. The water was colder too.

She rose up on to her knees and straddled me and then we had sex. One for the road. The water sloshing around us.

When we left the house and the Lake District an hour after that, Ivy was quiet and I didn't know what to say to her. What was there to say? Goodbye. Only it wouldn't be goodbye – I'd see her at work in two days.

I turned Bear's Den 'Auld Wives' up, and when their album finished I played Coldplay, then Muse and Mumford & Sons. When we hit Birmingham, I stopped at the services. 'I need to stretch my legs and I need a coffee.'

She glanced over. 'And I need a pee. I was going to ask you to stop soon.'

Awkwardness piled in on me as I got out of the car. I remembered the journey up. Sexual tension had hovered all the way through the drive. Now... We'd probably put out the lust torch. We'd certainly had enough sex to do it. We'd drenched the lust torch.

I ordered coffee while she was in the toilet and bought us a blueberry muffin each, and then I picked up serviettes and forks.

When I got to the table, I asked a woman behind me if I could borrow a pen.

I was writing on the napkin when Ivy walked over and found me. 'Hey, what are you doing?'

'Hoping you still want to work for me.' The repercussions would be massive if she didn't. Em would know.

'Yes, why?'

I finished what I was writing. 'Here.'

I officially re-recruit you, Miss Ivy Cooper, as my employee. If you want your job back. Your boss again, I hope.

I signed it.

She looked up with an odd expression, and she didn't smile, but she nodded.

'You'd better sign it too, then, to make it official.'

She did.

I turned and handed the woman her pen back.

When we finished our coffee, Ivy would have just left her new contract on the table, but I picked it up and shoved it into the inside pocket of my leather jacket.

I dropped her off outside her place a couple of hours later – where I'd picked her up a week ago. She didn't accept my offer to help carry her case up to her room. She said goodbye to me on the kerb. I kissed her, but it was only a press of lips. I think we both knew we had to get back into work mode. From January 2nd we couldn't touch – we'd need to be professional again.

'Thanks for taking me with you. It was fun, Jack.'

I gave her a restrained, twisted smile. 'You're welcome, it was fun for me too. You were good company.'

'Thanks,' she said again, then she carried her case up the steps of the house she had a room in.

When I sat in the car, I looked at my phone, then I picked it up and texted Victoria. 'Can I come over and see Daisy now? I thought she might feel better about spending time with me tomorrow if I agree with her what she wants to do.'

'Okay, but you'll only have half an hour – we're going out.'

I was sitting on the desk in my office looking out at the angular skyline of different-shaped buildings of varying heights. My spirit longed to see hills. But the city did have a charm of its own, and I got the city vibe too; when I was in the mood. I loved being in the city a lot of the time because it was so fast-paced. But tonight... Tonight everything seemed out of place.

For the last couple of New Year's Eves Sharon and I had held parties in the office. We had a good view of the fireworks over the top of the buildings, so we'd invited people here to watch them and supplied several bottles of champagne, so a lot of naughtiness had followed the fireworks.

This year I had no idea what to do with myself. I'd been at home and I'd smoked a couple of joints and thought about going out to a bar... But I wasn't in the mood.

Everything was planned with Daisy, a hot chocolate in Hyde Park was about all we'd have time for by the time I'd driven her into the city and home again. But Daisy had wanted to go out for a hot chocolate, and I thought her first time alone with me she'd probably prefer to be in an open space among other people.

My heart beat steadily. Tomorrow I was picking up my daughter and taking her out for the first time. For the first time in her life I was going to be her proper father.

Me... a father.

It was bizarre. My life had tipped up on its head this year.

I sat on my desk looking out at the city as my hands gripped the edge. It was New Year's Eve. There was something fucking wrong in this.

My phone was on the desk beside me. I'd put Arctic Monkeys on, then switched it off – it brought back too many memories of sex with Ivy and I wasn't in the mood to recall it. It made me want it.

But it wasn't the end of the holidays yet…

There was still over twenty-four hours.

Fuck it, why was I fighting the urge. I picked up my phone. Maybe I hadn't drenched my lust torch enough to douse it. Or maybe I was bored. Whatever. I wanted to see her.

Her phone rang.

'Hello.' Her hello said *why are you calling?* We'd said our goodbye.

'Hi.'

'Jack?'

'I…' I took a breath.

'You what?'

'I'm at the office, with some bottles of ale. No champagne. If you want to come and join me? I'm going to watch the fireworks at midnight. You could watch them with me…'

She took an audible breath, as though she was deciding. 'Okay. I'll see you in half an hour-ish.'

'See you then.'

'Bye.'

She ended the call. My heart thumped a steady bass rhythm. I probably should've brought up something to eat too.

It was fifty-five minutes before I saw her at the door. She didn't wait for me to go over and open it, but keyed in the entrance code. She smiled at me when she came in. She had on the woollen hat I'd bought her when we were away, with her loose parka coat and her stripy gloves. But below the coat she had black patent stiletto heels on her feet and sheer black, what I'd guess were stockings, decorated with pretty silver stars.

I walked out from my office. 'Thanks for coming. It's boring alone.'

She unzipped her coat and turned as she stripped it off.

I stepped forward and took the coat off her shoulders.

'Did you see your daughter?'

My daughter... The word kicked me in the stomach. But... 'Yes. We're all signed up for hot chocolate in Hyde Park.'

Ivy turned around and smiled as I hung up her coat. 'Sounds fun.'

'Or scary... I'm probably as scared as you were of that cliff. What if she hates it, hates me?'

'Kids are hard not to impress.'

'I hope so. But I don't have any safety harness.'

'Her mother is on the end of a phone...'

'Yes, I suppose so, but I don't want to use that get-out.'

She smiled. 'No, you wouldn't... But you'll be in control, you'll be fine.'

My gaze travelled down Ivy's body, then up again. 'Did you dress up for me, or were you planning on going out and I stopped you?' My lust devil was definitely not dead, not for her. She had on a silver dress that slipped off one shoulder at an angle, and the hem was also on an angle, rising up to show an awful lot of thigh coated in that black starry stocking.

She pulled her hat off and threw it on a desk. She'd done her hair too, curled it so the curls fell in a less-cluttered cloud of mauve. 'I was going to my best friend's party, but her boyfriend, Steve, is Rick's best friend, and she rang me an hour ago to say don't come. Apparently Rick has been a pain in the arse for everyone. Even Mum is on my side now. He got cross with her at Christmas when she told him there was no way she could change my mind, it had to be my choice. She said he expected her to ground me like I was a kid unless I took him back. I think he said some horrible things. She's not speaking to him any more, and so my parents have fallen out with his parents.'

163

'It's all been kicking off, then, while you had your phone turned off.'

'It sounds like it. Milly, my best friend, said Steve thinks if I go tonight Rick will make a scene. He's been around there every night since Christmas trying to find out from Milly what I've been doing and why I haven't answered his calls.'

'Are you okay about not going to their party?'

'Yes. But it was nice to hear your voice. I thought I was going to end up watching the telly. How dull is that for New Year's Eve?'

I smiled. 'Dull. I never watch TV.' I turned and picked up one of the bottles of ale I'd left on the reception desk. I don't know why I'd chosen to buy ale, I didn't drink it very often – but I'd been drinking it all week with her.

I flipped off the lid with a cheap bottle opener I'd bought to accompany them and held it out to her.

She took it. 'I'd already guessed you never watch TV. Do you even own one in London? You never had one up there, either in the house or in the cottage.'

'I do own one in London. Sharon has one. I haven't got one in the place I'm in now. I can't concentrate on TV – my brain is too busy thinking about work, or whatever comes next.'

She looked hard into my eyes for a moment. 'Have you been smoking a joint?'

'A couple, but over an hour ago. Why?'

'Because your pupils are dilated.'

'Are they…' I smiled at her; she'd probably been looking up FRANK since we'd got back; what did that scary grass do to me? 'Let's sit in my office.'

'And what?' She looked wary of me.

'Talk, maybe… Look at London…'

I held my hand out for her to walk ahead of me. This may have been a bad idea, asking her here. It was going to make things a hundred times harder when we had to work together the day

164

after tomorrow. It had been selfish taking Ivy away. I was still being selfish.

Sharon had yelled at me numerous times in the last few months that I was a selfish bastard because I'd fucked off and taken all my money and her free ticket to a good time with me. That hadn't been selfish. But Ivy should be yelling it at me right now – she had good cause.

If I hadn't asked her, though, she'd be at her place, alone.

I sat on the desk and slid back on it, with my legs dangling from the knee. She leaned her bottom against it and looked out over London.

We talked then, about nothing and everything. We said more about ourselves than we'd probably said in the whole time we were away, while the cannabis ebbed from my blood. We didn't drink much, either. It was like catching up with a friend, chatting over a drink.

But then I turned and looked at my phone, it was nearly midnight. I found a radio app and we left it playing on a show that would do the countdown.

When we heard Big Ben's first chime, it silenced our conversation, and we looked at one another counting the chimes as they rang-out.

'Eight. Nine. Ten. Eleven. Twelve.' Midnight became the first minute of the new year!

The first fireworks boomed into the air, a splendour of colours, red, white and blue. My arm wrapped around Ivy's shoulders as the fireworks continued, explosion after explosion, while my phone played out the music they were erupting to. Colour filled the night sky above London, bright and bold, and when the last firework died out and fell, I turned to Ivy. 'Happy New Year.'

'Happy New Year.'

I pressed my lips to hers and she leaned her body up against mine. My tongue slipped into her mouth and her fingers gripped my bum through my jeans. My hands slid down to grip her bottom cheeks through the cheap, thin fabric of her dress.

165

In the other room her phone rang out. We broke apart and she ran to answer it.

I heard her say, 'Happy New Year…' I didn't listen to her conversation beyond that, I turned my phone on to music and put Calvin Harris's album, *Motion* on. That wasn't breakup music.

She came back in holding her phone, by her side. 'My mum – she always calls me at midnight for New Year's.'

'I'd ring Daisy, but she'll probably be in bed—'

'There'll be lots of years to call her at midnight.'

Oh my God, a vision of the future played out before me, of me calling Daisy when I was old, when she was my age. I couldn't imagine where I'd be then? For the first time in my life I had no idea what the future was for me. The box of my life, that fate had shaken up, had left everything out of place this year – last year. I'd always had a plan, a vision I was working to. Now all I knew was I wanted Daisy in my life, but I couldn't see how that would fit with anything else.

I gripped Ivy's hand and pulled her close again. She put her phone down on the desk and then her hand came up to my neck and we carried on from where we'd stopped.

I didn't try to take her dress off, just slid it up and pushed down her thong, while our lips remained locked. Her thong fell on the floor and she unravelled her feet and high-heeled shoes from it, then I lifted her on to my desk, undid my jeans, slid my boxers down to my thighs and pressed into her as I kept kissing her. We kissed the whole time as I pressed into her over and over, while her hands ran over my hair and gripped at my hips and my bare bottom.

I'd imagined having sex with her in here. But I'd imagined her bent over the desk and I'd never imagined it would feel like this.

Her fingers gripped the back of my neck and my bum cheek while she kissed me like her life depended on it. I felt as if I depended on it and when she came I didn't even try to fight her body's call, my orgasm piled in on me, catching me in its white foam as if I'd been in the tunnel of one of those massive Hawaiian waves 'and it had collapsed on me. I sighed into her mouth, then breathed in the breath she breathed out.

Heady.

Her phone rang.

I was still inside her. I slipped out of her and started sorting myself out as she picked up her phone. She didn't answer it. 'It's Rick.'

Instinctively I snatched the fucking thing out of her hand and pressed the answer icon. 'Hey, mate. Fuck off. Can't you get the message? She's moved on. She doesn't want to talk to you.' I didn't wait for his answer – I ended the call and threw her phone down.

'Jack!' She yelled at me, but then she laughed and then she took a breath as though she didn't know what to do. 'He'll know I'm with you.'

'He won't, he won't know it was me. But hopefully it'll get him off your back.'

Her eyes said she was still deciding if that was a good thing as she pulled her dress down.

I moved between her parted legs again before she could jump down to get her thong. My hands settled on her thighs. 'We can't go back to mine, I'm sorry, Sharon's probably having the place watched to get more evidence for her divorce claim. But what about going back to yours?'

Her lips twisted up, in an uncertain look. But she answered, 'If you want.'

'I want.'

'Alright. But you'll have to bring the ale, I haven't got anything in.' I moved back and let her slide off the desk. She bent and picked up her thong, then slid it on awkwardly over the top of her high-heeled shoes. She picked up her phone then and turned it off when she walked out of the office ahead of me.

She glanced back over her shoulder. 'You do realise my place is one room with a kitchen in it, and a shower room attached and

I only have a single bed. You're leaving all your luxury behind. You don't pay me enough to have any of that.'

'Then maybe I owe you a pay rise.'

'No way. That would be paying me for sex... I AM NOT a prostitute, Jack.'

'I know. I didn't mean it like that. It was a throwaway comment.'

She turned around and waited 'til I caught up the couple of steps between us. I thought we were going back to the prostitute conversation, but instead she gripped my shirt either side of my waist and pressed a quick kiss on my lips, then looked into my eyes, trying to judge my thoughts. 'It's no big deal. But for the record, I earn what I should for my job. I'll work my way up to better pay, not earn it in bed with you.'

I nodded at her, then laughed. She was so different to Sharon.

Chapter 8

January the 1st

My phone vibrated on the the chest beside my bed. 'Hi Mil—'

'Ivy, you sneak. Who are you seeing? Rick told Steve he rang you last night and a guy answered your mobile.'

I took a breath to answer Milly, but I didn't get a word out.

'Why haven't you told me? Who is he? Where did you meet him? Are you sleeping with him? Is he fit? What does he look like?' The barrage of questions finally dried.

'Which question do you want me to answer first?'

'Are you sleeping with him?'

'Yes…' The word came out on a sigh of memory. I was still in bed, and my sheet was warm and creased from where the two of us had squashed up in my bed. We'd had sex and then he'd slept here. The smell of his aftershave lingered on the pillow.

'Oh my God, you whore!' Milly laughed. 'It's only been weeks.'

'I know, for God's sake don't tell Rick. Mum said he was acting weird enough over Christmas.'

'He was weird last night, crying into his lager and staring at his phone all night.'

'He wasn't just staring into his phone – he texted me ten times and then he rang at about quarter to one in the morning.'

'When he left here… Well, now Steve has taken him out, to take his mind off you, and I'm sitting here on my own. Come over and you can tell me all about this new fella. Is he fit?'

'Oh God, so fit… What other question did you ask? Oh yeah, and the sex is amazing… I spent Christmas with him too, and it's been the best time ever. He makes me feel alive, Milly. I've never felt like this.'

'You have to come over and tell me!'

'I'll be an hour. I have to get dressed first.'

'You aren't in bed with him now?'

'No. He left about two hours ago. He had somewhere to go.'

'He's not a player.'

'No, or maybe he is, but I know where he had to go, he wasn't running out on me. I'll tell you all about him when I get to yours.' I wouldn't tell her everything, though. I was keeping Jack's identity my secret.

'Okay. See you soon.'

'Yeah. See you soon.'

When I walked through the revolving doors into the ground-floor reception at work, the bass rhythm in my chest lifted to a heavy thudding sound. It made me think of the Arctic Monkeys' album, which had been Jack's sex soundtrack most of the time we'd been away.

When I walked up the stairs the memory of the music made me recall some of the explicit details of the sex it had accompanied.

But I'd thought about the sex all the way into work too and it had been really hot on the cramped rush-hour tube train. I'd been sweating inside my coat, and turned on, recalling all the stuff Jack and I had got up to. How was I going to look at him today and act as though it hadn't happened?

As I reached the office door, my heart beat manically: so fast I felt as if I'd run to work. I took a breath but the air wouldn't go into my lungs. Giving in to panic wasn't going to make this

170

easier. I could've called in sick, but that would've only delayed the inevitable. If I still wanted my job I had to do this.

I wish he'd talked about work before he'd left yesterday. He was the boss, he had to play the lead in this, and he could have said I'll see you at work and smile at you to say hi – or something like that, so I felt easier.

I felt embarrassed, terrified and awkward. It was like this was my first day again – only a thousand times worse. Because he hadn't said anything.

'Morning, Ivy. Did you have a good holiday?' Tina greeted me as she always did, like she did everyone when they walked through the door.

'Yes, it was okay. You…' I bet I blushed as memories of how okay it had been tumbled around in my head.

'Really good, thanks. But here we are back at work, and it's a new year.'

'Yeah.' A new year. A new start. 'Happy New Year.'

'Happy New Year,' she acknowledged.

I took my coat, scarf and the hat Jack had bought me off and noticed he was already in his office. I tried not to look. I couldn't remember how to naturally glance his way. Yet I'd watched him loads before we'd snuck off and been naughty together. Instead I stared bizarrely at the coat rack, hanging everything carefully.

My heart dropped to my tummy and bile gathered in my throat when I turned around. In my head the whole room watched me. Of course, no one was watching, not even Jack. I didn't even know if he knew I was here yet, and if he did know, I didn't know if he cared.

When we'd agreed on our naughty, nasty sex expedition, he'd said we'd come back and act like normal, and while we were away he'd focused on the moment, not the future – there had been no other conversations to use as a compass to help me navigate this. From what we'd agreed, he was supposed to be nothing but my boss today. But on New Year's Eve he'd blurred the boundaries, he'd asked me up here, and we'd had sex in his office and then he'd spent the night in my bed… and what now? I hadn't heard from him since he'd left yesterday.

I sighed when I sat down and turned my laptop on.

'Happy New Year,' Phil said across the desk.

I looked up. 'Happy New Year.' Then I looked at Mary, who sat next to me. 'You too, Mary. Did you both have a good time?'

Phil was replying when Tina's phone rang on an internal tone. 'Hi Jack.'

All my attention was pulled away and my heart pounded. I glanced into his office. I still wasn't sure if he knew I was here.

'Yes, okay, sure,' Tina said.

When she put the phone down she shouted out. 'Jack wants us all in the creativity room in fifteen! So he said get a drink or have a pee if you need one!'

Half the room laughed, some of the other half groaned. But that was Jack – full-on inappropriate. People stood up to fetch drinks, but then someone suggested a proper coffee run. I didn't volunteer, and I tried not to look when Tina went into Jack's office and asked him if he wanted an espresso.

When Tina came back with the coffees and Jack walked out of his office, a shiver ran up my spine. This was too weird.

I stood up when everyone else did and followed him towards the creativity room, picking up my coffee. But my heart raced like he was leading me by the hand and then backing me on to the cushions in the cottage.

At least when we were in the room I always sat in the same place, so it wasn't difficult choosing where to sit. But usually through the Monday-morning meetings Jack's gaze kept catching on mine and he'd give me a quirky little smile. Today when he started the meeting he looked everywhere but at me.

He talked through all the work we had on and made everyone do an update on where they were and say whether they needed any support. I thought he would look at me and ask about the

Berkeley account, but he didn't ask about it and all the stuff I'd been working on was still all over the wall behind his head. Surely that wasn't just strange to me.

'So that's it, then. Everyone get to it. New year, new start and all that jazz.'

I'd used that phrase in my head an hour ago. I hated it now. *New year, new start…* What did *he* mean by it? That I was forgotten – over and done with.

The prick.

Anger bubbled up when I left the meeting. I probably had volcano spume coming out of my head when I sat down at my desk. Phil came to stand by me a couple of minutes later.

I was working out a way to go into Jack's office and tear up at him.

Phil leaned on my desk and spoke in a quiet voice. 'Jack just asked me to manage the Berkeley account with you—'

'What? Why? I'm managing it. He said I could. It's my start-up account.'

'I know. I'm not taking it off you. He just said would you report to me about it, not him. He's busy with the Mack's account.'

He wasn't fucking busy! I glanced into his office. If he hadn't been on the phone I'd have gone in there and made a huge scene that would've given us away. But he was on the phone. Instead I bit my lip, looked at Phil and nodded.

It meant Phil would be asked to update next Monday. It meant I had no good reason to talk to Jack at work.

'I saw all the stuff on the wall in there. It looks like you've some ideas forming if you want to talk about them…'

'No.' I couldn't talk to anyone right now. I swallowed back my anger. 'The plans aren't ready yet. I'm still coming up with ideas.'

As soon as Phil turned to sit down, I pulled out my mobile. Jack's number was near the top on my stream because he'd called me New Year's Eve.

'Why did you pass my account to Phil? And why didn't you even look at me in the meeting!!!'

I watched him through the glass surrounding his office, Captain fucking Control! He read the text and he looked pissed off – but he still didn't look at me.

My phone vibrated in my hand. 'Don't text me here, people will notice it.' Was that all. Don't text him. I wanted to go in there and chuck his coffee in his face.

He'd sold me the heart-pounding rush of thrilling, desperate-feeling sex. I'd had a whole sack full of it over the holidays. But the deal was over now – all I had left of his thrill rides was the rush of anger.

He'd dumped me. Without even saying he was dumping me. And the bastard had called me into the office for sex New Year's Eve like I was one of his high-end fucking prostitutes – the only difference was I'd been free.

Jack was a prick.

It felt like I did the walk of shame around the office all day. So I spent most of it in the creativity room – hiding. But I was even more determined to come up with a fabulous idea so I could shove it in Jack's face and make him feel guilty. He was an asshole.

Emma came into the room at one point and she rubbed my arm, in a big sister, not a boss, way. 'Are you alright? You seem quiet today… Did you have a bad time? Are things settled with Rick?'

I smiled at her, with gritted teeth holding in the words… *I had a great time, until your shithead partner screwed me over.* I wouldn't have cared if the sex had ended and been left at the cottage. But he'd called me New Year's Eve! 'I'm fine. Everything's alright. Thanks.'

When the hands on the wall clock ticked over to hit five, I went back into the office, grabbed my bag and coat and walked out without saying goodbye to anyone. I put my coat on as I ran down the stairs.

When I stepped out the other side of the revolving doors, the polluted London air hit me. My lungs longed for the fresh air around Jack's cottage.

'Ivy. I want to talk to you and you won't speak to me on the phone.'

Oh shit. 'Rick.'

He held my arm

Someone came through the door behind me. Feminine heels struck the pavement. 'Ivy…' I glanced back. It was Emma. Her eyes said, *do you need help?*

No. God, I'd been grumbling to myself about Jack dumping me without words all day, and we'd only been together a week. I'd played with Rick's feelings for years. I owed him a little more explanation time and more time to make me feel like shit for walking out on him. 'I'll see you tomorrow, Emma.' She nodded and walked on.

I faced Rick. He was a big guy – broad and bulky, with his classic rugby build. I suppose he could look threatening and maybe Emma had thought that, but Rick was a giant teddy bear. 'You can walk with me to the tube if you like.'

He breathed in as if that meant the world to him.

I turned and started walking – he fell into pace beside me. 'How are you?' I asked, to break the silence.

'Why did you stop replying to my texts or answering my calls?'

There hadn't been any since Jack had answered the phone, but that had been less than forty-eight hours ago.

'I'm sorry, Rick, but you have to get that it's over.' I slid my hands into my pockets, trying to speak as gently, but as bluntly, as I could. I hadn't wanted to hurt him, but nor had I wanted to continue hurting myself.

'You don't have to marry me; it doesn't have to be over. Things can stay as they were.'

I breathed out. Why was he finding it so hard to get that it had ended?

'When you asked me, you made me realise I didn't see us as forever, and if we aren't forever then I've been wasting your life. You shouldn't want me. You should move on and find a girl who wants to marry you.'

'And if I don't want anyone else? All the guys have always said you're way above my league. I'm not going to find anyone as good as you... and I don't want to.'

We'd reached the subway and I didn't know what to say, but he managed the moment – he slipped his arm around my shoulders to steer me through the human traffic and walked down the steps with me. He paid for my ticket too, with his card at the barrier, then paid for his, and then stepped on to the escalator behind me. Of course the flat we used to share was in the same direction as my new place, just a couple of stops away.

I leaned against a pillar when we stood in the tube carriage and he gripped the bar over my head with both hands. Rick was as big as an ox but as soft as snow. He'd been bullied at school but then he'd discovered rugby and put on inches in height he'd worked hard to swell out, and he hadn't ever worried about bullies again.

'Who was the guy who answered the phone?'

'Just a guy, Rick. He's nothing to do with you.'

'A one-night stand?'

Yes. No. A one-week stand. Except neither of us could walk away from the other after the week. Unless I chose to pack in my job – it was an option floating around in my head. 'No. It's just a guy who's a friend.'

'What sort of friend?'

'It really is none of your business.' The carriage swayed along the track and jolted his body against mine. I was glad it was winter and I had my coat on, otherwise it would feel too awkward.

I glanced away from Rick, hiding from the unspoken question in his eyes: *did you have sex with him?*

He knew he'd been my only guy – it would shift everything that had been between us.

It had shifted every bit of ground I'd built my life on so far.

A woman looked at me from across the carriage. She looked like she was worried for me. I smiled at her, then caught a couple of other people looking. Maybe Rick's body language looked aggressive. But he was upset. If the tables were turned, I'd be upset. I understood why he was so pissed off with me. But I didn't know how to break the chain I seemed to have wrapped around his heart.

'You did…'

He sounded broken. I looked back at him and saw anguish in his eyes. 'It was nothing, okay, and it's already over. But that doesn't mean there's ever going to be a you-and-me again. He shouldn't have answered the phone to you. That would have annoyed me too. But it was only because—'

'Did I interrupt you? Well sorry for, fucking, that.' He pushed off the bar and turned to look as we pulled into a station. It was my stop. It wasn't his stop, but he followed me through the doors when they opened, then his hand came down on my shoulder, steering me through the people.

When we reached the street, he said, 'Which way?'

I sighed. 'Right.'

He walked with me, his arm still around my shoulders, even though I'd confirmed I'd slept with someone else. 'Steve said you told Milly you were with the guy over Christmas.'

Oh shit, was it fair of me to expect Milly to keep stuff from Steve? I was going to have to either swear her to secrecy on everything or not tell the one person I felt able to tell everything to.

But I wasn't Jack; I wasn't Mrs Secretive and I wasn't a liar.

'He's a player. So now you can get why it's all burned out already. I'm over him and he's over me, and maybe that's something you need to learn to do, move on to someone else.'

'Maybe it's something I never want to do' His hand slid from my shoulder, which was probably what I'd subconsciously wished for when I'd said that. 'Nor do I want to think of you doing it with someone like that. You aren't like that, Ivy.'

I looked at him as I walked. *That is exactly where you went wrong, Rick. Because I am like that. I am very like that. I loved every minute of it, and I want it repeated ten times over. I do not regret it. I didn't, even though Jack had ignored me all day, even if he ignored me forever.*

Before we turned into my road, a big guy walked past us, he had his hood up, but it looked like he smiled. He looked like the guy I'd seen the night Jack had picked me up.

When I stopped outside the house my flat was in, Rick looked up at it. 'So this is where you're living?'

'Yes.'

He followed me up the front steps. My heart thumped. I didn't know if he expected me to invite him in, but it was only a tiny room. I didn't want him in there, sitting on the bed, even to drink a mug of coffee. It would feel screamingly awkward. 'I...' *don't know how to get rid of you.* 'I'm really sorry, Rick. I don't mind being friends, if you want to be friends. But I'm not sure it's a good idea...'

'It's not such a bad idea if that's all you're offering.'

'Okay, then, let's be friends. Friends.' I held my hand out to him.

He shook it and nodded, once. 'Friends.'

I turned to press the code in to open the door, then turned back; he was watching me, he hadn't turned away. I didn't open the door. 'And no crazy texting, Rick. Please. No pleading messages. No middle-of-the-night calls... It was getting ridiculous. I care for you, but I don't want to be with you. I'm sorry.'

He stared at me for a moment, his eyes shimmering, but if it was tears, he held them back, and then he said, 'Okay.'

I turned to look back at the keypad and pressed the code in again. Then glanced back. Rick was still standing on the step behind me.

'I'll see you around.' *Go away.*

'Yeah.' He turned and finally walked down the steps. I pushed the door open, then looked back just as he did too. I lifted a hand.

He lifted his hand.

Pride stormed through my soul as I walked inside and checked my post box. I'd handled that really well. Better than Jack. And better than Rick too. I'd intended to get in and immediately ring Jack and let rip… But now… I didn't want to be like Rick. If Jack wanted to sweep Christmas and New Year under a rug, let him. I could deal with it. I could even deal with his cold-shouldering me at work. Christmas had been a wonderful experience, but now it was time to get back in the present and move on. I had more memories to make. So fuck Jack. I was not going to let myself react to his arrogance.

I felt better – like I was on top of the cliff.

In a few weeks I'd look back and be proud of myself for handling this so well and taking control of it.

Greg, my landlord, came out of his flat on the ground floor. 'Hi, Ivy.' He smiled at me.

I hadn't got the measure of him yet; he was nice, but almost too friendly. He was up-in-my-face friendly.

'Just got in from work?'

'Yes.'

'I'm going to the pub – you can come if you want?'

I smiled awkwardly. 'Thanks, but no thanks. I'm not really in the mood.'

'Well, okay, but if you ever fancy it…'

He smiled again as I walked past him.

He was probably twenty years older than me, and his over-friendliness bordered on creepy sometimes. I'd never feel like going for a drink with him. I had a sense he'd take it the wrong way and I didn't have any desire to make any memories with Greg. 'Have a good time.' I started climbing the stairs.

Chapter 9

I looked at my phone as it vibrated again. Another vicious outpouring of threats to rip my balls off from Sharon. I leaned back on the sofa. God, the place was so silent.

I'd got used to Ivy being around.

I went into my texts, not to reply to the one from Sharon, but to look at Ivy's. The first text she'd sent me. My answer was what showed, 'Don't text me here, people will notice it.'

She hadn't texted me since she'd left work though, either. I looked at my watch. Seven. It was still early. Ivy's text stream was third down on the screen. Above it was the last text from Victoria agreeing to me taking Daisy out next Sunday afternoon. I was hoping it was going to become a regular Sunday thing.

I opened up Ivy's text stream. 'Why did you pass my account to Phil? And why didn't you even look at me in the meeting?' Because every time I think about you I think about sex. It's not professional.

I'd been stupid to think we could go back to work and everything would return to normal. Shit, all I'd been able to think about all day was her. I couldn't look at her and not think about the sex.

I didn't know what to say to her, either.

My phone vibrated again, but this time it rang and my solicitor's name flashed up. It was late for him to be calling, well past proper office hours, but he was like me – he worked until the job was done. I answered. 'John. Hi.'

'Hello, Jack, I have some news you need to be aware of.' That sounded ominous.

I stood up and turned to look out of the floor-length window behind the sofa, at the nightlights of London. 'What?'

'I heard some news from a friend who works with Sharon's solicitor. He thinks she's put a private investigator on to you since we locked down the accounts.'

Awesome.

'She's trying to dig up evidence that'll help get more money out of you. So if I were you I'd keep yourself clean until this is all over. No women. Work and home, and nothing else, I can fight anything she raises to claim a higher settlement but when we're putting the case forward for you to have Daisy stay over, I wouldn't put it past Sharon to use any information like that to blackmail you, so keep yourself on the straight and narrow.'

'I am on the straight and narrow.'

John laughed. A while ago Sharon and I had been stopped by the police because I'd been speeding. They'd found cocaine in the car. John had helped us get away with it. It had been a hired car; we hadn't even received a warning. But John wasn't stupid, he knew it was ours but he'd claimed, how could it be ours when we'd only picked the car up an hour before and neither of us had left fingerprints on the plastic packet in the glove box; I'd been wearing gloves.

'I am clean, John. I wouldn't be going for joint custody of Daisy if I wasn't. If Sharon's hired a PI they won't find anything.'

'Good. That's okay, then. But I just thought you should know.'

'Thank you.'

'Bye, Jack.'

'Bye.'

My heart raced. Shit. I looked at Ivy's text again. It wasn't fair to drag her into this. Maybe I should let it rest for a while. Maybe it was better to play it cool, as we'd agreed in the beginning.

I didn't know what to say to her anyway and it was the wrong time to get involved with anyone.

It was better to leave things as they were.

Chapter 10

I looked up and watched Phil. He was checking over my final presentation. I'd worked hard on it. I'd thrown myself into work because Jack had continued to be a bastard and I wanted to show him I was good at this. But I ignored him, like he ignored me. He didn't deserve any of my attention.

'That all looks great. I think they'll love it.'

We'd had a couple of meetings with the Berkeley people and narrowed my ideas down to three, around one theme – we were doing the final pitch to them next week.

'Do you want to practise the pitch this afternoon?'

'If you have time…'

'Yes.'

Phil had been good; he'd played the role Jack would have done, checking my stuff and coaching me, and he hadn't tried to take my project over.

'Have you thought about how you're going to go through it?'

'Yes, I have it all planned out.' I smiled at him over the desk divider.

Jack picked that moment to come out of his office; he was pulling his coat on. I guessed he was on his way to lunch. I focused on my computer.

'Hey, Jack.' Phil caught his attention. 'Did you see this stuff Ivy's done for Berkeley?'

I didn't look up.

'Yeah, looks good,' Jack said. I sensed him glance at me, but I still didn't look up. I was done with looking at him; my lust had died. He'd put out my flame, but not with sex, just because he was a dickhead.

Jack walked away.

'When do you want to run through the presentation?'

'Two?'

'Okay.'

After I'd gone through the presentation with Phil and ironed out some of the weaker points, I shut myself in the creativity room and went over and over it. I thought if I went through it a few times each day around my other work, I'd know every word and be ready to do it with no cards and no ums and ahs, or hesitations.

It was six o'clock when I came out of the creativity room; everyone other than Jack had gone. He was in his office, working.

I bit my top lip as I walked over to my desk to put my stuff away, hoping Jack wouldn't decide to suddenly start talking to me. I didn't want to talk to him any more. He'd made it clear what he wanted – to forget he'd had any relationship at all with me outside work. All I was interested in was doing my job.

I locked my pedestal, threw my bag on to my shoulder and then walked across the room to get my coat. I was going to carry it out, to get out as fast as I could. I hated it when it was only Jack and me left – it was too uncomfortable.

'Ivy!'

Shit.

I turned around; he was standing outside his office. His hand lifted and ran over his hair. 'You okay?'

My expression twisted into something that must say, *what? Really...* Why are you talking to me?

'I wanted to say—' he began.

'You don't need to say anything.' You saying nothing has given me the message well enough.

'I know but—'

'Look, if you want sex, I'm not in the mood.' I turned to leave.

'Ivy! That wasn't what I was going to say.'

I looked back. He started walking towards me. 'I've been sorting things out with Victoria, over Daisy and—'

'Whatever, Jack. I need to go.'

His face twisted in an expression that said he didn't understand. I turned away again and walked out, my fingers gripping my coat like it was a rope attached to the top of a cliff.

I breathed out in the lift as I travelled down and put my coat on.

I wondered if Jack felt guilty.

He didn't act as though he felt anything.

When I got downstairs I walked out through the revolving doors and looked along the busy street, then turned towards the tube station. Ever since Christmas I kept getting a feeling that someone was following me, but not here – it was at the other end of my journey, when I got off the tube and walked from there to home. I think it was because I kept seeing the same guy.

I gripped the strap of my bag tighter as I walked down the steps to the tube station, then pulled my card out of my pocket and pressed it against the sensor. The gate opened to let me into the system. I glanced around as I travelled down the escalator, standing on the right, letting the people in a hurry run past me.

I knew where to stand on the platform for the quiet carriages, so I got a seat.

I pulled out my phone and started playing games, to take my mind off the pitch, and Jack. No matter how much I ignored him, he still danced around in my brain.

It was New Year's Eve that had ruined any hope of me being able to feel normal at work. I didn't regret Christmas, but New

Year – I shouldn't have gone when he'd called. It had been that one last element of control that had tipped the scales too far his way. He'd completely controlled how things were between us that night and ever since. He'd called me into the office, played out his desk fantasy that he'd told me about in the cottage. He'd told me about it even before our affair had really begun, and then fulfilled it before he let our affair end. Then he hadn't let me go back to his, and since leaving mine he hadn't spoken to me.

Until this evening, nearly three weeks after he'd left me in bed.

The whole thing had a nasty feeling about it, which was not exciting and adrenaline-pumping; it made me feel dirty.

When I got off the tube, I glanced around at the other people. I didn't see the big guy who'd kept smiling at me.

I breathed out and slipped my phone into my bag.

When I travelled up on the escalator I glanced around, looking at everyone. I think I was getting paranoid. But when I walked out of the tube station, the guy was there, on the other side of the street. He was about to come over the crossing. I turned, holding the shoulder strap of my bag tightly, and walked quicker.

But I was being stupid – how could he have known I was about to come out of the tube station?

Unless he'd been waiting – and what were the odds of us happening to keep seeing each other? *Lots. You live in the same area.*

I glanced back. He was walking the same way as me. Mostly I saw him walking the opposite way, but one way must be home and one way must be back. He had to go the other way at some point.

He was walking quickly. He was a big guy. He had long strides. So I walked quicker. I didn't want him to catch up with me. I didn't want him to prove it was nothing and he wasn't following me – in case I was right and he was following me. The street was busy. Lots of people were coming home from work.

I breathed out. *Stop panicking.*

I glanced back. The guy was still behind me. I half-ran around the corner into my road, then looked back to check no cars were coming and crossed over. I walked on down to the house where my flat was and reached the door as the guy turned into my road. He walked past the steps as I keyed in the code to get in, my hand shaking.

Oh, this was stupid. If he was following me it was probably because he fancied me. He'd smiled a few times when I'd seen him. He didn't speak and I didn't look back. When the door unlocked I pushed it open and hurried in. Then breathed out a deep breath and went over to check my post. I was looking forward to a glass of wine, some brain-numbing TV and maybe a phone call to Milly – anything normal.

'Hello, Ivy.'

I looked over. Greg stood in the doorway into his place, holding the door as if he hadn't been planning to come out – he'd just seen me and opened the door to talk. 'Have you only just come in from work?'

'Yes.'

'Good day?'

'Yes, okay.' *Why?* Every time Greg talked to me there was an undercurrent of ulterior motive in the tone of his voice and his manner.

'Are you doing anything tonight?'

Shit, I wished he'd get the hint. Maybe if I said, 'I'm far too busy painting my toenails'. 'I have stuff from work to catch up on. I'll be staying in. I don't have time to go anywhere.'

'You work too hard. You're young – you need to enjoy it while you can.'

I nodded, but I was too tired and worried about work and Jack to hang around to be nice and listen to his diatribe. 'See you, Greg. Have a good evening.' I left him where he was and ran up the stairs to get out of there.

Annoyingly, when I got up to my room, the first thing I thought of was Jack – because he'd left memories in my room. It was as though when he'd come back here he'd managed to set things up so he'd control my mind forever. If I could turn back time I wouldn't go into the office on New Year's Eve and I wouldn't let him come here.

Wine. TV. Don't think.

My phone vibrated. It was a text from Rick. I wouldn't get back with him. But at this moment in time Rick's niceness was a comfortable place. He hadn't been over the top since we'd talked. We'd kept to our agreement, friends. And as a friend, he was a good consolation. We'd started sharing texts in the same way as I did with Milly, although not as many, but he helped me keep my mind off Jack. We were helping each other get over our breakup. I was helping him with a slow withdrawal; he was helping me forget the mess I'd made of things since I'd left – only he didn't know it. The mess I was in was my secret.

Chapter 11

Mid-February

I looked up when someone else walked into the office. Ivy. I'd been watching everyone come in, waiting for her. She hung up her coat and walked across the room to her desk, then picked up her mug and walked back across the room to the kitchen.

She didn't look into my office. She never did any more. I hadn't seen her look directly at me since New Year. But playing it cool was what we'd agreed on, and apart from her angry text the first day back, she'd honoured the agreement. I sighed. Problem was, I didn't want to keep up my end of the deal any more. I was days away from getting a court agreement for joint custody of Daisy and once I had that signed off then I could let Ivy into my life, and I wanted to.

I still thought about Christmas and New Year at least once a day.

But I wasn't sure, after her explosion at me a couple of weeks back, if she'd want to come back into my life. She'd made it plain then she wasn't interested. I'd probably left it too long.

I should have texted her after New Year. But it had been easier to leave things as they were while I was working on winning Daisy and losing Sharon – and I hadn't realised then how much I'd felt for Ivy. I had a craving for her.

Ivy came back from the kitchen carrying a full mug. I picked up my mug and went out to get a drink. I was struggling to concentrate today, but that was what happened to me when I thought about Ivy, which was why I'd been avoiding her, and the subject of her.

When I came back with my drink, Phil came into my office.

'Have you got some time, Jack?'

'Sure, sit down.'

He shut the door. 'Ivy went through the progress on the Berkeley account with me yesterday. She's really confident, she's doing well.'

I nodded while he sat down. The mention of her name made me awkward. I never knew how to respond when people mentioned her.

'I wanted to go over a couple of the accounts I'm working on with you.'

'Great.' I pushed up my sleeves and sat forward as he put his laptop down on the desk, then opened it up.

When it came to the end of the day, Ivy and me were the last ones in the office. She was in the creativity room. I was ready to go but I hung around because I didn't want to have to kick her out. I wouldn't know what to say if I went in there. Anything I said would be wrong.

She came out of there at six and hurried across the room. She knew I was here, but she didn't look into the office – just put her stuff away, grabbed her coat and left.

I turned off my laptop and packed up once she'd gone. Then looked at my phone. I had an urge to text her. To say something like, 'I miss you,' I'd had the urge tens of times in the weeks since New Year, but I'd never texted because if she'd replied, what then? It would have been too complicated, with everything else going on.

Now I'd have time. But I couldn't just text her, it was too late for that.

I shoved the problem aside for another day. I'd wait until

everything was finalised with Daisy and then I'd worry about how to get Ivy to look at me again.

If I could. Sometimes her level of acting cool edged on disdain, so maybe the lust torch had burned right out for her since New Year and she wouldn't have anything to do with me – my flame was roaring.

I'd have to offer to take her away again. Get her out of here and give us chance to get to know one another all over again.

I smiled to myself. Thinking about some of the conversations we'd had over Christmas. I'd *sales-pitch* her – she'd give in.

Chapter 12

The beginning of March

Today felt good. Berkeley had loved the screening of the completed ad campaign. Jack had even walked by my desk and said a swift, 'Good work'. I think probably because it would have looked odd if he hadn't.

But he had to crack and talk to me sometime – he couldn't cut me forever. People were noticing. Three people had said, 'What did you do to Jack?' Of course it had to be my fault, because Jolly Jack had sun shining out of his arse.

I keyed in the code to get into the house and went to the post boxes. It was obvious I had some because the letters were only half-jammed in the slot. I opened the box with my key and pulled them out. The folded-over part that sealed two of them looked really creased and they were torn, like they'd been opened and stuck back down again. That was weird. The third one was a hand-written letter from my nan. She preferred snail mail… That envelope looked odd too. There were two creases along the top like tramlines, as though it had been opened and then resealed.

Maybe someone was checking the post for cash, or looking to steal identities.

Tomorrow I'd stick a note on the box for the postman, telling him to check the letters couldn't be pulled back out.

'Hello, Ivy.' Greg. I swear the guy spent his evening looking out of the window watching for when I got home. 'You alright? You look ruffled.'

Ruffled… 'Why?' Would he have?

'You look a bit pale and confused. Has something happened?'

'I'm okay.' I didn't want him to know that he'd got to me if it was him who'd opened my post.

'Sure?'

'Yes. I'm just tired. It's been a long day.'

'I keep telling you, you work too hard.'

'Yeah.' My voice was probably rude. I turned to go upstairs.

My hands shook. It felt creepy, like I'd been assaulted or something. Who would look at my post? What if it was the postman? How could I prevent it, then? When I got up to my flat I threw the letters on the bed and hung my bag up on the back of the door. Then stripped off my coat and shoved my hat and gloves in the pocket before I found my phone. My heart pumped like it was trying to shift an ocean around my body.

'Hello, sweetheart. How are you?'

'Hi, Mum. Something weird's happened. It's freaked me out.'

'What's happened?'

'It looks like someone's opened my letters.'

'Really?'

'Yes. It's weird isn't it?'

'Tell the police, love. Don't ring 999 and block the emergency number, but call 101 and tell them, and don't touch the letters so they can take fingerprints – in case it turns into anything. Maybe it's happening to lots of people.'

I looked at the letters. I'd already touched them. 'Now you're really scaring me.'

'Then why don't you come home tomorrow? We haven't seen

you since your birthday. You can get a train in the morning and go back Sunday evening.'

I took a breath. The idea made me homesick and there was no reason not to go home. Especially since Rick and I had begun tiptoeing our way into friendship, so it didn't matter if I saw his parents. He and I had been out for a drink twice now. We'd talked, laughed and got along okay – as well as we used to in the beginning, when we'd just been friends.

'Alright, I'll try and get there for midday.'

'That would be lovely, sweetheart. We'll look forward to seeing you. But on Monday you're to take those letters into a police station.'

'Yes okay, Mum. I'll see you tomorrow. I'll text you when the train leaves London.'

'Bye, darling.'

I hung up and put the TV on – on the news. Then looked at what food I had in the cupboard. But I wasn't really that hungry after the thing with the post. My stomach was an upside-down mess. I pulled out a can of baked beans and put a slice of bread into the toaster. I ate sitting on the bed. I didn't have a table or even a chair; just the bed, my tiny kitchenette, the TV and me.

The intercom buzzed as I finished eating and Emmerdale came on. I jumped. Shit. Who…? No one ever called on me. I always went to other people's.

I put my plate in the sink, then went over to the intercom and pressed the button. 'Who is it?' I listened to the crackle from the speaker, as though this was a horror movie, expecting some crazy person to answer with a deep laugh.

'It's Jack. Can I come up?'

'Why?' If I sounded defensive, it was because I was defensive. What the fuck was he here for? He had control of my life in the office, but I wasn't going to let him start playing his Captain Control games with me at home. He couldn't suddenly turn up. But he had… It was Jack playing everything his way again.

'Because we need to talk.'

'We don't. We've had plenty of opportunity to talk at work. You chose not to speak to me. So, no, I don't want you to come up here and talk. Go away. I'll see you at work on Monday.'

I lifted my hand off the sound. The intercom buzzed again. I ignored it. My phone rang. I didn't answer it. It buzzed with a message.

'Come on, Ivy. You know I can't talk to you about personal stuff in the office. Don't leave me standing out here like an idiot.'

'Maybe you are an idiot. You've acted like one since New Year.'

'Look, hey, calm down. I didn't know you were so pissed off about it, otherwise I'd have come over sooner. You never said.'

'You don't speak to me, so when was I meant to say?'

There was no reply.

I tossed my phone down, realising that after weeks of being brilliantly cool, calm and professional, and acting like I hadn't been bothered, I'd blown it all and given myself away. Bum. I'd sounded as pathetic as Rick last year. I should have let Jack talk and looked bored. Or made him talk through the intercom and laughed.

Footsteps struck the stairs outside and then someone knocked on my door.

'Ivy?'

Shit, someone had let him in. What the fuck was a security system for, for God sake? That was probably how whoever had tampered with my post got in.

I got up and reached out, grasping the door handle, so if he tried to turn it I could stop him getting in. But he couldn't get in unless I opened the lock anyway. 'What are you doing here?'

'I want to spend the weekend with you.'

What a prick! I opened the door. 'Fuck off. I'm not having sex with you, Jack.'

'What's wrong with you?'

'What do you think? You haven't spoken to me as an individual since you were last in this room. You can't come up here expecting sex. What's wrong with you?'

'Let me come in, so we can talk?'

'So you can run your sales pitch and twist everything out of shape, so it turns out your way, like it did before. No. Please? Go away.'

His arm lifted and his elbow rested on the doorjamb by my head. It meant I couldn't shut the door. It was an arrogant, domineering gesture – completely alpha-male and completely Jack – and, annoyingly, it twisted something in my stomach and thrust a memory of having sex with him into my head. A memory of the last night in the big house. 'Go away. I don't want to talk to you if you can't talk to me at work. Oh, no, I forgot, there was one time you spoke to me, when you wanted sex and I was working late and there was your *good work* comment today.'

'I've been busy.'

Too busy to even text after having left me in bed... I didn't say that, it sounded petulant, like Rick had been with me. I needed Jack to think that it didn't matter. 'I don't really care, Jack.'

His arm dropped and then his hands slid into the pockets of his leather jacket. He wanted sex, that was all. Maybe that was even the reason he'd complimented my success at work. That was a shitty thought. Everything he'd done since Christmas kept spoiling my memories of Christmas.

'I couldn't see you; Sharon's lawyer has a private detective watching me and I've been fighting for a legal agreement to see Daisy, so I didn't want to mess it up. But I've been seeing Daisy every Sunday for a couple of hours since the New Year and now I have a legal agreement. I get her every other weekend. So this weekend I'm free, before the new arrangement starts.'

And you want sex. I stepped back and sat on the bed. I didn't like his excuses. Excuses were a sales pitch in the opposite form – reasons to forgive me, one, two, three. 'I'm not free anyway.'

'Why?'

'I'm going to see my parents.'

Jack had stepped into the room. He leaned against the wall behind him. 'I was going to take you somewhere on the bike.'

'No thanks.'

'Why are you being awkward? This isn't just about sex, Ivy.'

'I'm not being awkward. You're being controlling. Everything gets played your way, *come to my cottage, come into the office and celebrate New Year with me… Don't text me, people might know*—'

'I only said don't text me at work. You could have contacted me in the evening, but you didn't.'

'I wasn't the one who said 'don't text'. I said something; you shut me down. The next move was yours. But anyway, I don't want to know what you have to say, I don't care. I have stuff going on in my life too. I'd rather you left.'

His brow furrowed. Had he really thought I'd agree to go away with him?

Maybe he had, because he was a control freak.

'I didn't know I'd done anything that wrong. I was playing it cool, as we'd agreed. I thought you might have moved on but…'

'You haven't even looked at me at work; you asked Phil to work with me so you didn't have to. Yes, that was really cool. Thanks. And everyone's assumed it's my fault. They all think I've insulted you somehow.'

'I'm sorry. I didn't mean it like that. I can't deal with you, that's all—'

'Deal with me… You don't need to. I can—'

'I keep saying the wrong thing. I knew I would. That's why I haven't tried talking to you in the office. I can't deal with what I think about you, that's what I mean. I think about us having sex. I can't be professional with you. So it was easier to not work with you, sorry. You've still done well.'

'Like I said. Thank you.'

His hands slipped out of his pockets, then he picked up the

post and moved it so he could sit next to me on the bed, uninvited. His elbows rested on his knees, but he didn't look at me, he looked at the floor. I noticed his heel tapping. I wondered if he'd had a joint since leaving work. He was still wound up.

'I'm sorry I've upset you. I'm not good at chasing women. I don't usually have to chase them. But we got on at Christmas. I enjoyed your company. Now I have a weekend free... I've been debating with myself all week how to approach you, and I didn't want to text. So I'm here.' His head turned to look at me, but he didn't straighten up. 'I'd like to see you again. I'd like to see you for more than one weekend. We could spend every other weekend together if you want—'

'Not if you're going to treat me like shit at work, and not if all you want is sex. I'm not into being used like that.'

He straightened up, his hands falling on to his thighs. 'If I promise to be more relaxed at work, will you come out with me? No sex required.'

My innards jumped, back-flipping at the chance of being with Jack again, even after all these weeks of being ignored. It made me loathe my bad side. But I wasn't going to forgive him just like that, or let him think he could come and pick me up, like a takeaway order, whenever he wanted. 'I told you I'm busy this weekend. Maybe in a fortnight, when I can see whether you're really sorry.' I lifted my eyebrows at him.

'And now?'

'You can go.'

'Really...'

I bet no other woman had told him, and all his raunchy, bossy, masculine energy, to fuck off. 'You can't order me in when you want, Jack, just because you have a weekend free. Not like New Year's Eve. The way you treated me then was mean. I'm not the type you're used to.' A prostitute.

He stood up. 'I know. So what is this? Am I on probation?'

'You have to earn the opportunity to be on probation. Pass the test in the next two weeks and I might believe you and put you on probation and try you out.'

He smiled. 'That's fair, if I get a chance. I'll see you at work, then.'

'You might, if you bother looking at me.'

'I'll see you at work, Ivy.'

When I shut the door behind him, I pressed my forehead against it, my hand on the handle again. I couldn't believe he'd come over. I really didn't need the complication of Jack playing with me again. I'd got over that. But my tummy was turning a dozen somersaults with stupid, blind excitement, from the adrenaline rush Jack always brought with him.

My phone rang.

Jeez, I was Miss Popular tonight.

I picked up my phone and touched the answer icon. 'Hi, Rick.'

'You okay? You sound pissed off.'

'I'm alright. Bad day at work and a bad day with the post. Why did you call? How are you? Mum was telling me this week you've had some time off work, are you alright?'

'I'm fine. The doctor signed me off with stress, that's all. Work's been too busy. It was getting to me. I'm only off for a couple of weeks 'til I get myself sorted. I wondered if you wanted to go for a drink tonight.'

'I was going to go and see Milly.' I hadn't planned it, but after the post and Jack's visit, I needed to talk to her. 'Are you feeling really down?'

'I'll survive. Sure you don't want to get together? What about tomorrow?'

'I'm going home tomorrow. Sorry. Maybe next week.'

'Okay, let's make a date for next Friday. I could meet you outside work and we could go out for dinner if you want?'

'Friday sounds cool, but pick me up here so I can change before we go out and text me and let me know what time.'

'Okay. I'll look forward to it. Bye.'

'See you later.'

I touched the icon to end the call.

Rick and I had become grown up about our breakup, and now Jack and I had become childish.

I sighed. But as I did I looked up Milly's number, then rang her. 'Hi. What are you up to?'

'Steve and I are curled up watching TV and eating Chinese. Why?'

'Can I come over? I want to talk to you, but if I do, you have to swear not to tell Steve?'

'Why?'

'Because it's about my hot guy from Christmas and Steve might mention it to Rick and that's not fair on Rick.'

'Okay, I promise. Come over, we'll talk in the kitchen, and I'll turn the TV up so Steve can't hear.' She laughed as I heard Steve say something in the background. 'But give us half an hour to finish eating and then come over.'

'See you later.'

'See you in a bit.'

I threw my phone on the bed, had a shower and then dressed up, purely to feel better.

I slipped my coat back on, wrapped a scarf around my neck and put the hat Jack had bought me on. Then went out and locked up. I'd left my bag. I just had my phone and purse in my pockets. I preferred not to carry a bag at night when I was walking alone. To be safer. I still had loads of Rick-like risk-averse habits.

My black-heeled boots clicked on the pavement as I walked along the path. Milly and Steve lived one stop along on the underground. I could walk it but at night I preferred to use the tube. The sound of my heels on the pavement echoed along the quiet street, dancing about the trees, which ran the length of it. My breath steamed in the air.

I heard a noise behind me and looked back. It sounded like someone else walking, but no one was there.

Maybe a cat or a fox had knocked something over.

When I got to the end of the road and turned the corner, I still had a feeling someone was there. I glanced back again. But the street looked empty.

My hands in my pockets, I carried on until I reached the tube station. But I kept looking over my shoulder as I rode the escalator down. I still had the sense that someone was following me. There were about ten people on the escalator; it could be any one of them – there was no one I recognised. But no one seemed to care what I was doing.

Maybe I was jittery because of the thing with the post.

I sat in the tube carriage looking around at everyone. No one was looking at me and yet I still had the sensation when I walked to Milly and Steve's that someone was behind me.

When I left Milly's I got Steve to run me home in the car and when I went to the railway station the next day to get to Mum and Dad's I splashed out on a cab.

Chapter 13

My heart pounded out a manic garage rhythm as I walked into the office on Monday morning. Ivy was already in, sitting at her desk, staring at her computer.

'Hi, Tina.' I carried on watching Ivy. She didn't look up.

'Hi, Jack, your post is open. I put it on your desk.'

'Thanks.'

Ivy still hadn't looked up.

Everything she'd charged me with on Friday was true. I hadn't even felt guilty about it before. I'd thought I was doing the right thing. The right thing for me, yes. Obviously not for her. Captain Control – I heard the name spoken in her voice. But I hadn't known how to act normally around her. There were too many memories, too much had happened between us – so I'd controlled the issue by avoiding it and forgotten about how she might feel.

I looked around the room and sighed out a breath. I *was* controlling; I knew I was. It was my instinct. It was partly why I'd achieved so much with the business and the properties. It had advantages and it didn't make me a bad man, and I hadn't meant New Year's Eve or what had happened since, to feel like that to her. I hadn't meant her to feel controlled. But looking back... I could have phrased the text telling her not to speak to me at work better, and I could have said something to her the next time we'd been alone, or gone to her flat, or… done something to break the ice after New Year's Eve.

'Morning everyone. Meeting in twenty. Time for a coffee run to Nero's, if you'll go, Tina?' I glanced back. She nodded at me. 'Put your orders in, people, and I'll buy the round.'

I left them to sort themselves out and headed for my office. Ivy still had her head down. When I walked past her desk, I said, 'Morning, Ivy,' in a low voice. The others hopefully didn't hear; they were putting their coffee orders in. I didn't hang around for a response but walked on. I didn't want it to be obvious, and I didn't know how not to be obvious with her.

When I walked into my office, I threw my keys on to the desk. *Get it together…*

I took my coat off and hung it up, then looked through the post. Tina knocked on the open door. 'Everyone's ready, Jack.' *I wasn't.*

I stood up. I had to do this.

Tina handed me my espresso.

'Come on.' I led the way to the creativity room, drinking my coffee, then I tossed the cup into a bin before I went in. *Play it cool. Look at her, but look at them all.*

My brilliant team were all in there, mine and Em's. I glanced at Em and smiled. She smiled back. That made me feel better. 'Okay, morning everybody…' I ran through the agenda, covering the workload for this week, getting everyone to share their progress and their next objectives, so we all knew where we were and I knew my clients were happy.

I breathed out, then I looked at Ivy. I'd used to always look at her, but I couldn't look at her any more without feeling weird, and I'd lay odds people could see I felt weird. '… and congratulations on the Berkeley account.' Ivy's lavender gaze lifted and tangled up with mine. But it wasn't like it used to be, because now there was knowledge and experience and memories between us. I looked at Phil. 'Well done, you two. Good work, they're really impressed.'

'Cool.' Phil answered. Ivy didn't say a word. But I guess half an hour of improvement wasn't going to cut it. I had two weeks.

'Well, that's it, then, guys. Get to work!'

Ivy stood up and filed out with the others. One old habit hadn't died – my gaze dropped to her bottom.

'Jack.' Em caught my arm. 'Can we talk?'

I shut the door when everyone else had left. Then turned around. 'Yes, how can I help?'

She gave me a twisted look. 'What did you do?'

'What do you mean?'

'I mean Ivy. She's been quiet as anything ever since Christmas. Everyone's noticed she isn't herself, and you two haven't been speaking, and then today when you do single her out she turns bright red. Why?'

I swallowed. Shit. I'd always known Em would kill me for it, but I didn't regret it. I wasn't going to say sorry.

I sat down with a sigh on a bright-yellow fabric square. The creativity space was the only room we had with no windows, and I guess that was why Em had waylaid me here. But, God, I needed to talk to someone about this. Em was not only my business partner but my best friend. It had been tearing me up for weeks and I'd been shutting it out. 'I had sex with her.'

Em punched my shoulder. Hard. 'Jack! What did you do that for?'

I looked up and smiled. 'Um, let me think, because she's shit-hot and sweet-natured.'

'Jack, it's not funny. She's trying to pull her life back together. When did it happen?'

'Christmas. She came away with me. We were working late. She was at a loose end and I was at a loose end, so I offered to take her to the cottage and she accepted.'

Em's hands curled into fists at her sides and her face rouged-up with anger – or maybe she was embarrassed by me. At work my behaviour reflected on her.

'Then you left her feeling so awkward she doesn't know where

204

to put herself when she's in here… Have you seen her outside of work since?'

'No. But I want to. I called around there on Friday now all the stuff with Daisy's sorted. She told me to get lost.' I looked up at Em, still sitting, while she stood. Behind her was the image of the blue sky. '*Future horizons*,' I'd said when I'd had the posters put up. I hadn't been able to imagine my future since the New Year.

'I don't blame her!'

'She's given me two weeks to stop being stupid and not ignore her at work. But I was feeling the same as her. I haven't known where to look either. Or what to say.'

'So this morning you dive right in and let everyone know something else has happened between you two that no one's seen. That's not sensible, Jack. You shouldn't have done this. It's your fault it's awkward! You don't bring your sex life into work. Didn't you learn about appropriate choices from Sharon?'

She was serious. I stood up, on the defensive now. 'Sharon was entirely different, I—'

'I know. You're the problem. I'm not blaming Ivy for any of this. I know what you're like, and I know what she's like. She's the wounded party. You're lucky you don't have a claim for sexual harassment on your head.'

I made a face at her. Now she was being dramatic.

'Leave her alone, Jack. She's been seeing Rick again anyway. Just treat her like normal and keep away from her outside work. She's one of the best people we have, and you know it. She has a ton of potential. Please don't fuck it up.'

Em didn't swear – except when she wanted me to take notice.

I smiled and took no notice at all. I was a contrary-bloody-bastard, so I'd been told nearly every day at university. It was part of my need to be the one in control. I'd always done what I wanted. But Em didn't need to know I wasn't listening. I nodded and pulled on my forelock. 'Yes, miss. Do you want a hundred lines: 'I'll keep my hands off Ivy Cooper'?'

'It isn't your hands I'm worried about.'

I laughed.

She didn't.

'Jack. Be sensible,' she said before I opened the door.

I wasn't sensible, though, either. Sharon had helped prove that. I was a full-on risk-taker. It was that that had given this business its break and my control had helped hold it up – and those things defined me.

I couldn't be who I wasn't.

Fuck it. When I got back to my office I rang Ivy's desk phone. She picked it up without guessing it was me, or she didn't look over, anyway. 'Hey. Will you come in and talk to me? I need to tell you something.'

She took a breath as if she had something to say in answer but other people would hear. She swallowed it. 'I'll come in, in a minute.' I loved that she'd started controlling my controlling nature – *what goes around, comes around*, my dad would've said to me. I smiled as she made me wait, deliberately not rushing. She finished typing something on her computer, then pulled a pad and pen out from her drawer. When she stood she looked into the office and caught me watching, I didn't look away, I clung to her gaze as she crossed the room and opened my office door.

She shut it behind her, then turned and looked at me. 'What do you want, Jack? Don't start playing games with me here. It's not fair. I can't stop it happening here.'

'I'm not.'

She gave me a hard look as she sat in the seat on the other side of my desk. The last time she'd been in this room I'd fucked her on my desk. That was why I'd asked Phil to play middle man on the Berkeley account. I couldn't speak business to Ivy in here without thinking about sex. But I had to set it aside.

'I want to talk to you about picking up a new account. If you think you're up to it.'

'You know I'm up to it.' She sat forward in the chair, perching on the edge.

'Well, then, it's the Pitkins account. Do you want it?'

'Yes. Of course. Thank you.' The thank you was said with a wealth of gratitude. Her voice was full of pleasure over being given another chance to just be good at her job. It sounded like she'd given up on me ever speaking to her – until today.

Em was right; I should forget about me and Ivy. But I didn't want to let things go.

When she stood up and walked past the end of the desk to leave the room, I rolled my chair over and grabbed her wrist to stop her. 'Wait a minute.' I let go of her and looked out through the glass to check who was watching. No one. She stood there staring at me.

'Em told me you're seeing Rick again…'

'I'm not. Not like that. Just as a friend. That's all. But it's none of your business, anyway.'

No. I'd upset her so much I'd probably lost the right to care. I let her walk away. I'd earn the right to care again.

I shut the door of my apartment, took my jacket off and hung it up, then pulled out my mobile phone and called Ivy. I'd wanted to take a hold of her and kiss her when everyone was saying goodbye. If she'd been last out, I'd have tried it. But she'd left on the stroke of five, before I could get near her.

She let her phone ring about six times before she answered. 'Jack. I'm busy.'

'It's not a long call. I'm doing a bit of customer evaluation. How am I doing?'

'What do you mean?'

'I mean, am I paying you enough attention at work?'

She sighed out a breath. 'Yes, you're fine at work. Now everyone wants to know what we did to make up.'

I smiled to myself and chuckled. 'As long as you're feeling better. That's all I want. Have you decided about next weekend?'

'Yeah, the answer's no. I'm over Christmas – Christmas is forgotten. And I don't think I want to resurrect it. It isn't sensible to go backwards. Live for the moment, remember.'

'It is sensible sometimes, Ivy.' My heart flipped into a hard pump. As if I'd put my foot down on the accelerator pedal and revved it up. I wanted Ivy in my life. I knew it with a vivid clarity. I'd felt different around her at Christmas, and I'd been different since we'd come back here, focusing on Daisy as much as work, and nothing else. I'd been looking for something else when I'd split from Sharon and Ivy fit the new me. She'd already become a part of the new me at Christmas. 'Give me a chance. I want to be your boyfriend—'

'Really… Jack. You'd hate anyone at work to know that. It wouldn't work, and I don't even believe you.'

'Believe me. Please? I wouldn't tell anyone yet, no, but only because of Sharon. She'd make your life hell. But the divorce is nearly through. As soon as it is, then we can come out of the closet—'

'There is no 'we'.'

'There could be a 'we'. If you come away with me next weekend.'

'Call me next week. I've got to go. I'm having dinner with someone.'

'Who?'

'It's none of your business.'

'Tell me who?'

'Oh, if you must know, Rick.'

'God, that man is really clingy. Or are you interested in being unfulfilled again?'

'Bye, Jack.'

She cut me off, the bitch. But I laughed. I liked her ballsy. I threw the phone down on a low table and tumbled back on the sofa next to it. 'Shit.' I wanted her. With her lavender eyes, and her purple hair, and her pale, slim body. I wanted her. She was perfect for me. She knew how to manage my crap. She knew how to have sex with me. She even liked some of my risky games. She knew everything... I could be the real me with her.

I looked up at the ceiling and shut my eyes. I felt like smoking a joint but I'd stopped smoking cannabis and thrown the last lot I'd bought away. I was a reformed character. I'd made up my mind I didn't want that stuff in the apartment when Daisy was here. I wouldn't want her getting involved with drugs, or thinking it was okay to be involved with drugs because there were so many people who didn't know where to stop and then couldn't control it. I didn't want my Daisy to be one of those people.

But giving everything up and going clean-living left me wired up with no outlet. Not even sex. I hadn't had sex with anyone since New Year's Eve.

I turned my new TV on – which had been allowed into the apartment solely for Daisy to watch. It was some dumb soap thing. I could go out for a drink but I wanted to be sober and clear-headed all weekend. Daisy wasn't sleeping over this week. I was going to pick her up Saturday, take her out for the day and then take her home, and then Sunday I had her all day again. That was the plan for my first two weekends and then if she was happy about it she was going to come to me Saturday mornings and stay until Sunday evening.

How cool was that? I'd be an actual practising father. My lips lifted and parted with an emotion that I'd only discovered less than twelve months ago. Unconditional love.

Ah, shit. There was someone else I should call. I picked up my phone, stood up, then crossed the room to look out through the floor-length windows. The flat was a penthouse place but it wasn't huge, not like the one I'd shared with Sharon; it was a small two-bed apartment, but I had a view of the Thames. I'd spent hours watching the boats on the river.

'Hello, Jack.'

'Hi, Mum.' I hadn't told her I'd won access rights to see Daisy yet. 'It's official, Mum. I get Daisy every other weekend. We're working our way up to her staying over with me. But it's all signed and sealed by a judge.'

'I'm happy for you. I know it's what you wanted. But you know how important it is that you look after the girl. No messing around while she's with you.'

'I know, Mum.' I hadn't told her anything about me cleaning up my life because she had no idea how dirty it had been, and I didn't want her to know.

'You haven't always acted in the right way…'

The dig hurt. But I'd gone out of my way to piss my parents off most of my life. *What goes around, comes around.* I heard the words in Dad's voice again. It was only since I'd discovered Daisy that I'd really realised what a prick I'd been to them. Or maybe since I'd left Sharon.

Before Sharon had come along Mum had been pushing me to marry Em – she didn't get that Em was not my type. Em was a brilliant friend and a wizard with numbers in the office, but there was no chance of anything else.

Then Sharon had come along and they'd hated her, and I, being a contrary controlling bastard, had married her anyway. Probably half to spite them all – certainly to control them all and make them see they could not control me. But then most of the things I'd done since I was a boy had been done because my parents had hated an idea and I'd wanted to control the situation, and them. That was what being away at boarding school did to people. To me, anyway. I'd always been an arrogant, independent little brat when I was child. But I'd needed to be. I'd needed to be in control at school because there had only been me… I had no brothers to stick up for me or sisters to run to. It had just been me mastering the world, because it had been better to be the one on top of it than the one running.

My child wasn't like that; she hadn't had to fight for things. I was glad about that.

And even better, Daisy had been pure accident. There was nothing planned or controlled about her. She'd had nothing to do with that part of me. She was a precious, beautiful accident. I wasn't letting the problems I'd created with Mum and Dad, or my stupid hang-ups, affect her. 'I wondered if you wanted to meet her?'

Mum was silent. Then she swallowed. I think discovering Daisy so late in my life had embarrassed them – most people did not announce a grandchild to their friends when she was already seven, and their friends could count and had worked out the age I'd been when I'd fathered her. It had been a kick to my parents' self-righteous lifestyle.

But so what? The smile on my face was massive. The old self-centred, pleasure-seeking me had created a life. For everything I'd done wrong in my life, I'd done one thing right.

And that accident had created more than one life; Daisy had given me my life to live again too.

'Yes. We'd love to.'

Thank God. My heart raced. I wanted this for them, as well as me. A new start. 'I think we'd have to leave it a couple of weeks. Give her chance to get used to coming to me, and then maybe you could come to London?'

'We could go out to The Ivy for lunch. Do you think she'd like that?'

'Probably, but remember she's eight. She might be fidgety and she'd probably like McDonald's as much, if not more.'

'I did have you, I know how children are, Jack. But I think we can give her more of a treat than McDonald's.'

'Your father wants to speak with you...'

The phone was passed over. 'Jack...' Oh God, and this was why I didn't call them, because I constantly received lectures on respon-sibility and accepting my role in life. It was no wonder I'd become so determined to be the lord over my own world.

I kept saying, 'Yes, Dad,' as he ran through his speech.

'Generations of us... Years of responsibility... You're my only son...'

'Yes, Dad.'

Once we'd said our goodbyes, I ended the call, looked at the TV and sighed.

I could go out to the climbing club but none of my friends would be there on a Friday – they had lives beyond climbing, and I'd been there every night this week. I needed to find a new outlet. I looked at my other acquisition for Daisy's sake, a PlayStation, and stood up, then went over, turned it on and picked up the controller. I'd messed around with it once to check it was working.

Daisy's little hand slipped into mine and gripped tight as I led her into Harrods. 'This is the coolest place, Dad.'

That word, dad, gave me a sharp stomach-punch. It did every time. 'I know. But you're not to start thinking this is normal, and I can't afford everything in here. But you can pick some nice things for your room.'

We'd already chosen a bed online, and furniture, but I'd told her we would come here for the curtains and bed linen and some pretty stuff to fancy it up however she wanted. We'd had our traditional hot chocolate in Hyde Park and requested the usual pile of cream and marshmallows on top and now we had another three hours before it was time for me to take her home, but our first full day together had gone amazingly. It didn't feel awkward, probably because she was a chatterbox, so the conversation never dried – not now she knew me.

'Can I have some toys too?'

'Save toys for another week; we'll go to Hamleys for toys.'

'Hamleys…' Her bright eyes looked up at me. She was as sharp as a pin. I was already planning on bringing her into the business, even though she was eight.

I gave her wink. 'It's the best toy shop ever. Save your toy money for there.'

She started skipping along beside me as we walked through

the handbag section, then the jewellery section. I had no idea where I was going. It was like a journey of discovery, and everything was gold and glittering, which had Daisy's gaze darting everywhere. This was a good plan.

'Look at that, Dad.' She pointed at a sparkly something.

'Oh yeah.'

I don't know whether the sign-free warren of rooms was a ploy to make you amble around and spend far more than intended, or what, but if it was, then Daisy fell for it. And seeing as I'd completely fallen for Daisy, I pulled out my credit card over and over again – for dresses, dress-jewellery, hairslides and hairbands.

When we reached the children's bedroom things we bought two duvet sets, curtains, a lampshade and a set of fairy lights to go over her bed, a stencil to paint flowers on the wall and a mirror. She smiled the whole time and kept glancing at me like I might say no when she asked for stuff. I think her mother would have said no. But I had the money. Well, I had it now, although Sharon was doing her best to get it all off me.

We wasted the entire last three hours in Harrods, ended up in the sweets' department and bought some of those too.

I was ten minutes late getting her back home, but Victoria was good about it. She smiled at Daisy then smiled at me when Daisy ran into the house with her bags of dresses, jewellery and hair stuff, to show her other dad.

'Daisy! Come and say goodbye.'

I never went into the house. Victoria's husband, David, still hated the whole idea of me muscling in on his family. I'd only seen him twice. He kept out of my way, and I didn't push it. As long as I got to see Daisy, I didn't care what he thought.

Daisy came back into the hall. I squatted down and her arms wrapped around my neck. 'Goodbye, Daddy.'

'Did you have a fun?'

'Yes.'

'Cool. I'll see you tomorrow and we'll paint the flowers on your wall, okay?'

'Okay.'

I patted her back. I could feel her spine and ribs – she was such a tiny, pretty little thing, but full of jumping beans. Her arms slipped from around my neck. 'Goodbye sweetheart.' We were not on I love you terms yet. I did love her; it was a complete obsession – she was a living part of me. But I wasn't sure if I should say it first or wait until she expressed the attachment.

'Bye, Daddy.' She turned and ran off again.

I handed Victoria Daisy's backpack. 'I bought her some sweets. They're in there. I'll see you in the morning.'

'Yeah.'

'Bye.'

'Bye.'

Then I was at a loose end again. As I drove back into central London, I thought of Ivy. Of just turning up at hers – but she'd been adamant that I gave her two weeks, and maybe I'd blow it if I broke the rule. I went home and played 'Assassin's Creed', which had become my new favourite adrenaline detox.

On Wednesday, I spent most of the day at work watching Ivy, without her knowing.

She was working on the new account with Phil and the two of them were in a deep debate at her desk, working out the finer details of a pitch. I was sitting in my office wondering if she was going to forgive me for the period I'd ignored her.

I knew Ivy was what I wanted. I'd been blind when I'd met Sharon. Or rather arrogant and easy to fool. I wasn't blind any more and I knew, one hundred per cent, Ivy wasn't interested in my money. She was the sort of woman I should've chosen in the first place – the sort of woman I could take home to my parents and introduce to Daisy.

I was completely sold on the idea of me and Ivy becoming

214

something. I could see a future again. I'd spent the last days of my testing period developing the image in my head. I had two days of test left to go, and then I just had to convince her.

I didn't hang around when five o'clock came. I got up, grabbed my coat off the rack in my office, then I walked past Ivy and said, 'Goodnight, have a good evening.'

She looked at me oddly, but she'd been busy all day so I hadn't had chance to say anything to her, and I didn't want to blow everything because of not talking for one day.

'You too,' she said unemotionally, looking back down.

I carried on walking. Maybe I'd made an irreparable mess of things with her. Maybe on Friday she'd tell me to fuck off again. There'd been no sign to say she was interested in me now. She never watched me any more.

I rode the lift down to the basement, then changed into my leathers in the toilet down there. I put my stuff in the pannier on the bike. I was going to spend my evening building the flat-pack furniture in Daisy's bedroom, ready for when she came to stay. The room was painted the colour she'd chosen, and on Sunday we'd decorated it with flower prints and lights and all the other stuff we'd been gathering to make it pretty.

I got on the bike and turned the key in the ignition, then twisted the throttle and revved the engine. It purred between my thighs as I let the break go. I lifted my feet and pulled away.

I held a hand up to Richard the attendant as I rode out of the car park.

I stopped at the entrance, watching for a gap in the traffic with my feet on the ground and straightened up a little. There was a car parked opposite, on the double yellows. The guy in the driver's seat had his hoodie pulled up over his head. I stared at him when I pulled out across the road. Then in my wing mirror, I saw his indicator go on and he pulled out behind me. He was following.

When I hit the junction where I turned right, I watched the car turn behind me.

I pulled away from it, speeding up. But then I saw a police car turn into the road behind us. Shit. I slowed down again and the car kept on me.

What the hell? It followed for four streets, then we lost the police and I lost the car.

I parked the bike in the basement parking for my apartment, slipped off my helmet and found out my mobile phone, breathing hard. I slid up the contacts and called her.

'Hi, I—'

'What the fuck, Sharon! Call your fucking dogs off, will you! One of them just followed me home from work while I was on the bike! What are you trying to do now, fucking kill me? Seriously, I'm telling John, so if I do die you won't get shit!' I took a breath, ready to rip loose again—

'You're paranoid. It's all the weed you smoke. I haven't got anyone following you—'

'I saw them.'

'It was probably coincidence. I told you, it's the cannabis. I don't need to have anyone follow you. I know what you get up to. Like I know there was someone with you when you were up at the cottage over Christmas.'

Fuck. I didn't answer. I didn't want Ivy dragged into Sharon's poison.

'Who was it, Jack? You slept in the house with them, whoever it was. You never sleep in the house.'

'How do you know?'

'The housekeeper. You never tidied up in the house, and she rang here because she thought someone might have broken in. No one broke in, did they? It must have been someone special… Who was it?'

'Me.'

'Liar.'

'Whatever. Call off your fucking watch dogs!' I ended the call.

Shit. If she knew the girl was Ivy, she'd go for Ivy just for fun, and as Ivy and I worked together probably accuse Ivy of having an affair with me for months in the divorce papers.

Ivy wouldn't welcome being cited in my divorce. I'd lose her then, for certain.

Chapter 14

I glanced at Jack. He was still in his office, on the phone and scribbling something on a pad of paper. I looked at the clock on the bottom right of the screen. It was nearly five. He hadn't asked me yet.

A long breath slipped through my lips. If he did ask, I still wasn't sure what I was going to say.

He'd been nice to me; he'd spoken to me in some way every day, but it wasn't the same as it had been before Christmas and I didn't think it could be the same.

That was the thing making me hesitate. The bad girl in me desperately wanted to go. I still fancied him physically. But what would it be like when we came back to work if I did go away with him? Even more awkward...

This was like one of his dares or his high-risk games.

But Christmas was like a dream now and my heart might be racing, but that didn't feel like a good thing any more.

Oh forget it. It would be stupid to go.

I clicked shutdown on my computer and packed up to go home.

Jack called my phone when I was in the lift. 'Hey, where are you going? I thought you'd hang around until everyone else had gone.'

He was convinced I'd say yes, then. Well, decision definitely

218

made. He wasn't getting control. 'You thought wrong.' I ended the call.

My phone rang again when I reached the ground floor. It was him.

My tummy started playing dodgems. I did still fancy him. But I didn't answer.

In the street, as I walked to the underground station, I had that weird feeling of being followed. I looked around, but no one stood out as though they were looking at me. I had the feeling all the time now, though, not just when I got off the tube.

I hurried, walking quicker. My phone vibrated in my pocket.

When I was in the underground system Jack couldn't call, but when I got out the other end there were no more missed calls anyway. He'd given up. I half ran the rest of the way, as best I could in a tight skirt and heels.

There was a noise behind me, a cat jumping off a wall – or a scuffed footstep, someone walking behind me. I glanced back. That guy was there; the one I kept seeing.

When I turned into my street he was about fifty meters behind me.

Sometimes when I saw him he turned into my street after me, and sometimes he walked straight on up the main road. When I reached the house, I looked back. He walked around the corner into the street.

My hand trembled when I tapped the code into the keypad. I pushed the door open and hurried in. My heartbeat slowed after the door shut. I looked at my post box. The postman always pushed the post right in now. I slid the key in to open the box. The police had said they were sure someone had opened my post but the fingerprints didn't match any on their records, so there was nothing they could do.

There were no letters. I shut the box up.

I ran upstairs to my room, shut the door and put the chain I'd acquired after the thing with the post, in its slot. I hadn't told the police I felt like someone was following me. It was just paranoia; I knew I was being silly. The guy had never spoken to me, he probably just lived near me… and the sensation I had outside work couldn't be anything to do with him. I'd never seen him there.

My heart thumped heavily as I walked over to put the kettle on and started thinking about eating tea. I switched the TV on and changed the channel to Channel 4 plus one to watch *Couples Come Dine With Me*; a bit of silly normality would sweep away the ghost of my imaginary stalker.

My phone vibrated – it was still in my coat pocket, but I could hear it. I fished it out.

'Jack: Hey, why did you run? I'm downstairs. Let me in.'

I didn't reply but pressed the button to free the lock downstairs. A part of me leapt. He hadn't given up. A few moments later he knocked on the door to my room.

I took a breath then released the chain and opened the door. But I wasn't sure I was ready for this.

'Hello.'

'Is that all you have to say?'

I threw him a tired, impatient smile, turned around and carried on making my coffee. 'Do you want one?' I glanced over my shoulder.

His brow furrowed. 'Seriously, instant…'

'Stop being so stuck up.'

His eyebrows lifted. 'Who ate up your good mood?'

'I'm tired.'

'So you don't want to go away…'

'I don't know.' I spooned coffee into a second mug, then sploshed the milk into both. The kettle boiled.

Jack didn't speak.

I finished making the coffee, turned and held one out. 'Here.'

'Thanks. I think.' His lip curled.

'You're too fussy.'

'Am I allowed to sit down?'

'If you want to.'

Chapter 15

I glanced around. Her place was tiny. I hadn't been kidding last time when I'd joked about her needing a pay rise. That was why I'd booked a weekend away. We couldn't go up to the cottage, someone was renting out the house and I didn't want to take her to mine because of Sharon's spies, and this place was way too small, so I was getting us out of London for a couple of days – if she'd come.

Every element of my body hoped she'd come: all my muscles were tight, holding on in anticipation of her decision. I'd been revved up for this all week.

I took a seat on the bed. The mattress dipped when she sat next to me. As the TV babbled on.

I sipped the coffee. It was what I expected, pretty awful. I looked at Ivy. 'So tell me, what's holding you back?'

'I'd have thought you could guess. Last time we got together you then ignored me for weeks. I'm happy as things are now.'

'You weren't happy when you came away with me at Christmas, then? Because you seemed happy to me.'

'But what happened after made me unhappy. I don't want to be unhappy again. One weekend of fun isn't worth the risk.'

The risk… That was what was wrong with me. I was all about risk, controversy and control. But I did worry for other people who were at risk. 'So let's do a little risk assessment. What is the highest risk?' I put my disgusting coffee down on the floor, then twisted around and slipped one knee up on to her bed so I faced her.

Memories of the cramped night we'd spent in this bed wedged into my thoughts. We'd laughed a lot that night and the week of sex I'd had with her had been like no other week of my life.

Her eyes said she wasn't thinking about that. She was thinking about the things I'd done after that, and they told her not to believe in me. I wasn't even sure she was attracted to me any more. Maybe she no longer felt the pull like I did. Maybe I'd entirely smothered her lust torch by ignoring her—

'The highest risk is that on Monday you'll completely ignore me.'

'Okay, so what's the likelihood?'

'High. Very high.'

'Low. I'm not even asking you away for an isolated weekend; I want this to be something. Dating. Going out. A relationship. Whatever label you want to stick on it. We'll have to play it cool because Sharon is a bitch on a mission, but that doesn't stop us seeing each other outside work now I have everything sorted with Daisy and I promise I don't expect sex this weekend.'

She sighed. 'But you didn't ask me about the impact, and the impact is still very high. You hurt me. A lot.'

That punched me in the middle. Her emotions were involved… Did it scare me? No. But I'd never had anything with someone who really cared. I'd kidded myself with Sharon, and maybe she'd kidded herself with me. But I didn't think any of our emotions had been genuine or had any depth.

But I knew what love could feel like – my heart was all tangled up with Daisy. 'I can't change the impact, Ivy, but I swear, I don't want you to be hurt. I just want to spend time with you… I don't know. I feel like we had something special at Christmas.'

She stared me.

'Next risk…'

She blinked. Her long, dark lashes dropping and lifting. Then her lavender eyes focused on me again, glistening. Did she have tears in her eyes?

'That's the only risk, and Christmas was special for me too, but it feels like a long time ago.'

'I know. But there's been no one since you, Ivy. Am I worth the risk, then? Will you give me another chance?'

She sighed. 'Give me a minute to decide. I still don't think the likelihood is low. More like medium to high. You have a reputation to take into account.'

'Yes, which I established before I knew I had a daughter, and when I had a grasping, manipulative, gold-digging, party animal for a wife. I've turned over a new leaf. I don't even smoke dope any more. I haven't since I've been seeing Daisy on Sundays. The last time was New Year's Eve—'

'Do you see Daisy every week? Will you—'

'No, I told you, the court agreement is every other weekend, so you and I have alternate weekends, and every evening in the week, if you want them.'

She looked away from me and sipped from her mug of cheap coffee.

'If we're going to date and you expect me to spend any time up here, though, I'm buying you a cafetière and some proper fucking coffee.'

That cracked open her smile.

'Come on, Ivy. Come away with me. I've booked us into a hotel. Give me a second chance.' I leaned forward and gripped her thigh because I couldn't take her hand – it was wrapped around the mug. 'Please?'

'Jack Rendell, saying please…'

'I keep saying please to you, you just don't listen. And, yes, it tells you how much I want you. Give me a chance. I'm crap at chasing women. I don't have to do it. I never bother with women

223

that aren't into me. So again, more proof. You're different. You're special. I'm chasing you and you're worth the chase and the pleading.'

She got up and tipped the last of her coffee into the sink, then left the mug in the sink and turned around, holding the side behind her. Her lips twisted sideways and her thin, plucked brows arched. 'Okay, I think you're worth the risk. But just to be safe, I'm agreeing on no sex.'

Excitement leapt in my chest like I was a kid; like Daisy spotting something pink and sparkly. I stood up. 'God, I'm glad you said yes, otherwise I'd have wasted a pile of money on that hotel.' I held her waist and leant to kiss her. She slapped my shoulder but she didn't try avoid it. My lips pressed on to hers and hers pressed back with firm agreement.

I patted her bottom when I broke the kiss. 'Get a bag packed. Then let's go. And I'll write you a contract in the services if you like, no sex.'

She threw me a smile, which, now she'd made her decision, looked a little excited too.

I sat on the bed as she pulled out a bag and then opened the one wardrobe she had in the room – then she looked at me. 'Dressy or non-dressy.'

'Both, we'll eat dinner somewhere nice, maybe, but we're going to the coast. We're going to Lyme Regis. Expect to be walking along a pebble beach, so you'll not be doing it in heels.'

'But you don't expect me to climb the cliff.'

I laughed at her. 'No. No cliffs.'

When she'd packed the bag, I picked it up to carry it downstairs for her. She held the door for me to pass, then pulled it shut and pushed on it to check it was shut and when she past her post box she weirdly pushed on that too.

'You, okay?'

'Yeah.' Her voice sounded bright and dismissive, but there was some undercurrent beneath it.

'Ivy?' A guy walked out of the ground-floor flat. A tall, lanky guy. 'Are you going out?'

He gave me a hard look, as if to say, who are you?

What the fuck?

'I'm going away for the weekend, Greg.'

'I'll look out for your flat, then.'

'The flat will look out for itself,' I answered. It wasn't a cat.

Ivy gripped the sleeve of my leather jacket. 'Thanks, Greg. See you next week.' She pulled me out the door.

'Who was that?'

Her eyebrows lifted in a 'shut up' gesture. 'My landlord.'

'The guy's strange.'

'He's okay. I ignore him mostly.'

I unlocked the car and encouraged her to get in while I put her bag in the boot.

When I looked up, before I walked around to the driver's side, I noticed her landlord looking out of the window. Weirdo.

As I got into the car when I looked ahead I saw a man standing on the corner at the end of the street, illuminated in the light from a lamp post. He was more worrying. He had his hood up and his hands buried in his pockets. It felt like he was watching us; certainly he was facing us. But I couldn't see his face – his hood hung down over his eyes, so I couldn't tell if he really was looking at us.

When I drove past him, as we left the street, he pulled his hood further forward and held it in place, as if he was hiding, but he turned, as though his gaze followed the car.

'Do you know that guy?' I pointed over my shoulder with my thumb.

Ivy looked back through the gap in the seats, but the man was probably totally obscured by his hood.

'Who. Why?' She sounded concerned.

'I thought he was watching us, that's all.'

'Why?'

'I'm sure he was looking at us getting in the car. It's probably nothing.' Or I'd led Sharon's spies to her door.

Ivy looked ahead and swallowed. I saw the movement in her throat out of the corner of my eye. 'You okay?' She looked nervous.

She swallowed again and looked ahead. 'It's nothing.'

'What's nothing?' I stopped at lights and touched her knee while three women crossed the road.

She glanced over, but I had to look back at the road when the lights changed.

'Someone took the post out of my post box and read it and I keep feeling like someone's following me.'

'What? Why didn't you tell me?'

'You weren't talking to me. Why would I tell you?'

Because… There was no reason. Shit. 'I told you about Sharon's investigator.'

'But you haven't been seeing me, so why would it be anything to do with Sharon. I feel like I have a stalker.'

'Have you told the police?'

'Yes, they confirmed someone opened the letters, but they had no match for the fingerprints, so what could they do? They told me to be careful and call if anything happened.'

'Has anything else happened?'

'No, but I have this creepy feeling all the time.'

'Well, someone followed me home from work one night this week. I think that was Sharon's private investigator and she knew someone had been to the cottage with me, so it could be that. But if it is, they wouldn't hurt you. Just be sensible.'

'I know. I don't need you to tell me. I have been.'

But I didn't feel comfortable about it. The man at the end of her road had been a big guy. I'd have to tell John. Maybe he could get a legal block on what Sharon was up to. It was going too far. But the call to John could wait until Monday. We were going to be miles away from London.

We walked into the hotel lobby at about ten-thirty. The place was all wood panelling, creaky floors and wonky ceilings. When I pressed the bell on the counter the hotel manager arrived to greet us with a smile. He had someone carry our bags up to the room while he booked us in and I signed the paperwork. Then he gave us the directions to find the room. We were in a room that looked down on the high street, facing a shop that had a massive tyrannosaurus rex skeleton head lit up in the window.

I walked over to the long sash window and leaned a shoulder on the wall next to it.

'It's like Jurassic Park...' Ivy walked up behind me and her hand touched my arm. When we'd been away before her hands would have slipped around my middle and her head would have rested against the back of my shoulder. I'd missed her touches.

I turned to face her, longing to kiss her thoroughly and get her clothes off. But we'd agreed no sex. I needed to be patient.

'They call it the Jurassic Coast – there's fossils in them there cliffs.'

She laughed at the accent I put on, but definitely at me, not with me.

Even though it was late, I decided to go out. 'Come on, change your shoes and let's go for a walk along the front and see what it's like. It's ages since I've been to the seaside.'

She looked at her watch, then lifted her eyebrows.

'It'll be more fun this late. There'll be hardly anyone around.'

Chapter 16

I held Jack's hand tightly as we walked along the pebbles in the darkness. The stones shifted and rolled awkwardly under my feet.

The sea roared beside us each time a wave washed up on to the pebbles and dragged them around, then rolled back out. Moonlight glistened on the sea further out, catching the sway of the waves and then the white foam when the waves broke on to the beach.

I hadn't been to the seaside for years. I'd forgotten the thrilling feeling when you heard the waves, and how the air tasted and felt different. Refreshing. 'I love this.'

At the edge of the beach on our right there was a long row of old houses looking out to sea, with a road in front of them. They looked like dolls' houses in the electric lamps, which were decorated with ammonite shapes. It was all a little magical. 'I wasn't even sure this morning I was going to come away with you. I left work because I'd made up my mind I wouldn't.' I looked sideways at him. 'I'm glad I'm here. This is such a beautiful place. I'd forgotten how great the seaside is. You feel in awe, don't you? Like we did in the Lake District.'

'Yes.' His hand gave mine a squeeze. 'I know what you mean, and that's why Christmas was so good. Because we feel the same.

I was being serious when I said I want to keep seeing you. You get life like I do.'

That wasn't true. 'Not like you do.'

'Okay there are differences, but I told you, I'm changing. I'm more responsible.' He gave me a smile. 'Mum would say, at last.'

Maybe he was changing. He'd spent most of the journey here talking about his daughter. He'd turned his spare room into her room, and it was now a pink flower garden, apparently. He'd said he didn't smoke dope any more too.

I didn't want him to change completely, though. I liked the man who arrived with a suitcase already packed and dragged me away to places that were beautiful. My heart thumped just as much as it had when we'd gone away at Christmas. I liked him being heart-pumping, and breathtaking; they were the things that had persuaded me to give him a second chance – and there was a king-size four-poster bed in our room at the hotel. I kept seeing it and wondering if I was going to let anything happen in it.

He turned me around and hauled me into a hug, then kissed me hard, his palm bracing the back of my head.

It felt like coming home, like a part of me had lain dormant and dead for all the weeks we hadn't been speaking, and now it came to life again. I'd been waiting for him to kiss me properly.

I slid my tongue into his mouth as the sound of the sea roared around us, washing up on to the beach. 'Ah!' My Converse were drenched as it swept right up over our feet. He gripped me about the waist in a bear hug and lifted me up. I bent my legs back to make it easier as he carried me higher up the beach, laughing.

When he set me back down on my feet literally, figuratively I was still floating. His hands pressed either side of my head and he kissed me again, like he was the thirstiest man alive and I was his only source of water.

My heart thundered, but it was a beautiful dance rhythm.

When we broke apart he said on a breath into my mouth. 'Shall we walk back?'

'Yes.' I thought of the bed but we'd agreed no sex, and I knew he'd honour it, and sex would raise the risk of this going wrong. But adrenaline rushed in my blood at the thought of taking that risk.

Our room was huge and old-fashioned, with a high ceiling and an ornate plaster cornice about the walls, and at the centre of the uneven floor was the huge dark-wood, four-poster bed. I was in awe of this room too, but he wasn't. This luxury was normal to him.

I watched him take his jumper and shirt off, my heart racing. He had his back to me. 'Jack.'

He turned around. 'Yeah.'

'You know we said no sex…'

He didn't answer, just looked at me.

'I want to take the risk.' If I was a fool, so what? I still fancied him.

When he came towards me it was as if no time had passed since Christmas. His fingers clasped in my hair, holding my head steady as he kissed me. Then, after a moment, his fingers were pulling my jumper up and taking it off, then undoing my jeans, and before I knew it we were tangled up in bed. But in the bed it wasn't like the early days we'd spent together when we'd gone away; it was like the last night.

He used his mouth to make me come once, as I gripped his shoulders and writhed under the onslaught of his particular brand of passion and intensity. Then he knelt over me. His pale-blue eyes bright. He'd left the light on tonight and he was as awe-inspiring as the sea, and the Lakes. I'd felt it at Christmas, but having known this and lost it, the emotion in me was triple the strength it had been then. I was excited, grateful that he'd come back to me, but terrified he'd step away again.

He urged my legs open wider with a knock on each thigh. Then he looked down and watched himself press into me.

'Ah.' It was bliss. I'd loved having sex with him before. I loved it now.

He smiled down at me, his hands pressing into the mattress either side of my head, above my shoulders, his arms only a little bent so he was raised above me, as if he was doing press-ups while he pushed in. It was the second time we'd done it in the missionary position. There was nothing wrong with the missionary position when it felt like this. In fact, maybe it was now my favourite position because I could look into his eyes.

'I love your eyes,' he said it to me like he'd read my mind. 'They're the most amazing colour. You know they're lavender.'

'I know.'

'Of course you do. They're beautiful.'

He was moving with a slow rhythm; it was the second time we'd done it without music too, without a set rhythm.

His gaze dropped to watch himself entering me, again. I guess that was what men liked, the porn show. I liked looking at the muscle in his chest and his shoulders, and his arms – and when his head lifted, I liked looking at his mouth and into his eyes.

My fingers held his biceps as he moved and the sensations inside became tangled up with the things I was hearing, seeing and feeling outside my body, as his weight pressed against my hips when he filled me, joining the rhythm of the bed creaking and our breathing breaking the quietness of the room. Everything combined to create something all-absorbing and overwhelming. I came not just because of his movement in me, but because of the aura in the air around us.

He was breathing hard when I was aware of anything again, and watching my face not our bodies as he shoved into me with firm thrusts, his pelvis striking mine and making my breasts rock and the bed jolt against the wall – and it was a sturdy bed. My thighs were going to ache in the morning.

'Jack.' His name was a word of acclamation.

He came with one last hard thrust, then he pulled out just slightly so I could feel his tip pulsing.

I grasped his head, my fingers buried in his hair and watched his expression. He'd shut his eyes and it looked as though he clenched his teeth, because the muscle in his jaw was taut.

Feelings broke inside me like a rushing, rolling white wave, washing up on to the beach with a roar. I wanted to call the feelings love. But he'd messed me around for months; I couldn't call it love. That would be stupid.

Something hit my arm. 'Hey, sleepy-head.'

I opened my eyes. I was tired, and achy. We'd had sex for hours. I think he'd come four times. I'd come about twenty times. The people in the next room probably hated us – the bed had been creaking half the night.

'I think every beautiful lady deserves breakfast in bed. Sit up.'

He was standing beside the bed, wearing loose, thick cotton pyjama bottoms, and no top, and he looked gorgeous. I could go another round, even though my legs ached. But food and coffee would be nice. I sat up, pulling the sheet and blankets up so they covered my breasts and tucked the covers under my arms as he set the tray over my lap. Then he got into bed with his own tray.

'There's loads on here.'

'I wasn't sure what you'd want, so I ordered everything.'

'What time is it?'

'Eleven. I didn't want to wake you up early, but I want to go down to the sea.'

'So do I.'

Once we'd eaten breakfast he chased me out of bed and we went down to the sea front. It was different in the day; busier, and the energy from the sea seemed stronger, and the vastness of it was clearer. It was a beautiful day, the sky was blue and it was even warm enough to take our gloves off in the sun.

We walked all the way along the beach to the serenade of the pebbles rolling around in the waves, and then we reached a little corner that was sand, where a few people were playing with dogs, tossing balls into the waves. We walked on around the cob, right to the end of the ancient harbour.

The last part, the truly old part, was cobbled, slippery and slanted, and the waves crashed over the top, catching the seagulls that were balanced on the end of it.

Jack had a hold of my hand and he kept walking when I would have turned back.

'We could get washed off...'

'In a storm maybe; it's just blowy. If it was really dangerous they'd have it blocked off.'

He yanked my hand and made me move. My heart pumped quicker, in the way he had of calling it into a particular rhythm.

I followed his lead, but when we were showered with the salty spray from a wave crashing against the other side I turned and hugged his waist, ducking my head.

He laughed. 'Chicken.' Then he grabbed my hand and pulled me into motion again, making me run on the uneven, slippery cobbles until we reached the end.

Dangerous Jack Rendell. Captain Control. He probably believed he could even order the sea not to do anything to hurt us. I held his waist again as he stood looking out at the waves crashing over the rocks and sending up spray.

'It makes you feel like a king watching nature.'

He'd kept saying things like that at Christmas. But I knew what he meant. 'Nature is probably the most awesome form of art.'

He looked at me as my head lifted from his shoulder. 'We're going to have to remember that for an advert. I'm sure there'll be ideas in there somewhere.'

I nodded.

'Come on. Let's get something to eat, then we'll walk along the bottom of the cliffs and see if we can find any Jurassic sea monsters.'

Something to eat turned out to be a small shell of prepared crab meat, which we bought from one of the old huts that the fishing boats in the harbour supplied. We sat and ate on the harbour wall, watching the waves smashing up against it beneath our feet. Then we walked down on to the beach on the other side of the harbour and along beside the cliffs, where numerous fossils had been found over the years.

'I heard you can break the pebbles open and there's fossils in them.' Jack started picking up the pebbles.

I walked up to the cliffs. 'Oh my God. The cliffs are warm and damp. Feel this.' It was weirdest rock I'd ever felt.

Jack set his palm near mine and laughed. 'Definitely not climbing. That feels horrible.'

'What is it?'

'Clay.'

'It's gross.'

'Yeah. It breaks up easily. Good for finding fossils; bad for climbing.'

The cliff was in soft layers and it just crumbled when you touched it.

We spent hours walking along there looking for fossils but we didn't find one.

When we walked back, I was tired and achy but in a wonderful way. It had been a good day, even better than Christmas, because we'd talked more. We'd talked about family and friends, and all the stuff we didn't know about each other.

When we neared the road that would lead us back to the hotel there was a wonderful smell of frying fish in the air. I gripped Jack's hand with both of mine. 'Let's not have a posh dinner, let's have fish and chips. You have to have fish and chips at the seaside. It's illegal not to.'

It stirred memories of childhood holidays as we queued, following the line in the shop around.

My tummy growled when Jack ordered cod and chips twice. I smothered mine in vinegar, then sprinkled the salt over them, then took the wrapped parcel of heaven outside to find a bench to sit on, where we could look out at the sea and eat them with our little wooden forks.

'I'm going to label this one of the best moments of my life.' I swallowed my first delicious mouthful of battered cod. 'God, this is amazing.'

'I know.'

What followed was lots of sounds of pleasure, along with some shivers, as it was cold now the sun was disappearing beyond the horizon at the far edge of the sea. But the sunset made the moment even more magical. I added it to my bank of memories to keep.

Jack scrunched up his empty packet. 'That was a good call. They were the best fish and chips I've ever eaten.'

I screwed my packet up, although I hadn't eaten them all. I was full. 'I bet you never normally eat fish and chips.'

He smiled at me and took my packet, then threw it in a bin nearby. 'No, but I'll start if they taste as good as that.'

'London fish and chips never taste as good as that. That is the magic of the seaside.'

'Where do you want to go now? Seeing as you are into making me slum it.'

I stuck my tongue out at him. Then pointed at a pub behind the fish-and-chip shop. 'Let's go in there for a pint.'

It was an old-fashioned pub. The people at the bar looked like they had roots growing into their bar stools they were so at home in their seats, and of course Jack stood out. His clothes made him look rich. He was preened and perfect, even though he dressed down most of the time. The guys in there stared at him when he leaned on the bar and called for the bartender to serve him.

I didn't want trouble, but I fancied a normal drink in a normal place.

Jack looked back at me when the barman came over. 'What do you want?'

'I fancy Guinness. I'll have a pint of Guinness.'

Jack looked at the guy. 'A pint of Guinness, and what local ales do you serve?'

When he pulled out his wallet to pay, I hoped it wasn't loaded with cash. It wasn't the sort of place to be loaded with cash.

We took our pints over to a table for four near the back of the pub and sat down. 'Do you drink in places like this?'

'Ivy, I'm human. Of course.'

'With who?'

'With the guys I climb with mainly.'

An old couple sat next to us and we began talking to them. They had a little black poodle they'd got from a rescue place. I cuddled the poodle.

Then someone put 'Delilah' on the jukebox and the pub full of people began singing along. I sang too as loudly and raucously as everyone else. Jack laughed at me, then started singing, and then we were no longer outsiders. The sing-along progressed into another song, and then another. I went and picked a couple of songs on the jukebox.

It was fun. Normal. The pub, the conversation and the music were good and we drank three pints. It was a really good night, because it had been so spontaneous and unexpected, and when we walked out a couple of the people at the bar lifted their hands to say goodbye.

It wasn't far to get back to the hotel. I walked it with Jack's arm hanging around my shoulders.

He felt like mine and I treated him like that when we got back to the room. I climbed on top of him, with no belt to tie him up. It was just my body teasing his, my fingers, and lips and tongue, and other parts…

'Hey.' Jack's voice woke me as his fingers stroked through my hair. 'Do you want to go for a walk on another beach to watch the sunrise?'

I loved Jack's view of life, his way of life. So maybe he'd been right on Friday – I was like him in a way.

I nodded, blinking the sleep out of my eyes to see him. It was still dark.

I'd slept deeply. I couldn't remember anything from the moment I'd lain down on his chest after we'd had sex until now. In fact, I'd been on top of him then so at some point he'd pushed me off on to my back. But he'd made the best mattress.

We shared the shower, hurrying to get to the beach before the sun rose.

He drove around the coastal road to Charmouth. It was entirely different to Lyme Regis; the sea front wasn't built up at all and the beach wasn't all pebbles, either.

The sun peered over the horizon as we pulled into the car park. I yawned and stretched before we got out of the car. I'd put my walking boots on at the hotel. He changed into his with the boot of the car up.

We walked across a bridge over a river that ran out into the sea. Ducks swam around on the clear water. Then we walked around past a closed kiosk, through the dry sand, to face miles and miles of beautiful cliffs, glowing sand and endless sea. It was a pretty view, highlighted in the first red light of dawn. The tide was right out and we walked down to the shore line, which revealed a layer of dark-grey rock, and oh my God. When I looked down at our feet, every so often there were fossils, embedded in the stone.

'Wow.' I laughed.

'Look at this one.' It was an ammonite; bigger than Jack's boot. A wave rolled in and the last of it swilled over Jack's foot and over the fossil.

'This is amazing. I'm so glad we came down here.'

'I know. Someone told me about this place when we were in the pub. But they said to get down here early, while the tide was out.'

The only other people here were a couple who were way ahead of us in long wax jackets carrying a spade. They looked like proper fossil-hunters.

A Jack Russell dog ran along beside them.

'I'm going to have to bring Daisy here. She has to see this.' Jack's eyes always brightened when he spoke about his daughter. He looked at me, his hand squeezing mine. 'I want her to meet you, but we'll have to give it time. I can't introduce you for a little while. When she stays over for her first weekend she's going to meet her new grandma and granddad – that's all arranged, but I'm taking everything slowly. We're moving at her pace.'

I knew nothing about kids. 'I guess that's wise.'

He gave me a smile and we carried on walking.

When we went back to the hotel we ate lunch then packed up our stuff and loaded up the car. I didn't want to leave. I didn't want to go back to work and my reticence was worse than after Christmas because I felt as if Jack would slip through my fingers when we were back in the office, away from another awesome place. I thought maybe it was beautiful places that made Jack like he was with me, and in the office it would change again.

When we got to my apartment, he carried my case up for me.

'Do you want to come in and stay for coffee?'

'For your coffee… uh-uh, thanks, but I'll pass.'

'For anything else, then.'

He laughed and hugged me, his arms wrapping around my shoulders. Then he kissed me, a hard press of lips, before whispering in my ear. 'Thanks for the temptation but I need to be on my game tomorrow at work. I have some stuff to do. I'd better go. I'll see you in the morning.'

I caught his arm before he could turn away. 'Please don't ignore me tomorrow.'

'I'm not going to.'

We shared another, more amorous, kiss. Then he left me. When I'd shut the door, I called Milly and poured out all the details of the weekend.

Someone was doing that 'Lord of the Dance' jig in my tummy when I woke up, I was so nervous. I'd dreamt that Jack ignored me. I'd dreamt of him in his office, refusing to look at me. I looked at my phone to check the time. Seven. It was time to get up.

It was time to go to work and discover my fate.

Was Jack going to be true to his word – or not?

I rolled on to my back. There was a text on my phone, from Rick, it must have come in late last night. 'Are you still up for a drink on Thursday night?'

'Yes. Sure. No worries.'

I got up and showered, then blow-dried my hair and did my makeup.

Seeing as it was spring, and also maybe to prod Jack a little, I put on the chequered trousers he'd told me he liked, with a thin purple sweater that matched my hair, then slipped my feet into my black-patent heels.

My heart thumped when I hurried downstairs. I loved that Jack was a heart-pounding guy, but I wished I didn't have to feel afraid. I wished I had more faith in him. But then faith had to be earned and he'd kicked it away.

'Ivy!' Greg was coming out of his door.

'Greg.' I turned around.

'A man was looking for you at the weekend, he didn't give a name, but when you didn't answer the intercom he was asking if I knew where you were. I'm sure I've seen him here before.'

'Oh.' Who?

'I told him you were away. I hope that was okay. He said he'd call again. He said he was a friend.'

I nodded. I didn't know what to say. *My stalker?* Had he called here? It gave me the shivers.

There was only one man I knew, though, who might call here and say he was a friend. When I left the house I called Rick. 'Hi—'

'Hi, I got your reply about Thursday. Same time, same place, yeah?'

'Yes. But…'

'What?'

239

'Did you call at my place over the weekend?'

'No. Why?'

'I was away and someone was asking for me.'

'Not me. I was at Steve's most of the weekend watching rugby. You sound upset about it, are you okay? It wasn't a problem?'

'No. No. Not really, I just wondered. It's just weird, I don't know anyone else who'd call on me.'

'Neither do I. But if you're feeling nervous, if this man comes back, if it's a problem, you can call me?'

'Thanks, Rick, but I'll be alright.'

'I'll see you on Thursday.'

'Yes. Bye.'

'Bye.'

I thought of the man Jack had seen on the corner. Someone had definitely checked my post and now someone, who didn't want to leave a name, had been looking for me here. Maybe my stalker joke was not a joke?

On the escalator down to the platform at the tube station I thought I saw the guy again; the one I kept seeing, a few meters behind me, but I didn't see him on the platform, it was too busy, and I didn't see him on the tube either. When I got off, I looked over my shoulder about ten times on the walk to work.

When I reached the building and navigated the revolving doors into the ground-floor reception, my heart set up a bass-beat rhythm. What would Jack do?

The room was full. I was one of the last to arrive.

Jack was in his office.

I took a breath and tried to breathe as though this was nothing. Like any other Monday. Only this Monday I'd walked into the office having spent the weekend having sex with the boss.

When I sat down, I glanced into Jack's office. He was on the phone. He didn't see me look.

I took another breath to calm my nerves and switched my laptop on.

240

An email popped up a minute after my inbox had opened. 'Good morning, beautiful.'

My heart did a little victory leap.

I checked no one had read it over my shoulder, then sent back a smiley face. I was so happy I went into the Monday-morning meeting grinning like *Alice in Wonderland's*, Cheshire Cat.

Chapter 17

I smiled broadly at Ivy when she came into the room for the meeting. She threw me a big smile back and it never left her face. She grinned at me while I tried to talk without looking at her constantly. She'd really feared I'd ignore her. I shouldn't have done it before; it had been an error of judgement, but it couldn't have happened even if I'd wanted to now. She was in my blood, like a drug. I'd had an injection over the weekend. I was now a sworn addict. I wasn't going to let there be any distance between us again. She did things to my stomach, made it all wobbly, made my head feel like it did when I circled on a roundabout with Daisy, and my chest a mashed up mess of feelings.

When I'd thought I'd been in love with Sharon, my feelings had been lust for the different sort of sex and greed for the rush of rule-breaking. I'd been a naïve-idiot and self-absorbed. Thank God Daisy had come along and given me the push I'd needed to walk away from that life.

I glanced at Ivy and caught her gaze, then smiled again. She gave me a nod when she stood up to walk out of the room. I looked down. She'd worn the chequered trousers that made her bottom look exquisite.

Wow.

When I got back to my office I sent her another email. 'Will you come into my office?'

She got up and walked around the desks, her bottom swaying. She looked really good today.

She pushed the door open, a pad and pen in one hand, then closed it, looking back to check it had shut before looking at me with a quirky smile. 'Yes, boss. How can I help?'

'Well, you could help by taking those trousers off, that you know I love, and come over here, unbutton my trousers and sit on my lap. But that may wind us both up arrested for indecent exposure. So I guess, aside from that, I want us to tell Em what's going on, together, if you're up for it?'

'Oh, okay.' She sat down as though she deflated into the seat. 'It's better she knows.'

'I know. I just… It'll be weird. But I agree.'

I leant forward, resting my elbows on my desk. 'There's something else I need to tell you first, though.'

She nodded.

It was strange to have her on the other side of the desk when I wasn't talking work. I wanted to be closer to her, especially as what I had to say wasn't nice. 'Ruth on reception downstairs told me a man came in and asked where I was on Saturday. I've called my lawyer; John is on to it. But… If Sharon works out I'm involved with you and she tries to contact you, don't get caught up in any discussion with her. She can be nasty. Not life-threating, or dangerous, but she'll chew you up and spit you out with words. Don't bother getting into a verbal battle with her, just put the phone down.'

Ivy sat forward in the chair. 'Jack…' The words seemed to dry up on her tongue and her eyes shone, with the concern showing on her face. Her eyes had changed colour too; the lavender became greyer.

'What?'

'Someone was looking for me too. They asked at the flats. Do you think that was Sharon's investigator?'

'Was it a man?'

'Yes.'

'Was he big?'

'I didn't ask what he looked like.'

'The guy I saw at the end of your street was tall and big built, and the guy that came here was too. It was probably the PI. I'll call John again and get him to have another go at Sharon's solicitor. But, Ivy, leave early and tell the police about it too, just in case it's not what we think and it's some random man, and if you're worried, call me. I don't care if it's late, whatever, call.'

She smiled, telling me I'd said the right thing.

But it wasn't only for her benefit that I'd said it. Captain Control wanted to be all over this. I needed her to be safe – needed not wanted – any idea of her not being safe made a sharp pain stab into my chest. I breathed in. But she lived over half an hour away from me. 'And if you're really concerned, call the police and then me. Yeah?'

'I will.' Her hand lifted shakily and tucked her hair behind her ear. She was scared. If it was Sharon, she needn't be. Sharon was annoying and embarrassing, but she wasn't physically violent. For the first time in my life I hoped Sharon was up to something.

'Are you okay if we call Em in? We can put it off for a day or two, if you'd rather wait, but I want her to know, and I think it's better it comes from both of us.'

She bit her lip before smiling slightly. It was not the wide grin she'd had on her face all through the meeting, it was self-conscious, as if she didn't have that much faith in how long *us* was going to last. 'I can't sit down, though. I feel weird sitting down on the other side of the desk from you.'

I gave her a smile. 'It feels weird for me too.' I wanted us to last, I really did. Other good things that I had in my life had lasted. This could too.

She stood up and walked over to look out of the window. I picked up the phone, but I didn't dial, my head became full of memories from New Year's Eve. But that had been weeks ago. I was a different man, even from then.

'Do you want to go out with me Wednesday night? We could take the bike and ride out of London somewhere for a meal in a pub?' She glanced back. 'Do you still have the leathers and the helmet I bought you?'

'Yes.'

'Then Wednesday, I'll pick you up at six-thirty and we'll ride out of London.' I looked back at the phone and dialled Em's extension.

'Hi, could you come in here for a minute?'

'Sure. See you in five seconds.'

She obviously hadn't noticed Ivy was in here because when she walked through the door she stopped. 'Oh, sorry, Ivy. I didn't realise you two were talking.'

Ivy smiled awkwardly. 'It's okay.'

Em hesitated, as though she expected Ivy to leave, but when Ivy didn't move, Em shut the door. She looked at me.

'I want to talk to you, Em. Well, I wanted us to talk to you.' I stood up, because they were both standing. 'Ivy and I are seeing each other outside work. We don't want everyone to know yet, but we wanted to tell you.' I looked at Ivy. By choice I'd have lifted my arm and let her come to me so I could hold her, but there was a glass wall in front of us which everyone else could look through. She bit her lip.

I looked back at Em. It was important to me that Em got this – as my business partner and my friend.

She looked shocked. She looked like she'd murder me, but I wanted her to understand – this wasn't a fling.

'It's your choice.' She said to me. Trying not to hurt Ivy's feelings, I guess. 'You're happy, Ivy?'

Ivy nodded.

I suppose, as we were her employers, this must be painfully uncomfortable for Ivy.

'Well then, I'm happy for you. I hope it works out. Was that all, Jack?'

'Yes.'

A sharp nod tilted Em's head, but when she turned she gave me a slight shake of her head.

As soon as she'd left, Ivy said, 'I'd better get back to work too. I'll see you Wednesday.'

'Yes, but I'll call you after work tonight.'

'Okay.'

When I sat down, the arrival of an email chimed on my desktop – from Em. 'I hope you know what you're doing. If you offend or hurt one of our best people, I'm going to string you up, Jack, and not by the neck.'

I laughed and sent her a reply email with a smiley face. Then I rang John on his personal number.

'Hello, Jack, what is it?'

'We have to get that decree nisi in. I want things over and done with.'

'You know we've found some holdings in Sharon's name. You need to give us time to investigate.'

'Two weeks. That's all. I cannot give you any more. She's been harassing Ivy already.'

'You'll risk losing a lot more than you should if you push for two weeks.'

'I don't care.'

'Okay, I'll see what I can do.'

'Then, after that I just have to wait six weeks, right? And then I can have the absolute and that's it, all done?'

'Yes.'

Then all my ties with Sharon would be broken. 'But, John, you need to tell her lawyer that she's been spying on me again, and she needs to stop. My new girlfriend and I have had people asking after us.'

He sighed. 'Okay. I'll tell him.'

246

When I finished the call, I rang Tina. 'Would you bring in the files I need for the meeting?'

'Sure, Jack.'

'Thanks.'

Chapter 18

The intercom buzzed. I breathed in. I was wearing the leather all-in-one Jack had bought me. I pressed the talk button. 'Hi, Jack.'

'Hi. You ready?'

'Yes, I'll come down.'

'No, wait. I'll come up to you. I want to tell you something first.'

I let him in the door downstairs and I could hear him running upstairs when he got near. I opened the door before he reached it. He was in his leather all-in-one too, carrying his helmet. He looked sexy like that, edgy.

'What is it?'

'Go into your room and sit down a minute.'

'Why?'

'If you go in and sit down, I'll tell you.'

I backed up and let him in, standing in the small kitchen area.

'Sit, Ivy.'

I did, but. 'Why?'

'I had a conversation with my lawyer before I left work. Sharon claims she hasn't had anyone tailing either of us.' He leaned a shoulder against the wall. 'I think she's lying. I still think it's her. But there's always the outside chance it really is some random guy stalking you. I just… I wanted to tell you to be careful.'

'You said that the other day.'

'I know. But I'm worried about you.'

So was I; I didn't need him spooking me more. I stood up. 'Okay. Can we go now?'

He smiled as his arm came up, then his fingers gently held the back of my neck and gave it a comforting squeeze. 'Yes.' His hand was still on my neck as I walked downstairs, with him walking two steps behind me.

When we got down to the hall, Greg was there. He looked at me as I came down the last flight of stairs, then looked behind me at Jack. But he must have seen Jack arrive and known I'd let him in. I swear Greg spent hours looking out of the window watching everyone come and go. 'Nice bike,' he said to Jack.

'Thanks,' Jack answered, his hand letting go of my neck as we both walked into the hall.

Annoyingly, Greg stood directly in front of us, preventing us from walking out.

He looked at me. 'You riding pillion, Ivy?'

'That's the plan,' Jack gave another short snappy answer, that really said, *fuck off and get out of the way*.

'Have you had any more ideas about who that man was?' Greg asked me.

He'd been asking every night when I got in if I'd heard anything from my friend who'd come round. 'No.'

'And we're just on our way out,' Jack pushed.

Greg looked at him. 'Okay, mate.' There was, a *no need to get annoyed* pitch in his words. 'Have a good time,' he said, looking at me. Then he stepped out of the way.

Jack clasped my arm and led me past Greg.

When the door shut behind us, he said, 'Your landlord creeps me out.'

'I think he is harmless, just annoying.'

I looked along the street both ways about six times as Jack got on the bike and lifted it off the stand. I didn't see anyone odd. I put my helmet on.

I was suddenly very glad I lived in an attic flat – at least I needn't worry about anyone looking through my windows.

I climbed onto the back of his bike. It was the first time I'd been on a proper, big, bike with him. I wrapped my arms around his waist, holding on.

'Hold me nice and tight,' he said through his helmet.

'Uh huh.'

'I won't go fast until you're used to it. Okay?'

'Yeah.'

I wasn't ready at all. I was terrified. I turned my head sideways so my helmet pressed against his shoulder. He started the engine and revved it. My stomach lurched when he pulled away. But as he rode out of the street, my mind was on trying to spot my stalker as much as thinking about the bike. I didn't see any big guy standing around looking out of place. But maybe he didn't stalk me every day…

And maybe it wasn't him who had called at the flats – maybe that was a different man. Maybe that *had been* the person investigating Jack. I'd had that sense of being followed for weeks – when I was having nothing to do with Jack and no one had called at the flats then – but they had got in and taken my post.

Jack drove out to Windsor and we ate venison in a pub there. He had a thin long-sleeved top on under his leathers and he stripped his suit off to his waist while we ate. Half the women in the pub stared at him all the time we were in there because, with the tight top hugging his chest and his midriff, and his leathers gripping his legs, he looked like the fittest man alive. If we were going to keep seeing each other I'd have to get used to other women staring at him.

But I hadn't worn anything under my leather onesie thing except a bra. So while all the women ogled him, I sat there eating in my biker gear, despite Jack continually telling me to unzip the front at least, 'It won't matter, it's just like a bikini.'

'In March…'

He had changed since Christmas – he was more relaxed. But he still had a dirty, dark humour; after every other mouthful, I was given a look and then there was a comment. 'Go on pull the zip down just a little bit, *for me*…' 'What colour bra do you have on under there, anyway.' 'I bet the guys in here would pay you just to pull the zip down seven inches.'

I silenced him in the end with a smack on the arm. 'Shut up.'

He laughed.

What I didn't tell him was that his persistent teasing was making me horny, although it was partly to do with the fact I'd been ogling him as much as the rest of the women in the pub. All I wanted to do was get him home and strip the leathers off his bottom half.

We went for a walk along the riverside after we'd eaten. The Thames wasn't as wide as it was in London or so built up. We walked through a park, gripping our helmets in one hand and holding each other's with the other.

The whole evening was good. But we had work tomorrow, so we didn't drag it out.

When we got back to mine Jack walked inside with me and followed me upstairs.

I glanced back at him. 'I'm not going to get attacked on the stairs.' As soon as we'd ridden back into London my mind had been on whoever was watching me again.

'I'm not thinking about any of that right now – my mind is on other things.' His eyes told me what other things.

I slid the key in the lock and opened the door, my heart skipping at the idea that he'd stop over.

When we got in there he pushed the door shut behind us, then dropped his helmet and took mine and dropped that down too. 'Now I get to see.'

He gripped the end of the zip and yanked it right down, so the leather parted, revealing my fluorescent-green lacy bra and nothing else but skin.

'Wow. You do have a beautiful body. I hope you know that and I hope you know what it does to me…'

'I think I worked that out.'

He kissed my collarbone as his hand snuck inside the leather running about my waist, just feeling my skin. 'Silk.' He breathed against my neck, then he started sucking and biting my skin there gently.

My head fell back against the wall and my body floated into sensation. One of his hands lifted and cupped my breast. The other slid around beneath the leather to grip my bottom, so I had no choice – I had to arch into his grip as his kiss lifted to my mouth.

He made me feel beautiful. The way he craved and hungered for me. I could feel it in his hands and his mouth all the time.

His hand pulled my bra down to one side so that he had access to my breast and then his mouth left mine and instead absorbed my nipple, tugging on it with a hard suck as his hand found my thong instead and slid into the front of it. His other hand was still at the back gripping my bottom.

He carried on sucking my breast as his middle finger slipped into me. I felt like the queen of sex with him. I laughed at the use of one of his favourite sayings and I rocked against his invasion, getting sweaty as his hand on my arse urged me to follow the rhythm he wanted to control.

I guess he'd wound himself up into a horny volcano in the pub too.

When I came, he sighed, looking down like he wanted to get at it with his tongue, but with my leather suit still on he couldn't. He sucked his fingers, then stripped the leathers off me, pulling off my boots and his boots.

'On the bed, on all-fours,' he ordered. The old-style Jack.

252

'Control freak,' I said.

He growled in answer.

I didn't care. This was a part of the old-style Jack I wanted to keep. It was just who he was. He couldn't change who he was. I didn't want him to.

I crawled on to the bed, the last orgasm humming through my nerves. I had my bright-green thong and lacy bra on, and a breast protruding from one cup. He unzipped his leathers and stripped them off the top of his body down to his thighs, and pushed down his boxers, then climbed on the bed behind me.

He was going to do it like that; with his leather suit hanging loose but coating his thighs, and his top still on, and his boxers wrapped around his thighs. He gripped his erection, stroked it in his hand, then rubbed it up against me. 'Ready to begin?' I smiled. He was giving me a little bit of control back, proving again that he had changed a little.

I love you. 'No. Take your top off...' I think the words I spoke disguised the words I was shocked to hear in my head. But they were true. I loved him. Shit... That was a crazy thing to do. To fall in love with him.

He smiled and conceded. My head turned, straining to look back, as he pulled my thong aside and held it aside with a thumb, which pressed into my bottom, then pushed into me. I watched the muscles across his abdomen move beneath his skin. *I love you.* My heart raced, kick-started by adrenaline. Since Christmas Eve Jack had led me into loads of risky things. But falling in love with him was by far the biggest risk.

He looked up and smiled. He was wow. Really wow.

I shut my eyes and drew on all the sensations as his fingers gripped my hips and controlled my movement until I came and then I broke his rhythm because nature had me pushing against him so hard, and paralysed with pleasure. When it died back he had me moving again, and I think it took me three orgasms to finally bring him to his. He came with a low, gravelly sounding shout like a cry of victory.

253

When he withdrew, he tumbled on to my bed and we ended up in a tangle of limbs, Jack still half- clothed. But he didn't move to get up and dress, or undress – he just lay there. His head turned so he looked at me as I looked at him.

I love you, Jack.

Chapter 19

I woke up and looked at the clock on Ivy's cooker. It was two a.m. My limbs were heavy, weighted down by a deep after-sex relaxation. They were also weighed down by Ivy, who was asleep half on top of me in her cramped single bed. 'Hey,' I brushed her shoulder. 'I need to get home. We have work tomorrow.'

She nodded as her eyes opened. The room wasn't too dark, the half-moon was bright and its light seeped through the thin blind she had over the attic window.

When she didn't move, I slid her leg off me and untangled my other leg from between hers. I still had my leather suit half on.

I pulled my boxers up over my sorrowful penis, which would much rather stay with Ivy, then picked up my top and pulled that back on.

Her eyes opened when I stood over her pulling my leathers back on to my arms. I smiled down at her sleepy eyes. I wasn't sure if she was awake or if she was dreaming.

I slid the zip up, pulled my boots on, then picked up my helmet, leant down and whispered over her lips. 'See you at work. Sorry, I have to go.'

'Bye,' she breathed quietly.

'Bye.'

I walked out the door and shut it quietly, but I made sure it locked. Then I ran a hand over my face to try and wake myself up at bit more, before jogging down the stairs, my helmet in one hand, and my other hand on the rail.

'Hey.'

Fuck. There was a guy in the hall, and he was tall and broad, plus the dark blue hoodie he was wearing looked like the hoodie the guy who'd stood on the corner the other night had worn. But I hadn't seen the colour the other night – the electric light had bleached it out. All I'd been able to tell was that it was a dark colour, and a thousand hoodies looked just like it. 'Do you live here?' I challenged, standing at the foot of the stairs, blocking his path, but he didn't try to walk past me. He turned to a post box that was open.

'Yes. I was just coming in. I'm getting my post. But who are you, mate?'

'I was visiting someone.'

He looked at me. 'Yeah…'

I stared at him. He stared at me. He could be the one who was stalking Ivy. The thought that it could be someone inside her block of flats gave me a jolt of alarm like an electric shock. I'd been thinking that she was safe in here, but whoever it was had got access to her post box.

Shit.

'Goodnight,' the guy said as he turned to go upstairs. I think it was a statement to say *you should be going*.

'Goodnight.' There was an awkward moment when neither of us moved, but then he walked on.

I opened the door, but I didn't go out. I held it open, stood still and listened. His footsteps stopped on the first floor and I heard a key turn in a lock and then a door open – and shut.

I walked out.

But if her stalker was someone inside her block of flats, they didn't need to stand on the corner of the street to watch where she went. She'd mocked my controlling nature again tonight, but

256

it was screaming. I wasn't going to trust anyone until I knew what was going on.

I checked that the door lock clicked into place behind me before I walked down the steps.

No one stood in the street, but there was a car down the road with a man huddled up in the front seat. I could see his silhouette formed by the streetlight behind the car. His head was covered, but he must be cold. Maybe it was someone who'd got kicked out of home after an argument. I tried to memorise the number plate just in case. I repeated it five times. But I'd forgotten it ten minutes later as I rode back to mine. I was too tired. I could remember the first three digits, though.

I wrote them down. Then went to bed.

Chapter 20

I set out for work smiling. Happy. Although I looked over my shoulder when I turned the corner out of the street. No one was behind me. I actually didn't feel as though anyone was following me. Maybe it had been Sharon's investigator. Maybe he'd stopped following me now Jack had warned him off.

When I got into work Jack was in his office on the phone. He lifted his free hand off the desk when he saw me to say, *hi*. It was something he might have done for anyone, so it didn't stand out. But once I opened up my emails there was a message in my inbox from him. It just said, 'Hi' in the subject line. I opened it up and shrank the box to read it.

'I've been thinking I really don't like you walking between the tube station and your house. I want to pay for you to get taxis.'

'Don't be stupid :P'

'I'm not being stupid. I'm trying to keep you safe until we work out for certain who messed with your post and who was asking after you.'

'I'm fine.'

':(I worry.'

'I'm fine! Captain Control.'

There was a pause, then he sent another email. 'What are you doing tonight?'

'I'm busy. I'm meeting Rick for a drink.'

'Go to the kitchen.'

I rolled my eyes when he walked out of his office. He only glanced at me, making out as though he hadn't been communicating with me.

I deleted his email chain and then picked up my mug. 'Does anyone else want a drink?'

'I will.' Phil lifted his mug.

I took his mug with me and followed Jack.

When I went in there, Jack was filling his mug with hot water, nothing else.

'What?'

'Are you kidding me? You're going out for a drink with Rick…'

I put my mug down, then started rinsing Phil's out. 'Yes.'

'Why?'

I glanced over at him and laughed at his outrage, which made him even more outraged, judging by the look on his face. 'Captain Control's in his element today. Did you bring your cape? And you should swap your underwear around so it's over your trousers. Because I like him. We're friends. He's a nice guy. I just wasn't in love with him. He wanted to stay friends and so we're friends.'

Jack sighed.

I spooned coffee into my and Phil's mugs, not looking at Jack. 'Don't go possessive on me, Jack.'

Suddenly his hands were at my waist and he leaned around and kissed my cheek, then he said into my ear, 'Do I need to be?'

I twisted my head around and looked at him. 'No. I don't like Rick like that, do I? And I'm not going to cut him as a friend because you're jealous. If you're jealous…'

'I am jealous. But I guess I'll shut up. Just take care.'

I laughed at him. 'Yes, boss.'

He smacked my backside. 'Don't be cheeky.' Then he said, 'I'd better go back.'

I nodded as he turned away, then filled my and Phil's mugs with water and milk.

'There you go.' When I set the mug down on Phil's desk I glanced into Jack's office. He was focused on work.

When I shut the front door of the flats behind me I was looking forward to seeing Rick, but maybe a bit less than I'd looked forward to it in the last couple of weeks. I'd rather be with Jack. Which seemed a disloyal thought because Rick had been a friend and never turned his back on me, even after I'd walked out on him. He'd been there for me for years.

Greg was at the bottom of the steps, about to come up. He stepped back out of my way with a smile as I ran down. I hadn't dressed up but worn my Converse, slim jeans and a loose top under my parka.

'Thanks.'

'Wherever you're going it's obviously somewhere nice – from the way you're hurrying.'

I smiled and lifted a hand, to acknowledge him, but kept going.

'Have a good time!' he called after me.

I walked quickly along the street, but glanced back over my shoulder. Greg was letting himself in and there was no one else around. I speeded up as I turned the corner, desperate to get on to the busier main road. But then I nearly walked into someone.

Shit.

It was the guy. Up close he was really big, his shoulders were bulked up.

He looked at me and his lips twisted with a smile. I stepped back.

Shit.

Nausea turned my stomach over. If I vomited over him, would that put him off? 'Sorry.'

I stepped sideways to walk past him, but he stepped the same way.

Shit.

'Sorry,' he said. Then he walked around me and carried on.

My heart thumped hard in my chest, knocking out a deep bass rhythm. I'd never been so scared in my life. I ran the rest of the way to the tube station.

Rick was in the pub when I got there. He was sitting at the table we'd always sat at. I walked across the room and smiled. Seeing Rick still gave me a sense of comfortable slippers. He was a piece of home to me, even though we'd split months ago – and today he was also a refuge. My heartbeat slowed a little, but I was breathing hard, out of breath.

'Hi.' I hung my coat over the back of the chair. He stood up.

'Hi.' He rubbed my arm in a gentle gesture, then leant to kiss my cheek. 'How are you? You okay?'

'I'm fine, thanks. I think… I just had a bit of a shock… I'll tell you why in a minute. You?' I wasn't okay, though, I was still shaky from bumping into the guy, but he hadn't done anything. I had no evidence he was the person who'd tampered with my post, or that he'd been following me… I was probably being a drama queen.

'I'm good. What do you want to drink?'

'A gin and tonic, please?'

Rick nodded, then turned away and went to the bar to get my drink.

I sat down and my hands rubbed my arms. I was cold – when the pub wasn't that cold.

He set my drink down, then sat down facing me. 'So tell me about this shock?'

'It was nothing really, but a few weeks ago someone looked at my post, and the police found suspicious fingerprints but they couldn't match them and—'

'Ivy.' He gripped my free hand as it lay on top of the beer-stained wooden table. 'Why didn't you say something?' His brown eyes watched me.

'Because I told you, it's nothing really. It's just I keep getting this silly feeling that I'm being followed and I told you someone was asking after me at the weekend. I'm overreacting I know.'

'Did you find out who?'

'No.'

His fingers squeezed my hand. 'I wish you'd told me. Text me if you need to, if anything happens. I'm not far away. I'll come over.'

I smiled at him, turned my hand and gripped his for a moment in a gesture of thanks, then pulled my hand free. 'Thank you.' It was good of him to offer, but I'd call Jack first.

Heat flared in my skin as I probably blushed. It was odd thinking about Jack when I was with Rick.

'There's something I have to tell you too, but it's nicer than your thing. At least, I hope you'll think it's nice.'

'What?'

'I've met someone.'

'Rick!' Wow, I hadn't seen that coming. 'That's great! I'm really happy for you.'

'It feels weird telling you. But I wanted you to know...'

'Yeah, yes I should know. What's her name? Where did you meet her? When? How long have you been seeing her?' Why did I feel a little funny inside?

He laughed. 'Do you want the answers in order?'

I nodded, then rested my chin on my fist to listen. The idea of him moving on made my tummy have a weird queasy sensation, but it had to happen. It was the thought of losing the security that I got from Rick. He couldn't keep being that for me if he had someone else.

'Her name's Jessica. I met her at a rugby match. I've known her a few weeks, but it's become something in the last couple of weeks.' He smiled. 'Anything else?'

'And you really like her?'

'It's early days. But yes...' He smiled more widely.

God, this was strange. I'd never imaged what it would feel like to think of Rick moving on. But that was selfish of me. A part of me wanted to tell him about Jack, but it was too early. I wouldn't tell him until I knew for sure that Jack and I were a thing. I was hoping it would be okay because he'd been doing everything right, but even though I kept telling myself that, at the back of my mind I didn't believe it enough to tell others yet.

The problem was, I wasn't over the way he'd treated me after New Year's Eve. I'd thought everything was right when I'd woken up with him in my bed on New Year's day, and I couldn't have been more wrong, and the cutting feeling of being ignored by him that first day at work had left scars. I didn't trust him not to do the same again. Not yet. It was too soon, and the scars were too deep, and I wasn't sure he liked me enough. I wasn't sure of my place in his life. I couldn't imagine it being anything more than temporary, from my experience of Jack, and I'd fallen in love, and it would be even more embarrassing then to tell everyone we were a thing if Jack then decided we weren't and dumped me.

The conversation progressed into general topics and I got another round of drinks. We stayed until last orders – then Rick walked me home.

At the end of the street I lived in, he held my arms and pressed a kiss on my cheek like he always did now. 'See you. I'll text you and organise something, yeah? Maybe we could do the pub quiz night if you want to?'

'That would be fun. But I won't be insulted if you dump me for Jessica.'

He laughed. 'Or maybe I could bring her? Would that freak you out?'

Yes. Maybe… I didn't know. It would certainly be different. 'No. Bye.' The idea didn't feel comfortable. I could work it out later, though. I was being stupid.

'Night.'

I turned and hurried along the street then ran up the steps to the front door, but my hand was shaking again when I pressed in the code. I just wanted to get inside and feel safe. It was so strange to think that Rick wouldn't be there to turn to. He'd been my security blanket for years.

My heart thudded as I walked up to my room and let myself in.

I wanted to call Jack, but if I rang him I wasn't sure what I'd say. *I love you.* I didn't call him.

When I lay in bed I couldn't sleep. Thoughts of Jack and Rick tumbled around in my head; Jack being jealous and controlling today – Rick moving on.

Why did I feel bad about Rick moving on? That was mean. Maybe the way I'd been hanging on to him was as controlling as Jack... only in a quieter way.

I'd been hanging on to Rick for years and maybe I'd been manipulating him. And now I'd walked away from the bits of him I didn't want and kept the bits of him I wanted as a friend and I'd assumed that his security was always going to be there for me to use when I needed it.

The office was quiet on Friday – we were all focusing on projects and keeping our heads down to get deadlines completed before the weekend – so when Sharon walked in, then leant on to Tina's desk saying, 'Is Jack free?' everyone looked up.

She stood out like a massive throbbing sore thumb.

I liked my heels and I liked dressing colourfully, but she had on a pair of nude patent platform heels about five inches high, and a leopard-print top that opened down the front and exposed half her breasts, and a black skirt that must have been painted on, because God knew how she had pulled the thing up past her bum. Jack must have been on something stronger than cannabis at the point he decided that Sharon was the right person for him.

'Sharon.' He'd heard her too. He came out of his office and

crossed the room. I looked at my laptop, although I wanted to stare. I wanted to know what he said to her.

'I heard that you want to rush everything through now. Is that true?'

She'd come here to make a scene. I looked up again. She caught me looking and stared back at me, but then she looked at Jack. I looked down.

When I glanced up again Jack held her arm and was walking her out of the office, talking in a low voice.

Sharon looked over again and gave me a bitchy look that said *fuck off*.

I looked away, my tummy flipping with a rush of fight-or-flight adrenaline. Maybe I could see what Jack had seen in her. He'd have liked that edge; she was scary.

I saw now why he'd told me not to get involved.

Chapter 21

God, she was aggravating me. 'Sharon. I have clients arriving in fifteen minutes. Go.' She had such a skill for getting under my skin.

'And you also have something going on with that purple-haired girl.'

I didn't answer. Whatever I said, she'd draw her own conclusions. The lift doors opened but I didn't shove her in there. I decided to get into the lift with her. I didn't trust her to go to the ground floor. I pushed the button to go down and let her go when the doors had shut.

'I want what you owe me, Jack.' She pouted, leaning back against the far wall. She'd given up trying to get round me and seduce me months ago. Whatever feelings I'd had were well and truly dead – and she knew it.

I hated her now. 'You never worked a day in all the years since I met you; I owe you nothing. You can keep the apartment and have a one-off settlement, of a reasonable amount, but that's it. The end. I'm not going to be your cash machine. Invest what I give you wisely or get a job.' Or bleed some other fucker dry.

She smiled.

She was such a bitch.

When we reached the ground floor the lift doors opened. I

pushed the closed button. The doors shut again. I held the button down as my other hand grasped her wrist. 'And, Sharon, if you have someone watching me, call them off. It's not going to win you anything.' I wanted to say, and if you have someone following Ivy… But mentioning that might cause more trouble. I didn't know it was her. 'It's over and as soon as possible it will be over completely and you can move on with the guy you're screwing. Marry him, you'll have the cash from me and his open pockets.'

She made a face at me. 'I told your lawyer I haven't got anyone following you. I don't need to. I have memories. I have enough dirt on you.'

'What you don't know is how much dirt I have on you. I won't see you in court. I'm not going, but my lawyer will have a lot to say. Good luck, Sharon.' I let the lift button go so the door opened, then walked her into the front reception and waited until she'd gone through the revolving door before turning to the desk. 'That woman, Sharon Rendell. Please don't let her in again.'

When I got back upstairs I sent Tina out for coffee to charge myself up ready for my clients and headed back into my office.

'You okay?' Ivy's email pinged into my inbox.

':) Yes, fine. Sorry you had to see that.'

'Call me tonight.'

'I'll do better. I'll come over if you want me to?'

':) Okay. I'd like that.'

The rest of my day was too busy to think about Ivy or Sharon. But the minute I walked out of the office I thought about Ivy with a longing that was as dry as a desert in need of rain.

When I rode out from the basement car park at my apartment, on the bike, the traffic was still dense from rush hour. I would have weaved through the jam, but a police car had me in its sights, so I decided I'd better not.

I put my feet down on the tarmac to hold the bike steady as I waited for the light to turn green. The engine hummed between my legs. I watched the traffic around me through my dark visor. Then I checked my mirrors. I couldn't see the car with the first three digits of the number plate I'd remembered. Everything looked normal, but it was busy.

It was busy all the way out to Ivy's and I kept looking in the mirrors to see the police car following me most of the way, so I couldn't duck and dive through any of the queues. But when I turned into Ivy's street, leaning slightly over on my bike and checking the mirror as the indicator ticked, I noticed a car following me that I hadn't spotted because I'd been focusing on the police car. But this car I knew. This car I'd bought.

I pulled up in the street and the car passed by me, then the indicator went on and it pulled in a few places ahead.

Here we go. I sighed as I slipped my helmet off, but I didn't get off the bike.

'Hello.' Sharon used her bright voice as she walked up to me. The one that said she wanted to play nice games.

I didn't answer, just sat on the bike with my feet steadying it, my helmet on the saddle in front of me.

'What are you doing here?'

'Isn't that my question?'

'I wanted to know why you're so bothered about me having someone following you. Is there a woman in there?'

'Piss off, Sharon. Go home.'

'I knew you must be hiding something. Is this place one of yours?'

'No. Go.' I looked down and unzipped a pocket in the chest of my leather suit, then pulled out my phone and looked at her. 'Calling John, right now, and if you fail to go, I'll call the police and have you arrested for stalking.'

She smiled. 'Going.' Then turned away. She knew we'd been badly matched. She'd probably known it from the beginning – she didn't want anything from life other than sex, drugs and the money to buy them, it probably didn't matter to her that we'd never had anything to hold a conversation about.

I breathed out, pulled the bike up on to its stand, climbed off it and then ran up the steps to the front door. Sharon was in her car, on the phone.

I pressed the buzzer.

'Hello.'

'Hi. It's Jack. Let me up.'

The door clicked.

I ran up the stairs, my heart racing. Ivy was holding the door open for me when I got up there. 'We've got a stalker tonight.'

'What?' Her pupils flared.

'It's okay. Not like that – it's Sharon. She's outside. I told her to go, but I'm not sure if she's gone.'

'She saw me watching you earlier. She probably knows.'

'She didn't seem to know it was you living here, though. She followed me.'

'Then the other stuff wasn't her…'

I gave her a one-shoulder shrug as the fear that statement sent through me struck between my ribs like the puncture of a knife blade. Who then?

Ivy hadn't dressed up because I'd texted and told her not to, for which I'd had a twisted-face reply on the text, implying *what are you going to get me doing?* I didn't think she was going to like my idea, but it was important to me, and so I wanted her to give it another go.

'What are we doing?' she asked.

'Going to the climbing club.'

She immediately slapped my arm. 'Jack.'

'It's different in that setting.'

It wasn't controlling – I'd been fighting with myself all day on that point. It was something so important to me I wanted her to be able to share in it, that was all.

She stuck her tongue out.

269

'Get your climbing kit and your leathers on – I'll put your shoes in the carrier on my bike. Then let's get over there and have some fun. It'll be quiet on a Friday.'

'I don't call doing something that freaks me out fun.'

'It'll be different at the club. I promise. Go on. And if Sharon follows, she can't get in there.'

'You can be a bastard, Jack. You didn't tell me where you were asking me on a date to tonight because you knew I wouldn't go if you said.'

'Correct. But at least I didn't lie.'

Her fist hit my tummy lightly. 'That's playing Captain Control. You should've asked me.'

I laughed at her petulance. Which was cruel, I suppose. Maybe I hadn't got a handle on my alter ego yet, but at least I was trying. She made me want to try. 'Come on. It will be your choice. I can't force you to climb. But you know I love climbing – I want you to try it. For me… I want us to be able to climb together. No sales pitch; I am only asking.'

'But I hate heights,' she grumbled, as she turned around to her cupboard and started pulling out the clothes she needed.

I sat on the bed and watched her body as she dressed, her pale, slender arms and her flat, washboard stomach, and remembered her saying she did yoga to work out. 'Where do you do yoga?'

'A place near work.'

'I'll tell you what, I'll come sometime, if you like, so you can get your own back on me.'

She glanced across at me and shook her head.

'Thing is, though, yoga doesn't exercise your heart, it's too slow.'

She slid her arms into her top and bunched it up to pull it over her head. 'Believe me, my heart does not need any additional exercise – your randomness is keeping it worked out.'

'What?'

She slipped the top over her head, then straightened up and looked at me as she pulled it down over her middle. 'You make

270

my heart race. I never know what you're going to suggest. You have me terrified half the time.'

'And the other half.'

She gave me a twisted smile. 'Excited.'

I laughed. 'You make me feel excited too.'

'Yes, but I don't scare you and make you do the things you hate, and my ex isn't a she-devil, or even a he-devil.'

'Don't be a chicken.' Those were my last words on the subject as I helped her pull on her leathers. Or maybe Captain Control's last words.

When I went outside I checked the street. Yes. Sharon was still there.

We walked down the steps and I held Ivy's hand as Sharon climbed out of the car. I weaved my fingers in between Ivy's as Sharon walked closer. 'Sorry,' I said glancing at Ivy. 'The she-devil is out of her lair.'

'It's okay.'

It wasn't okay.

'The purple-haired girl…'

I didn't answer.

'She doesn't look like your type.'

I turned to tell Ivy to put her helmet on, but she let go of my hand and stepped forward. 'Hi.'

'So he's got you all kitted up to go out with him.'

'Yes.'

I moved forward and wrapped an arm about Ivy's waist. 'Come on, Ivy—'

'Ivy… Nice name. But you do realise, he's not your type either. You look too tame.'

'Shut up, Sharon.'

'No, it's okay, she can talk. You told me what you were like before.' Ivy dived right in.

'Yes, and then I realised what an asshole I was.' I stared at Sharon.

'He loves prostitutes; did he tell you that? That's his type.'

'That isn't my type—' I protested, but Ivy interrupted me.

'He told me anyway. He also told me you bought them for him, and he sent most of them away.'

'And they really were not my type.' I braced Ivy's waist more firmly.

'Whatever, she doesn't look like something you'd want. There's no fire in her eyes.' Sharon looked from me to Ivy. 'He'll get bored of you in a few months, love.' She turned and walked off, then she looked back. 'And I haven't been following you. I have better things to do.'

I breathed in and faced Ivy. 'Sorry.'

She shook her head. 'It's okay. It's probably better we got it over with.'

'I guess. Come on.' I kissed her on the lips before I slipped my helmet over my head. But things did not feel over. Sharon was still legally my wife and Ivy had just endured one of Sharon's finest outbursts.

And if Sharon wasn't the person following Ivy, then who had been?

Chapter 22

The rope tightened and pulled the harness I had on. 'That's me.'

'Climb when ready,' Jack called, to say he had the rope at the right tension.

I was learning to climb in the formal way, not his Spiderman, I'm-too-clever-to-fall-and-break-my-neck way. He'd gone through all the calls, and the safety requirements of the club with me.

He was right, it wasn't so daunting here, and gripping hold of plastic things, which had been designed to be gripped, was very different. Plus there was the secure knowledge that I was one-hundred per cent safe.

'Climbing,' I answered.

'Climb on!'

My heart thundered as I gripped the first pink-resin hold with my hand. Then I reached for another. Then I lifted my foot and found a hold and began to go up. I was using any colour hold that I could reach and grip, or stand on, but Jack had said the different colours were different routes, so if I got into it and I liked it more then I could climb different colour sets and they had varying levels of difficulty.

When I was only about a third of the way up the wall, he shouted, 'Test the rope, Ivy! Just act like you fell!'

I looked back at him. 'What? Why?'

'Just do it. It'll give you more confidence. You'll feel securer. *In control.*' The last words were said with a smile.

I let go of the holds on the wall. The rope took my weight, or rather, Jack on the other end of it did. He lowered me to the ground, grinning at me as I made a face at him.

'Now climb again.' He pulled the rope. 'And you can jump off as many times as you like. I've got you; you can feel safe. Climb when ready.'

I took a breath and looked back at the wall. 'Climbing.'

'Climb on.'

This time I climbed more determinedly. He was right; I did feel safer. I focused on the lumps of bright-coloured resin, grasping one then another, and I didn't even considered the distance between me and the floor.

When I got to the top, I was breathing hard and sweating, as though I'd done a work-out. I didn't know how he could climb and make it look so effortless. 'Go, Ivy!' Jack shouted.

'Woohoo!' I yelled, but then I looked down and realised how high up I was.

'Just let go of the wall and I'll let you down slowly.'

I did as he said, and he did as he'd said. I was absolutely fine. 'That was fun,' I breathed when I got to the bottom and he started to unharness me.

He smiled. 'Good. Then you'll come again?'

'Yes.'

'I'd like that.'

I met his blue gaze. 'I'd like it too, Jack.'

I was trying not to think about what Sharon had said... but she was right about one thing: I was tame compared to him. Dull. I really wasn't sure about Jack's interest in me – the depth of his attraction – whether he just liked me for now and it was a shallow thing that would fade quickly.

What if I ended up being his Rick, and he got bored of me as she'd said he would? That thought kept kicking at me every time I looked at him. I'd only just started believing I was more than a fling to him…

Jack undid my helmet. 'We could go to a pub for a drink if you want to, now we're done here? Or we could go back to mine for the night? Seeing as Sharon knows there's no need for us to keep hiding.'

He turned to pick up the rope we'd been using and started winding it around his hand to his elbow.

'Let's go to yours.' I hadn't thought about the fact that Sharon knew meant we didn't need to be secretive any more. But that was nice.

And his place was nice… 'I like it,' I said, as I walked in and he put the lights on. It was open-plan, with a row of windows along one wall. I could see the lights of London's landscape through them. I bet on a clear night it was beautiful.

I glanced about the room. It was sparsely decorated but then I knew he wasn't a man who liked fuss and frills. The colour scheme was cream, grey or light brown, and his sofa was a black-leather L-shape and everything was straight lines or square, and it was all ruthlessly tidy and spotlessly clean. He probably had a cleaner, though, so the cleanliness wasn't his doing. But it still seemed over the top for a single-man cave. But maybe a playboy pad was not the same as a man cave… And I bet Captain Control hated untidiness.

'You have a TV.'

'I bought one for Daisy.' He was stripping off his leathers. 'Do you want to see what we've done with her room?'

'Yes.'

He walked past me, I presumed leading me to Daisy's room, but as he passed he pulled the zip down on my leather suit. 'You're staying, aren't you?'

Yes, but I didn't really feel at ease.

I followed him, stripping my leather onesie off my arms, so it

275

hung from my waist. He opened a door off the hall on to a very different room: it was *all* frills. I laughed. 'That is pretty, and really girly. I like it.'

'Daisy chose it all. She loves it.'

'Good for her. I like her style.'

He turned around and smiled at me. 'And my bedroom's just along there. I have red wine, but I wasn't expecting you here so I don't have any ale. Sorry.'

I stepped forward and touched his cheek. 'You don't need to apologise, wine's okay.'

'Then why don't you go into the bathroom and start running a bath for the two of us and I'll bring the wine. The bathroom is there.'

I stripped off my leather suit and boots in the hall first. 'Where do I put these?' I shouted. It echoed through the apartment.

'I'll take them.' He appeared from along the hall, then walked past me into a huge bathroom. It had a black-and-white marble chequered floor, and pale-grey tiles on the walls, and a huge white cast-iron, roll-top bath, with the taps rising in a pillar from the floor. The shower took up a whole corner of the room; it had two showerheads and it was probably big enough for four people, not two. On the other side of the bathroom there were two sinks embedded into a black-marble top with white cupboards beneath it.

He put the wine and the glasses down beside one of the sinks, then turned on the taps to run a bath before taking my stuff and disappearing again.

When he came back I was stripping everything else off.

'Do you want bubbles? I have some. Daisy bought a load of bath-bombs for when she stays over.'

'Yeah, let's have bubbles.'

He opened a cupboard under the sinks and took one out of a paper bag, then threw it into the water under the tap from a distance away. I remembered him skimming stones in the Lake

District and my stones plopping into the water. That was a good comparison to the way we lived our lives; he skimmed along it, testing and trying anything and everything. I dropped into places – stayed there and sank. That was what I'd done with Rick, until I'd realised how unfair that was on both of us. I'd wanted to be like Jack – like the Jack of today. But Sharon was right, I wasn't like him. I loved bouncing along with him, I loved the excitement and variety of his life, but I wouldn't be doing any of it if I was on my own.

In the weeks I'd been single after Christmas I'd stayed in and done exactly what I'd always done – gone to yoga, spent time with Milly and Steve and gone out to the pub with Rick.

My heart pumped when I climbed over the edge of the bath, but not with a thrill-inspired feeling, with a fear that I'd got myself into something that was going to end up very painful and messy when it fell apart and he moved on. This was different to Christmas. At Christmas I hadn't had any expectations, I'd been involved for the experience. Now I wanted him, not just moments and memories of him.

I loved him.

He watched my body move from across the room as I sat down in the water. He'd taken his top off, but he was still wearing his tight legging-style bottoms as he held the bottle of wine, busy taking the cork out.

'Unless Daisy is really tall, you're going to have to get her a stepladder to get into this thing.'

He looked at my eyes. The white light in the room made his eyes bluer.

'I hadn't thought of that. I'll have to get a step or something. She's not with me tomorrow, she has a friend's party to go to. That's why I said I'd meet the people about the Italian account, but Sunday is the last of my single days. In a fortnight, if she's happy to stay over, I get my first full weekend with her. If she isn't happy, though, I said we'd just spend Saturday together, like we've been doing, and then I'll drive her back and pick her up again on Sunday. I'm trying not to put any pressure on her.'

'You sound like you're doing the right thing.' Now I understood why he'd been changing; his control side slipped away when he talked about Daisy. 'I bet she really loves you.'

He laughed, but turned away to pour the wine into the glasses. I watched the muscle play across his back, beneath his skin. 'That's a tricky thing.' He turned back and came over, holding out a wine glass to me. 'I love her. My tummy turns upside down every time I see her. She's precious and she's so like me it kicks me in the stomach every time I look at her. But I don't say 'I love you' because I feel like she might feel uncomfortable.'

'Thank you.' I lifted the glass from his fingers. 'I think you should say it. Maybe she's waiting for you to say it before she does. She's the kid. You're the adult. You should take the leap. You're a risk-taker, Jack.'

'You're such a fountain of good advice…' He sipped from his glass, then put it in a special gold thing attached to the bath for holding glasses.

I wondered how many times he'd done this before and who with. Not Sharon, because this was the place he'd moved into when he'd split with her.

No prostitutes, then.

But there must have been some others. I wanted to ask, but I didn't. I didn't want to be the jealous girlfriend. God, that would make me even duller.

He stripped off his leggings and his tight boxers all in one, flashing me his bottom and his athletic- shaped legs. All the hours he spent climbing were worth it even if I only ever sat at the bottom of cliffs watching.

I picked up my glass and sipped from it as he got into the water. It swayed around me as he sank into the bubbles. 'Ah, that feels good.' His legs bumped with mine. 'Did you want to sit facing me, or do you want to come cuddle?'

'I don't think cuddle is the word you're really thinking of.'

'Maybe not, but whatever, come over here.'

I swivelled around, trying not to spill my wine or slosh bath-water and bubbles over him. Then I settled between his legs, my back against his chest.

His arm came around me and his fingers began idly playing with my breast as his forearm rested against my middle. My head fell back on to his shoulder. *I love you.* I wasn't brave enough to be the first to say it either. But it was true. He made me feel good inside. I loved all his excitement and the thrilling fear ride, and his alpha-male control levels. They were Jack's charm, his Unique Selling Point; the things that made him who he was. I'd fallen for them and him, head over arse. But it made Sharon's words burrow deeper into my head. What if he didn't ever love me because I was too dull? It *would be* Rick and me turned the other way around.

I sighed out a breath. Wet fingers brushed my hair from my brow.

But I wasn't going to let any risk of the future ruin now.

But the impact…

That would be massive.

And the probability…

I didn't know what it was. Medium to high, maybe… He'd slept with a lot of girls before me.

'Ivy, whatever you're thinking about, stop. Relax.'

I nodded. My hair rubbing against his chest.

We didn't have sex in the bath, we just lay there and talked while his fingers played with my breast and my nipple, or stroked over my tummy, or skimmed along my inner thigh, or brushed over the sensitive skin in the cleft between my legs.

But when we got to the bedroom, all warm and wrapped up in towels, then it was a feast of sex like we'd had at Christmas, both of us playing like ravenous gluttons, and he pulled out silk scarves from a drawer and tied me up, leaving me pressed on my tummy, and smacked me, the bastard. But later on I got him back and did the same.

It was fun, because it was so different for me. But was that because I wasn't like him – and who else had he used the scarves with?

'Would you like another cup of tea?' Jack leant down and took the plate off my lap. He was waiting on me and looking after me just like he had when we'd been away at Christmas.

'Yes, please.'

He kissed my cheek. There was a sentiment there that hadn't been there at Christmas, though.

He smiled when he pulled away. He was walking around in loose jogging bottoms, which hung low on his narrow hips, but he was bare-chested. I'd like to wake up to the view of him like that every morning.

His fingers tapped my cheek. 'You know, you'll have to go after that. I have to work. I have the people coming from that Italian company. I'm picking them up at the airport, then taking them to the office to talk shop before we go out to dinner.'

'That's okay.'

'And tomorrow I have Daisy.'

'I know. I'll get up and get out of your way.'

'You don't have to rush. I just need to leave by twelve.'

I nodded. But when he left the room, I got up anyway and disappeared to have a shower. When he found out, he joined me in there and we did a lot of touching, then he lifted up my legs and we had sex against the wall under the shower heads, talking and laughing as we did it.

I wanted this life with him. I didn't want him to get bored of me.

When we left, he was late, so he dropped me at the nearest tube station, not at home. He held the back of my neck when we said goodbye, leaning across from the driver's seat, and kissed me hard, his tongue sweeping across the seam of my lips. I opened my mouth and indulged in a full-on snog, parked on the double-yellow lines right outside the tube station, clinging to the arm of his duffle coat.

He'd dressed in a dark-grey suit with a dark-blue shirt for his meeting and he looked handsome to the extent he made my thong wet just looking at him. 'See you,' he breathed into my mouth.

'Yeah.'

I got out and he waved when he pulled away. I moved my helmet to the other hand, which held my leather suit too, and waved back. A part of me drove away in the car with him. I watched him all the way along the street.

I smiled to myself when I turned and ran down the steps into the tube station, my heart racing – with excitement, we'd had an amazing night – but with fear too. I didn't know how long this was going to last.

People looked at me oddly because I carried my leathers and my helmet and I was, weirdly, wearing my climbing gear that I'd had on the night before.

I worked out what line connected to a route out to mine, then got on the escalator down. My life felt like a dream world whenever Jack became tangled up in it.

On the tube a young guy opposite me had his earphones in and his music playing loudly. But my heart played a louder dance rhythm. Jack was everything I wanted. I was happy, so happy, but shaky. We were destined to crash. I knew it. I had to keep living for now and not think of the future.

I was deep in thought when I got off the tube at the other end and I climbed up the steps to the street level thinking about Jack. I didn't even concentrate when I walked home. I was walking on auto pilot, my thoughts a mile away, until I had to cross the road to get to my flat. When I looked to see if any cars were coming, I caught someone step out from a gap in the hedge, where a gate must be, and then step back out of sight. It looked like the guy I'd kept seeing.

I crossed over quickly and pulled out my keys. Then pressed in the code to open the door. When I went in, Greg was in the hall.

'Ivy.' He nodded at me.

I nodded a greeting but hurried upstairs before he could start asking questions and delaying me. I wasn't in the mood. But when I reached the last flight of stairs...

Shit. The door was open.

It looked open...

My heart smacked against my ribs.

It was open! The wood was splintered around the lock. Someone had forced it open. My fingers shook as air stuck in my lungs. I pushed the door open wider with the back of my arm and walked in. Nothing had moved. There wasn't much there, but nothing seemed to be missing or disturbed. It looked like they'd broken in and lain on the bed.

Oh my God. I dropped my leathers and my helmet and then bent to fish out my phone.

Oh my God.

I felt like I'd collapse but I couldn't sit because the only place to sit was on the bed and I didn't want to sit on it – or touch the bed. Whoever had been in here had lain on it.

I walked out on to the landing and sat on the top step of the stairs, then rang Jack.

'Hi, it's Jack, sorry I'm busy. I'll get back to you. Promise.' Damn, he probably had his phone turned off. I didn't leave a message. I couldn't put the words together on a message. I needed to hear a voice.

I called Mum.

'Hello, Ivy, your father and I were—'

'Mum, someone broke into my flat. The door is broken. They've been on the bed...' It was said through sniffs as my shock became tears. I swiped the back of my hand over my cheek and under my nose.

'Have you called the police?'

'No.'

'Okay, dad will call them now and get them to send someone over.'

'I can't go in there, Mum.'

'What did they take?'

'Nothing.'

'And there's no one around. No one saw them?'

'I don't know…' I was confused and desperate… Frightened. My heels started bumping on the step as my legs shook and I huddled up, holding the phone tight to my ear. I wished Mum was here. I wished Jack was here!

'Dad is calling the police.'

'Thank you. I can't believe somebody did that. Who would do that? Why would they do that?'

'Do you want to come home?'

'No, I can't. I can't leave. The door's open. I can't lock it.'

'I'll get Dad to call for a locksmith too.'

'But the wood is damaged. The door is damaged.'

'Brian. Can you call a locksmith, and Ivy says that the door itself is damaged. Can you tell them in case they have to do anything about that? It might need a carpenter.'

I gripped the phone tighter, trying to breathe.

'The police are on their way, sweetheart.'

'Thank you.' They were the last words I managed before I began crying uncontrollably into the phone as my free arm clasped across my middle.

Mum carried on talking, trying to reassure me. I couldn't listen. I didn't know if it had been one minute or one hour since I'd come home when the police eventually arrived. They'd pressed my buzzer but I hadn't answered because it would have meant going back into my room and I didn't want to be in there.

Someone else let them in.

I heard them talking as they came upstairs. Greg, was leading them. 'Ivy didn't say she'd had a break-in. I just saw her.'

'Did you see anyone else?'

'No, no one suspicious.'

It wasn't the policeman I heard talking, but a policewoman who came around the corner of the stairs first. 'Hello. Ivy Cooper?'

I tried to stand up but I was shaking too much. The lady hurried up the stairs and held my arm. 'It's okay. Take it steady.' She helped me stand. 'Is this your room?'

'Yes.'

'Do you want to go in and sit down?'

'No.' I looked at Greg, who came round the corner of the stairs with the policeman. I didn't know Greg really. I didn't want him here. Anyone could have broken into my room. He could have…

The policewoman looked at Greg as the policeman walked past us. 'Thank you for showing us up. If you can stay in your flat we'll come and speak to you in a moment, but please leave us now.' She was perceptive. But then, I guess they faced things like this all the time. I didn't.

The policeman walked around in my room making notes.

'Can I call someone for you? Do you have family?'

'I've already rung my mum. She rang you. But they don't live near here.'

'Is there anyone else?'

'No one who can come over.' Milly was visiting her parents, she'd be back this evening.

'Have you contacted a locksmith to get the place secure?'

'My mum and dad are sorting it out.'

'Okay. That's good.'

The policeman came out of my room. 'When did you find it like this?'

'When my mum rang you?'

'How long were you out for?'

'I was away last night. I went out after work.'

He was making notes every time I answered. 'Have you any idea who did this?'

'No.'

'Is there anything missing.'

'No.' My hand trembled as I wiped my nose on my sleeve. 'Not that I can see.'

'Has anything been moved or touched?'

'Only the bed covers.'

'Molly, if you stay with Miss Cooper I'll do some door-knocking and see if anyone saw anything.'

'Okay.' She looked at me. 'If you don't want to sit down in the room, would you like to come out and sit in the car until the locksmith arrives?'

'Yes, please.'

'I'll see if I can get the man downstairs to make you a mug of tea too.'

'Thanks.' My brain echoed with a numb silence.

When she left me in the car, I thought of someone I could call. I looked up my contacts. Then pressed the call icon.

'Hi, Ivy. Are you in need of a night at the pub?'

'Rick. I… someone broke into my flat. Milly's busy. Would you come over? I feel sick.'

'What about the police?'

'They're here.'

'I'm getting my coat. I'll be there as soon as I can.'

'Thank you.'

The policewoman came back holding two mugs. I opened the window and she handed mine through, then she opened the front passenger door and sat in the front seat.

'I phoned a friend. My ex is going to come over.'

'Is he reliable?'

'Yes. He'll look after me until my friend is free.' I couldn't stay here tonight and Jack was with the clients, so I'd take my stuff to Milly's. But that meant I had to go back into the flat. 'Would you come with me while I pack some things? I don't want to be in there alone.'

'Of course, let's finish our tea first, though.'

She spoke to me, sipping her tea between sentences, and asked lots of questions, about various things, I think mostly trying to calm me down, but she did ask a little bit more when I spoke about Jack and Sharon, as if she was considering whether they were the culprits.

I felt better when I went back into the house, a little less in shock. More in control of myself. But my heart banged against my ribs like a fist when we walked upstairs. I could hear the policeman questioning one of my neighbours on the first floor; a man I didn't know at all.

When I turned the corner on to the stairs that only led to my little room in the attic, the open door loomed ahead of me. My flat was nothing special, but I'd liked it. Now I didn't know if I could ever stay in it again.

'I'd get your lock changed to a chub lock. They're more secure.'

'But someone let him in downstairs, so…'

'I know. But at least then you'll feel safer when you're in here and we'll remind the other residents not to let anyone through who's calling for someone else.'

'Thank you. That's twice someone's let them in, and I've been feeling like someone followed me, and…' I remembered. 'When I came in today, just before, I thought I saw someone in the street who'd followed me around the corner and then turned back. I've seen him a lot.'

'Okay. Well you get packed and then we'll get a full statement.'

She stayed with me while I packed. It didn't take me long – my hands shook too much to pack properly, so I threw things into my rucksack. I didn't even know if I had what I needed; my brain was too messed up to think.

I sat in the police car again to go through my statement. Then the locksmith arrived to look at the door. His verdict was that I needed a new door, but he knew a carpenter who could fix it. The door was Greg's responsibility, though, and so the policewoman handled all the conversations with Greg. He called his insurance company to see if they would cover it. The whole thing screamed like a nightmare.

When Rick finally arrived after nearly an hour, I threw myself at him, flinging my arms around his neck, then cried my eyes out against his shoulder. 'It's okay.' He rubbed my back gently. 'I'm here.'

That sense of being home swamped me, the feeling of slippers and sofas to curl up on – that sense of security that had always surrounded Rick. 'What took you so long?' I said against his chest.

'I'd stayed at Jessica's. But I'm here now. It's okay,' he said again as he looked at the policewoman while I continued gripping him in a bear hug and sobbing. 'Is everything sorted? Have you got any idea who did it?'

'We're doing a full investigation.'

Rick patted my back and I think he looked at the policewoman a bit helplessly because she said, 'We'll refer you to victim support, Ivy.'

'That's cool.' Rick replied for me. 'Thank you.'

'I suggest you wait until the carpenter arrives and finishes what he needs to do, then you can leave. Our team might even be finished by then.'

In the end, I gave up my fear of Greg maybe being involved and agreed to go back inside to wait, but with Rick. I wouldn't have gone in there on my own. We sat on his sofa, with me hugging Rick like he was the last human on earth, as I kept crying. Rick's arm hung around me and he stroked my hair. 'I called Steve on the way over. He didn't know.'

God how stupid. I was planning to go to Milly's and I hadn't even asked her. 'He and Milly went to her parents; they're not home until later. I didn't ring her. But they'll let me go there, won't they? When they get back, they'll let me stay there…'

'You can kip at mine if you want? I'll take the sofa. You can have the bed.'

'No. I'll go to Milly's.' It would be too weird staying in the place we used to live in together and— 'You have Jessica now. She wouldn't like it, would she? I'll call Milly.' I sat up and got my phone out of my pocket, rang her and told her everything, and she said I could stay.

Once the carpenter had put a new door and lock on and the police had finished going over everything, I locked up and walked away.

The police said they'd let me know what was happening and Greg said he'd keep an eye out for any weirdoes. I still wasn't sure if he was the weirdo, though; he was always appearing when I came in, like he waited for me, and he'd been the same with Rick as he was with Jack, staring too much, and he'd said in a knowing way when Rick arrived, 'Oh your friend came then…' in a sarcastic voice, like he was judging me for having men call here.

When Rick and I walked down the steps to the street my eyes looked everywhere as my body felt like I had creepy crawlies all over me. I couldn't trust anyone.

Rick and I waited in a café near Milly and Steve's for them to get back. I left my phone on the table by my elbow, hoping Jack would call back. After about an hour, it vibrated, shaking on the tabletop and sending a tremor through me. I snatched it up. 'Jack,' I breathed, before I'd even got the phone to my mouth and ear.

'Hey, what is it?' His voice gripped at my soul. 'I'm between the meeting and the dinner, but I saw your missed call.'

'Someone broke into my flat.'

'No.'

'The door was forced open. The police said it was done with a crowbar.'

'Shit. Why?'

'I don't know. The person didn't take anything. But the police have taken fingerprints and pictures and it has to be the same person who looked at my post.'

'But why, Ivy? That's not Sharon's style at all. She likes public showdowns. She wouldn't do that. What has she got to gain from that? Shit.'

His voice sounded shaky. 'I'll call, Em. I'll get her to take over here and I'll come and get you.'

'No. It's okay, I'm going to stay at a friend's. It's all organised and you have Daisy tomorrow. You need to focus on that. I was shaken up but I'm okay now. I'll be alright.'

'Are you sure? I'm willing to drop this if you need me to? I'm sure Em would stand in.'

'Emma doesn't do sales. You're the sales person. You carry on, I'm fine.'

'You're sure?'

'Yes.'

'Then promise you'll call me if you need me. I'll leave my phone on vibrate on the table. If you need anything ring and I'll go to the loo or something and ring you back.'

'Thanks. But I'll be okay.'

'I feel like shit now. I want to be with you.'

'It's fine.'

He took a breath and blew it out harshly. I could tell he really wanted to leave the clients and come over, but he couldn't do anything here and he had to be with Daisy tomorrow, so I couldn't go to his.

'It's okay. Just have a good day with Daisy tomorrow.'

'I'll call you later.'

'No, don't if it's late, I know Milly has some Valium stashed away for emergencies. I'll probably take one, I'll be wiped out.'

He made a sound like he wasn't happy he wouldn't be able to talk to me.

'I'll see you on Monday – it's alright.'

'See you then, but take care and call me if you need me.'

'Thank you.'

'Bye.' He blew me a kiss down the phone.

'Bye.' I didn't blow a kiss back, Rick was sitting opposite me and his eyes were asking, *who?*

As soon as I ended the call the question was voiced. 'Who was that?'

'I… the guy I'm seeing. I've started dating someone too.'

'You didn't say…'

'I know. But it's only been days, it was too soon.'

His mouth set in a line and he nodded slowly.

'It's the guy I spent Christmas with. We've got back together, but it only happened a couple of weeks ago.'

'Well, I hope he's good to you.'

'I'm hoping he's good to me too.'

Things went silent for a minute. 'Are you angry that I called you, when—'

'When you're seeing someone else.' He shook his head. 'No, I'm glad you still feel able to call me. And I'm seeing someone else too, remember…'

'Yes.' I reached across the table and clasped Rick's hand. 'Thank you for coming. I appreciate you helping me. He's working and I had no one else to call.' Was this me controlling Rick still? Hanging on the safety line he was willing to keep hold of at the other end. Maybe I *was* as controlling as Jack, in a more subversive way, still pulling on Rick's kindness when it suited me. But so what? I didn't care at the moment. I needed Rick.

'It's okay. I didn't mind. Where did you meet this guy?'

'At work. It's Jack.'

'Your boss?'

'Yes.'

'I thought he was married.'

'They've been separated for ages, they're getting a divorce.'

'You and him haven't been going on longer?'

'No. I wouldn't have done that to you. I'm not like that.'

290

He stared at me for a moment, then sighed out a breath. 'It feels weird you seeing someone else.'

'It felt weird for me when you told me about Jessica. It's strange isn't it?' But that made the point. It wasn't fair of me to keep holding on to him as my safety line when he had Jessica at the other end of it too.

'Yes.' He shrugged as his lips twisted into a bitter smile. 'It is weird. To think we spent all that time together. I thought it was going to be you and me forever.'

I swallowed against the lump suddenly grasping at my throat. My face twisted in a strained expression too. I'd hurt him when I left. He hadn't deserved it. A piece of me ached for the comfort of the easy life I'd left, when I hadn't been afraid of anything. But I ought to let that life go completely. I needed to move on and I ought to let him move on without me jerking on the safety rope that kept pulling him back.

He stood up. 'Come on. Milly and Steve should be home by the time we walk there.'

Chapter 23

I pressed the button in the lift to travel up to the office. I didn't feel able to work. But I'd spent my weekend in a parallel universe and I wanted to do something normal. I didn't think I was going to get much work done, though.

I walked into the room. Jack was in his office. He stood up as soon as he saw me. I took my coat off and hung it up. When I turned around Jack was there. 'Ivy. Are you okay? Are you sure you should be in here? You're a sickly white.'

He pulled me towards his office by a gentle grip on the sleeve of my sweater.

As soon as we got in there my tears welled up. I wasn't feeling good. I was feeling lousy – numb. 'Be warned, if you ask me to talk about it I'm going to cry, and there are glass walls and everyone will see me crying.'

'Shit. I didn't realise you were so upset. You should have called me last night. You should go home.'

'I can't go home. I don't have a home any more. Someone violated it. Homes are meant to feel safe. Mine doesn't. And the place is so small that I can feel him everywhere in it. I hate it.' The tears I'd promised him ran down my cheeks in rivers. He stepped forward and his arms wrapped around me and hugged me hard. Not in the way a boss gave an employee a little empathetic hold, but in the form of someone who cared about me hanging on to me because they needed to, to give me comfort that reached as deep as my heart and my soul. My arms wrapped about his waist and I hung on to him too.

'I guess we're going to have to come out to the office,' he whispered in my ear.

I lifted my head and looked out through the glass. Yes. They were all looking. 'Sorry.'

'Hey, I held you first and I was going to say to you we'd tell people today anyway. We don't need to care about Sharon any more. Do you want me to take you home to my place after the meeting?' My forehead toppled against his shoulder and I nodded. His hand stroked over my hair. 'You can knock yourself out with Jeremy Kyle and I have a PlayStation as well, so loads of entertainment.'

'Thanks.'

'You can stay for as long as you want.'

'Thanks.'

'You're welcome. But I guess we'd better go and face the music.'

If Rick's comfort had been like turning to home and safety, Jack's comfort was like being inside a fortress. He gripped my hand when we went into the open-plan office, and I saw Emma notice the gesture. Then he shouted. 'Meeting time! No time for coffee.'

We walked ahead of everyone and he kept a solid hold on my hand, the tension in it said, *everything's going to be okay*.

He didn't let me sit – he kept me with him at the front. Then, when everyone was sitting down, he said, 'You've probably already guessed this, but Ivy and I want you to know we're seeing each other outside work.'

I'm sure I turned red as they all looked at me. I tried to smile as some of the guys lifted eyebrows and other people said congratulations. Emma just looked at me weirdly.

'Anyway, now that cat is out of its bag. Also, be aware that Ivy's place got broken into at the weekend and she's a bit shaky.' He looked at me and then said quietly, 'Do you want to sit down?'

No, I wanted the floor to open up and swallow me whole.

I did sit down.

I didn't absorb anything anyone said through the rest of the meeting. Afterwards he left me standing by my desk and went into his office to fetch his coat and his keys.

Emma came over to me. 'Ivy. How awful about your place. Are you okay?'

'Yes. I think so. I spent the weekend at a friend's, but Jack is going to let me stay at his now. I can't concentrate on work, I'm sorry.'

She smiled at me. 'You don't need to be sorry. I hope you feel better soon.'

'Thanks.'

Phil looked up at me when Jack came back, but he didn't say anything. Jack clasped my arm and started walking. He looked at Tina as we walked past her. She was all big eyes and knowing smile. 'I'll be back in about an hour. If anyone calls don't transfer them to my mobile. I won't answer. I'll call them back later.'

He took me home by taxi as he had the bike and I didn't have my leathers, and through the whole journey I leant against his shoulder crying, my arms gripped about his middle while his arm stayed tightly wrapped around my shoulders.

He still had his arm around me when we travelled up to his place in the lift, and when we got out he gently squeezed my shoulder as he steered me in through the door.

The place was different in the day. The view from all the windows was awesome.

His hand fell away. I turned to look at him.

His hand cupped my chin. 'I wish I'd left them to it on Saturday. I should have got Em to take over and fetched you.'

'No. You couldn't have come over anyway. I was at Milly's and I couldn't have come here because you had Daisy on Sunday, and then where would I have gone?'

He stared at me, his eyes expressing empathy, guilt and a desire to hang around here with me. 'I have to get back. The Italians signed up to one of my ideas, I need to get the contracts set up, but I'll get someone else working on it, then I'll come home and lounge around with you this afternoon. But while I'm gone, treat the place like it's yours. Riffle through my stuff. Raid the fridge. Whatever.'

I nodded. I was not really capable of riffling or thought, or anything.

'Do you want me to stay? The account stuff could wait until tomorrow.'

'No, it's alright. I'll be fine. I'm only dopey from taking Valium.'

'Are you sure you should've taken it?'

'Says he who took all manner of non-prescription drugs a few months back.'

'Yes, but now I've stopped and the Valium weren't prescribed for you, they were prescribed for your friend. Still illegal, sweetheart.'

I stuck my tongue out.

'Lie down on the sofa. Do you want me to get you a drink, or anything else?'

'No. I think I'll put the TV on and try to sleep.'

'I'll get you a blanket and a pillow.'

'Thanks.' When he went off to get them, I slipped my shoes off, then sat down.

He threw the pillow and blanket next to me, then bent down and held my cheek with one hand, and kissed the other cheek. 'See you in a while.'

I nodded. I felt rotten – I'd needed Captain Control to take over. And it was a nice feeling, that by taking control of me he was letting go of control at work. He did really care about me, then.

When he came home it was about three in the afternoon and I was lying on the sofa watching an old film on Film 4. He made

295

me a hot chocolate with some stuff he'd bought for Daisy, then changed into chill-out clothes – a t-shirt and the loose jogging bottoms he'd worn Saturday morning. Then he sat down at one end of the sofa and lifted my head on to his lap. I hadn't really slept over the weekend, even with the Valium, because I'd kept dreaming and waking up, but as he stroked my temple I fell asleep.

April

'Healthy porridge or unhealthy bacon butty for breakfast?'

'Porridge. But I'll cook it. You want to get to work.' I hadn't been into work all week. I'd been going to attempt it yesterday, but he'd told me, no, as my boss. He'd insisted I stayed at home, at his.

'Okay. I'll go and shower.' He had his phone in his hand. He looked down and sent a text. Then left his phone on the kitchen worktop.

I looked down and saw a blue-and-white string of messages between him and Emma. The last one that he'd sent said, 'I don't give a shit what they think, she's still freaked out over the break-in. I wouldn't expect any of them to be in work in this situation. But if you're worried, I'll cover her wages out of mine, okay?'

Oh God, I couldn't help myself. As he disappeared, before his phone had chance to lock, I picked it up and then I scanned through the chain of texts he'd been sharing with Emma all week. The last one from her said: 'You know we're paying her. Everyone is noting everyday she's not here and noticing that it's all very well to take a ton of time off when you're sleeping with the boss.'

Tears clouded my view of the texts. I flipped back to the main message menu, cut up by how harshly she'd had a go at him. If everyone thought I was getting favours – they were right if he was going to pay my employer's sick pay himself. But he'd told them what had happened. I'd have taken the time anyway.

The next name in his text stream was Sharon. The urge would not be denied, because the last text it showed under her name from Jack said, 'At least she's not after my fucking money!'

My heart thumped a hard rhythm as I opened the stream to look at the text above it. 'You know she's too quiet for you. You're gonna get bored.' The rest of the stream was not about me. She'd sent the comment after she'd seen us last Friday. The earlier texts were jabs about Daisy or requests for money. But it still stung. I'd forgotten about her and her bitchy attitude. Now it smacked me in the face. I'd been hiding here, sulking like a child, and he'd let me. He would get bored if he spent too much time around this me.

I needed to pull myself together. I needed to go back to my flat and back to work – and get over this. It wasn't asking too much; it was clear that's what everyone else thought they'd do.

I made the porridge. It was probably crap, but I sprinkled a little brown sugar on top and poured a little maple syrup on it, then some cold milk. When he came back in he was wearing a light-blue sweater with a white shirt under it, and the grey suit trousers he'd worn at the weekend.

'If I dress quickly, can I come in to work today? I think I'm being childish hiding like this. I think it would be better for me to get back to something normal.'

He sat down on a stool on the other side of the worktop. 'You can if you want – of course you can, but do you think you're up to it, really?'

'I'll be up to it, Jack. Stop fussing over me. You're playing Captain Control and I need to just get on with it.'

'You're allowed to feel bad when someone scares the shit out of you, Ivy. And looking after you isn't controlling you.'

'Yes. But not forever.' I was being mean. He hadn't been controlling, just kind. It was my fault; I'd wanted the comfort of being looked after.

His hand touched my shoulder. 'You'll get over it. You're way too sensible.'

Ouch. I wished he hadn't used the word *sensible*. It was too like *boring*. God, Rick was what I called 'sensible'; he was the beware-of-this, think-about-that person. I didn't want to be sensible.

Jack drove us in to work in the car. It was weird. And riding up in the lift with him from the basement was weird. He took my hand and squeezed it. 'If you feel like you need to go home, tell me.'

'Okay.'

He kissed me when the lift passed the last floor before ours, then let go of my hand.

When the doors opened he lifted his arm, encouraging me to walk out first, then held the door into the office for me.

Everyone looked. Heat flared in my cheeks. I didn't look back at Jack. I went to my desk and sat down. Embarrassed. Jack didn't make a fuss – just went into his office and got on with his work.

'Hi.'

I looked up at Phil.

'You okay?'

My hands were actually shaking. It was strange to be outside the cocoon of Jack's apartment. The whole world was different because some bastard had decided to invade my very small place of safety. I took a breath. 'Not really. I still feel violated, but I have to try and get back to doing normal things sometime. But I'm grateful to Jack for letting me stay at his place. I haven't been home yet. I can't stand the thought of it. I guess I'm going to have to try it tomorrow, though. I can't stay at his forever.'

Phil shrugged at me as if to say 'why not?', and then I thought he probably didn't even know about Daisy.

'His daughter comes over every other weekend, so I can't outstay my welcome. It would put him in a difficult situation.'

Phil's jaw dropped, pulling his mouth open a little. I wanted to stick my tongue out at him. He was older than Jack, nearer thirty. In fact I think he was thirty this year. So he should know better than to judge people.

'Do you want to come round here and look at the work I've done on your accounts. You can take them back over now.'

When I pulled my chair round to Phil's desk I glanced into Jack's office. He was leaning one arm on his desk – his other hand was scribbling away, probably recording some genius idea. I didn't care what anyone else thought, I was glad I was with Jack. I just had to not be boring and make sure the office knew that this relationship was not about money for me – it was just about him.

At one o'clock, Jack came out of his office. The back of one curled finger brushed my cheek. I glanced up. He had his coat on. 'Do you want to come out for lunch with me?'

Phil coughed. I ignored him and stood up. 'Yes, okay.'

Jack walked ahead of me to get my coat, then held it up for me to put on. He wrapped his arm around my shoulders as we walked out of the office, but when we got to the coffee shop I told him, 'I'm paying.'

He looked at me. 'You don't have to.'

'I know I don't have to, but I want to, because it's not right that you pay for everything.'

'But, remember, I pay your wages. I know what you're budgeting on.'

'Cheers.'

'I could talk to Em about giving you a pay rise?'

'Wow, that would look good. Like you were asking her if you could pay me for sex. Awesome. Thank you.'

His forehead scrunched up. 'Don't be stupid.'

'If you give me a pay rise, you'd have to give the same to everyone, so we all earned the same.'

As we moved along in the queue his hand cupped the back of my neck. 'You are so wonderfully naïve. You don't seriously think you're all on the same money, do you?'

'We're not… I mean I know people like Phil earn more for managing bigger accounts. But—'

'Ivy, you're all on different amounts, dependent on your skills,

299

knowledge and contacts, and you're on the least. One of the other factors is how bad you were at negotiating when you started, and you were shit – you didn't try and push us up at all.'

'I'm on the least!' I smacked his arm. 'You asshole.'

He laughed, 'It's not my fault you were too timid to push for more. You should always push for more, Ivy.'

Timid. Ouch. That was as bad as 'sensible'. 'Okay, I want a pay rise, then; there's a law against women being paid less than men.'

'Yeah, exactly, because men push harder. But you couldn't screw us over with that – on an average we're about level. It's you who is paid low – nothing to do with you being a woman.'

I made a face at him and when the woman asked what we wanted I ordered everything that was most expensive and said, 'He's paying.'

Jack pulled out his wallet, laughing. But when I picked up the tray and turned to find a table he said, 'Em and I were going to look at your salary anyway since you took on the Berkeley account successfully; we should have just upped it then. I'll talk to her.'

But that made me feel bad because I thought Emma would be annoyed, but I couldn't tell Jack I'd seen the texts.

'Here.' He nodded towards a table.

I sat down opposite him. His pale-blue eyes smiled at me. I'd felt crap sitting around his apartment alone all week; I felt better with him.

It was going to be awful when this ended.

Don't think about it!

When I dropped into the passenger seat of Jack's car after work, I looked over at him. I'd been debating with myself all afternoon – and in the lift down to the basement. 'I need to go back to my flat, Jack. Can I go back to yours and get my stuff? Then will you take me there?'

'Why?'

'Because I have to face it. I can't keep running from it and I want to get it over with. I need to be me again. If I don't try, I'm letting whoever broke in win.' And when things go wrong between us it'll be even worse if I'm not living my own life. I couldn't let myself get into the routine of being dependent on Jack like I'd been with Rick.

It took two hours to get back to his, pack, and then come back across London in the early evening.

Jack parked, then got out, and as I got out he fetched my bag out of the boot. He carried it up to the front door. I pressed the code in. Greg had changed it, on the advice of the police, to be safe, but he'd texted me the new number. He'd also had a CCTV camera installed on the insistence of his insurance company. I should feel safe. I was protected now, or as protected as it was possible to be.

I delayed going upstairs by opening my post box. I hadn't even thought about checking for any post all week. I had eight letters, three of which were postmarked as letters from the police station. I gripped them tightly as I turned to climb the stairs.

I glanced back to check Jack was close. He smiled.

'Thank you for coming with me.' It was a heartfelt statement.

'Why wouldn't I come with you?'

I focused on getting myself to the top of the stairs. My heart thumped and a spasm gripped so tight around my chest it was hard to breathe. I glanced at Jack again. 'I think I'm having my first ever full-on panic attack.'

'You'll be okay.'

I nodded. But I really didn't feel okay as I turned around the corner to see the stairs leading to my new front door. Bile spun up in my throat and time flashed back to the moment I'd seen the door standing open.

I stopped.

Jack gripped my shoulder. 'It's alright.' I leaned back against him and didn't move for a moment. He stayed silent and squeezed

301

my shoulder, then after a minute whispered against my ear, 'Climb when ready, I've got you.'

I breathed out and straightened as I answered, staring at the door, 'Climbing.'

'Climb on. There's no one up there, you know.'

I nodded, but I didn't move.

'Come on, let's go and face it.' He got me walking again. Breathing hard as my heart pounded so much it made me dizzy. He took the keys from my hand and when we got upstairs I saw him notice the change of the style of lock. He opened it.

I stepped into the room. My leather suit, boots and my helmet were still on the floor where I'd left them, but the duvet cover had been taken by the police to be tested for forensic evidence. Everything else looked normal, as if nothing had happened.

Jack put down my bag and then he picked up my leathers. 'Where do you keep this?'

'I hang it up over there.' He did it. Then he picked up my helmet. 'This.'

'On the shelf in the wardrobe.'

'Put the TV on, Ivy. I'm sure the noise will make you feel better.'

I did. *EastEnders* was on.

He took his coat off and hung it up over my leathers. 'I'll make us coffee.'

I laughed. 'This situation is so fucked up – you're even going to risk my shitty coffee.'

'I'll risk several mugs. I'm staying with you. I'm not leaving you here when you're scared. We'll live here over the weekend.'

'It's tiny for two people.'

'It's fine. We can squash up in the bed – we've done it before. It's cosy. I'll make us coffee. You put a new cover on the bed.'

I turned around. But I couldn't. I couldn't touch it. It made me shiver. I didn't want to ever be on that bed again.

'Have you opened your letters?' He was trying to distract me as he filled the kettle. I'd completely forgotten about the letters I was holding. I opened the ones from the police. One was a copy of my statement, for me to sign and send back. Another was to tell me that they'd seen someone like the person I'd described walking behind me on local CCTV; there was a picture in with the letter. It looked like the guy I kept seeing but the letter said he had appeared to legitimately turn back, he'd dropped something near the gate of one of the houses and turned to pick it up, then walked on and was seen walking on other CCTV footage further along the main road.

The last letter… I read, then held it out to Jack. The paper trembled violently and a tear fell on to it before he took it.

The fingerprints in my room had matched those on the post they'd checked weeks ago. But worse, there'd been semen on top of the bed.

'I don't want the bed in the room, Jack.' I turned into him. 'I don't want to go near it.'

His arms came around me, protective and secure. My new fortress. 'That's okay. Forget the coffee. We'll go buy a bed. You were right; you need to be here to get over this. But you don't have to sleep on that bed.'

He took me to a late-night-opening department store and paid them ridiculous money to deliver the bed we'd chosen within two hours. Then we went to a hardware place and bought a hammer and screwdriver so we could take the old bed to pieces. The new bed arrived at ten-thirty p.m. and when the old bed was carried out of the room I felt as though the presence of a demon went with it. It was packed on to the lorry the new bed had come on and driven away.

Jack put the new bed together, then we put on a new duvet, pillows and sheet, which he'd bought at the store too.

'Let's cuddle and find a film to watch,' Jack suggested when we were done.

The air in my room was full of the smell of new linen and Jack's aftershave.

We changed for bed. He stripped down to his boxers as he hadn't brought anything with him, and I changed into pyjama bottoms and a t-shirt. Then we snuggled up under the covers and I slept leaning on his chest with the TV playing. It was then I knew I one-hundred per cent loved him. I'd fallen in love with him. I'd been calling it love for days, but now I knew that if Jack got bored of me and dumped me, my heart was going to shatter into a million tiny little pieces. This was love. This was the sort of love I'd been longing for when I'd left Rick. It was in every cell of my body.

Captain Control ruled my world, and with him in it, it was a beautiful world. I didn't ever want to lose him.

So what would happen when I did?

Chapter 24

At some point in the night, when Ivy had been asleep for a while, I clicked the TV on to standby.

Captain Control… I heard the words in her voice and I smiled. Yes, maybe. But sometimes Captain Control was the good guy – in a situation like this he wasn't bad to have around. She hadn't been her vibrant, smiling self all week. She'd been scared and shaken up. Captain C wasn't leaving her. I was wrapping her up and holding her so tight she felt safe again. Captain C would look out for her as if I was her guardian angel.

When I woke up Ivy was plastered to my side still and her head gently lifted on my pec muscle as I breathed in.

I looked at the clock on the oven. It was nearly nine.

I remembered looking at the clock last time I was here.

Shit. It weirded me out to think that someone had been in here on her bed, fucking playing with themselves. I understood why she'd needed to change the whole bed. I got why she'd struggled to come back here too.

I brushed her hair off her cheek.

Her dark eyelashes fluttered and lifted.

'Sorry. I didn't mean to wake you?'

'What time is it?'

'Nine, not early.'

She nestled closer against me instead of moving to get up, her arm slipping about my middle and hugging me. A rumble of humour rolled through my chest.

I gave her a squeeze of reassurance. I thought the world of her. I'd never felt like this for a woman. My innards had been mush for days and the empathy inside me was burning a hole through my chest. I was so attached she could melt me with a smile. And my lust for her… It hadn't quelled. I was hard for her a dozen times a day, thinking about stuff with her. But we hadn't done any of that all week. She'd been in need of hugs not sex.

I took a breath. My body wanted to flip her on to her back and have its wicked way. But this was her first night in here. She was not in the right headspace. I'd take her out of here for the day and then tonight I'd sleep over again if she was happy for me to do it, and then maybe… 'Shall we get up and I'll take you out to breakfast, then we could go out for the day somewhere, if you like?' It would be better for her to do something. 'We'll have breakfast in Hyde Park, where Daisy and I go for hot chocolates.'

'Okay.' But she didn't get up. Her fingers slid to the back of my neck and she reached up to kiss me, destroying my plan to be chivalrous as the pressure of her fingertips urged me to roll her back. My hand slid to her waist as I leant over her and kissed her, my erection probably peeping out of the top of my boxers as it brushed against her hip.

Her hand slipped down underneath the covers and freed it. I was painfully hard. 'Sure you're up to this today?'

'Yes.'

Well, if she was sure, I was sure. I lifted to let her slip my boxers down over my backside and then helped her strip them off my legs, and then we dealt with her pyjama bottoms. I didn't try to make this anything fancy, or wild, and yet – like the first time we'd done it in the missionary position at Christmas – it felt so special I was never going to forget it.

I slipped in and out of her slowly while she licked her lips and her sleepy lavender eyes looked at me, and her warm, long legs wrapped around my hips and squeezed me tight. Each time I moved, the muscle in her abdomen clasped at me.

She came after about ten minutes and so did I, but it had been ten minutes of heaven.

I was jumpy today. Fidgeting. I hadn't been able to concentrate on the advert I was developing because my brain was shot at the minute. It couldn't settle on thinking about anything work-related.

Ivy gripped my hand to stop me turning the Café Nero drink mat, and tapping it, then turning it again and tapping it.

'You're a ball of energy today. What's up?'

I hadn't told her I was worried because she was busy trying not to be worried about the stuff going on in her life. She'd spent three nights in her place alone, and she said she felt secure now there was CCTV and a new number on the door and a better lock on her room. But the guy, whoever he was, had sent her a letter, typed not written, just saying, 'I'm watching you,' nothing else.

The fucking bastard. I wish I knew who he was. I had a desperate urge to slam him up against a wall and hit him – then watch him dragged off and thrown into jail.

But his letter had meant that the slightest thing was freaking Ivy out. Like, some guy had bumped into her accidentally in the High Street and she'd panicked. That had been a proper anxiety attack. A woman walking past had sat Ivy down and made her relax. I hadn't been there. I was being pulled in different directions – I wanted to be with her all the time, but I couldn't be, because there was Daisy too, and work was busy.

I wanted to employ my own private investigator to follow her, to make sure she was safe, but she said it would just scare her more and she was safe in her home now and the streets were always busy, so she'd be okay.

But she was being brave. I wished she'd be less brave and move into my place. We'd work something out for the days Daisy came,

307

but at least then when I had to work late and I wasn't with her, I'd know where she was and that she was okay.

Captain Control – he'd been yelling in my head for days. He wanted to get a hold of everything and put it in order. I wanted Ivy safe, but I couldn't do that. She'd made me drop the safety rope because she was determined to not let the bastard who was stalking her alter her life – or me control it. And Daisy… how did I control things with Daisy…? I wasn't even sure how things worked with a child, not really.

I leaned back and sighed.

'Jack, come on, what's up, tell me?' Her slender fingers squeezed my hand. She had gold nail varnish on.

It wouldn't harm to share it if she was getting herself worried over what I was worrying about anyway. 'It's Daisy.'

She smiled in a wry way. 'Why? What's happened? Isn't she coming for the weekend tomorrow?'

'Yes, but I'm thinking about what I'm going to do with her? What if she's bored? I'm worried she won't have enough to do and she'll hate it.'

She shrugged at me as if to say 'so what'. My worries were on a scale of one to her ten.

'She won't be bored. You aren't boring, so she won't hate it. You're going out with your parents on Sunday for lunch, aren't you? And you said she's excited having spoken to them on the phone so many times. She'll be looking forward to meeting her new grandparents. Imagine that in a child's view – two extra people to buy presents for her for Christmas and birthdays.'

My lips twisted; she made me laugh. I hadn't thought of it like that, but I bet Daisy had. But my fears were not alleviated. 'Yeah, and then there's the whole awkward evening in between Saturday and Sunday. What do I do with a little girl when it's the two of us sat there like lemons?'

'That's Captain Control talking, and it's the first time I've heard him speak in a sentence mentioning Daisy. I thought Daisy is his

Kryptonite; he can't be around her. You always say you're going at her pace, so stick to your gut feeling and go with it. Don't plan to fill the time with anything, just ask her what she wants to do. Download her favourite movies, make popcorn, get your pyjamas on and then you sit in front of the TV and chill out.'

'Seriously?'

'She'll love that. She'll probably fall asleep watching a movie, so you'll have to carry her to bed and tuck her in, and you said she loves the room, and you put a lot of effort into making her feel comfortable to stay in it. It'll be awesome. She'll be happy and you'll be happy.'

'I feel like an idiot worrying over this with all the stuff you have going on.'

'It's okay.' But I could see in her eyes, she wasn't okay with what was going on. She wanted the guy, whoever he was, caught. *Like I did.*

When we were back in the office I got a text at three p.m. from John. 'Your decree nisi has been agreed, you should get a letter confirming it on Monday, and the court upheld our stance; Sharon has no monthly allowance, just our agreed severance amount, the apartment, and no right to apply for any more in the future.'

I thumped the air. 'Yes.'

'Thanks, John. Good work. That's good news.'

I emailed Ivy. 'Hey, come in here.'

I think every time she came into my room two-thirds of the office looked. I hoped at some point they were going to get over it. I stood up but waited until she shut the door, then said with a big grin. 'My divorce is agreed. I just have to wait until the decree absolute is signed and then no more Sharon.'

She smiled. 'I'm glad. That'll be one thing off your mind.'

'Look, Ivy, I don't mind paying someone to work out who's been following you. Let me do it?'

'No, it's alright, the police are dealing with it.'

Yes, but not fast enough. I sighed, then I went over and kissed her – just a touch of lips against lips as I held the back of her neck. I kept my hand there. 'Are you still up for tonight?'

'Yes, I liked climbing at the club last time.'

'Okay. Then shall I sleep at yours?'

'No, go home. You'll want to be ready to pick Daisy up in the morning.'

My lips twisted. There was that tug of war going on in my chest. Daisy would always win out, though, she had to; she was my child. 'You're seeing Rick on Saturday night, right? So you're not going to be alone.'

'No, Sunday evening now. He's with his girlfriend Saturday, and I'm spending Saturday with Milly, and Sunday with Mum and Dad. You don't need to worry about me. I'll be alright.'

'You're good for me, you know that, don't you?' I pressed another quick kiss on her lips, mindful of everyone outside potentially watching. I didn't look to see if they were. 'Thank you.'

She smiled and then her neck slipped free from my hold.

Chapter 25

Mid-June

I felt like skipping into the office. That would make everyone laugh. But Daisy had been skipping everywhere all weekend and my heart was dancing.

I felt like a kid. I couldn't wait to talk to Ivy. I could have rung her last night, but I didn't want to tell her my news on the phone, so it was probably going to be shared over lunch in Nero's because I wasn't going to tell her in the office either. I didn't want everyone peering through the glass while I spilled my soppy guts.

It was one hell of an awesome day, though. I had the decree absolute tucked safe in my jacket pocket. I was officially a single man… and Daisy loved me. I was a dad with a kid who loved me.

Ivy was in. That was a miracle; she'd been out for a drink with her ex again last night, so I'd expected her to sleep in and arrive bang on nine.

I'd decided weeks ago I didn't dislike her ex. He'd been cool with her over the break-in, helping her out and keeping her from panicking too badly, and he'd been good ever since. She always seemed calmer after she talked to him. His sensible head seemed to level out her anxiety. I wasn't jealous. I didn't need to be, because on some of the nights she went for a drink with him she came back to mine afterwards and had sex with me; she wasn't getting that from him. She didn't think of him like that. She saved her sexy, passionate side for me. And I got all her other sides too: her kindness, humour, concern, adventure.

I ruffled her mauve hair as I walked past her, messing it up. She gave me a mock-annoyed face. About three people looked. I felt like stopping and turning around and saying, *When are you all going to get over this? You've known for weeks. We're two people dating. It's perfectly normal. I just happen to be her boss.* My eyes probably gave that little speech anyway. Everyone who'd looked, looked away.

At the meeting I was all revved up and bubbling over with positive energy. We had chances at some really influential accounts and I had some great ideas. There was one concept I was going to run past Ivy – I wanted her to take it on. She'd had her pay rise, a thirty per cent increase, but Em's warning was 'She has to earn it, Jack. I want to see her doing the work.'

To which I'd replied, 'She's been doing the work. You said so yourself when she took on the Berkeley account, and you've been going on at me since I told you I'd started seeing her outside work about how she's one of our best people, so don't then moan when I say let's pay her as if she is. She's up to this.'

Ivy was grinning at me through most of the meeting. I kept catching her lavender gaze. She knew me well enough to know that something had charged up my adrenaline. She must be guessing it was a good weekend with Daisy, but it was way more than that.

She hung back to talk to me when everyone else filed out. 'You're in a good mood…'

'I am. I'm in an amazing mood. I'll tell you why over lunch. We'll go at twelve.'

'Alright.' She turned – she had her hair up in a ponytail since I'd messed it up. I tugged the end of it. She glanced over her shoulder and laughed. I bet we'd really annoy everyone in the office if we got flirty.

'I got another letter this morning.'

'You didn't.' Shit, that spoilt my news.

'It was just a stupid picture of a flower. It wasn't threatening.' None of the last four letters she'd had, had been threatening. I think we'd both decided the guy following her was just a weirdo and nothing else. He'd never actually hurt her physically and now he couldn't get into her place, he'd resorted to sending letters – and that was all. She didn't even feel like he was following her any more.

I still wished they'd catch whoever it was, though.

When the clock hit twelve my phone buzzed at me and vibrated. I turned the alarm off and went out to get Ivy. It was a bright, warm day outside, so I didn't bother with my coat. 'Hey, beautiful, you've pulled. Come on, I want lunch.' *And you.*

Phil glanced up. I smiled at him. *Fuck you. What are you? Jealous.* He actually smiled before he looked away. Maybe people were getting used to it.

She stood up, smiling at my over-the-top happy mood.

I set a hand at her waist when we walked out. Her small handbag hung off her shoulder and she carried her coat like a comfort blanket – or a shield to defend herself against evil stalkers.

We were lucky, we found a quiet seat at the back of Nero's on a comfy sofa and settled in. I twisted sideways to face her, bent up my leg and rested an elbow on the back so I could sit facing her as she nibbled on a wrap.

She swallowed her first bite. 'Go on, then, what's put you in such a happy mood?'

'Two things, the first being that I have my decree absolute. It's official. I'm a free man, still reasonably young and now single again.'

She smiled at that. 'I'm glad for you. Congratulations. Is that the right thing to say for a divorce?'

'I think we should go out after we've been climbing tonight and have dinner to celebrate.'

'That would be nice.'

'So subdued. Be happier for me.' I hoped it would affect her too. 'But you haven't heard my second bit of news. I told Daisy I loved her at the weekend and she said it back, and it wasn't just chatter, I said it properly. I hugged her when I tucked her into bed, after we'd finished reading her story, and said, you know what Daisy, I know I only discovered you recently but I do love you, you're my daughter and my heart is all involved with you. I love you. And she said, *I know Daddy, I love you too*. My heart exploded with a boom when she said that.' Nothing had ever hit me with a rush quite like it.

Ivy smiled that heavenly little smile of hers that had captured my interest from the moment I'd met her, and had enchanted me when all I'd known about her was that she looked good, fancied me and had a sweet nature.

My arm dropped and my hand touched her hair. 'You told me to just say it to her. You said there was no harm in being first, and that as I was the adult I should be the first to say it. And, okay, it took a few visits for me to pluck up the courage. But, I just said it and she said it back...' I took a breath... 'So I'm going to try the same trick again.' Her long eyelashes descended as she blinked then opened up her eyes. 'I love you, Ivy.'

She'd taken a bite out of her wrap and now she choked.

I slapped her back, then she swallowed her mouthful. 'Oh my God... Sorry. I didn't expect that.'

'I think Daisy's reaction was better. It definitely wins.' Ivy hadn't said it back.

She took a breath, then a sip through the straw in her Frappuccino thing, then smiled at me. God that smile. 'I love you too.'

'A little clinical. Are you sure?'

She laughed, putting down her drink, then she turned to face me and wrapped her arms around my neck. 'I love you,' she said into my ear.

'I love you too,' I said against her hair. She pulled back and looked at me like she didn't really believe me, though. 'What?'

'It's just… What Sharon said when she saw us together a few weeks ago – I've been thinking ever since then that at some point you're going to get bored of me and end it. I've been waiti—'

'Waiting for me to get bored… That's stupid.' I held her hand.

'Yes. Because she's right, I'm boring compared to you. You do everything so full-on, and you keep using words like 'sensible' to describe me, and when we went away at Christmas I kept hearing myself saying sensible don't-do-it things. But it was sensible that made me walk away from Rick, and now I feel as though I'll be the one holding you down, I'm—'

I let go of her hand. Disappointment tightening around my heart. 'The only thing you're doing is talking rubbish. Why did you listen to Sharon? Remember, I left her because I didn't like the way we were living – or her. And why are we even talking about her when I just said I want to celebrate my divorce and that I love you? You're being weird, Ivy.'

'I'm not weird. I mean if I scored you out of twenty, Jack, you'd be twenty-five, and you've been with a ton of girls. Why are you going to settle for me?'

'Settle… This isn't settling. I'm choosing you, and remember, we fancied each other for years from the moment you started working for me – that's hardly settling. I waited for more than two years to get my hands on you, and I happen to like your form of 'sensible'. God knows, I've had too much of stupid in my time. I like you, as you are, whole package, brains, personality and definitely looks, but more importantly I'm emotionally involved with you. When your flat was broken into I didn't realise that something happening to someone else could affect me that much… I care about you, I love you, and if you don't even trust me to love you, I'm not going to lie, it makes me feel like shit—'

'When you bounced into the office this morning so full of happy. Sorry.' Her eyes held the apology too. But it didn't feel good enough.

'I said I love you and you basically said you don't believe me…'

'I didn't mean to…'

'Don't listen to other people. Lots of them could tell you a lot of things about me. None of it applies to you.' I stood up. 'Let's get back to work. There's nothing like having a smack in the face on one of the days in your life you expected to feel like the best. I'm going to always remember the first time I said I love you, you said – I thought you'd get bored of me. Thank you.'

'It wasn't meant as an insult.' Ivy snatched up what was left of her wrap in its carton and her Frappuccino.

'Yes, well, it was taken as an insult.'

'Jack!' she shouted at me when I walked ahead.

I stopped and turned around.

'I'm sorry. I read your texts when I was staying at yours after the break-in. You'd replied to Sharon and said 'at least she isn't after my money'. I couldn't help looking – you'd left your phone on the counter and I looked at the text chain—'

'Not making it better, Ivy. You checked my phone… That is not good. Also still not cool that you'd listen to a single word out of Sharon's mouth.' She knew what I felt about Sharon, so why was she hearing Sharon's words over mine. She'd even seen what a bitch Sharon could be. I turned around, hanging on to a torrent of abusive words. Fuck.

After about an hour of being back in work, Ivy sent me an email. 'Are we still going climbing tonight?'

Shit. I was mad at her but I wanted to spend the night with her still. 'Yes, and guess what? It's pretty weird – I've been climbing since I was a teenager and, strangely, I'm not bored of it.' I sent the email back. But I'd shelved the idea of dinner afterwards. I wasn't in the mood to celebrate any more.

316

But a minute later I sent her another email: 'And guess what? I've been running this fucking business for years, weirdly, worked my arse off to build it up, and NOT BORED.'

'Jack. I said I was sorry.'

I got up and walked out into the office, over to her. She looked up, her eyes saying, *what are you going to do?* I leant down, gripped her neck and pressed a kiss on her lips, then whispered over them. 'Not bored of the taste of your lips either.'

Phil coughed. Then he said, 'If we did that in the office you'd have something to say about it.'

'No I wouldn't. Hook up with whoever you want in the office, only seeing as none of you are single it might be a little awkward back at home if your other halves found out.' I looked along the room at Em. 'Em, you wanted to go over the accounts, let's do it now.'

'Okay.'

I got it in the neck when she came into the office – for being childish and mixing up work with my personal life. 'This is exactly what I was worried about. Things go wrong when relationships fall apart.'

'I just told her I love her; we aren't falling apart. I'm just pissed off with her. She didn't say the right thing back—'

'So you're sulking.' She laughed.

'Shut up. Not you as well.'

When Ivy was in the kitchen later I followed her in there and when I leant past her to fill a glass with water I touched her bum. 'Sure as hell not bored of that.'

I walked back out before she could answer.

Even when we were climbing later, I kept jabbing. She was halfway up the wall and I shouted up. 'Hey, honey, hurry up, I may get bored down here and let go.'

She glanced down. 'Shut up! It was a legitimate fear.'

'It was a sick accusation.'

'Jack, don't argue with the woman while she's climbing.' Paul,

317

one of the instructors who was near us, knocked me back for it. He was right.

When she finished her climb, I got her to hold the rope for me. She hated doing it – she was terrified I'd fall and she wouldn't be able to hold me, no matter that all my weight was on the pulleys. But I'd kept telling her I could climb anyway, so I wasn't going to fall. I climbed the same wall she had in about four minutes, then climbed another, much harder, wall and deliberately took a non-direct route to try and calm my mind. But when I dropped her off back at hers, I wasn't in a mood to stop over.

She leaned across the car and touched my cheek, like she was going to say something but didn't. I gave her a kiss and she tried to make it passionate, but I wasn't playing. I pulled away. 'I'll see you tomorrow.'

'Okay.'

By the time I got home she'd texted me, 'I do love you. It was because I don't feel as good as you. That's all xxx <3'

I looked at it. I didn't want to not reply, I'd learned from that error, and she'd said something nice, and I loved her... 'I do love you too. And you're better than me! See you tomorrow.'

I sat down and played on the PlayStation. I couldn't sleep. I'd been going to say so much more to her... I'd been looking forward to today for fucking days and she'd ruined it.

This was what was wrong when I couldn't control stuff – sometimes things worked out and sometimes they didn't. I hated it when they didn't. It was like going to a boarding school and losing all control overnight. It was that feeling of sheer panic that had set me up to become such a driven person. As much as I was controlling, life controlled me; life had had its foot down on my accelerator ever since I'd been a kid, pushing me to fight, to get in charge and keep everything ordered in a way that I could manage and come out on top.

I'd thought with Ivy I could be different – that I could let go...

318

Chapter 26

I got into the office early so I could speak to Emma before Jack came in. She was always the one who opened up. I hadn't slept and my eyes were red from crying. It was stupid. He'd said he loved me and I'd spent the night in tears.

'Emma, can I talk to you, in private, in case anyone else comes in?'

She gave me an impatient smile that said, *I don't want to get caught up in the middle of you and Jack.* But she was the only person I knew who knew him well enough. I picked up a pen out of the pot on Jack's desk as I waited for Emma to come in, and my fingers began clicking the nib in and out.

'You spent the night upset, I take it.'

I looked up and put the pen down as she came in. 'I'm sorry, I know you don't like me seeing Jack. But I love him and I upset him; he didn't upset me. But he's still angry and I don't know how to fix it. We haven't argued before.'

She sighed. 'Ivy, I'd rather not get involved. It's awkward you two dating; it's awkward for everyone.'

'I'm sorry.' I was going to walk out, but she caught hold of the sleeve of my coat.

'Jack flares up sometimes; it burns out quickly. Just ride it out and don't let it get to you. He told me he said he loved you. If he said it, he meant it. He wouldn't say it lightly. But for the record, I did hate you two dating, but I was coming around to the idea until you fell out yesterday. Just don't fall out very often. The rest of us do not want to be involved in your arguments.'

When Jack came in about half an hour later he frowned at me. I didn't acknowledge him. I thought maybe I'd start crying again if I did.

I saw Emma go in and talk to him and my cheeks heated. But she could be talking to him about work – except he came out of the office when she did and came over to me. 'Come on, let's do a coffee run. I'm paying for coffee!' he said the last sentence to the room. 'If you want something, you'd better tell Ivy quickly!' The orders were shouted out and I wrote them down.

He gripped my hand as we walked out to the lift. 'Your eyes are red. Have you been crying?'

I nodded.

'Why?' he said it in a dry voice – not a concerned voice.

'Because you're angry with me.'

He sighed. 'I am allowed to be angry when I say I love you and you throw it back in my face.'

'That wasn't what I did.'

'Well, that is what it felt like.'

I slipped my hand free from his as we reached the ground floor.

He didn't speak as we walked around to the coffee shop, but then he said, when we were in the queue, 'Em just had a go at me. She reminded me how vulnerable you must be feeling with that guy still sending you stuff. I'm sorry. I probably overreacted.'

'There is no "probably" about it.' I turned into him, clutching either side of his jumper and began crying against his chest. 'I do love you, but I was too scared to risk saying it and—'

'Because you thought I couldn't love you.' His arm came around me and his hand settled on my back. 'Well, you were wrong. I'm a risk-taker, remember. I thrive on it. So if you think you and I are a risk, I say take it. I think there's good odds I can stay with you and not get bored. So does that mean you think I'm worth the risk?'

I straightened up and thumped his shoulder. 'Yes.'

'Well, thank the Lord for that, because I was going to ask you about moving in with me, after I said I loved you.'

'You what?'

'It doesn't have to be right away, but I was going to suggest we took a week off work from this weekend and go away to the cottage to celebrate the divorce too. Then the weekend we come back is my weekend with Daisy and I want to introduce you. I thought the two of you should get to know one another so that as soon as you're ready you can move in – if you want to.'

Tears clouded my view of him. I wished I'd kept my mouth shut yesterday. 'Yes.'

'To what?'

'To everything. To going away, to meeting Daisy, to moving in with you. Yes. But we'd better leave it a month or two before I move in – until Daisy is used to me being around.'

'She'll love you. There's no risk in that. I talk about you to her all the time.'

'What can I get you?'

'Good morning, Susie…' He rolled off the list of orders.

The woman walked away. 'Sorry I messed up yesterday. I spoiled your day.'

'Yes, you did.'

'I'll make it up to you tonight.' I lifted to my toes and pressed a kiss on his cheek.

'Not tonight you won't, you're seeing Rick.'

'Oh poo, yeah, I forgot. Sorry.' But then I smiled. 'I'll come over after.'

His arm slipped around my shoulders and squeezed. 'It's a work night, go home. You can come to mine Wednesday and make it up to me, and then we'll pack up and go away after work on Friday and escape to the cottage for a week. It's beautiful up there in June. There are loads of wild flowers – you'll love it. We could even ride on the bike up to Northumbria. Now there's another beautiful place…'

I smiled. It would be strange going back to the cottage – and going there with a Jack who'd said he loved me.

Half an hour after we got back into work an all-staff email landed in my inbox. 'Ivy and I are going away for a week next week, so if you need me to do anything urgently you best get on and talk to me about it.'

I emailed him back. 'God, you're so abrupt, Captain Control ;) xx'

':D and looking forward to next week, when I intend to let Captain Control take a hike and relax with you.'

Rick slid my pint glass across the scratched wooden table. 'There you go.'

'Thanks.' We'd met up to do the pub quiz. As usual we'd been pretty shit at it, but we didn't do it to win, we did it for a laugh. We had once debated asking Jessica and Jack to join us, but the verdict, led by Rick, had been no because they might be good. It wouldn't have been fair if they made us look bad.

'One day, Ivy,' he said as he sat down. It was what he'd always said when we didn't come anywhere near winning.

I smiled. 'Yeah. One day.'

He smiled back at me, then sipped from his pint before leaning his elbows on the table while one hand gently gripped his pint glass. 'How's things, anyway? Have you heard anything more about the guy who broke in?'

'I got another letter today.' I hadn't even told Jack, because we'd fallen out.

'What did it say?'

'Just I love you. Jack's convinced it's some poor, sad fool who's fallen for me. I don't think the guy ever really wanted to hurt me, whoever he is, and I don't feel like he's following me any more—'

'He must watch you, though, if he's still sending letters.'

'Yes, but it doesn't bother me so much. Not now the place is secure. I don't feel scared and, anyway, I'm moving out of there soon.'

'Where to?' His forehead screwed up.

'Into Jack's.' I smiled.

His knuckles turned white as his fingers gripped his pint glass tighter, and his gaze clung to mine.

'What?'

I'd thought he'd be... Not happy, I suppose, but okay. Things had changed between us since the break-in, but in a healthy way. I didn't think of him as a safety rope; he was just a friend. I turned to Jack for everything else.

'Jack said he loved me, and I love him, so we're taking the next step. I'm going to meet his daughter, we—'

'Aren't you too young to be bringing up his kid?'

What? Why did he care? And he'd wanted me to have his kid. 'No.'

His eyes became a darker brown, as they did when he was upset.

I gripped his hand. 'Hey.' I didn't know why he was being strange about it.

'It's weird, that's all. Just weird... To think of you living with someone else. I shouldn't care, though, should I? I have Jess.'

I guess if the table turned, though, I might feel the same. We'd been together a long time. He still felt as if he was a part of me because he was a big part of my history. 'Do you love Jessica?'

'Yes.' It was a quick, emphatic answer, spoken in a hard tone.

It would be him and Jessica soon, and it did feel weird. We'd grown up together. But we'd moved on.

'I'm happy for you,' he said, and his hand pulled free from mine. The tone of his voice was flat. 'I hope it works out.'

I was still in hope-mode too, even though I'd told Jack I believed him.

323

Rick picked up his pint and drank it down. Then said, 'Shall we head off? I might go around to Jessica's'

'Yes.' I drank the last of my pint, gulping it down, then stood up.

'Will you be okay to get yourself home?'

Since the moment Rick had known about my stalker, he'd walked me home whenever we'd been out. But I'd just told him I wasn't scared any more. Shit. That had been foolish. I was a little.

'Are you sure you'll be okay getting home?' he asked as he held the pub door open, like he'd sensed my trepidation.

I'd have said no, but he wanted to go and see Jessica. 'I'm alright, honest.'

'I'll see you, Ivy.' He kissed my cheek. I felt like that was goodbye. Maybe we'd moved on so far it was time to stop looking back at all.

Rick turned and walked in the opposite direction to the way I walked.

The night was really quiet.

Even though I didn't feel as if anyone was following, it was so long since I'd walked in the dark alone I was nervous. Maybe I hadn't been scared for a while, but I hadn't been vulnerable either, not like this. The light evenings had meant when I came home from work it was daylight.

I turned the corner and began walking along another street. Rick wouldn't hear me if I shouted now, but there were a few other people around, and the guy stalking me had never attacked me and never indicated he would. I kept telling myself that, while I walked, regretting that I'd worn heels and not flats. But then I could just slip my shoes off and run.

You'll be okay. He isn't dangerous, even if he is following.

I breathed slowly, trying to stop myself slipping into panic while my heart pounded out its anxiety.

I'd have called Jack, but he'd taken the opportunity of me

324

meeting Rick to climb with some of his friends, and then he'd been going for a drink. I didn't want to bother him when I was being stupid.

'It's okay,' I said aloud. I could take the tube. That would mean I only had a short walk at the other end. It was only one stop, but I'd rather do that than keep walking in the dark. I saw the underground station sign ahead.

It was okay.

The station wasn't busy either, but there were enough people around so that I didn't feel like someone could do anything to me. When I sat down on a seat in the carriage, I looked at all the guys, to make sure they weren't looking at me. They weren't. Most of them were looking at their phones playing games or listening to music with earphones in.

I breathed in and out steadily.

When I walked out of the tube station I couldn't keep controlling my anxiety, though. I gave in and rang Jack. There were two people in the street; my anxiety swept up to overwhelming and my heart felt as if it hit my ribs with the pace of the woodpecker I heard in the trees at the back of my flat sometimes.

'Hi, what is it? You okay?' It was noisy around him; he was in the bar.

'I'm walking home. I'm scared. I just wanted someone to walk home with.'

I heard him move, as if he stood up and walked away from the table where his friends were. 'Where's Rick?' Jack's control had eased a lot, but in the case of my stalker he and Rick passed the baton of looking after me. Whenever I was with Rick Jack didn't worry, and Rick looked after me and walked me home.

'He's gone to see Jessica.'

'And you're scared. It's okay. I don't think you need to be. I seriously think the guy doesn't intend hurting you. You're alright.' He'd had a drink, obviously, otherwise Captain Control would be grabbing his cape.

'Thanks. But will you stay on the phone and walk with me?'

'Yes.'

I was about halfway along the street and my heels clicked on the pavement as I walked. I looked over my shoulder, two people were walking the opposite way, but no one was behind me.

'Do you want me to come over? I can get a taxi.'

'No, stay with your friends. You haven't had a drink with them for ages, and it'll take you an hour to get here. I'll see you tomorrow. I'll stay at yours, tomorrow…' I'd reached my place. I walked up the steps and pressed the code in.

I breathed in when I walked inside and then let out a long breath when the door shut behind me. I hadn't even realised I'd been holding my breath for the last few strides. 'I'm home. I'm inside now anyway. I'll see you in the morning. Have fun, and don't get too drunk.'

'I'm as sober as a judge.'

'As a judge who's had a few shots.'

He laughed. 'See you in the morning.'

'Bye. I love you.'

'I love you too.'

I ended the call, then held the phone against my chest. It was a wonderful novelty to say 'I love you' to him and hear it back. It made my heart flutter. I smiled when I walked upstairs.

I'd ribbed him about being tipsy, but I was too. Which was probably why anxiety had got the better of me.

I swayed a little and it took three attempts for me to get the key in the lock of my door.

Relief breathed through me when the door closed. I was safe. Cocooned.

I looked at the bed. The bed Jack had bought and lain in with me loads of times. Being in the bed made me feel better, whether Jack was there or not, because the bed held so many good memories. That was my safe place. I put the TV on because I preferred to have noise around me, then I changed and got into bed and thought about Jack.

I still felt bad for upsetting him yesterday. I'd book a table at a restaurant tomorrow, a nice restaurant, and pay ahead so he couldn't pay.

It wouldn't be as nice a restaurant as he could get us into, but I'd make it a good night.

We were going to be alright. We were good together.

I smiled when I lay down to sleep. I love you… I heard the words in his voice. They were beginning to sink in – seeping into my heart like water absorbed into the ground. I wanted to believe him.

Chapter 27

I'd discovered something this week. I hated falling out with Ivy.
I still had a little simmering anger over her accusation, but the
other thing I'd discovered was that she was good at make-up sex.
She'd been working to convince me how sorry she was all week
and I was milking it dry.

I smiled as I zipped up my leather suit and shut the pannier
on the bike. I'd packed what I wanted to take to the cottage this
morning, so I only needed to change, pick up my case and then
I was ready to collect Ivy and head off on holiday.

She'd left work half an hour before me to get home on the
tube, but she'd said she was packed too, so we should be able to
head off quickly. I was looking forward to a night of great sex, in
the house. I'd kept telling her we were going to the cottage, but
I'd had the house made ready.

But it wasn't sex I was looking forward to anyway – it would
be a great night of *making love*. It was different. Really different
from having sex.

I straddled the bike and its weight between my legs provided
its usual sense of stimulation for risk and speed.

I leaned over the handlebars, rolled the bike off its stand, then
turned the ignition on. The engine hummed between my thighs

as I rolled forward and lifted my feet up. I rode out of the car park slowly.

The views from the windows in the house filled my head.

The lights were on red, so the traffic was stationary across the front of the car-park exit and some stupid asshole had parked on the double-yellow lines about a hundred meters away.

When I breathed in, the ring I had tucked safe in my pocket, pressed against my chest, near my heart. It had been there since the day before I'd fallen out with her. I'd been sounding her out in the café. I'd intended to propose if I'd received the right signals – not in the café, but I'd planned to take her somewhere for the afternoon. To celebrate my divorce. I'd bought the ring knowing I had the decree absolute. I wasn't planning a quickie marriage, though, I wanted Ivy to meet my parents and me to meet hers, and do it all properly – maybe even have a really big wedding in a year's time if that was what she wanted. But I'd just wanted her to know, when I asked her to move in, I wasn't thinking short term, I was committed. I was certain I'd got it right this time.

Then she'd thrown her accusation at me. Bored…

Was it any wonder I was still a little pissed off with her?

The lights changed and I leaned lower on the bike again and pulled out. The dickhead on the double yellows revved his engine and then it was just a massive roar of sound as the thing came at me.

I tried to swerve. To avoid it. But he aimed for me.

Shit! Shit! The wanker! I couldn't get out the way.

Ivy!

Shit!

Fucking hell… I swerved and the back of the bike slid out as the car hit me, smashing into my leg. My head hit the floor as the bike came down on its side on top of me. I went under the car. 'Daisy! Ivy!'

Chapter 28

I rang Jack again. I was getting pissed off. 'Jack you're really late. I thought the plan was to go early.' I ended the message. I'd left five messages so far. They were getting angrier.

It was seven-thirty. Where was he? He could be stuck in traffic, but if he was in traffic his car would pick up my call on Bluetooth, so he could answer – and if it was something else I couldn't understand why he hadn't called to say he'd be late.

He'd kissed me at work, before I'd left, with a glint in his eyes. It had been the most passionate kiss we'd risked at work. Phil had shaken his head at me after, but I think people were starting to get used to Jack and I being a couple, and since our fall-out there had been a lot of touching and kissing going on around the office. I'd wanted Jack to know I believed he was committed and he'd taken it as permission to be touchy. So we'd held hands and he'd put his arm around me when we were talking, and kissed me before he disappeared back into his office.

But our last kiss, when I'd said goodbye today, had included a tongue dance.

'I'll see you soon. I'm looking forward to being alone in the middle of nowhere with you. I love you.' Those had been his last words to me. They were not words that implied he'd stand me up.

I rang his mobile again; it still didn't answer.

By ten o'clock I was sitting on the floor in my room with my back pressed against the wall, trying not to throw up and ringing his mobile on constant redial. He hadn't answered and I'd tried his landline at home and at work and no one answered. I'd rung Emma once at about eight, really embarrassed, but I'd been desperate. She'd thought he was with me. She hadn't heard anything else.

My hand ached and trembled as my thumb continually touched redial. How could he do this to me? But he wouldn't do this. He wouldn't.

Something was wrong.

I swiped the tears off my cheeks with the back of my hand and stopped dialling. Then I just stared at his picture on my phone as if I could will him to call me, as if the strength of my need for him would make him call me.

He didn't call.

I slept in the position I sat in on the floor with my forehead resting on my bent-up legs, clutching my phone in my lap, so I would feel if it vibrated.

Where was he?! The words shouted through my dreams as I drifted in and out of sleep.

Why hadn't he called?

What was wrong?

I dreamt of our time at Christmas – of his hard edges and hidden depths. Captain Control in his cape; my fortress. I was shaken awake when I dreamt of my door being broken through – only in my dream the room had been smashed up and was unrecognisable.

It wasn't really daylight but it was getting lighter outside.

I got up. I'd go over to his apartment. He'd be there. Maybe he'd lost his phone.

Maybe something had come up and he'd lost his phone.

I called his landline there again, but he didn't answer. But it didn't mean he wasn't there. Maybe he was asleep. I used the bathroom then grabbed my coat and left.

I ran downstairs and I ran as fast I could to the bus stop. The tube line wasn't running yet. I looked at the bus times. They'd take ages. I saw a taxi and lifted my hand to hail it – I had the money on me. I'd drawn cash out to go away with. The cabbie talked, but I didn't answer.

When he stopped at Jack's I threw thirty quid into the money tray. 'Keep the change.'

My heart pounded as I ran through the main door and pressed the code to access the lift, but when I got up to his floor and knocked on the door, there was no answer. Silence.

Silence.

I turned and slid down the door, then pressed my head back against the wood. *Why?*

Was I going crazy? Was this a nightmare?

I wanted to wake up.

I shut my eyes and cried, making a noise that echoed around the small, square lobby outside his apartment. The sounds of pain tore my throat.

My heart was paralysed, cold and solid. What if he was hurt? He'd been travelling from work to here, and then from here to me – what could have happened?

He'd been on the bike. Hospitals… Maybe I should go to the hospitals. I stood up and went over and pressed the button to call the lift. I could go down to the car park and find out what time he'd got back here on his bike last night, and what time he'd left in the car, then I'd know—

But what would I know? He'd still be missing. Maybe I should go to the police.

My phone vibrated and rang out. I snatched it out of my pocket, my heart skipping, hoping it was Jack. It wasn't Jack. It was Emma.

'Hello.'

'Hi, Ivy. Where are you?'

'Outside Jack's. He never showed.'

'I know. His mum just called me. He had an accident on the bike. He's at the Chelsea and Westminster Hospital, in intensive care. He's badly injured.'

'No.' My palm hit the lift button. I kept hitting it. *Hurry! Come on! You fucking thing!* He'd been in hospital this whole time. 'How do I get there? What tube station?'

'It's on the District Line going out to Wimbledon. Get off the line at Fulham Broadway, then walk up Fulham Road. I'll ring and let his mum know you're coming. But, Ivy, someone drove into him when he pulled out of the office car park last night. He's unconscious. They aren't sure if he'll survive—'

The lift doors opened.

'Thank you for telling me, Emma. I'm going to him.' My heart beat with a heaviness that felt like stone smashing against my ribs, and the motion resounded in my legs and my arms and hands, and my head.

'Bye,' Emma said.

I ended the call. It would take me almost an hour to get to the hospital. I wanted to grow wings and fly there.

Chapter 29

The intensive-care unit was in the basement and the hallways were like a rabbit warren. It was as if the hospital didn't want me to reach him, there were so many signs and so many turns. I ran. People stared at me. They couldn't understand. The real world was miles away. They couldn't know a catastrophe had hit my life.

He had to live.

He had to.

When I found the end of the maze it wasn't the end. The end was barred beyond locked doubled doors. He was lying unconscious behind them. I pressed a button that had a sign above it saying 'press to let us know you're here. Then please take a seat'. It took ages for a nurse to come. She was dressed in the blue pyjama style clothing I'd seen people wearing for operations on the TV.

'Yes.'

'I want to see Jack Rendell. I was told he's here. Is he here?' I was breathless from running and my hair was probably a mess I'd gripped it so many times during the night – and my makeup must be half on and half off.

'I'm sorry, we're only allowed to let family in. His mother is with him.'

'But I'm seeing him. I'm going to move in with him. We were going away yesterday. He was meant to pick me up and he never came.' The tension of not knowing where he was for twelve hours broke. I wiped the tears off my cheeks on to my sleeve as my hand shook. I hadn't eaten anything since yesterday lunchtime, or even had a drink yet this morning and I was so tired – and scared. 'Is he alive?'

The nurse smiled. 'Yes. I'll ask his mother to come out and speak to you. If she's happy for you to come in, then you can see him.'

'I've never met his parents…'

'Sit down. I'm sure she won't be a moment.'

His parents. His mother…

I sat with the heels of my Converse tapping against the floor. I wiped my cheeks with my sleeve again. I probably had black streaks of mascara all over my face now.

My hands gripped my elbows.

A very stylish woman with brown hair came out of the doors. She had eyes the colour of Jack's. She looked at me. 'Ivy?'

I stood up. 'Yes.' More tears leaked on to my cheeks. I wiped them off. Her eyes and her expression implied that she was in pain, in the same way I was, but she didn't look as though she'd cried; her makeup was still perfect.

'How's Jack?'

'Very sick. Some mad man drove straight into him. The witnesses told the police it was deliberate. He's broken Jack's femur in his right leg and in his left leg the tibia and fibula and the bone at the top of his right arm. He's also broken two ribs and torn ligaments in his knees. They've operated on his arm and his legs, and pinned all the bones back together, but when he came around the nurse said he turned blue – he couldn't breathe. He has an embolism on his lung, which means his body cannot absorb oxygen. They have him on the machines to keep him breathing and oxygenated. But unless he recovers enough to breathe for himself…' Her stiff upper lip trembled, then curled in a pain-filled expression and fluid glossed her eyes.

I stepped forward and hugged her, a stranger, but she did not seem a stranger because there were tears in her eyes, and there were tears dripping from my cheeks for the same person. Jack meant we weren't strangers.

'Come along…' She let me go and took my hand, 'Let me take you in to see him. I'm alone and it would be nice to have some company. Jack's father is abroad on business.'

She spoke very properly, with a classic plum in her mouth, as though she'd stepped out of *Downton Abbey*. Jack spoke well, but it was almost accent-less, only British, but his mum spoke with a strong upper- class lilt.

She squeezed my hand as she led me along a wide hall with white walls and clinical washable skirting boards. My heart skipped a dozen beats. I was not here. Jack was not here. He was at home safe and this was a dream.

'This young lady is my son's friend, Ivy Cooper,' his mum said to a nurse at the desk. 'I'm happy for her to visit Jack whenever she wishes. It's what he would want.'

She turned me towards an area with a central nurses' station, where two nurses watched a dozen monitors, and on either side was a bank of small rooms. Within them I could hear more monitors beeping and machines. Bitter-tasting bile rose in the back of my throat as nausea twisted through my stomach.

'Has he talked about me?'

She glanced at me after she'd acknowledged a nurse with a smile. 'He has, Ivy, yes. A dozen times. I believe he's been building his father and me up for the moment he intended introducing you.'

He'd been thinking of the future, of us in the future, and I'd doubted him. The guilt hung heavily around my neck. I wanted to have the chance to believe – to really believe.

She let go of my hand. 'He's in here.'

A nurse was in the room doing something with the machines. Emotion wrapped its fingers about my throat and squeezed and my whole body became cold. He was so pale and he had a dark black-and-yellow bruise across half his face and across his side. His arm, which lay over the top of the sheet, was covered in a dressing that had blood seeping through it. His hair, which was always neat, was messy and sticking out at all angles. Then there were tubes coming out of him from everywhere, out of his nose, his mouth, chest, neck and his arm, and there were wires everywhere too, where he was attached to all the machines around him.

'Jack.'

A machine, which I presumed was helping him breathe, carried on a noisy rhythm, pushing air into the thick tube going into his mouth, while a monitor with green lines beeped out a steady pattern of sound. I would've taken his hand, but there was a peg thing on one of his fingers. I gripped his thumb instead, leaned down and kissed his cheek. His skin was cold.

'Ivy's come to see you, darling,' his mother said, as though he was awake and just couldn't see.

I thought of him climbing. I saw him in my mind. He'd been going to climb in Cumbria this week. I'd promised to watch him… Would he be able to climb now? *I've been climbing since I was a teenager and, strangely, I'm not bored of it.*

This wasn't fair. He didn't deserve this.

I looked at his mother, then looked at the nurse. 'Will he hear me?'

'We can't know,' the nurse replied. 'But we say it's best to talk to people as though they can hear.'

'Hi, Jack,' I said close to his ear, conscious of his mum. 'I was waiting for you. You didn't come.'

'You were waiting…'

I looked at his mother. 'We were going away, to the house in Cumbria.'

'It's pretty there.'

'We spent Christmas there.'

337

'Ah, so you were who he was with over Christmas. He didn't say.'

Heat burned under my skin. But he'd told them about me since then. I wondered if he'd said he wanted me to move in with him. 'Does Daisy know? Have you called Victoria?'

'Yes.' His mother walked around to his other side and laid her hand on Jack's arm as the nurse stepped out of the way. 'Daisy sent you her love, Jack. She's going to make you a get-well card. I suggested she didn't come and visit until you're a bit better.'

My stomach churned. I hadn't eaten for about eighteen hours, but I doubted I could eat even if someone put food in front of me. I slid my hand under his and let my thumb slot around his, longing to feel his hand grip mine back but there was no response.

His mum sat on a high stool on the far side and began talking to him about me being here, about Daisy and what she'd said, and she spoke about a meal she'd had with him and Daisy, and spoke about his dad trying to get back so he could come and visit too.

I didn't say anything. I didn't know what to say. My heart just cried out silently.

It was dark when I finally had some time alone with Jack. His mother had been in the room all day, and there were no opportunities when she went to the toilet or to eat because the nurses regularly kicked us out to change a tube or something so we used those times to use the toilet and eat. But finally, at nine o'clock, after they'd turned the lights out, his mother had said she'd leave for the night because she was going to meet his dad at the airport. I thanked her for the offer of a lift home, but declined. I wanted to be alone with Jack.

A different nurse, a woman with dark hair, who'd taken over for the night shift, was in the room. She replaced the bag that was dripping clear liquid into a tube going into his arm, then checked the machines.

I was sitting on the stool beside him. I leaned down to whisper. The longing in me… the screaming, shouting fear of last night… was now a quiet sleeping terror that was breathing slowly, waiting to know if Jack would get well… 'Jack. I love you.'

The machines kept playing their rhythm around us. I looked at the white tape holding his eyes closed, hoping to see some movement. There was nothing.

'This is a strange way to meet your mum.'

There were another few seconds of the machines playing.

'I missed you. I was terrified last night. I didn't know where you were. I'm sorry I wasn't with you…'

Tears slipped out. I'd controlled them for most of the day since I'd come in here, but… He looked so broken.

I looked up at the nurse. 'Will he wake up?'

The woman stopped what she was doing and turned to face me. 'It's hard to tell. He's not in a coma, he's been given medication to induce a coma, it's paralysing his body so that he isn't able to fight against the machine that's helping him breathe. It makes it more comfortable for him. We've been running x-rays of his lungs all day and he's not absorbing oxygen properly. He wouldn't survive at the moment if the machine was switched off.'

'But he'll get better…'

'We hope so.'

Her words rang through my head as I looked back at Jack. Hope. Was that all my control freak had? Hope… I hated that word suddenly. I wanted control. I wanted certainty.

I lifted his hand and held it against my forehead. I wanted him to feel me here. I wanted him to know how much I felt, that I loved him with desperation.

I sat with him and kept whispering in his ear for an hour, talking about the things we'd planned to do when we'd got to Cumbria, and how, when he was well, we'd go there and do them – like swim in the tarn at dawn, naked. He'd climb again; he had to be able to climb. He'd hate it if he couldn't. He had to get well.

'You should really go home now,' the nurse said to me at ten-thirty.

'What time can I come back tomorrow?'

'Any time.'

I wondered what Jack would think of himself lying here.

I stood up, my hand squeezing his, as I tried not to disturb the clip on his finger. Then I leant down. 'I love you. You'll be okay. I'll come back tomorrow. Don't be afraid.' I didn't even know why I said that, I'd never known him be afraid, and yet if he could hear and couldn't move I imagined, for Jack, that would be the worst nightmare.

'I love you,' I said again, then I let go of his hand, crying as I turned away.

The nurse said goodnight, but I couldn't answer. The reply was stuck in my throat.

Chapter 30

When I walked out of the hospital on to the busy Fulham Road I took my phone out of my pocket. I felt like a ghost. Either I wasn't real or the world wasn't; the pavement swayed as if I was on a boat and the noise around me was fuzzy, as though it wasn't tuned in.

I slid the contacts up to Mum's number and touched it. 'Mum.' Her name came out as a sob as the tears fell again. I hadn't seen myself in a mirror but the way people were looking at me... I must look a wreck. 'Jack was in an accident. He's hurt. They aren't even sure he'll make it...' I choked on the tears.

'Oh good Lord, sweetheart. We'll come up to London. Brian! Jack has had a serious accident! We need to go to London!'

I sniffed and wiped my nose on my sleeve. 'I'm going to be in the hospital with him.'

'That's okay, we'll be there when you come away from the hospital. I'll call you tomorrow when we reach Paddington Station and we'll find a hotel near you.'

'Thank you.'

I called Milly afterwards and she asked me if I wanted to go to hers – she promised to have a bottle of wine waiting. But this wasn't a pain I could talk or drink away. I just wanted to cry.

When I reached home, I pressed the code in, went inside and

walked upstairs. I felt as if Jack should be next to me, pushing the door wider and holding it for me.

My case stood on the floor by the door, with my leather suit thrown over it and my motorcycle helmet and boots beside it. I looked at the place where I'd sat through the night panicking because he wasn't here.

I couldn't believe he was in hospital. It wasn't Jack. Jack was full of life. I lay down on the bed, but I didn't undress.

I was too exhausted not to sleep.

When I woke up I looked at my phone. Five a.m. My heart hoped for a text from Jack, or a message from him.

I got up, had a shower and changed, then walked to the hospital.

The woman doing the night shift was still working and she let me in to see Jack. He looked the same, quiet and peaceful, but totally reliant on all the machines, tubes and wires he was attached to.

I held his hand and kept kissing the back of it and whispering to him, about nothing, only stupid things. I didn't have the confidence his mum had to speak as if he was conscious. But I spoke for my sake as much as his.

'Music is good too,' the nurse said.

I looked over and smiled. 'It's all on his phone.'

'His mother, Lady Rendell, has that.'

'Lady…' My eyebrows whizzed up. *What?*

She laughed. 'You didn't know? His parents have a title.'

I shut my eyes and lifted the back of his hand to my forehead. For God's sake, Jack, you could have told me. I think I'd even said Mrs Rendell yesterday and she hadn't corrected me. He'd talked to me about his lonely childhood and boarding school and the weight of responsibility he'd felt his dad had always ground into him, but he'd never said he came from a family like that.

'I'll ask her if she has his phone later.' I looked back at Jack.

At Christmas, when we'd been in the Lake District, we'd said we'd only focus on now – but now all I could do was think about the future we'd started planning. I wanted to live that future with Jack.

His mum came in with his dad at ten o'clock. His dad was well-spoken too. But now I understood why. They didn't sound upper-class; they were upper-class.

His dad shook my hand. He was perfectly nice to me, although his gaze kept turning to Jack's face and the muscle in his jaw twitched occasionally. He hadn't come to meet me. He'd come to see Jack.

I mentioned the music on Jack's phone, then left them to talk to Jack alone. His dad had flown back from the US. He'd come a long way to get here.

I didn't leave the hospital because that would be leaving Jack. I went to the café and got a coffee, then I drank it alone, suspended in time. Waiting. Hoping.

His parents came in after about an hour and bought me another coffee when they bought theirs. They said the doctors were taking another x-ray of his lungs.

The awkwardness that had hung around me yesterday, when I'd first met his mum, was back – now I knew about their title.

'You were up early…' His mother smiled at me. 'They told us you were in here before seven.'

'I couldn't sleep.'

'I should imagine,' Jack's father said. He gave me the impression he thought I was odd; he kept looking at me with a frown, as though I was a puzzle to be worked out. 'But you had some time with him alone, to talk.'

'I begged him to get better.' I laughed at my stupidity, but it was a bitter sound.

His mother smiled. 'Well, it is probably better you are the one to do that. He would never listen to me or his father. I told him to avoid the woman he's just divorced, when he brought her home, and he married her a month later.'

Maybe that was why he'd ended up with Sharon. To spite his

parents. I could imagine it in a young Jack; he'd have loved to show them that he was the master of his life. But what a stupid reason to waste years – and now he'd had a second chance and… I saw his face as he twisted around on the sofa in Nero's, to tell me he was single again.

When we walked back down to the intensive-care unit, my phone rang. 'Mum…'

'We're at Paddington Station. We're booked into the little hotel around the corner from your old flat.' Where Rick had proposed to me. 'We'll drop the luggage off, then we'll come over to the hospital.'

'No, Mum, it's okay. I'd rather be at the hospital alone. I want to be in the room with him and you can't go in there.'

'That doesn't matter; we can sit and wait outside, and when you're ready to go we'll be there. I'm not leaving you to go through this on your own, darling. You've been going through so much recently.'

I smiled as if she was in the room. 'Thank you. I'll see you later, then. But I might be with Jack when you get here.'

'We'll be in the waiting room, don't worry.'

I looked at Jack's parents as we reached the doors leading into the intensive-care unit. His dad pushed the door open and held it for me, in the same way Jack would've. 'My mum and dad have come to London too. They're coming to the hospital. But I've told them to wait out here.'

His mother nodded.

The next time I came out. Mum and Dad were there.

The doctor had asked to speak to his parents alone, and so I'd had to leave, but my heart was thumping and my hand trembled as I tucked my hair behind my ear.

Mum wrapped her arms around me. I hung on to her and cried on her shoulder, longing for Jack's fortress of comfort.

Then Mum took me to the café and bought me a cup of coffee and a piece of chocolate cake, insisting I ate. The chocolate cake tasted like gravel. My mind wasn't on food – it was focused on what the doctors might be saying about Jack.

After about half an hour, Jack's parents walked in. His mother had been crying; there were tear stains cutting through the foundation on her cheeks and her eye makeup had smeared.

I lifted a hand to say, *over here*. They acknowledged me before they queued to get a coffee.

'Jack's parents,' I told Mum and Dad, 'they're a Lord and Lady.'

'Good grief.'

'I know, Mum, but don't make a fuss.'

'I'm not going to—' She was cut off by his father approaching.

Dad stood up and held out a hand. 'Hello, I'm Brian, Ivy's father.'

'George,' Jack's dad said, as he put their tray down. Then he shook Dad's hand.

'Elizabeth.' My mum stood and held out a hand too.

Jack's mum came up. She'd been to the toilets to repair her makeup. 'I'm Catherine.' She held out her hand.

I touched his mum's arm, to get her attention. 'What did the doctor say? Is it okay for me to go back?'

She looked at me, her eyes so like Jack's. They had a depth that spoke of soul-deep sadness.

It was bad news.

'In a moment – sit down and let George tell you what the doctor said first.'

My parents moved the chairs round so Jack's parents could sit with us. I felt time stop and hover on pause.

When everyone was settled, George's Adam's apple shifted as he swallowed.

I looked at Catherine. Her eyes were shimmering.

'The doctor told us that there is no sign that Jack is improving, so we should prepare ourselves to consider donating his organs, in case he does not recover.'

My mum was sitting on my right. She gripped my hand as it rested on the table.

'That isn't to say that he will not recover, but he is seriously ill, and unless he improves in the next week then...'

They'd switch off the machines... George didn't say it, but that was what he meant.

I screamed inside as the café turned into a blur of people, seats and noise.

'We thought you should know. You should have the chance to prepare yourself for the worst too, if...' his mum picked up a serviette and touched the corners of her eyes, as though catching the tears before they rolled out.

'Excuse me.' I couldn't say how I got through that packed café. All I focused on was the door into the toilets, and when I was in there I pushed past a woman changing a baby and shut myself in a cubicle and cried with loud sobs.

I suppose if I'd been anywhere else other than a hospital, then people would have shouted through the door and asked what was wrong, but in a hospital I bet they were scared of the answer. It was Jack's mother who eventually came and fetched me. By then my crying had become quiet streams of tears and catching, short breaths, as the pain tightened about my throat and my chest, screwing the hurt up tighter and tighter.

She knocked on the cubicle door. I was hunched up, leaning against it.

'Ivy... Dear... Come out.'

I couldn't; I didn't want to face this. I wanted Jack back. I wanted to be in the Lake District. I wanted to be standing at the bottom of the cliff watching him play Spiderman. I wanted to be sitting on the back of his bike, feeling the roar of the engine, and the wind, and the speed as I hung on to him.

'Come along. We're going to see him.'

I didn't answer.

'You know it would hurt him to think of you upset.' It was said gently, but it was said to make me think of Jack, not myself. He was downstairs, lying motionless on a bed, maybe able to hear and all he'd be able to hear was the machines.

I wiped my cheeks, pulled myself together and opened the cubicle door. 'I'm sorry, Mrs... Lady—'

'Just Catherine.'

She gave me a hug. I held her too.

'Don't worry. I had my own moment before we came upstairs. I think we would be abnormal if this did not make us cry.'

As we walked back out she told me that she'd called Victoria and asked her to bring Daisy in tomorrow, just in case...

In case he died. The words breathed through me. Words that were impossible to believe.

His father was waiting with my parents. He had a face like stone, locking every emotion in. He would not cry, I could tell. He was not the sort to cry. He was where Jack had got his need for control from.

But Jack would cry. He'd showed me numerous emotions: desire, fear, passion, anger... I think he would have cried for me. I knew he would cry for Daisy.

After his parents had left, I was alone with Jack in the dark, with the sound of the monitors and the occasional appearance of the same nurse who'd been on the nightshift yesterday.

I wanted to lie down beside him, curl up on his bed, with his chest for a pillow. I wanted to feel his arm around me and hear his deep, sarcastic laugh rumble in his throat. I didn't want to listen to the rhythmic sounds of the machine keeping him breathing and the monitors tracking his heartbeat.

I even prayed, bargaining with a God I hadn't spoken to since primary-school assemblies. Please save him. Please. Please. Please let him be alright. Please. *Please.* The word rewound and replayed through my head. Please. Please. I held his hand, my other rested over the white blanket on his hip.

I bowed my head and pressed my forehead on to the sheet by his side as I prayed again.

The nurse touched my shoulder. I jerked.

'I think you should go home and get some rest.' I'd been asleep. 'Your parents are waiting for you outside.'

I'd forgotten they were even here. I blinked the sleep from my eyes and stared at Jack. He was yellowish today and I couldn't see his beautiful eyes; they were still taped shut, while his mouth hung open around the tube going down his throat to help him breathe.

'Go home. You'll be better company for him tomorrow if you've had some sleep. You need to look after yourself. Jack isn't going anywhere; he'll be here in the morning.'

I sighed. I knew I couldn't stay here all night. I squeezed Jack's hand and leant to kiss his forehead. He was so cold. 'I have to go for a little while. I'll come back as quickly as I can. I love you. Goodnight.' I kissed his forehead again and then whispered into his ear. 'Get well.' Then I let him go.

I stepped out of a horror-filled fantasy world when I pushed open the double doors into the room where Mum and Dad were waiting. My heart was left behind, lying on the bed, cold and unconscious—with Jack.

'Hi.'

'It's eleven o'clock, sweetheart,' Dad said.

I nodded. But what did time matter? Mum picked up my bag. I'd left it with them and not even remembered.

Mum led me upstairs with an arm around me. We walked to the tube station.

Taxis passed in the street, cars, buses. People walked all around us, some shouting and laughing, on their journey from one place to another. The sounds were echoes in my head. I was too numb.

Mum and Dad took me to a McDonald's near where I lived and made me eat. But even chewing and swallowing didn't feel real. I wasn't in my body. I was at the hospital with Jack. Still holding his hand and praying.

'Why don't you come and sleep at the hotel with us,' Mum suggested. 'I'm sure they'll have a room.'

'No, it's okay. I'd rather be at home.' Jack's atmosphere was there. His smell. My memories. The things he'd bought me.

When I woke up, it was dark outside. I reached over and picked up my phone. Four-thirty a.m. I got out of bed and showered. Then dressed in a hoodie, jeans and my Converse.

Dawn broke as I walked across London.

It was a little after six when I walked along the hall to the ICU and into the waiting room, then pressed the buzzer to call the nursing staff. A blonde-haired nurse, who I'd not seen before, answered the door. 'Hello.'

'Ivy Cooper. I'm Jack Rendell's girlfriend. Can I come in and see him?'

'Ah, oh, you're really early, I'm sorry, the doctor…' She stopped talking and smiled at me. 'You'll have to wait here, I'm afraid. The doctor is with him.'

My hand lifted to catch hold of her arm. 'What's happened?'

'I'm not supporting him, but I'll ask his nurse to come and speak to you when she can, but she's really busy.' Then she was gone.

Why was the doctor with him at six a.m.?

My heart whacked against my ribs like it wanted to be freed from my chest. I bit my lip when I sat down, but ten minutes later I stood up and walked across the room, then back again.

Twenty minutes later I was still walking; no one had come out to talk to me. I looked at the door. They were busy, but I was worried to the point that I felt I was going to collapse from hyperventilating. I pressed the buzzer, then sat down and my heels tapped on the floor as my hands clasped together in my lap.

After ten more minutes a woman, dressed in a hijab and normal clothes, not the pyjama things all the nurses wore, came out. 'Ivy Cooper?'

'Yes.' I stood up.

'Hello.' She held out a hand. 'I'm Dr Gymer.'

'Hello.'

She sat down, so I sat down, turning sideways to listen to her. 'Okay, so we took an x-ray early this morning and it was good news. Jack's lungs are fully inflated, so we decided to try and take him off the machine that's been helping him breathe to see if he could breathe alone.'

I bit my lip.

'He's doing fine. He's breathing and his lungs are inflating. We're just bringing him round from the medication. Hopefully you should be able to go in and see him in a while. But I'm sorry, it's going to be a little longer, so we can get him settled. His oxygen levels and his blood pressure are still very low, and the medication we've been using to keep him asleep is going to take a while to work its way out of his system.'

I nodded. 'Does it mean he's going to be okay?'

She smiled at me. 'It means that if everything is fine for the next twenty-four hours then he's probably out of the woods, certainly the risk of any major problems will be low.'

'Thank you.' I wanted to hug her.

'You're welcome.' She stood up.

So did I.

'Why don't you get a drink and something to eat? As I said, it's going to be a while longer before you can go in.'

'Thank you,' I said again, before she disappeared back through the door.

Jack was behind there, in the bed, *breathing*. 'Ahh!' I squealed, then looked up. 'Thank you.' I walked on air up to the café, my heart racing with excitement. Maybe he'd talk to me today. The future rolled into motion, like I'd pressed play on our film. I could see *us*.

I drank my coffee outside in the street, while birds chirped in the trees calling out a good morning to the world. It was full daylight and the street was packed with people on their way to work.

Work.

I pulled out my phone and texted Emma. 'Hi, I'm with Jack at the hospital. They think he's going to be okay.'

I should've got his mum's number. I couldn't contact her and tell her. But his parents would be here in a couple of hours.

I texted my mum. 'Jack's okay! They've taken him off the machine! I'll see you later.'

I went back inside with a smile on my face. The lift was too slow, so I gave up on it and ran down the stairs, then along the corridor.

No one else was in the waiting area. I pressed the buzzer.

After a few minutes another nurse I didn't know came out. A man with brown hair.

'I'm Ivy Cooper, for Jack Rendell.'

'It'll be a little longer, I think. But I'll tell the nurse who's looking after him that you're waiting.'

I breathed out and nodded. 'Thank you.'

I was waiting alone again and walking back and forth across the room. But this time with excitement, as I tried to be patient.

Chapter 31

When I opened my eyes, my eyelids were weighted down with stones, and sticky like they'd been stuck together with glue. I blinked a few times because the room was hazy.

My body felt as if it was made of lead and there were weird noises: a rhythmic beeping and the sound of plastic rattling by my ear. And I was in a strange-feeling bed; the sheets were scratchy. Everything was wrong…

I breathed in deeply and then realised I had something on my face. My hand lifted and touched a tube that was going into my nose.

'Leave it. It's just to double your oxygen intake while you're getting better.'

I blinked. My eyes focused on a dark-haired woman in a pale-blue uniform that looked like a set of oversized cotton pyjamas. 'Where am I?'

'Hello, Jack, you're in the intensive-care unit at the Chelsea and Westminster Hospital. You've been very poorly. You got your family worried.'

I lifted my arm – it looked swollen and there was a dressing on it, and there were dark brownish, dried bloodstains on that.

'You were in a motorcycle accident.'

'When?' My throat was so dry.

'Three days ago.'

'Can I have a drink?'

'Yes, would you like me to sit you up a little bit?'

'Please.'

Sitting me up involved raising the back of the bed, then she held a cup with a straw to my lips. I swallowed. The cold water tasted like the best champagne I'd ever drunk.

'One of the other nurses is calling your parents to tell them you've come around—'

'My parents are here?'

'In London, yes, but your girlfriend is here in the hospital if you'd like to see her. She came in this morning at six.'

'What time is it now?'

'Eight.'

'May I see her? Will you let her in?'

'Sure. I'll fetch her. She'll be thrilled to see you awake. My colleague told me she was quite upset when she left last night. I think she'd have slept here if she hadn't been told to go home.'

I gave the woman a weak smile.

When she'd gone I lifted the blanket and looked at my legs. I was naked and one leg was in a dressing from the knee down, the other from the knee up, but both were swollen. That was why they felt so heavy.

This was like living in a horror film. I couldn't remember why I was here. I'd woken up as Frankenstein's monster.

'Jack!' Ivy came through the door. Her hair was a mess and her eyes were red-rimmed and puffy. They shimmered with tears, sparkling in the white light in the room, but her lips parted in the biggest smile. Then her tears ran over.

'Ivy.' I lifted a hand. I felt like I'd been out of action for years not days I was so weak. She held my hand, but then immediately let it go and wrapped her arms around my neck, ignoring all the tubes she knocked, which pulled at my skin.

'Hey,' I breathed into her ear. 'It's okay.' It was weird I was the one in the bed covered in dressings and wires and yet I comforted her.

'I can't believe you're talking to me,' she said into my ear. 'I prayed so hard last night.' When she let me go she smiled down at me and brushed her fingers through my hair, which must look like hell.

I hated the thought of lying here with no control over what had been happening to me. 'Ivy, what happened, because I don't remember anything? All I remember is us going to lunch on Friday. We were going away weren't we? What day is it?'

'It's Monday?'

'What about our week off? I wanted to go away with you.'

'It can wait, we'll do it.' Her fingers touched my cheek and then she held my hand, as if she didn't want to break contact with me. But then her lavender eyes became greyer. 'You were knocked off the bike – outside work.'

I couldn't remember. My stomach gripped hard in my middle like it clasped into a fist. It made me want to vomit.

'It was a hit-and-run. They haven't found whoever it was. Your mum said the police are looking through the local CCTV, but it wasn't caught on any cameras. They have witness statements describing the car, though.'

'What did I do to my legs?'

'You broke your femur at the top in one leg and in the other one you broke the two lower bones, but they operated on you and put a load of metal in you before you got sick. Your mum said you should be able to walk as soon as you're well. You'll be like Ironman.' That was said to make me feel better. It didn't. I had friends who'd broken bones; they took ages to heal and they made it hard to climb.

I leaned my head back against the pillows and shut my eyes. Both legs and my arm…

'You'll be okay. You'll climb again and do everything again. I know you will.'

I looked at her and smiled weakly. 'Can I have some water? I can't hold it.'

She held the cup and the straw to my lips so I could drink.

'The room's spinning.'

'That's probably all the drugs they've been pouring into you.'

I nodded. I was losing the energy to talk.

'You'll be okay. I thought I was going to lose you. The doctor warned your parents—'

'You met my parents?'

'Yes.'

'Do they like you?'

'I think so. They're nice.'

The heaviness inside me started dragging down my eyelids. 'I'm sorry, Ivy, I'm tired. I think I need to sleep.'

'That's okay. I'll be here.'

I shut my eyes.

When I opened them again, it wasn't Ivy in the room, it was Mum and Dad. 'Hi,' I croaked.

'Hello.' Mum looked up. Dad was standing on the other side of the bed, talking to a male nurse. He turned.

Mum held my hand. 'Ivy said she'd spoken to you, but since then you've slept all day.'

I smiled. 'Sorry, Mum.' I looked across the room. 'Dad.'

'What have you got to be sorry for?'

'I'd straightened out and stopped being a thorn in your side and now this…'

'It is hardly your fault, Jack,' Dad said.

No. 'Where's Ivy?'

Mum smiled. 'You're with us for two minutes and your first question is where is your girlfriend.'

I smiled at her weakly. 'Can I have some water?' She stood and held it for me as Dad hovered.

'We have your things,' Dad said. 'The police gave them to us. They had to itemise everything, including the thing in the

355

pocket of your motorbike suit...' he said that, like it meant something.

His eyebrows lifted. Mum took the straw from my mouth. 'What, Dad?'

'The ring...'

I'd forgotten. 'I was going to propose.'

'Inside a serviette...' He went on staring at me. 'Written by Ivy Cooper... Resigning as your employee and accepting the role of something else.'

Oh shit. My skin burned and I shut my eyes. My eyes were about the only part of my body I could move without help. Now he was going to hate Ivy as much he'd hated Sharon. I opened my eyes. 'You don't like her? You don't approve? But she isn't, she's—'

'I don't dislike her. I've not spoken to her as much as your mother, but she is pleasant enough. Certainly she's attached to you. But what's your motive for proposing to this purple-haired girl. I hope it's not out of stubbornness, to spite me, like you did before.'

'It's not, Dad, I'm over that.'

I looked at Mum. 'Do you like her?'

'Yes, I do. I approve of her entirely. We will look after the ring until you want it.'

I wanted it now. I wanted to be on holiday with Ivy, getting down on one knee in the house, not laid up here, broken and useless.

'Excuse me Lord and Lady Rendell.' The nurse walked back into the room. 'Jack. Your daughter is here. Her mother would like to bring her in.'

'So we must move on. We have had our turn, Catherine.'

'Dad...'

'It's alright, I am joking, Jack, the child comes first.'

Mum kissed my cheek. 'We'll be back later.'

'Thank you. Thank you for coming.'

'Do you think we would be anywhere else when our son is at death's door,' Dad said.

I never knew with them. But no, that was mean. I did know they loved me, in their inexpressive way. It was just that the world Dad had been brought up in was different.

Dad's eyebrows lifted as though he'd heard what I thought. Then he walked over and held my hand firmly. 'Jack.' I think it was the most emotional gesture he'd ever shared with me. But it was him saying, *I love you. I was scared I'd lose you.* Dad was not sentimental or outspoken, or tactile.

When Mum and Dad walked out of the room, the nurse said to me. 'I can get rid of these tubes from your neck before your daughter comes in, if you want me to?'

'Yes please.' I didn't want to scare Daisy and scar her for the rest of her life, and I couldn't see what was going into my neck, but it sounded like a bank of tubes. They must have been pouring a cocktail of drugs into me.

He pressed a cotton wool pad on my neck, then pulled out what felt like a really long needle. 'Bloody hell,' I said when I saw it. 'Was that in me?'

He smiled. 'I'll go and tell her to come in, shall I? And if you don't tell anyone you have more than two people in here, I'll let your girlfriend back in to.'

I laughed, but it came out more like a groan.

'Hold this on a minute more.' He lifted my hand and pushed my fingers down on top of the dressing pad. 'Press it.' Then he went out. I lay there, just me and the machines... It was so strange. My mind was outside the hospital, on the bike, riding somewhere – fast.

Daisy came in looking nervous. The first thing her eyes went to was the drip going into my forearm. Then she looked up at my face. I lifted a hand and leant forward a little, wishing I could just get up. 'Hello, sweetheart.'

'Daddy... You're all bruised.'

357

Victoria had her hand on Daisy's shoulder and she carried a bag with flowers poking out of the top.

Ivy walked in behind them. I smiled at her. My heart said, *hi*, through my eyes. Her presence caught like a hook in my chest.

'Can I sit on the bed with you, Daddy?'

I looked down at Daisy. She looked terrified of what was happening to me.

'No, but you can sit here.' The male nurse pulled over a high stool for her to climb up onto.

I looked at Victoria and smiled. 'Hi.'

She actually came over and kissed my cheek, then leant to my ear. 'Your mum said you might die last night. I prepared Daisy to come and say goodbye. We were thrilled to hear you felt better this morning.' She straightened up, but her eyes were glistening.

Had I been that ill? 'Honey. What have you been up to?' I gripped Daisy's hand as it lay on the bed.

'I made you a card, to help you get better. But Mum said she didn't think you were going to get better—'

'But I am better, Daisy, and I will be all better soon. So your card-making worked before you even gave it to me.'

'You look sick.'

'I've been sick. But I'm going to be okay now.'

'We brought some grapes.'

'Thank you.'

'And flowers. Mummy said you wouldn't want them. But I said you like flowers. We did my room in flowers, didn't we? You do like flowers?'

'I love flowers.'

'Shall I go and find a vase?' Ivy offered.

I looked at her. 'Thanks.'

Ivy took the bag from Victoria, then went out of the room.

Victoria looked at me. 'She's nice. I like her.'

'You've been getting to know her?'

358

'Uh-huh. We've been outside for an hour while your parents were in here.'

Daisy's hand closed around mine. 'I like her too. I like her hair. You said it was nice. It matches her eyes.'

'It does, doesn't it? I told you so.'

Daisy grinned at me.

This was not the way I'd wanted Ivy to meet my parents and my daughter, but the deed was done, and it looked as if, despite the setting, it had gone well.

'Daisy said when she saw Ivy: 'Oh you're the lady with the purple hair.' I guess that's how you've been describing her.'

'Yes.' I winked at Daisy as Ivy walked back into the room. 'You weren't meant to tell her we call her the lady with the purple hair.'

Daisy laughed.

'I don't mind being called that, but your joke will be ruined if I dye my hair a different colour.'

Daisy looked back at her. 'Make it pink.'

A sound that was a very low-energy attempt at laughter escaped my throat. 'Do not make it pink.'

Ivy held up the full bag of stuff. 'I'm sorry, I got told off. We aren't meant to bring food or flowers in.

'Sorry, I should've told you that,' the nurse said. 'I always forget to make people obey the rules.'

'Never mind, you can take them home, Daisy, put them up in your room and think of me.' I smiled at her.

She nodded.

They'd turned the lights out in the room and down in the main room outside, to make it look like it was night when Ivy and I finally got more time alone. Mum went to fetch her as Dad said goodnight.

'Goodnight, Dad.' He clasped my hand for a moment.

'Sleep well son.' He smiled at me before he turned away and left, leaving me waiting for Ivy.

Daisy and Victoria had stayed for an hour and Ivy had left the room with them, so Mum and Dad could come in. I'd fallen asleep while they were in here so they'd hung around until I'd woken, late, and I hadn't wanted to tell them to go away.

Mum came back in with Ivy. 'Goodnight, Jack. We'll come back in the morning.'

I nodded and squeezed her fingers as they held mine. 'Goodnight.'

Ivy hovered at the end of the bed while Mum leant and kissed my cheek.

I wanted Ivy closer.

She came close after Mum had walked out and she reached for my hand as the nurse who'd taken over for the night shift slipped out the door too.

'Come here.' I lifted my other arm, drip tube and all. She leaned down and hugged me as best she could, ignoring all the monitor pads on me. 'It's okay. I'm okay.' I'd spent half the day telling everyone that. But maybe I'd been busy trying to persuade myself.

'I know.' She kissed my lips and I held the back of her neck.

When she broke the kiss, I said. 'I wish we were away in the middle of nowhere, where we'd planned to be.'

She smiled.

I pulled her back for a second kiss. 'I love you.'

'I love you too.'

Dual tears escaped from her eyes; they glimmered like jewels in the low light. 'I didn't know what happened, Jack. I spent all Friday night waiting for you.'

'Sorry.'

'It's not your fault.'

I threaded my fingers through hers. 'I wish you were in this bed under the covers with me. I'd feel a lot better.'

'I wish I could take you home.'

'Sneak up on the bed and lie next to me.'

She smiled, then looked back at the door as she slipped off her shoes. Then she climbed up on to the side of the bed that didn't have the drip, or any cables coming off me, and lay an arm over my middle. I set my arm about her shoulders and everything felt right.

I fell asleep, but I was woken by the nurse coming back in and telling Ivy to move off the bed because it was unhygienic.

She tumbled off, looking ruffled and exhausted. I think she'd been asleep too.

I caught hold of her hand. 'Go home and sleep. I'll see you tomorrow. But would you bring me in some underwear and a t-shirt?'

'Yes.'

She kissed me goodbye as I held her hand and she touched my check. Her touch slipped away, then her hand slid from mine.

'Bye.' I lifted my hand to her.

She blew me a kiss from her fingers.

Chapter 32

I slept easily when I got home, my dreams were full of Jack smiling, and Daisy with dark hair like his, eyes likes his and a cheeky smile like his.

I woke up at ten-past five and lay in bed staring at the lines of light leaking around the blind covering the window. It was weird, because now I knew the daughter he'd spent so much time talking about, and the parents he'd always sounded like he was wary of. But his parents seemed nice; mine had spent half the day getting to know them and they got on. Mum had put on her posh phone voice the whole time, though.

I got up at five-thirty and went to find a twenty-four-hour supermarket and bought him some clothes to wear. Then I went into the hospital. He was already awake. The nurse, another guy, was feeding him porridge because Jack wasn't strong enough to do it. The nurse left us alone and I took over, spooning it into his mouth like he was a kid. I tried to make a joke of it, but he hated it.

He was in a different mood today.

'I've had enough.' He clasped my wrist and pushed my hand away when I tried to persuade him to take another spoonful.

I put the spoon back in the bowl and left it on the side. He was in a bolshie mood, like he'd been in when we'd fallen out the other day. I didn't know what I'd done wrong.

His teeth gritted and he looked up at the ceiling, silent. Helpless.

'Do you want me to go?'

'No.'

I felt like saying, *then what do you want, because you're confusing me?* I was too close to the emotional rollercoaster I'd ridden over the weekend to take awkwardness and silence.

'What's wrong?' I said quietly.

Jack looked at me, his eyes dark and cagey.

I touched his cheek. 'Why are you in a bad mood?'

'Maybe because half my body was smashed to pieces and I'm stuck in here.'

His mood had been okay yesterday.

'I want to get up. I want to get out. I want to be free from all these fucking wires.'

The nurse came back in. 'I just heard; the doctor said you can go up to a private ward today, Jack, there's a room for you. We'll get you moved in an hour or so.'

I looked at the nurse. 'Can I help him get dressed? I brought some clothes in. It might help him feel more normal.'

'Sure.' He looked at Jack. 'You're a bit down today, aren't you, Jack, but it's the medicine wearing off. People always get the blues for a couple of days after they come off morphine.'

'God he's patronising,' Jack whispered when the nurse walked out of the room, and now I got it; he might be down because of the drugs, but one thing Jack, my *Captain Control*, would really hate was a stranger treating him like a child, especially when he could do nothing for himself. This was Jack's hell as much as that cliff in the Lake District had been mine.

'Well, you're getting out of here now and I presume you'll be able to get out of bed and move around on the ward.' I'd help him find the footholds and get up this cliff.

'I don't want to be on a fucking ward. Can't you get a wheelchair and take me home?'

'And if you got really sick again—'

'I won't.'

'Just stay in here a few days, maybe until the weekend.'

'The weekend – I'm holding you to that,' he said as he unsteadily tried to swing around sideways, to hang his legs over the edge of the bed, but there were long white dressings on his legs, covering where they'd operated on his bones, and his legs were swollen, so he couldn't bend them easily. I opened the pack of boxers, pulled out a pair and threw the others back in the bag I'd been forced to pay five pence for, then carefully slid them over his feet and up his legs.

He stood up at the end, so I could pull them up, but he had to hold my shoulders and his fingers clasped tight as he wobbled, and he turned white.

'Should you be standing? Shall I call the nurse?'

'Don't you dare. I don't want that bloke back in here. Help me get that t-shirt on. I can do whatever I want to. It's my body I don't need his permission. If I wanted to walk out of this hospital I could and I would. I'm not his prisoner.'

'But you just had surgery.'

'I saw the surgeon just now and he told me everything is fine and I should get my limbs moving as soon as possible to avoid another blood clot.'

'Jack…' Captain Control was angry and fighting.

'What? My bones are bolted back together. He said it's fine to stand. Movement gets the blood to the bones and helps them heel. And if they'd pinned me together that badly that everything would fall apart, it would fall apart whether I stood up today or in a week.'

But getting the t-shirt on was impossible with the drip in his arm and the monitors on him. He was all for ripping them off himself but I went out to get the condescending nurse.

As Jack was going up to a ward so he would be taken off the machines soon anyway and probably because he knew Jack was an awkward patient, the nurse agreed to take it all off now. He took the drip line out, then told Jack to press on a pad of cotton wool to stop the bleeding. Jack was too weak to do it for long, so I took over as the man detached Jack from the machines and switched them all off.

Jack was getting well again, but there was no way I was going to let him discharge himself when he was still this unsteady. He'd been near death two days ago.

When the porter came with a wheelchair to take him up to the ward, Jack had jogging bottoms and his t-shirt on and he looked more like Jack, just a pale version of himself, but he got paler and paler as we travelled up in the lift.

'Are you okay?'

'Yes.'

I didn't think he'd admit it if he wasn't; he was in full on control mode now. He was going to get better no matter what his body thought about it.

The nurses up there were nice. They got him settled into a room with a TV, a view of the city and an en-suite with a shower.

He wanted to sit in the chair in there, to escape the bed. 'Jack you look as if you're going to faint, get on the fucking bed.'

He laughed at me then, because I didn't swear loads so he knew my patience was running out.

I smiled at him sarcastically, but held his arm to help him move.

When he'd lain down, as he shut his eyes I touched his arm. He looked as pale as the sheet. 'You rest. I'll go down and get some breakfast. My parents are probably here now.'

He caught hold of my hand and his eyes opened. 'Your parents...'

'Yes, they haven't been in to see you – they just wanted to support me. But now you're up here, do you want to meet them?'

'You've met mine so, yes. But give me an hour to recover from the move.'

'Okay.' I stroked his hair off his forehead. Maybe later, if the nurses agreed, I could help him use the shower, I could wash his hair for him. That would make him feel better and give him another foothold. 'I'll leave you to sleep. I'll see you later.' I leaned down and kissed him. His hand clasped my wrist and tried to hold me down, but his hold was too weak.

'Thanks, Ivy. I'm sorry I'm putting you through this.'

'You aren't putting me through anything. I'm here because I love you—'

'I love you twice as much as that.' He shut his eyes and almost instantly fell asleep.

I didn't leave him for an hour, I left him for two; from the colour of his skin he'd needed a really good rest.

Chapter 33

I was sitting up in bed struggling to lift a beaker of tea to my mouth and chew a sandwich when Ivy tapped the open door. An emotional guitar solo played through my heart. What I'd said to her earlier was true. After this, I loved her more; every emotion I felt was a dozen times deeper. That aggressive nurse downstairs would have said it was an aftermath from the medication. I didn't think so.

'Hello, Mr Angry Invalid. I brought you visitors.'

I made a face at her and twisted sideways on the bed, trying to let my legs, from the knees, dangle over the side, but it felt like the stitches in my legs were going to tear open. I twisted back round, but sat upright, stuffing the pillow higher behind me.

Ivy's dad stepped forward with his hand out. I held my hand out. My arm trembled. I wondered how her first meeting with Mum and Dad had gone. This was the wrong setting for all of this. 'Mr Cooper.'

'Jack.'

I'd bet they were dubious about me, about my intent. I was her boss and now they knew my parents they might think I was messing around with Ivy because she didn't have my background.

The room did a spin as her dad shook my hand then let it go. 'I'm Brian, not Mr Cooper.'

'Mrs Cooper.' I looked over and nodded at her.

'Elizabeth.'

'I wish I was meeting you in better circumstances, over dinner or something,' I said, but at least now I had some clothes on.

'Sorry he's in a bad mood.'

'Can you blame me?' I gave Ivy a look.

Ivy's mum smiled at me. 'No. We know how poorly you are.'

'Sorry. I'd imagined this moment differently.' Like I'd imagined talking to her dad differently. Like I'd imagined introducing her to my parents differently. But she was okay with my parents anyway.

I looked at Ivy. 'Would you ask someone to get us a hot drink?'

'You have one,' she glanced at my half-empty beaker, 'and we had one downstairs.'

'I know, but I'm really thirsty, and that's cold.'

She nodded, but her look said I'd sounded rude. 'Okay.'

'Sorry, Ivy. Please would you ask if we can have a hot drink?'

When she disappeared I looked at her dad and smiled. I'd rather be on my feet looking him in the eyes. I felt so out of control stuck in a bed. But this was how things were. 'I want to ask your permission to marry Ivy, Mr Cooper, Brian. If that's alright. I'd intended proposing to her when we were away, and asking your permission to marry her after, but seeing as you're here. I don't want to rush anything. I know there's Daisy to think about and I've only just got divorced, but Ivy wasn't feeling secure with me, and I love her, and I want to marry her, and I want her to know it.'

He gave me a shallow smile, a little like his daughter's. 'Well I guess I don't need to ask you how you'll provide for her, as you're her boss. But thank you for having the decency to ask. You have my consent and she looks devoted to you, so I have no doubt it's what she wants.' And they'd seen her turn Rick down. They were positive words.

Devoted to me... They were pivotal words.

God Sharon had never been devoted to me, but I felt devoted

to Ivy too I'd do anything to keep her, anything for her. But I still didn't think she believed that.

She would get it, though.

Ivy came back in, smiling. 'They're going to bring a trolley—' She stopped and glared at me. 'Lie down. You had three major operations three days ago and you're white as the sheets. You shouldn't be sitting up.'

I made a face at her. A trolley... This wasn't Fortnum and Mason's.

As I lay down again, I caught Mrs Cooper's gaze. She winked at me. On first impressions I liked Ivy's parents; they were homely, normal, nice people.

While we drank our cheap tea, Mum and Dad arrived.

Just how down to earth and nice Ivy's parents were flashed like a beacon when Dad came in and did his stiff-upper-lip thing and Mum greeted everybody in her ladies-who-lunch voice.

But apparently they knew each other, and my parents liked them... It was as if they'd been friends for weeks.

I was tired and struggling to keep my eyes open after half an hour.

Ivy held my hand, standing on the far side of the bed to the others, saying without words: *You're alright, I'm here.*

After that weirdo had broken into her room I'd had her safety rope – now she was gripping mine.

When it got to the end of visiting time I persuaded the nurse, with a bit of charm, to let Ivy break the rules and stay with me and while I said goodbye to my parents and her parents, Ivy went downstairs to get some stuff from the shop so she could wash my hair.

When Ivy came back, the nurse came in and took my dressings off. Ivy hovered in a corner. There were vicious red scar lines on my legs with regimental rows of black stitches, and there was a matching wound on my arm. All my muscles were tight and sore; it was going to be a long time before I climbed again.

Shit.

The nurse told Ivy that she could help me into a wheelchair and help me wash in the shower and do my hair, if we were careful not to get shampoo on my wounds. So she left the dressings off.

Ivy shut the door to the room when the nurse went out after leaving a pile of warm towels in the room.

'Strip off and get in there with me.' I said as Ivy helped take my t-shirt off.

'You're meant to be too ill to be thinking stuff like that.'

'I haven't had sex for nearly a week.'

'More like half a week, and you've been unconscious.'

'It would make me feel better. At least take your top off.'

She gave me a grin and stripped off the sweatshirt and t-shirt she had on. She had a blue lacy bra underneath. I stood up and pushed down my bottoms and my boxers a tiny bit, my bad arm shaking. Ivy had to help me get them off the rest of the way. I felt foolish, but I was glad it was Ivy helping and no one else. 'I couldn't imagine Sharon helping me like this.' It was a joke, but it wasn't so sarcastic. Ivy looked at me as she straightened, folding my clothes.

She smiled.

Guilt punched me. 'Sorry. You shouldn't have to be my nurse; I didn't ask you to go out with me for that.'

She smiled again. 'You told me at Christmas, it was because you liked my bum.'

I smiled. 'And your eyes. I've always loved your eyes, and your face, and your body. Well, just all of you, Ivy.'

Her smile twisted.

I took her hands and leaned heavily on to her to get into the wheelchair. The pain from the wounds was sharp, like knife stabs when I tried bending my legs. The nurses had offered me more morphine but I didn't want it. I was tough enough to deal with pain. But naked, I could see how much of a mess I was in. There were bruises on my inner thighs and across my chest, and all around the wounds, and then I saw my face in the mirror and

370

the disgusting yellow bruise over half my forehead and around my eye. It was a wonder Ivy still wanted anything to do with me – and that Daisy hadn't run out of the room screaming.

Ivy wheeled me into the shower room and angled the shower so it didn't run over my legs and the chair so I could tip back my head and then she washed my hair. God it felt good, not only to have clean hair but to have her hands on me.

After she'd finished washing my hair she helped me stand up under the water for a moment, to wash off the brown stains of the iodine they'd painted on my legs while operating. She got her jeans wet – and her bra was soaked.

When she turned off the shower she put a towel on the wheel-chair for me to sit on, then started patting my legs down carefully.

'I wish we were at home,' I said. The pressure of tears hurt at the back of my throat.

'You will be soon. I know you'll be going crazy in here, but just be patient.'

'Me patient...'

'Jack, I do know you, but you can cope.'

I growled at her as she wheeled me back into the bedroom. 'You know Captain Control is screaming?'

'I know. But he's going to have to shut up.' She smiled at me, lifting her eyebrows. 'Remember when you made me climb that cliff at Christmas?'

'Yes.'

'Think of this as yours. You can get to the top. I'll help you.'

God, that was mean. 'Are you trying to sales-pitch me?'

She laughed.

'It took you moments to get to the top of that cliff. This is going to take weeks.'

'So what, it'll be okay. You'll get there.'

I made a face at her, remembering her resistance and my sales pitch. No pitch could persuade anyone they wanted to be hit by a car.

She helped me get clean boxers on and then the clothes I'd taken off back on, and then she helped me on to the bed. I was exhausted.

'You look like a ghost.'

'Lie down and hold me.'

She put her t-shirt back on and then lay down. We put the TV on to some drama and cuddled up until a nurse came in and told her to get off the bed – then she was sent home. It was like being at boarding school again. I had no control over anything.

'I'll see you tomorrow.'

'I'll ask the nurses if I can bring your PlayStation in so you have something to do – there must be advantages to private care.'

I smiled. She may have reacted badly to my declaration of love, but everything she was saying and doing now said she loved me.

'I love that you know me so well.'

'I just love you, Jack. See you tomorrow.'

My first visitors arrived on the ward at eleven o'clock in the morning. It wasn't Ivy who walked in but Mum and Dad, who'd brought in some clothes and stuff from my apartment – Ivy had texted Mum and asked her to. They gave me my phone back too, so I called Em and found out what had been going on in the office. Then Ivy walked in with her absorbing smile and bright eyes.

'Hello, beautiful.'

Mum and Dad were sitting by the window discussing where to eat lunch. Dad was going to go back to America tomorrow and Mum was thinking about going home for a couple of days. I'd told her I'd be alright if she did. I didn't need them hovering around me.

But I wanted Ivy hovering.

I'd told Em I was keeping Ivy off work because I needed her. I'd said she could take Ivy's salary out of mine and tell everyone else she was taking unpaid leave. I wasn't going to let anyone malign her for being there for me. She had offered to help me face this cliff and I needed her. The doctor had said to me this morning it would be months before I'd be back to normal. The break in my femur had been complex and there was steel scaffolding holding me up when I stood now. It was going to take months of physiotherapy to get my knees moving and my range of movement would never be the same. That knowledge just made me want to fight harder; I was going to get better.

'Happy now you have your PlayStation?'

'Not until you play on it with me.' I couldn't face this without her. She was the only person I was prepared to relinquish my control to. I trusted her. I wanted her to be the one who hung on to the rope, while I climbed out of this hole. God it was dark.

She gave me another beautiful smile.

'I'm not in such a bad mood today,' I told her. I was resigned to facing the cliff. As long as I had her with me, I'd force the fear away and get up there.

'Yes. He is happier, but trying to do far more than he should,' Mum answered. 'The nurse told us he tried to walk along the corridor alone. They are getting him some crutches.'

'The doctor said it's fine for me to be on my feet.'

'Yes, but to take it steady,' Dad said. 'He didn't mean on your feet all the time.'

'Jack Rendell?'

I looked up. A policeman stood at the door to my room. 'Yes.' *Why?*

'I'd be grateful if you'd give us a statement. We believe we have the driver of the vehicle that hit you in custody.'

Ivy's phone started ringing. 'Hello,' she answered it.

'Are you able to tell us what happened that evening?' The man pulled out a notepad without even waiting for me to say it was okay.

I sat more upright on the bed. Mum came forward and moved the pillows to support my back. 'No. I don't remember. I can't remember anything after midday.'

'Yes.' Ivy spoke into her phone. She sounded anxious as she walked out of the room so she could keep talking.

'Well, we have the witness statements and we can do an identification check with the witnesses too if necessary, so that isn't a problem.'

'Who was it?' I wanted a name, a label to pin on the person who did this to me.

'The man in custody is called Rick Baker.'

'Rick...' I heard Ivy say his name outside at the same moment.

Chapter 34

My phone rang as the policeman started talking to Jack. 'Hello.' The screen said it was an unknown caller. But I never got sales calls; I never gave my number out to anyone I didn't know.

'Hello, is that Ivy Cooper?'

'Yes.' I couldn't hear because the policeman in the room was still talking. I went out into the corridor.

'It's Officer Martins, Molly, from the police force.' The woman who'd come out when my flat had been broken into. 'I have some news for you.'

My heart missed a beat. 'What?'

'We have a match for the fingerprints found on your post, and the man's DNA sample has been sent off to see if that's a match to the forensic evidence discovered when your apartment was broken into.'

I couldn't breathe. I felt like all the drugs Jack had had in his body four days ago were in me. I didn't even know if I wanted to know who it was. I'd overcome my fear. What did it matter? Jack getting better was all that mattered.

'The name of the person we have in custody is Rick Baker. Do you know this man? Quite often—'

'Yes.' The word left my throat in a growl of pain. I turned around, not knowing which way to look or what to do. 'Rick.' I said the name as I heard Jack say it. But how could Jack know?

'You know this man? He hasn't been questioned about the incidents involving you yet—'

'Yes I know him.' There was a door leading out on to a patio area on the roof at the end of the corridor; I walked that way and pushed the door open. 'He's my ex-boyfriend. My friend… We're still friends… He was the one who came to help me when my place was broken into.' I'd talked to him about my stalker, the weirdo sending me letters and following me. Him. Oh my God.

He'd been the one who'd smashed the door in! And… Rick!

'Where is he?'

'He's in a cell here. I didn't undertake the arrest so I haven't seen him. I didn't realise he was with you that day.'

'Can I see him? Can I come down and speak to him? I can't believe he'd do that. He was with someone else.' *What about Jessica?*

'Miss Cooper, he's been arrested on another charge.'

'What charge?' Did I not know him? Had I gone out with him for years and not known the guy I was sharing my life and bed with.

'He was involved in a traffic incident. He hit a motorcyclist.'

Oh my God. 'He doesn't own a car.' That couldn't have been him. 'He doesn't drive in London.'

'He hired a car, Miss Cooper, and we have the car on CCTV near the incident. My colleague is interviewing the witness who was knocked over.'

I looked back at the door into the hospital. Jack. 'Jack Rendell…'

'Yes, he was the gentleman riding the motorcycle. Do you know him too?'

'I know him. I'm here with him. Jack is my current boyfriend.'

'I'm sorry…'

Rick did it deliberately. 'Did Rick… Did he…'

'Miss Cooper, when he was questioned, he admitted the hit-and-run.'

Oh my God. A scream cried out silently in my throat. How could I believe that? He'd been my place of safety. The guy I'd walked away from for being too nice.

I dropped down, kneeling on the patio, pain grasping hard in my chest... I couldn't breathe.

'I think you should come down and make a statement, Miss Cooper. Where are you?'

'I'm at the Chelsea and Westminster Hospital in Fulham Road, with Jack. There's an officer in his room.'

'I'll give him a call and ask him to bring you down to the station.'

My heart bashed against my ribs as I sucked in the polluted city air, struggling to catch my breath. I wanted to be away with Jack, like we'd planned, miles away. In his quiet cottage. I wanted to turn back time.

All the times I'd been scared to death by someone following me, scared to go home...

Rick had offered for me to stay with him the day of the break-in...

What was wrong with him?

He was sick.

I looked up his number on my phone and sent a text. 'You are sick! I hate you!' Then I deleted his details and went into Facebook and blocked him. But he'd been seeing someone else... But I hadn't ever seen a picture of Jessica.

We hadn't spoken since I'd told him I was going to move in with Jack.

He'd tried to kill Jack because I'd told him.

Oh my God! My place had been broken into the first night I'd stayed at Jack's – if Rick had followed me there...

This nightmare was getting worse.

Tears were dripping off my cheeks as I walked back. I swiped them away with a shaky hand as the policeman walked out of the room to take a call.

Jack slipped off the bed slowly and stood unsteadily when he saw the tears on my face. His parents stood up.

Jack's eyes said he knew it was Rick.

'I'm sorry,' I leant into his neck as his arms wrapped around me.

'It's not your fault. I thought I was the one with the crazy ex,' he tried joking.

'How could he do that?'

'He loved you – the police said he'd been drinking in the car. He was off his head.'

'But he doesn't drive in the city. He'd hired the car to do it, Jack.'

'Miss Cooper. Are you ready to come to the station to make a statement?' The policeman came back into the room.

Jack looked at me. 'Why do you need...?' He looked at the policeman. 'Why does she need to make a statement?'

He only knew about Rick being the driver. My hands clasped either side of Jack's t-shirt. 'Rick was my stalker too, Jack. He's the one who broke into my flat.' Every belief I'd constructed my life on had gone. Nothing made sense. Good people did good things – not bad things. I'd split with Rick because he was too good for me.

I hadn't known him.

What if I'd stayed with him?

'I'm going to fucking kill him.' Jack tried to take a step forward but he'd have fallen if I hadn't caught him.

'Your language, Jack,' his mother warned. The policeman stepped forward and gripped Jack's other arm. He held on until Jack was back on the bed.

Jack looked at his mother. 'My language... You don't know what that guy did to her. She's been too scared to live a normal life for weeks. When I'm able, I'm going to hit that bastard so fucking har—'

'Mr Rendell. You'll stay out of it and leave it for the police to

378

deal with. Now, Miss Cooper, would you come with me to make a statement?'

I could see Jack grit his teeth, the muscle in his jaw flexed. I turned and held his hand. 'I'll see you later. I'll come back after.'

'I'll come with you,' his dad said. 'You shouldn't go alone, and I know your mother and father went home this morning.'

'I didn't know they'd gone...' Jack said.

'My nan called – she had a fall.'

His dad picked up his jacket. 'Come along.'

Jack's dad looked at him with the most affectionate expression I'd seen him give him so far.

Gratitude caught in my stomach as I looked at Jack too. His gaze flooded with concern – love.

I pressed a kiss on his lips. 'Sorry.'

'God, do not say sorry for that sick bastard, Ivy. I wish I could come with you.'

'I'll be back soon.'

'Yeah.' He held my neck and pulled me closer. 'Then you can sleep on the bed with me. I'll tell the nurses to piss off if they ask you to leave.'

I smiled. But I was shaking when I left the room with his dad.

Chapter 35

Jack's dad had been mostly quiet, but he was like a pillar of stone, silent but solid. His presence had helped make me feel more confident and helped me to forget that Rick was in the police station somewhere in the cells – Rick the traitorous, lying, not-nice guy.

If I saw him, I'd claw my fingers and charge at him, and I thought of him in the pub the last time I'd seen him, chatting as though he was so innocent.

But I was sure he'd said he'd been doing stuff when things happened. That he'd been with Jessica or Steve. The police told me to leave the investigating to them and to focus on their questions. How long had I known him? Had I seen anything that concerned me? Did I know his whereabouts at the times of the incidents? Could I think of any reason he might have to do this? 'Only that he was upset when I'd left.' Just that.

In the taxi on the way back to the hospital, my mind was spinning with confusion, anger and hurt.

When I walked back into Jack's hospital room with George, Jack looked pale.

'You look how I feel, sweetheart.'

Was I pale too? I did feel exhausted, and sick.

I nodded and went to use the toilet in his shower room. When

380

I saw myself in the mirror, he was right. I looked awful. There were dark rims under my eyes.

When I went back out a nurse came in. 'Sweet tea for the pair of you. And will you lie down, Jack! You might feel bionic with all the metal you have in you, but your body is still trying to heal.'

'He's always a fidget,' I said when I took my tea. I was trying to feel normal. I wanted to feel normal. But…

Oh my God. The thought of Rick driving at Jack grasped at my throat and he'd been the one in my room…

'Your father and I are going, Jack. I'll come back up to town in a couple of days, but if you want me to return sooner call me, please?'

'I'll be alright, Mum.'

I moved out of the way while she hugged him.

'I'll be in the US but it's only a phone call away.'

'I know, Dad.'

George patted Jack's arm.

I was numb. Cold. Empty. How could Rick do something like that?

In my head I was looking at Jack as he'd been the first moment I'd seen him in here, smashed up and attached to numerous machines. That image would haunt me.

Almost immediately after we'd got together again, I remembered Jack saying he'd been followed one night. Why? Because Rick had seen us together when he'd been following *me*.

'Goodbye, Ivy. It has been nice to meet you and get to know you a little, and when we meet again let's hope it will be in much better circumstances.' George held his hand out.

I shook it. 'It was nice meeting you and thank you for coming to the police station.'

'You are very welcome.'

His mum hugged me. 'Take care of him, Ivy. I think you'll be very good at that, but take care of yourself too, because he's not so good at thinking of others.'

'He's just fine at it.' I gave her a smile and glanced at him. 'But he is not so good at being a patient; so, yes, I will look after him.'

'Thank you, dear.'

'You're welcome.'

She lifted her hand with a smile. 'I shall look forward to meeting you again.'

When they walked out Jack added quietly, 'In some swanky restaurant somewhere. They do not slum it, Ivy, be prepared for fuss.'

'I wish you'd told me your parents were a Lord and Lady. Where do they live?'

'Not in a Palladian mansion, if that's what you're thinking. They live in a big house, but it's an average big house. The estate that went with my grandfather's title was sold off with its leaky roof years ago, and thank God, because I wouldn't have wanted to inherit the thing. It's a country hotel and golf club now. We can go and stay, if you want, and I'll show you the pictures of my ancestors in the halls.'

'Do you have a title?'

'No and I won't have one. Dad's a lesser son; his title goes with him. But he still sees me as having to protect the family name and honour. It's all very medieval.'

I shook my head at him. He hadn't lain down, and neither of us had drunk our tea.

He took a hold of my hand. 'I wish you'd told me your ex was nuts.'

I laughed, but it came out choked. 'Shit, Jack, a week ago things were perfect. I was looking forward to a week with you in heaven, and instead this is hell.' Tears leaked out.

'Oh. Come here.' He held me.

I pushed him away. 'You're meant to be lying down.'

'Then you'd better lie down with me. I'll find a film on the TV and we'll forget him.'

I went over and shut the door, then settled down next to him. My phone vibrated in my bag across the room.

I got up to get it. There was a missed call and a message from the police number.

'What is it?' Jack asked when I called the messaging service.

I put it on speaker. 'Hello, Miss Cooper. This is Molly from the police service. I wanted to let you know, Rick Baker has been charged and released on bail. He's admitted to breaking into your apartment and interfering with your post as well as attempted murder. He's been warned not to have any contact with you or Mr Rendell. If you have any concerns please call us, or if you feel it's an emergency call 999. Thank you.'

I looked at Jack as shivers ran up my spine.

'You must feel betrayed. Come on, come and lie down with me. I don't know about you but I feel like a bomb's hit me.'

I nodded, then I started crying again.

My phone vibrated again. Jack took it out of my hand.

'Look.'

Oh my God. Rick had texted. 'I'm sorry. I wanted to give you a reason to turn to me. I thought you'd come back, but he got in the way.'

'You could get him thrown into jail right now for that, Ivy.'

I thought of all the texts Rick had sent after Christmas – until I'd agreed to see him again as a friend. The texts had been constant. He'd shown signs of craziness then. But I'd known him since we were kids. How could I have guessed he'd do this?

'Are you okay if I text him back for you?'

Jack had answered my phone on New Year's Eve. Had Rick known it was him?

Jack typed one-handed, slowly because he was shaky and weak. Then he showed me the text.

'She can report you to the police for contacting her. You're lucky she hasn't. Piss off and leave us alone. Him.'

'You'll have him driving into you again.'

'I don't give a shit. I'm not letting him harass you. I wasn't happy when you started seeing him again after he'd been hassling

383

you at Christmas, but I wasn't really in a place to complain was I? I wish I had done now. But he'd even won my trust after the break-in.'

'Sorry.'

'I told you, don't say sorry for the freak.' He put my phone down on the bedside locker, then we lay on the bed together and he kissed me.

It felt like a first kiss. Because we'd seen things about each other that most people didn't ever see. He'd seen me at my worst, broken down by the break-in and the stalking and he'd stood beside me holding on to my safety rope and now his life was going to be changed forever, maybe, because of being involved with me, and he still wanted me and loved me. We'd been through things together and survived, and we'd survive this. I was a new person and I saw him as a new person. This was my Jack. I'd worried about him getting bored of me, because of his reputation and the way he'd been with Sharon; but *my Jack*, this new man I was with, was not that man. My Jack was a solid block of unmoving love and adoration. He'd been my fortress for weeks; now I'd be his too. Because now I'd seen how vulnerable he could be.

My tongue danced around his and he rolled a little over me, his erection pressing against my hip.

I broke the kiss. 'I'm not going all the way with you in here.'

'Coward.'

'A nurse might walk in.'

'So. The risk makes it exciting.'

'Yes, but you're not well enough to go on top, and I'm not going on top and being the one flashing my backside if they come in.'

He laughed. 'We'll get under the sheets.'

I slapped his good arm. 'Stop it. I'm not going to be persuaded this time. So don't try any sales pitches.'

His eyebrows lifted. 'This time…'

'I take it you're feeling a little better. But stop it, otherwise you'll be feeling ill again.'

He kissed my cheek and then my neck.

'Jack,' I said quietly. This was his sales pitch without words. 'Jack,' I said again as he sucked my neck. 'Stop it.'

'I bet you want it,' he whispered into my ear, like a caress. It gave me the shivers, for good reasons. 'Your heart is racing.'

'You always make my heart race. My heart beats like crazy every time you suggest something naughty.' I answered into the air.

'It's the rush. It's telling you to do it. Adrenaline is the best drug. It's taking away my pain already. It'll stop the shock spreading. You should get more of it.'

'And you're addicted to it. Stop pitching.'

He laughed and rolled on to his back, while the good arm he had around me tightened and pulled me closer. 'Probably. Certainly do not expect me to stay off the bike when I'm better.'

'I didn't, and I know you'll be trying to climb, and I'll be helping you to do it.'

'I love you,' he breathed the words into the air.

I leant over and kissed him on the lips, then said, 'I love you too.'

'You know, I'm going to be okay – to spite that bastard.'

I ran my fingers along the side of his cheek, which was coated with a shadow of four days' stubble. 'You'll be okay and I promise, I'll treat you with regular doses of sexual adrenaline as soon as you're well enough.'

He laughed. 'I'm well enough now.'

But this little romp had not been about him wanting sex, it had been about him trying to gain control of the world again. He would be okay. I was going to make sure of it. The control would be ours again – to fight over.

Chapter 36

End of October

I held the rope tighter as I watched Ivy looking at the rock face. She glanced back at me.

'You can do it.'

I knew what was going on in her mind – an urge to say she couldn't, and I knew her heart was beating like a manic rave beat. But she wouldn't voice her thoughts; she never did any more. Whatever crazy suggestion I proposed to her, she swallowed her fear and did it, for me. I'd been promised regular doses of sexual adrenaline while I recovered; she'd honoured that. Now I was returning the favour of adrenaline rushes – but not always in bed. I smiled.

'Go on, Ivy. I've got you. I promise.' But today she was facing her worst fear again. Heights. And solid awkward-shaped rock did look very different to perfect designed-to-be-climbed resin.

She'd climbed this rock face last Christmas, when I'd climbed up beside her. But now she knew I couldn't get up there, so she had to do it alone.

I was climbing on the walls again, but I couldn't do it properly yet. I didn't have the movement in my joints because of all the scarred muscle tissue, and metal, and my strength had gone. But

I was building it up and getting more movement back week by week, and I hadn't given up on the idea of being able to climb here again. But right now I was living it through Ivy. That was why she never said no, because she did things for me, travelling the thrill ride for me.

'Go on,' I encouraged again.

She threw me a look that said, *shut up*. She was harnessed up and I had a hold of the safety rope.

'Are you sure you're strong enough to hold me.'

'I told you last time, you can jump off anytime and I'll lower you down. So just take a step up and then test me if you don't trust me.'

'I trust you.'

'Well then, why did you even ask? I've got you and you aren't going to fall off anyway.'

'Okay.' She took a breath.

I tugged the rope so she felt the pull as she stepped up to the bottom of the rock.

'That's me,' she said. I was trying to make her feel like she did at the fake wall.

'Climb when ready.'

I heard her take a deep breath. 'Climbing,' she said, finding a hold with one hand. The first time she'd done this she'd clung on with two hands before lifting her foot; she was definitely more confident.

'Climb on,' I acknowledged. She started climbing.

She was slow, but steady and sensible; searching out secure holds before she moved. She was a confident, competent climber – if only she believed in herself.

She was one of the crowd at the climbing club too. We often went from the walls to the bar; the only thing I'd lost was the ability to get to the top of a wall myself, but I was still aiming for it. And right now I was just glad to be up here in Cumbria again. I could've got up here two months ago on the train, but I'd held out because I'd wanted to drive here and I hadn't wanted to bring Ivy back up while she was playing nurse. I wanted us level. I wanted everything to be as it should've been before Rick had smashed me off the bike. The only thing that was missing was me being able to climb.

Although that was a stupid thing to think. Nothing was completely the same. Ivy had packed up work in the summer. She'd loved the job but it was too awkward when she was spending so much time caring for me for weeks because I hadn't been able to walk very easily and then keeping an eye on me when I'd started hobbling around with a stick. And she was meant to be on the payroll, although she hadn't been for weeks – and with both of us out, the business had been working through some tough times. But so had I.

A month ago I'd got Em to get a loan to buy me out of the business. Phil had taken over my half.

Ivy and I were going to set up another agency and start from scratch, just the two of us. I had a feeling my customers who weren't tied to contracts would follow me. Em would probably hate me for it, but the old business would survive. I felt a little guilty for ducking out on Em, but Ivy was more important. I wanted to be with her. The business was not the thing that had got me through the last few months; Ivy had been.

Before Ivy all the women who had been important in my life had been the opposite of me, making up for what I lacked. Ivy was my true partner. She was like me in lots of ways, and yet with her… she made who I was better.

I watched her complete the climb, her hand reached over the top and gripped the turf and she pulled herself up on to a foot-hold, then her other hand reached over the top. She tumbled on to the grass on the top, then stood up and unclipped the rope, screaming with excitement and waving down at me.

I smiled. She didn't need my safety rope any more. But I needed hers. She had all the control. I waited for Captain Control to yell out in complaint. He didn't. My inner voice was silent. But Lord he'd had nearly a year to get used to shutting up, since he'd been introduced to me up here last Christmas. 'Do you want to go for the bigger face? You'll be okay! If you want to do it, we can get you on a rope?'

'Yes.' Her expression said she was seeking the adrenaline rush of challenging herself.

She did it too, a perfect climb, without a fault.

When we got back to the house I made her a risotto for dinner and we ate it with a bottle of ale, sitting at the long antique oak table in the kitchen.

I liked being in the house with her. It was becoming our special place. It was making me contemplate living up here. Maybe we could stay in town in the week and come up here every weekend, or every other weekend at least; it would be too awkward for Daisy to travel up here all the time. I was going to bring her up for a holiday soon, though.

After dinner Ivy came around the table and kissed me. Then whispered over my lips. 'Did you bring a suit with you?'

'Yes. Why?'

'Did you bring a tie?'

'Yes. Why?' I was smiling now.

'Because I have a use for it.'

'Well if it's to tie me up, the answer is no. Neither my arm nor my legs are up to that, but yours…' It probably wasn't true, I'd probably be okay with it, but I'd been through enough. I didn't feel guilty for using my injuries as an excuse when I wanted to.

'Well, maybe I will let you tie me up and maybe not…' She started backing towards the door.

I snatched up an ice bucket I'd left some champagne chilling in, ready for the moment. But the moment wasn't now. It had come and gone again – it kept doing that. There was always a reason not to say the words.

I wanted to say them during this holiday, though. I was going to find a time.

We went up to the little double bed we'd had sex in the first time we'd come up here. I was going to christen every bed in the house with her this time around, and every room.

She started undressing, and I undressed. Then she lay down on the bed, all naked pale skin. I turned and pulled my tie out of the drawer, then made her stand in front of me while I tied her wrists. 'You can tie the wrist of my good arm to the bed tomorrow night if you want.'

'It's okay, I enjoy you tying me up too.'

Laughter rumbled in my chest as I picked up a piece of ice. 'Lie down.'

'Yes, sir.'

I climbed on the bed and knelt beside her, which was awkward because my left knee only bent to about ninety degrees, but I was slowly forcing it into moving more.

I teased her nipple with the ice.

'Ah, ow. That's cold.'

'Makes the heart race wondering where I'm going to put it next, though.'

She laughed, her eyes watching me. It was sunset and the vivid orange-and-red sunlight spilled into the room, gilding her as I ran the ice down her beautiful sternum.

My vision caught the scar on my arm. I was trying not to look at my scars. I hadn't got used to them. They were memories I didn't really want. They made me think of her ex. But the cardigan-wearing nutter was in prison, serving out a couple of years for not being able to let her go. And she'd called me Captain Control.

If she ever decided to leave me, though, I'd probably go as mad as him.

The ice melted on her rigid stomach, dripping off the sides and then I shifted. Lifting a leg so she could move hers and I could kneel, awkwardly, between her legs.

I slid the last of the melting ice inside her, then raised her legs so she could lift her hips, and shuffled down the bed then licked the cold melting water out from within her. Her body was like silk, warm silk, compared to the water.

I messed around with the ice on her body, while I teased her with my teeth, biting then sucking and then her hips rocked up against me searching for the depth of my tongue as shameless as she'd always been, seeking the orgasm she wanted.

This was my passionate, perfect, Ivy.

When she came, her tied hands came down from above her head and clasped my hair, as her taste tingled sour on my tongue, and her inner muscle pulsed about the finger I slipped into her, just to feel it.

I tumbled on to my back. It was not what I wanted to do. I wanted to flip her over and do it that way, but she knew that our sex life was as limited as my climbing – the pain from the scarring in my muscle became too much after my legs had been bent for too long.

She didn't say anything about it, just rolled over and knelt up, balancing on her tied-up hands. She smiled at me as she straddled me; I positioned everything. I didn't untie her and she didn't ask me to. The side of her hands pressed down on my chest. Then she slid down on to me and took control.

Yes.

She had a lot of control in every element our relationship. Most of it. I loved her, regardless. I was over that. A recovered control addict.

She lifted up a little so I had to push up into her, pressing my heels into the sheets, as I gripped her thighs.

I held her gaze as the sun set behind her, the sky growing darker and darker.

I knew where and when I was going to propose. I knew the perfect place, and the perfect hour.

Chapter 36

Jack shook my shoulder a little. 'Wake up. I want to go out.'

I opened my eyes and blinked. 'It's still dark.'

'I want to go somewhere.'

'It's the middle of the night.'

'It's dawn in fifty-five minutes and you have fifteen to get up and get some clothes on or I carry you downstairs naked.'

'You're not strong enough to carry me.'

'Do you have to remind me? At least let me imagine I can do it in a threat.'

I laughed at him. But then he pressed a quick kiss on my lips. 'Get up.'

My hand lifted and grabbed his cotton t-shirt at his side. He was already dressed.

He turned on the light beside the bed.

I covered my eyes with my forearm.

'Come on. I made coffee. I'll go down and pour you one, then you can drink it and wake yourself up before you go.'

I didn't know what he was up to, but we'd waited nearly a year to get back up here, and he'd been looking forward to this like it was all he'd lived for over the last few months while he'd been recovering. This was him, clasping the turf on the top of his cliff and hauling himself over the top, with relief and excitement. So if he wanted to do something crazy at dawn, I wouldn't complain, I'd get up.

I rolled to my side as he walked out of the room. He had his tight black jeans and a black t-shirt on, and he looked good. Pride lifted my lips into a smile of appreciation. I liked that he was mine. I liked that we had each other. We'd become a team of two, at home and in a business soon.

Milly kept telling me I was overdosing on him. But I liked the overdose and I felt as if he needed me in an overdose. The last few months I'd been holding him together. He needed to get back to who he used to be, and he couldn't climb yet, he was too stiff, and he couldn't have sex how he wanted. He was holding on to his patience and bearing it, but he was not a patient man. In London, I'd thought, if he didn't see some improvement soon, he was going to break, but this had been the thing he'd been holding on to, climbing towards – coming up here. He'd smiled loads since we'd been up here, and I'd smiled too because it was good to see him happy.

I hoped this was the turning point. When we went back to London, at least he'd have work again. This was when we got back on the rails of normal life, or life as Jack liked to live it – wonderfully abnormal.

I pulled my pale-blue jeans on, then a loose t-shirt and stole one of his jumpers out of the cupboard to wear over it. I shoved the sleeves up as I walked downstairs, barefoot on the wooden steps, in the dark, following the light that was on in the kitchen.

He was leaning against the kitchen table. I walked up, tiptoeing over the freezing stone tiles, and clasped his middle, giving him a squeeze from behind. 'I love you.'

He turned around. 'Drink your coffee and let's get going.'

'Sure boss.'

'Not your boss, your partner.' He gave me a grin.

'Sure partner,' I corrected.

I found out some walking socks and my boots, because I guessed we were not going to a restaurant at dawn. He was doubled over lacing his boots, because his knees didn't bend enough to do it any other way.

Rick had affected so many small elements of Jack's life that put together…

Jack looked up and caught me watching him. I slipped my hands into the back pockets of my jeans. He straightened, then turned and lifted his leather jacket off a hook and put it on, giving me one of his wicked little half-smiles – the pure flirt that he'd always been.

Rick's meanness had not changed that.

Jack opened the back door and his hand settled on my shoulder when we walked out.

It was still dark mostly, but the sky to the east was a lighter blue and it created a beautiful silhouette of the hills. Autumn was beginning, but it wasn't too cold. I only had his thick jumper and my t-shirt on. I hadn't put a coat on.

I walked around to the passenger side of the car and saw Jack touch his jacket, as if he was checking for something in his inside pocket, but then he pulled his keys out of his pocket on the other side.

He pressed the button to free the lock and I got in.

I was half asleep and the world felt fairytale-like as he drove through the valleys between all the hills, while the sky on one side of the car gradually became a lighter and lighter blue.

He turned off the road at the sign to Keswick, then turned again at the sign to Castlerigg.

We were going back to the stone circle.

He parked the car in the roadside layby, then patted my knee. 'Let's go and watch the sunrise.'

He had the most beautiful ideas and the best sense of how to live life. Rick hadn't taken that from Jack either.

I climbed out of the car and ran around to where Jack waited for me by the gate. I was wide awake now, and the air was fresh and chilly here.

He gripped my hand tightly as we walked into the field, but as we climbed the slope, and the sky on the far side blushed with orange, his grip became more out of necessity and less out of an expression of love.

'I can't walk on fucking slopes,' he grumbled.

I turned and walked backwards a pace ahead of him, as he kept his death-grip on my hand.

He'd been on crutches for six weeks and then got it down to one crutch, then a stick. He'd given up the stick about three weeks ago because he'd refused to come up here walking with a stick. But at times he still needed it, really.

'You'll be fine.'

'We won't be able to get up to the tarn, though, and go for a swim like I promised you in the spring, will we?' His blue eyes asked me to forgive him for not being the person he used to be.

'We will next summer. I promise. But I don't think the physiotherapy you're doing is working well enough. I want you to do yoga with me. It'll build up your core strength again so you'll be ready to climb when you can, and it'll stretch your muscles out – and the heat of Bikram yoga makes it gentler, so if you ever can—'

'If I ever can?'

'So you CAN move your legs more.'

He'd been walking slowly, holding both of my hands, but then he stopped and laughed. 'What are you trying to make me do?'

'Be happy.'

'And sit in an inactive yoga class.'

'And be able to climb like Spiderman again. You promised me months ago you'd do yoga if I climbed. I'm climbing.'

'Okay, you're right. I promised. I'll go to your yoga class with you when we get back to London. I'll try anything to get my legs moving more, even lying on floors with you and standing on my head. But don't tell any of my friends at the climbing club.'

I laughed at him. He really wasn't a good patient. 'I promise not to tell anyone.'

We reached the level ground the stones stood on, and I let him go when he could walk alone. He touched his chest again as he looked at the view, then slipped his hands into the back pockets of his jeans.

I turned around and looked – it was amazing. The most beautiful view I'd ever seen.

'It's dramatic, isn't it?' Jack said as he walked ahead of me towards the circle.

'Yes.' It was. It was like some sort of statement about life, about how beautiful and precious it was. It was as if someone had put the stones here so people would come up here and breathe in life.

He walked into the centre of the circle, then turned around and watched me. His hands slid out of his pockets. 'I wanted to say something to you months ago.' His voice was low and serious, but there was a sweet note in it, like honey melting in coffee.

'I was going to say it when we'd planned to come up here in the spring, and since then there's never been a moment that felt like the right time. Not when you've had to do so much to help me out. But then I made up my mind that I was going to wait until we got up here…'

'Wait for what?'

'I'd get down on one knee, Ivy, but I can't… But…' He pulled something out from the inside pocket of his jacket. Something white… a tatty serviette. He held it in his palm and unfolded it and in the middle of it was a diamond ring.

It was the napkin I'd written on when we'd come up here last Christmas – the one contracting him to be my lover.

I looked up and met his gaze – his blue eyes said a thousand things. 'Will you marry me, Ivy? I want you to know how much I care about you. I know this is still pretty quick and you may want to wait and be sure you're not tied to an invalid before—'

I covered his lips with my fingertips to stop him talking. 'Don't be stupid, Jack. I don't care about what you can and can't do. You're still you. I want you to get back to normal for your own sake, because I love you. But I love you however you are. I will marry you. Yes.'

'Ivy…' He looked up at the sky.

The dawn light reached from one horizon to the other now the sun had risen fully.

He looked back down at me. 'I can't even begin to find the words to tell you how good you make me feel.' He grinned, then looked up again and thrust his good arm in the air. 'Woohoo!'

I laughed at him and his foolishness as he looked down and held my fingers, then slid the ring on. 'It looks beautiful on you, and it's waited a long time to get on that finger.' His gaze lifted to my face. '*You* look beautiful.'

'Thank you.' Before he let my hand go, I took the serviette that was now scrunched up in his palm. 'You kept it.'

'A contract is a contract.'

'Yeah, but you wrote one after this.'

'I didn't keep that one. If you ever want to revoke it, you'll have to try and prove it in a court that you reneged on me with no evidence.'

'Oh, Jack, you're crazy.' I wrapped my arms around his neck and his hands settled at my waist. 'I need to write you a new one now, anyway. I will be your lover, and your partner and your wife. Do you think John will draw it up for us formally – that I contract myself to you forever?'

'Yes. He'll put anything you want in writing if you pay him, but that's called a marriage contract, Ivy, and when we're married I'm going to hold you to it.'

'And I'll hold you to it.'

'You'll have my commitment, you'll have everything I can possibly give you. You have my heart and my broken bones.'

He picked me up then, the idiot, stumbled around a half circle and nearly fell.

When he dropped me down, I grabbed his arm to steady him. 'Let's sit on a stone and look at the view for a while.'

We did that, but afterwards we went down to Keswick and got hot chocolates loaded with cream and marshmallows and then walked beside the lake, and then went for a ride on the ferry. I wouldn't forget this day. It was going to be one of my best memories.

While we rode on the boat I rang Mum and Dad.

Dad said, 'Oh, he finally got around to it, then? He asked my permission the day I met him.'

I laughed.

He'd been waiting that long.

Then I rang Milly, who was quietly thrilled – quietly because she didn't want to overdo the excitement in front of Steve, who still blamed me for Rick going mad.

Then Jack rang Daisy, and when I nodded at him, told Daisy she would definitely be my bridesmaid.

We were going to be happy.

Chapter 38

When the organ started playing I turned to look down the aisle. She was late, but it was the bride's right to be late, and yet my heart was playing a tune of its own, worrying that something had happened to her. She kept going on about how she loved the way I made her heart race – she was making mine beat today for all the wrong reasons. It felt like a heart attack.

When I'd married Sharon it had been with a day's notice, in a register office, wearing what we'd worn to go to a club, and it had been quick, impulsive and stupid. This wedding had taken a year to plan. We'd chosen to get married in Keswick, a year to the day after I'd proposed. Everything beyond the place, though, and my suit – black tails – had been Ivy's sole choice. It was her fairytale wedding, and mine, because I only needed her to make it that.

Daisy walked up the aisle holding a basket of white flowers, wearing a pink dress that made her look like a beautiful little Disney princess. She'd stayed with Ivy and her mum and dad last night, and Ivy's friend Milly, with the promise of a thorough pampering and being treated like a grown-up with the other girls as they'd had their nails and hair done.

Milly walked behind Daisy, wearing a deeper pink, and then two meters behind them, Ivy. Her dress was less traditional: it was a soft white, which angled across her chest, leaving one shoulder naked as it clung to her body – but from her waist it flared with a gradual increase in volume, so when she walked it flowed around her legs. She was so beautiful, but the most stunning thing that I could see through the short veil she wore was that she'd changed the colour of her hair; it was dark.

I watched her, transfixed as she followed Daisy and Milly.

When Daisy got to the front I glanced down and winked at her. She gave me the biggest, happiest smile before moving to sit in a pew beside Mum. I looked up as Milly took the bouquet from Ivy.

My hands itched to lift Ivy's veil as her dad walked her forward. She smiled at me through the sheer fabric. Her hair was pinned in curls, with a few thin ringlets kissing her neck.

The vicar said something and whether I was supposed to or not, I couldn't help it, I stepped forward and lifted her veil, folding it back over her hair so I could see her face. Her makeup was sensitively done, in natural colours. which made her skin glow and her lavender eyes even more prominent – her dark hair, against her pale skin, made her eyes a dozen times more striking. I liked it. 'Your hair,' I whispered.

'I thought it was time I got a little more conventional.'

'I like it, but I liked you unconventional just as much.'

The vicar coughed.

I looked up and smiled.

When Ivy said, 'In sickness and health,' she squeezed my hand.

Tears blurred my vision, because she knew what that meant. She'd endured me sick, in moodiness and impatience. But she'd pulled me through it with hours of sweaty yoga.

I pledged my life to her in return.

'I now pronounce you man and wife!'

For whatever it was worth. Richer. Poorer. Sickness. Health. To have and to hold. She was mine and I was hers…

I was the happiest man alive. Love pulled like an anchor in my stomach holding me near her.

Chapter 39

'This is one part of our wedding I wish you had not persuaded me into.'

'Jack...' I hoped he wasn't going to back out on me. 'It's what everyone does these days—'

'So you said.'

'And I didn't persuade you. It was a fair trade. And I don't want to stand up for the first dance and sway, it looks stupid.'

'I've learnt the dance; you don't have to pitch it. I'm honouring the bargain. But expect me to be red the whole time we are doing this. My friends are here. Half of them are from private school, and my family...'

'They'll be impressed.'

'They are going to laugh.'

I braced the back of his neck. 'Don't think about them, look at me. Do it for me.'

'I am doing it for you, and the weekend of awesome naughty, nasty sex I get as the trade-off... be prepared to have a bottom as red as my face, I'm going to smack you so hard.'

I leant and whispered in his ear, 'Put your all into it and I'll let you spank me for all you're worth, as long as you kiss the pain away after.'

'Oh God. Giving my all.'

My hand fell to his shoulder. I'd picked my wedding dress for our dance. 'Ready?'

'As I'll ever be.'

A year ago, he could never have done this – it was testimony to how far he'd come. We were going to dance a foxtrot. I was smiling at him as the DJ called us into the middle of the floor. He was in on it, but no one else was.

He started playing Ed Sheeran's 'Thinking Out Loud', and the lights were turned off, so the room was only lit by the blue sparkling lights from a glitter ball.

This was my wedding. It had been dreamlike, but the church and the dinner had slipped past too fast. Yet I had a lifetime to follow, with Jack.

His hand held mine, low at my side, as my other hand rested on his shoulder and his other hand was at my waist as we swayed to the song. We smiled at each other as if this was all we intended to do.

We'd rehearsed this dozens of times. He didn't want to do it in front of anyone but we'd had fun learning the steps and the lifts with a dance teacher. We'd spent half the time laughing. It had taken him longer to get the steps because his injuries slowed him down, but he'd done it. Like he could climb now, albeit not quite like Spiderman – he was less agile – but he could climb anything he wanted. He did always use a rope now, though, because he didn't trust himself completely.

I trusted him.

'Ready,' he whispered in my ear, and then he gave the DJ a nod. The guy blended the slow beat of 'Thinking out Loud' with the violin which began 'Real Love' by Clean Bandit and Jess Glynne and Jack span me around a few times in a low-key way without changing the position of our arms. People who'd been talking and not watching looked over at us.

I stopped looking at the crowd and looked into Jack's eyes, smiling, as the piano and the cello played. Jack lifted my arm into

402

the formal hold and we moved into the structured steps of the foxtrot, racing across the floor. People started standing up as the beat suddenly flared, and then Jack did the first lift just gripping my waist and holding me up, before letting me slide down his body.

We did an intricate set of steps across the floor, chest to chest and legs moving in unison as we skipped out the steps. Then Jack spun me in a sharp turn before we did another set of intricate steps, then we stopped and spun again. He lifted me up and I wrapped myself sideways around his body as he turned, before he set me down and span me on the floor.

When I got up, we went into another intricate set of steps, going from one corner of the floor to another, not looking at anyone but each other.

I loved every moment of it, and I felt like a real dancer when I clung to his neck in the last move and he spun me so I lifted off the floor with my legs and my skirt flaring out.

When we stopped, we stared at each other, like two love-addicted idiots. The room broke into applause, wolf whistles and shouts.

'I guess I did it right,' Jack breathed hard.

'You did it right. You do everything right.'

'Daddy! Dad! I want to dance like that.' He turned around and picked Daisy up, to give her a heart-racing turn in the air. He had us both addicted to the rush of loving him.